PRAISE FOR ... RIES

'A first-rate police procedural by someone who ... knows what he's talking about.'
— HANIA ALLEN, author of *The Polish Detective*

'Audacious, Ritchie's street talk sizzles with wit and invention. *Cause Of Death* is engaging, eventful and original.'
— M.P. WRIGHT, author of the JT Ellington series

'Without a doubt the best crime book I have read in a long while that has true to life police procedural knowledge and great authenticity.'
— *Love Books Group*

'This book is a must read for any thriller fan! Action packed, fast paced and full of twists and turns. … This is THE BEST thriller book I have read this year!'
— *Orchard Book Club*

'All I can say is if you start reading this book, make sure you have no plans for the rest of the day or evening as I could not put this book down.'
— *The Secret World of a Book*

'If you like a crime read with an edge, a grittier story which sits in stark contrast to the beauty of the city in which is it set, one which walks on the precipice of a darker shade of fiction, then definitely pick up this series.'
— *Jen Med's Book Reviews*

'This is a brutal, raw and highly addictive thriller that definitely packs a punch (sometimes literally).'
— *Over the Rainbow*

'Explosive action and thrilling plotting make this a gripping read.'
— *The Quiet Knitter*

Also by Peter Ritchie

Cause of Death
Evidence of Death

Shores of Death

PETER RITCHIE

BLACK & WHITE PUBLISHING

First published 2018
by Black & White Publishing Ltd
Nautical House, 104 Commercial Street
Edinburgh EH6 6NF

1 3 5 7 9 10 8 6 4 2   18 19 20 21

ISBN: 978 1 78530 153 7

A CIP catalogue record for this book is
available from the British Library.

Typeset by Iolaire, Newtonmore
Printed and bound by Nørhaven, Denmark

At night, when the sky is full of stars and the sea is still you get the wonderful sensation that you are floating in space.

NATALIE WOOD

What terrified me will terrify others; and I need only describe the spectre which had haunted my midnight pillow.

MARY SHELLEY

ACRONYMS AND JARGON

Bampot	nutter
Bizzy	police officer
CHIS	covert human intelligence source (informant)
CROP	covert rural observation post
DEFCON 1	the highest level of defence readiness condition (US forces)
DO	detective officer
Doric	dialect spoken in the north-east of Scotland
Double tap	two shots fired quickly and close together on the target
Dug's baws	vernacular for dog's bollocks
Europol	European Police HQ in The Hague, Netherlands
Foxtrot Oscar	fuck off
Gimmes	abbreviation of give me: a case that almost solves itself (e.g. clues all over the place or someone just puts their hands up)
Goldie	whisky
Hee-haw	a way of saying 'fuck all'

Hibees	Hibernian Football Club
HOLMES	Home Office Large Major Enquiry System
Hooky	false
ID parade	identity parade
Intel	intelligence: human or technical
Jakey	a homeless alcoholic
Jambos	Heart of Midlothian Football Club
Lemon	lemon curd – burd (rhyming slang)
Locus	the place where a crime or other incident has occurred
malky	to attack someone
MISPER	missing person
MIT	Major Investigation Team
MSP	Member of the Scottish Parliament
Mumping	getting a freebie
Napper	head
NCA	National Crime Agency
Numpty	Scottish urban term for someone who's not that bright
PNC	Police National Computer
Pokey	prison
Polis	police
Radge	a nutter
Rammy	a brawl, fight
RCS	Regional Crime Squad
Rubber heels (squad)	anti-corruption/internal investigations
RV	rendezvous
Scoosh	booze
SIO	Senior Investigating Officer

Smack	heroin
SOCO	Scenes of Crime Officer
Square go	a punch-up; a fair fight
Squeak	old name for an informant
Sweaties	sweaty socks – a Metropolitan Police term for Jocks (the Scots)
Tipple	spot/recognise
UC	undercover agent
Weegie	someone from Glasgow
Wet work	murder/assassination (alluding to the spilling of blood etc.)

PROLOGUE

PROLOGUE

Tony Capaldi looked Italian, wore Italian designer gear and told a great story about his Italian background. From a distance he looked the real deal, but close up you could see the attempts to cover a hard life's wear and tear. There was something a bit Liberace in his appearance although his sexual orientation was definitely the opposite of the great ivory tapper. It didn't matter; although his appearance would have turned off the vast majority of the female gender, he did appeal to a certain kind of woman who only saw what she wanted to see.

The truth was that the nearest Tony Capaldi had been to Italy or an Italian family was when he was buying his favourite food, which consisted of a fish supper with lashings of brown sauce and two pickled onions, plus a full-fat Coke to complete his idea of fine dining.

The real name his waste-of-space parents gave him was Hugh Elvis McNally. The boy, however, despite his inspiring name and having the King blasted into his ears all day and every day of his young life, developed a deep hatred for both his moniker and the rock-and-roll legend. Eventually the day came when he couldn't stand

1

it anymore, stole his old man's benefit money and fucked off forever. His parents were only concerned for about a day then forgot all about him.

McNally had been brought up in Ballingry in Fife and spent the rest of his life trying to forget that particular fact. God hadn't given him a lot, but what he did have was Mediterranean looks and the gift of the gab, which he developed on his journey as a fraudster. He could con the fish out of the river, and he'd only suffered a couple of short spells inside, which was nothing compared to the number of crimes he'd *actually* committed. In his thirties McNally had latched onto the financial possibilities of online dating. At first it had only been to see if he could get for free what he normally paid for, but it had taken no time to realise the potential for conning lonely women out of their worldly possessions, or at least their savings, if he could get his sweaty little hands on them.

Given the type of life he'd led, he was fortunate in that he had no real friends or family to bother about or who might lead the police to his door. Half the forces in the UK were looking for him, and he'd even managed to get a blurred CCTV shot of his phizog on *Crimewatch*, so he was definitely a celebrity of sorts. More and more women were coming forward with stories about the Italian stallion who'd promised so much and left them with so little. Many of them had been devastated by their short, meaningless relationship with McNally and a couple of stories in the *Daily Mail* had racked up the pressure on the police to get their hands on him. He'd seen the headlines but thought if he was careful, kept on the move and canny about giving anything away, he could survive. He'd made a pile from his cons and planned to move to the Continent before his luck ran out. He fancied a country where the sun shone and he could rent a nice apartment by the sea. In his own deluded world, where guilt was something he just didn't recognise, he believed he deserved a bit of a break from the miserable British weather and the miserable British people. Most of his needs were simple so he was able to save most of his earnings, although he did have a weakness for young blonde prostitutes, who he used on a fairly regular basis.

That night McNally had booked one of the best restaurants in Edinburgh: it had attracted rave reviews for the standard of its food and service. He hadn't been in the capital for a couple of years and had been plying his trade across the south of England, but he'd probably taken one chance too many and now it was back to his homeland, where the women he met always adored the Latin-lover type. He'd arrived early at the restaurant and wanted to have a drink and think through his lines. He thought the latest one sounded interesting – not the type he would normally have expected to answer such a rank-cheese advert. The woman he'd spoken to on the phone sounded educated and her description seemed to suggest someone a bit younger than his normal dates. Grace. What a lovely name, he mused. He'd only had one other Grace, an unhappy widow who he'd actually found quite disgusting; however, she'd not only been loaded but couldn't wait to give him the money for his fictitious mother's cancer treatment in the States. She'd been convinced after their third wonderful date that McNally – or Tony as she knew him – was the man of her dreams; in fact she wished she'd met him before her bastard of a late husband, whose only redeeming feature had been his considerable wealth. McNally had already arranged to get a prostitute he'd been with the previous evening to call him during tonight's dinner and make it sound like an important business call from New York. He knew from tried and tested experience that kind of thing always worked a treat and was normally a sound investment.

The problem for McNally that night was that about a week earlier he'd been with another rather attractive hooker just after he'd arrived in Edinburgh. He wasn't to know that she was a registered 'covert human intelligence source' – or CHIS as they were known in the modern and politically correct police force. Another thing he couldn't know was that she was an avid follower of *Crimewatch* and the blurred shape of the Italian stallion, as the *Mail* loved to describe him, was enough for her to recognise her client even with his clothes off.

Right on the time they'd agreed to meet, the doors opened and a woman wearing a light raincoat appeared. McNally was just a bit more excited than usual and prayed to the god of fraudsters that she was in fact his date. Her hair was cut short, almost boyish, and her sharp, clean features were definitely a break away from his usual clientele. He watched her speaking to the waiter, who pointed towards his table. She looked round, smiled in his direction and he became even more excited because she was certainly over a decade younger than the women who tended to answer his adverts.

As she approached the table he smiled across the room and tried to give her the look that he always thought had a bit of Colin Firth in it. As the coat dropped from her shoulders the smile stalled, because unless he was very much mistaken the woman either had some kind of abnormality or she was well and truly pregnant – and very much nearer to birth than conception.

'Fuck that.' He said it quietly, but it was loud enough for the couple to his left to look round and the guy gave him a full glare. They shook their heads in concert and went back to their meal.

McNally liked the look of this one but pregnancy was a deal-breaker, so he decided that as soon as he could

4

make an exit he'd slope off to the toilets then offski and leave her with the bill.

'Hi, you must be Tony.' She stuck out a pale hand as he struggled to keep his cool and sense of frustration under control. He knew she could have been perfect for him – a real distraction after the acres of wrinkled or Botoxed flesh he often had to endure to make a buck. He stood up and took her hand. It was cool and soft. He stared into her green eyes, which even in the half-light of the restaurant seemed to glint with energy. Her smile suggested someone who was in control even though it was him planning a quick escape. He was fascinated even though he hadn't spoken to her bar the crap he'd given her on the phone. He wondered why this woman had answered his advert. There was a tingling along his spine as a thin bead of sweat ran its way down the small of his back and was absorbed by the elastic of his lucky red boxers.

'It's nice to meet you, Grace. You look wonderful.' He decided at that point to avoid her very obvious signs of pregnancy as the circuits in his brain tried to make sense of what he was seeing. There was a very slight tremor in his voice, which was unusual for a man who normally oozed confidence with his victims – vital where control was the key to unlocking their bank accounts.

'I've been dying to meet you, Hugh, or do you prefer that I call you Elvis? Don't know many people with the name Elvis,' she paused, 'apart from Elvis.'

The bead of sweat that had run down his back had turned into a stream. The sound of his real name put him on the edge of panic. Part of him said that she had to be a bizzy, but the woman sitting opposite him was pregnant and super tidy. It didn't compute – unless the police budgets had been cut so far they were keeping the women on till they produced.

'I'm sorry, what do you mean? My name's Tony.'

5

That was a useless answer because she clearly knew who he was. It occurred to him that she wouldn't be very nimble, being pregnant, so maybe it was time to fuck right off and not worry about meaningless conversation.

'I just need to go to the toilet for a moment and then perhaps we can come to some arrangement.' He said it as if it might work.

'Off you go, Elvis, but so that you know – I have no intention of coming after you, given my condition. If you decide after your lavvy break that you might need a bit of fresh air before saying goodbye, there's some of my team waiting for you. If you try to make a struggle of it, there's a guy there called Jimmy McGovern. Nice bloke but a mean bastard with anyone who wants to have a go. Don't get me wrong, he enjoys all that: ex-boxer and could have been a contender, as they say. What do you think, Elvis? The easy way or the hard way?'

McNally looked round the room and shook his head. He'd committed that most common of the seven deadly sins … greed. He'd just done a few jobs too many. It was over, and he knew that he was about to leave his world of fake dreams for a few years of good old Scottish-prison reality.

'Easy way if it's okay with you. Sorry, I didn't get your name.' He looked crestfallen – a date that had looked to have so much promise had car crashed in only a few short minutes.

'My name's Detective Superintendent Grace Macallan and you're under arrest.'

Her second in command, newly promoted Detective Chief Inspector Jimmy McGovern, took McNally away to the cell that would rest him overnight before his court appearance and a definite remand in custody while Macallan made her way a bit wearily back to the office and sipped some mint tea to try to ease the indigestion that was plaguing her days. McGovern eventually arrived back and smiled at his boss and friend who clearly needed to get away from the job now. She'd never fully recovered from the bomb blast all those months ago, so she was going to take some extra time off beyond her maternity leave. Today was to be her last day, and as usual he thought he'd have to surgically remove her from the office.

She looked up and smiled weakly. 'Okay. I know it's time to go. I'm knackered, but it was the business making an arrest before I went off.'

'An arrest!' he said. 'The health and safety gurus will be pissing blood in the morning when they find out you waddled your way into that restaurant to arrest our boy – and you hardly fit enough to sit down properly. Jack's probably waiting outside, so go have that baby and I'll see you soon. Don't ask me to keep you in the loop because I won't.'

She dragged herself onto her feet and despite the baby bump managed to give McGovern a big squeeze before she trudged down the corridor and out into the car park.

As she manoeuvred herself in beside Jack Fraser, she gave him a big grin and a wink. 'Okay, that's me on leave so let's do this.'

Jack smiled broadly and started up the engine. 'Just forget about it. The job will survive without you.'

She knew that – it was something that she thought about more and more. She put her head back on the rest and closed her eyes.

1

Eric Gunderson steered his sixty-foot trawler west–north-west towards his destination in the port of Eyemouth on the Berwickshire coast. He was a North Shields fisherman but his orders were to land north of the border.

Gunderson's blond hair, these days thin and lifeless, was sticky with nervous sweat. He had blue eyes that had once sparkled with the joy of a man who lived most of his life at sea and crammed all his human needs and desires into the short trips home. A product of generations of men who'd fished the shallow waters of the Dogger Bank from his home port on the Tyne, Gunderson had the looks of his ancestors, who'd harried then settled on the east coast of the British Isles.

The early summer weather had been kind since he'd navigated his boat, the *Brighter Dawn*, from Den Haag harbour on the coast of Holland into the cold waters of the North Sea. He'd left at the same time as two other British boats and they'd sailed in convoy across the unusually tranquil waters, never more than a mile apart. As night fell thousands of stars sparkled in the ink-dark sky, unspoiled apart from the boat's navigation lights.

He looked at the mirror-smooth blackness of the waters and saw the darting luminescence stirred up by a shoal of mackerel driven into high-speed terror by the approach of the rumbling engines. On a passing ship the watchman would just see the navigation lights of fellow sailors and nothing else, but he would know that below those small lights men lay in bunks built more like coffins than beds. He would recognise that feeling of brotherhood for the men he couldn't see but who thought just like him – the men who faced the uncertainty of life at sea and understood each other without the need for a common language. They carried a pride in what they faced from an element that could be the sweetest friend or the most terrible foe.

Gunderson felt nothing that resembled pride, and for the first time in his life he had a churning sense of self-loathing for what he, along with the men who skippered the other two boats, was doing. They'd all grown up in fishing families – had known nothing else but the sea and their trade. Life had always been hard, but they'd been there in the boom years when the British fishing fleets were making fortunes from the trade and an ever-increasing market. What they hadn't foreseen was the crash caused by muddled politicians in Brussels and London, or the problem of overfishing. Like the other skippers he'd invested heavily, getting his boat built only a year before it all started to go wrong. On top of everything else his wife had decided that the drop in his earnings meant an equivalent drop in her feelings for him. She'd taken the car and most of his worldly goods then threatened him with a call to the Inland Revenue about the 'black' income that he'd avoided paying over the years. She dictated a deal that he couldn't afford but would keep her in the comfort she thought she deserved.

Debt had crept in close then overwhelmed him.

Gunderson had always been a man who was prepared for almost anything and was afraid of no man. Debt – its consequences and especially the stigma – was something that made him shiver in his bed at night. In the good years friends were glad to shake his hand when he came home and smiled on cue when he bought their drinks, but they disappeared overnight when there was a problem. If they couldn't avoid him, they'd drop their eyes as if he was suffering from an incurable disease, and in a way that was the truth. In earlier and better times he would have said that what he did next was the act of a fool and didn't deserve a good man's sympathy.

It had been too easy, but he was a drowning man and would've grabbed any lifeline to keep him going. He had been introduced to someone with money to lend, and just like the most desperate junkie he'd believed that a cash hit would make all his problems go away. When he couldn't meet the deadline or the spiralling interest charges it seemed too good a deal to refuse the second and third loans. By that time he was drinking most of the day just to keep his mind anaesthetised and sheltered from the pile of dog shite that was the reality of his position. It wasn't just a pile of dog shite, it was a pile of dog shite on the pavement that people walked through then cursed. Unfortunately his creditors dealt in nothing but reality; the man who'd given him the loan and acted like an old friend morphed into his tormentor. It didn't matter what he did, the man seemed to be able to find him – and he didn't work alone. They were part of a bigger team, and when he'd told his few remaining friends and relatives who they were they'd stared at him as if he was insane. Everyone seemed to know them, and that they were bad news, yet no one had said a word at the time. No one wanted to help or have anything to do with the gangsters who were Gunderson's waking nightmare.

The threats increased, more deadlines passed and then he was given his final warning. Although the men knew Gunderson didn't have the money it didn't worry them – they had other plans for a man with a boat and the knowledge to sail it to the Netherlands and back. The other advantage was that he was clean as far as PC Plod was concerned, apart from a couple of convictions for being drunk and disorderly, plus a pier-side rammy with another skipper. For a deep-sea fisherman that was clean, and he'd always counted himself as an honest man.

He'd ended up staying with his mother, who wondered what had happened to the man she'd been proud to call her son. He was broken; if he wasn't an alcoholic he was the next best thing, and it was only the unproductive trips into the North Sea that kept him from drinking himself to death.

On his return from yet another trip where the catch had been slightly better than poor, it occurred to his mother that he seemed to have aged by five years each time he came back. She knew he had money worries but would have wept if she'd known the extent of his debt and who held the note on it.

Gunderson had kissed her tenderly on the forehead, but his throat ached for a taste of beer after a week at sea where the weather had been tropical and humid. Two minutes after he'd left his mother's door the heavens had opened and he'd run along the pavement cursing the water splashing in through the three-inch split in the sole of his shoe. He'd tried to cross the road and was waiting on the pavement for a space in the traffic when the Beamer drew up and someone inside opened the door.

'Get in, Eric. We don't want to have to chase you in this pissing rain.'

Gunderson leaned down and looked into the back of the car. He didn't know the guy perched on the rear seat, or the two in the front, but they looked fucking horrible and he didn't award himself a prize for guessing what they wanted. It dawned on him that they must know where his mother lived and that made up his mind to get in the motor with them. He was soaked and shaking but not with cold – just plain old-fashioned fear.

The deal was straightforward. He did what they asked, because otherwise they'd promised to bury him in the concrete under a set of Newcastle roadworks. Gunderson was a hard man, but these men were professional, and he knew enough about Northern criminals to know that they had his balls in a vice. They had merchandise that had to be picked up every so often in Holland – and he had a boat. They told him that if he mentioned one word to another human being they would get a couple of infected junkies to do his mother while he watched. That would be just before he got the concrete bath.

The first couple of trips had been straightforward and two heavies did the run across with him, picked up some packages in Scheveningen on the Dutch coast and went straight back to North Shields. He never saw what was in the cargo and the heavies hardly spoke a word, but he didn't need Sherlock Holmes to tell him what they were picking up. After the second trip he felt easy about it and asked how long it would take to pay off the debt. The main man had looked at his mate and laughed before grabbing Gunderson by the throat and spitting words into his face: 'When we say so. Do a few trips and then we'll see, but don't ask again, as a refusal tends to offend.' He'd turned to his partner and smirked at his own joke, but he wasn't finished humiliating Gunderson. 'Maybe we'll just get tired of looking at your face and call it a day,' he'd added, clearly enjoying himself as he pushed the fisherman away.

That was how it was, and he was caught in a trap with

few options – though the cemetery or lying under a new piece of road were certainly two of the strongest possibilities. The debts just kept going up from all sides though, and when the Inland Revenue told him they wanted to do a complete inspection of his finances, a fucking awful situation took a turn for the worse.

2

Forty miles from the Northumberland coast the two other boats changed course. The *Brighter Dawn* kept her line towards Eyemouth; the *Glory* and the *Horizon* headed further south for the Northumberland harbours of Amble and North Shields. They would all sail into port in the small hours of the morning and with as much cover of darkness as the early summer days would allow.

When the *Brighter Dawn* was less than two hours from Eyemouth harbour the streets of the fishing town were calm and quiet with most of the population asleep. The narrow streets were empty and even the occasional strutting fox raking for half-empty takeaway cartons was more than obvious to a watcher. The police tactical firearms and arrest teams came into the town as quietly as they could, but they couldn't hide until they were settled into their positions. In the circumstances, the operational commander was pleased with the smooth dispersal of the teams, and by the time they'd all settled down no one would have been any the wiser. It made no difference though because the two men who'd been watching the harbour area before the police arrived saw it all. They

15

looked at each other and realised that the presence of the heavy team meant only one thing – there was an informant; and that meant someone was going to die. The older man, Maxi Turner, calmly pressed the quick-dial button on his phone and it was answered after two rings. It was 1 a.m. but someone was waiting on the call.

'There's a whole fucking pig artillery unit arrived and no doubt they're waiting for our friends.'

There was a fifteen-second delay in the answer as the news was digested. 'Okay, stay out of sight but keep an eye on it till they arrive. The goods will have to disappear but the boat still needs to arrive as planned or those thick fucks will work out what we've worked out already. If they make a run for it they'll be intercepted before we can get them in somewhere else. As long as there's no cargo aboard we're fine, job done and we'll see what happens with the others.'

The phone clicked off and Turner slid back into his seat. He closed his eyes and spoke. 'Your watch, son, but nothing's going to happen till they arrive. Make sure and wake me as soon as you see their lights.'

The younger man looked round and cursed silently but accepted the privilege of rank. His name was Geordie Simms, a new recruit in the team, and getting up the ladder meant taking a lot of shit from people like the thug who was snoring quietly only a minute after having given his order. Simms pulled his collar up and wished he was back in Newcastle.

The man who took the call in North Shields put the phone back in his pocket and lit up a cigarette. Pete Handyside was a Geordie through to his black and white soul. An unusual-looking man for his chosen trade, where steroid-pumped muscle seemed to be a necessary requirement for acceptance and credibility, he looked more like a

16

bookkeeper and rarely put on a pound in weight through a good diet and running. His gaunt features had led a few people to underestimate him at their cost. What he had in abundance was speed and a vicious streak that surprised and frightened even those close to him. He was a career criminal and had no problem with admitting that to himself, his friends and his enemies. His family, however, were something else, and he protected his wife and infant children from the reality of his business.

He'd started young, when he realised that he didn't want to be like his father, a born drunk who got his kicks from beating his wife or kids, and sometimes all at once. The oldest of five, Handyside was stealing to help his mother and siblings before he was twelve years old. When he was sixteen every CID officer in North Shields knew him as one of the best burglars in the trade and someone who would admit fuck all if they brought him in. It didn't matter how much they threatened him or softened his ribs, he just took it and smiled back at them, even with the pain searing from the site of the blows. By the time he was eighteen he was running his own team, had a couple of detectives in his pocket and saw the drugs trade as his future. He'd been right on the money about that.

When he celebrated his thirtieth birthday he'd just stabbed to death his last remaining rival, an achievement that elevated his status to the main man in the North-east. It was about that time that he'd made a house call to a retired detective who lived on his own and on past memories. The policeman had been on Handyside's case since he was a kid, taking great delight in giving the boy a hard time, and Handyside's skin was still marked under the heart from the beatings he'd taken from the bastard.

A week later the neighbours had complained about the smell and the uniforms had found the old detective hanging from the back of his kitchen door with his trousers round his ankles. The heating had been left on full and he was starting to come apart already. They'd called a couple of detectives, who basically didn't give a fuck about their old colleague and were glad to see the back of a man even they'd regarded as a disgrace when he was in the job. His state of undress and the red top opened at page three beside him was enough to convince them that it was auto-erotic asphyxiation gone wrong (more common than Joe Public realised) so they'd just shaken their heads and written him off as a dirty old bastard. After all, he was a dinosaur and well known to have a serious drink problem, so who the fuck would be interested in topping him? The men who'd taken care of the late detective's last moments knew exactly what they were doing and how to dress it up so there was no need for the cops to treat it as a suspicious death.

On the night of the man's funeral Handyside had sat quietly at home, and although he wasn't much of a drinker he cracked open a bottle of champagne and poured his wife a glass of the best vintage in his cellar.

'What's the celebration?' she'd said, smiling at the man she loved so much – the man who treated her and the children as if they were sacred.

'You know how hard it was for me as a boy?'

The question had surprised the woman, who understood him better than most. She'd nodded, knowing his childhood had been scarred and that although it played on his mind he rarely brought it up. They had been raised in the same neighbourhood, but both her parents had smothered her with affection, and her father had worked long hours at sea to make life better for his only daughter. Handyside's family were the sort that people sneered at from a safe distance. She'd heard all the gossip about Peter's father and how he treated his wife and children. People had talked about it, sometimes with

18

too much relish, then made no attempt whatsoever to do anything about the abuse taking place so near their door-steps. She'd taken his hand as he spoke quietly, staring at some memory she couldn't see. 'I think I've finally left it behind. I paid off an old score this week and now I just want to concentrate on us.'

In his mind, killing the old detective had wiped part of the sins committed against him. He heard people talk about their fond memories of childhood and it made him grind his teeth at the thought that he'd never had one, only a series of adults who had stripped away his humanity piece by piece. He'd kissed his wife tenderly and she'd thought again how lucky she was to have this man. For a moment, the line in the local paper about the death of the detective who everyone said was as bent as a Westminster politician had made her wonder, but she knew to lock it away and love the man beside her. She didn't know the Pete Handyside mentioned so often as top of a criminal organisation and didn't want to meet him. She never even called him Pete, the name that made every criminal and detective in the North-east sit up and pay attention. Her man's name was Peter.

He loved only his wife and their two children, who he kept well away from his business, and they adored him right back as a gentle and loving father who had to work a lot of unsocial hours. His wife had only asked him once for the truth. He'd kissed her warmly, told her not to worry and she'd never asked again.

Now Handyside narrowed his eyes as the smoke drifted round his face. He was sure his gut instinct had been right. He'd suspected for months that there was an informant close to the heart of their operation and before the night was through they would know at least what part of the organisation had the problem. They'd lost two small consignments in transit, supposedly through

19

routine or accidental stops on couriers by the uniforms. He knew that had to be more than coincidence, and one of his bent detectives had told him that in each case anonymous phone calls had been made to the uniforms telling them that the couriers were on the road and where they were going. They'd both been headed to Scotland, which was clue one. It smacked of one of the heavy teams on a long-term operation and getting a few take-outs to build their case. On top of that, a couple of his boys had reported that they might have been followed. He knew there was always paranoia about surveillance, but the men who mentioned it were the best he had and cool heads.

Handyside pulled the phone out of his pocket, knowing he had to make the call. Other men would have flinched at what he was about to do, but he'd learned a long time ago that there was no room in his business for sentiment or weakness. Only the brute strong survived; the rest ended up in the ground or fed to the pigs – both animal and human.

The *Brighter Dawn* was in sight of the guiding lights on Eyemouth pier end and two of Handyside's men were on-board with Eric Gunderson. Alan Hunter was ex-army and had joined the team after six years in uniform and active service in New Labour's wars. He was brought up in Newcastle, ruthless and loyal, but the first to admit that even after all these years his boss was a bit of a mystery to him. But if you did the business for Handyside he looked after you. Unlike so many other so-called crime bosses, he was like the best football managers and took an interest in everyone, including their families. Hunter had done a spell inside for assaulting a uniformed cop who thought he could talk to him like a dog. The uniform had got what was coming and Hunter did six months in HMP Durham, which he thought was a worthwhile penalty for wiping the smile from the bastard's re-arranged gob. Handyside had been pissed off at his lack of discipline, but after the bollocking and final warning he'd made sure Hunter's partner received more than a wage every week he spent inside.

The other member of Handyside's team on the *Brighter Dawn* was Frankie Dillon, once upon a time a bent cop who'd taken one bite of the pie too many before the rubber heels ended his career and he went down for four years. He had the morals of a sewer rat, but Handyside recognised that he was useful as he knew how the cops worked and had added a couple of corrupt senior detectives to the payroll. He had nothing that resembled a guilty conscience and didn't see much difference between his life as the most crooked detective in the North-east and being an out-and-out gangster aside from a better standard of living. Handyside frightened him more than any man he'd ever met, and he knew that his previous life meant that if he fucked up he would die painfully.

The two men on the *Brighter Dawn* were both as tough as the brass on Tony Blair's neck and Handyside's best men for the job he'd given them. His gut had told him that if there was a problem then his money was on the Eyemouth cargo, and the news that a police team had arrived there shortened the odds a long way. Handyside had placed spotters out in Amble and North Shields, and before he'd finished another cigarette the texts and calls had come through from them to say there were no signs of police activity – or, for that matter, rival gangs. He'd already discounted the latter anyway, because the opposition were all dead as far as he knew. The other two boats had made port without a hitch and had unloaded not far from where he stood at the mouth of the great river, so he gave the order.

Hunter took the call then blinked several times as he tried to process the command. Finally he nodded and put the phone back in his pocket. He looked at Dillon and lit up a cigarette as he told him what they had to do. They were sitting on the afterdeck, chain-smoking and gulping coffee to keep themselves alert. They were brick hard, but they both knew that letting down Pete Handyside was not something they wanted to risk. Lung cancer was definitely a preferable option there. Handyside only gave an order once, and it had to be followed to the letter or there were guaranteed consequences. Both men lit up again before getting on with what had to be done. They were about to commit one of the worst crimes the UK had seen in years, outside of terrorist attacks, but they were professional and once they'd accepted the order they put away any doubts and just treated it as another job. Violence was nothing new to them, and by their calculation the victims weren't worth a fuck. They were wrong.

Hunter stepped onto the dimly lit bridge and tapped Gunderson on the shoulder. 'Stop the engines, skipper.'

'I don't understand,' he replied. 'What's the problem?'

Hunter blew a stream of smoke towards Gunderson's face to remind him that asking questions was not in his contract, then drove his knee into the fisherman's balls as hard as he could. He wanted him to concentrate on his pain for the next ten minutes rather than on what was about to happen on the deck of his boat. Gunderson collapsed in a ball of agony and curled up below the steering wheel, gasping at the fire in his lower abdomen before Hunter kicked him in the lower back to give him two seats of pain to keep him on the deck. He pushed the man aside with the base of his shoe then pulled steadily back on the controls until the deafening noise of the diesel engines reduced and the boat slowed to a stop, then drifted round till the light wind kept her on the broadside. She rolled gently without power and seemed peaceful under the starlit sky.

The first job was straightforward although it pained Dillon to weight up perfectly good dope and consign the cargo to the deep. But it had to be done. They already knew they were going to be run over by the filth when they hit port so it was a no-brainer.

Gunderson had hardly moved since the hydrogen bomb had exploded in his goolies. He lay on his side, a trickle of vomit trailing from the corner of his mouth onto the grating on the bridge floor. He didn't give a monkey's about the mess and his eyes were squeezed tight as he dealt with the rhythmic throb of pain in his lower body. He was oblivious to sight and sound and nothing else mattered at that moment, which was just as well. Gunderson was a tough and brave fisherman who could deal with most of what life threw at him, but not with what was happening as he lay in the darkness of the bridge. He knew there were women on-board; he'd seen four of them brought onto his boat in the middle of the night in Scheveningen. They'd been taken straight down into the cabin and Hunter had told him that it was off limits to him till they were clear in Eyemouth. He'd heard female voices when he went into the galley to brew up on the way across, but that was all. The only thing he could have remembered was that they were young and in the half-light looked beautiful. What he was sure of, and it had shocked him, was that they were terrified of the men who'd helped Hunter and Dillon bring them on-board. He'd picked up some of their voices and his best guess was that they were Eastern European or Russian, but they all looked like the kind of men who only their mothers could love.

While Gunderson dealt with his groin, Handyside's men got on with their job. There was a lot to do and then they had to prepare for the reception party waiting for them when they steamed into port.

There was always going to be a difficulty with the first girl, but it was easier than either Hunter or Dillon had expected. The fact that Dillon was sexually aroused by the thought of killing four women meant that only Hunter might have had any reservations, and if he did he was keeping them to himself. He wouldn't show them to a bent cop in any case. Once a rat detective, always a fucking rat detective as far as he was concerned, and he had no doubt that any signs of dissent would be passed back to Handyside.

The first girl was brought on deck for the first time since they'd boarded in the Netherlands and she looked out into the dark night and sucked in the fresh air. She saw the flashing harbour lights just above the horizon and smiled as she realised they were nearly on land. Even on the calm seas she'd felt sick all the way across with the combination of motion, diesel fumes and unwashed bodies. She'd been apprehensive when they'd brought her up to the deck alone but the sight of the distant shore lights reassured her that at least they could get their feet on dry land again. Her English was okay and she'd been well educated back home in Slovakia.

'Can I use the toilet, sir?' She tried to smile at the two Englishmen, who seemed less frightening than the Croatians who'd drugged and kidnapped her near the Slovakian border. Dillon smiled and said, 'Of course,' as Hunter came up behind her with the hammer. He didn't make any mistake and the girl knew nothing about it. The blow took her just behind the ear and penetrated the skull, killing her almost immediately.

'Christ, Al, that's how to fucking do it.' Dillon leered at the sight of the girl twitching on the deck as a plume of red blossomed round her head.

Hunter grabbed Dillon by the throat and held the hammer a couple of feet above the man's skull. 'Let's just make it quick. I've got a feeling you might enjoy this sort of thing and let me tell you now that if I see that stupid fucking smile again I'll put you in the water with them.' He pushed Dillon away in disgust and tried to blank out what they were doing. It only took them a few minutes to weight the girl and drop her over the side. The second girl went quickly and Hunter prayed that it would all go the same way.

On the bridge Gunderson had hardly moved but the pain had dropped one level and his senses started to search outside his own body. The boat rolled gently on the light south-easterly swell and the timbers creaked and moaned in reaction to the waves. The metal stays tapped against the masts and these were all noises so familiar to sailors that they barely heard them. The first sound that made Gunderson move his thoughts from his groin to the world outside his head was a heavy splash as the second girl was dropped into the water. Handyside's men had tried to drop the body in as gently as possible to avoid spooking the other women, but on such a quiet night it was difficult to conceal. Gunderson lifted his head an inch from the grating and tried for a moment to compute, but an unexpected spear of heat lanced from his groin up to his neck, and he dropped his head back onto the floor and groaned. The sensation passed and he tried to steady his breathing.

Dillon scrambled down the companionway leading to the cabin and looked at the two girls who were left. Like caged animals waiting for their turn in the abattoir, they were nervous – events were starting to panic them. Hunter and Dillon were no sailors and hadn't realised that on a boat drifting in quiet seas anyone below becomes sensitive to sound, which carries from the water like an echo chamber. Two women had gone on deck and the sound of something heavy dropping into the water close to the hull had followed. Dillon read the signs – the wide eyes and the slight recoil when he came into the cabin. If anything, their reaction made him even more aroused and he cursed Hunter, who refused to let him wield the hammer. He promised himself there would be payback as soon as he could blindside the bastard. No matter what he did for Handyside, Hunter always seemed to be top of the pecking order among the troops.

He pointed at the girl nearest to him and grabbed her by the wrist, which just confirmed what the young women were sensing. For reasons they couldn't understand something had gone wrong and they weren't even going to be allowed the indignity of being sold as sex slaves.

The girl who Dillon had selected was Ingrid Richter, born in Prague but of German heritage. She was the product of a stable, happy family who cherished her and her younger sister above all else in their lives. A brush with drugs at Zagreb University had brought her into contact with people who had an order for Eastern European females under twenty-five with glossy magazine looks. Rich, deviant businessmen in the West were paying fortunes for a particular kind of woman who could be held discreetly and used whenever and however they liked. As part of the deal the gangs who sold the women promised to dispose of them whenever the men tired of their purchase. It was win-win for the gangs, who would take the girls back and put them straight into the brothels or hire them out as escorts, depending on how much damage they'd suffered at the hands of their previous owners.

But Richter was no ordinary girl: her father and his forefathers were steeped in the military and had fought in European wars down through the ages, sometimes on different sides of the same conflict. Her father had taught her to be self-reliant, and through sport and self-development she'd become a model student. Only a climbing accident had prevented her representing her country in the winter Olympics. Her curiosity with dope had been stupid but she was no worse than the majority of other students who dabbled with new experiences at university. Her problem was that her looks made people stare: at her clear, pale skin and the long, thick black hair surrounding a face that seemed to have been carved into clean, perfect lines. She wasn't tall but it made no difference, and if anything her broad shoulders and slim, toned body gave her a look that was her own. Above all she was strong, and even when she was drugged and abducted by the traffickers she hadn't panicked. Instead of fear she'd used her hatred of these men to keep her in control, swearing that when the opportunity came she would seize the moment rather than let them win. She knew enough to work out that even though she had been abducted, she would never be that far from the world she knew – and thus safety. What had happened on the boat was not something she'd bargained for, but she'd already worked out that at the top of the ladders she would have only moments and few options if they were still at sea.

She looked at the man gripping her wrist and let her hate take control. She saw a trickle of saliva on his chin and the way his lips twitched with obvious pleasure. Richter had been part of the university judo team and could tell that this man had no idea how to restrain her properly; she'd already identified his first mistake in believing that their fear was all he would need to deal with the young women on the boat. That was an important mistake, and she had to use any weakness to her limited advantage. She wanted to hurt him badly, but she had no idea who else was at the top of the ladders and she'd already worked out that there was only one possible escape route – into the sea itself. At the very least she would fight rather than be slaughtered like some dumb animal, and if it was the last thing she did she would drive something into this man's eyes to make sure he never looked at another woman as long as he lived.

Dillon had to let go of her so she could climb up the narrow companionway ladders and into the small galley behind the bridge. On the last step of the ladders she looked round nervously, trying to take in as much information as possible, and she thought she could hear the sound of someone breathing heavily, as if in pain, coming from the direction of the bridge. She believed she had only moments to grasp life or die in the attempt, and her heart raced with adrenalin. Dillon had turned his back for a moment, but she had to wait, knowing there was another man called Al somewhere. He looked tough and smart compared to the man who'd dragged her from the cabin. She already knew that Dillon was an evil little bastard – every time he'd come into the cabin to put food on the table there had been no mistaking what was in his eyes. Someone or the fear of someone was the only thing that had kept him from hurting them before they'd arrived wherever they were going. The men were English so it had to be the UK.

Dillon grabbed her by the upper arm again, digging the points of his fingers into her flesh. That was another mistake and left her enough room for movement when she was ready. He would have to let her go again as he navigated through the narrow galley door and onto the open deck. She saw the glare of the halogen lights illuminating the afterdeck outside but nothing beyond. In microseconds her survival instinct saved another piece of information. She'd sailed many times and knew boats.

In darkness and with powerful deck lights on it was difficult to see beyond the arc of the lights and the waters close to the boat, so her first problem was that she had no idea how far she was from land, although the length of time they'd been on-board meant they had to be near enough to their destination. The other issue was that on her own in the chill waters of the North Sea with nothing to guide her she would die anyway. Her stomach trembled and fear weakened her knees for a moment before she remembered that there would be only one brief opportunity to save herself so she could either take it or let these animals steal her young life.

Richter couldn't have known that no more than fifteen feet from her Eric Gunderson had struggled to his knees, alarmed by the sounds he was starting to analyse. He pulled himself upright and waited till his legs felt like they could take his weight again. He was in near panic and knew that something had gone badly wrong with the original plan.

The young woman stepped out onto the deck and Dillon had to let her go for a moment as they both negotiated the narrow galley door. He turned and faced her square on and his eyes sparkled with the lust he was hardly able to control. She flicked her eyes round the deck space at the back of the galley. There was no sign of the other man, but she knew he was close so her next move had to be right – it would be the difference between living and dying. She'd taken in all she saw around her in an instant and had identified what she needed if she made it into the water. It was time, and what happened in fractions of a second moved through her mind in freeze frames. The battle for her life and what might lie in the future were all wrapped up in a brief struggle with the man who smiled at her and quivered with the excitement of what he thought was about to happen. She snapped her head up to meet his stare, bared her teeth and snarled like a dog just before letting her knees bend, dragging him down slightly through his grip. He didn't work out in time that she'd pulled him off balance, but her balance was perfect and she moved her weight onto her front foot and propelled herself upwards, bunching the fingers of her free hand with the middle knuckle out to form a hard wedge shape. She drove her balled fist into his throat almost exactly on the point of his Adam's apple. Dillon dropped in a heap, choking and struggling to cope with the excruciating pain in his neck. He clutched his throat and heaved like a dying man as she grabbed the life belt with the boat's name from its cradle next to the galley door. In one movement she pulled it free, stepped over Dillon and was at the boat's rail. She looked round and saw Hunter moving along the side of the superstructure, no more than three paces from her and holding a half-raised hammer.

'You fucking bitch.'

For a moment Richter froze, snared by the horror of the man moving towards her, his eyes blazing. She had expended so much energy in her fight to live, but in that moment her courage failed as she watched the man who wanted to kill her close in. Like a startled deer in the headlights she was trapped by her own terror.

Moments change lives, and as Hunter covered those last few steps towards the girl the *Brighter Dawn* tipped over ten degrees as a gentle swell ran past her. It threw him off balance for a moment and he gripped the handrail to steady himself, but he'd lost his forward momentum. It was enough to break the spell holding Ingrid Richter. She stepped onto the boat's rail and leapt as far from the *Brighter Dawn* as she could.

The shock of the cold water sucked the breath from her lungs, but she was in a fight for survival and dragging the lifebelt behind her she swam one-handed, trying to escape the boat's lights.

Hunter cursed and watched the thrashing figure of the girl fighting for her life. 'You bitch,' he yelled. 'I'll cut your fucking throat when I get you!'

It was a useless call and he knew it. He had to do something, but the man who could move the boat was nursing his balls on the bridge and Dillon was out of the game for the time being. He was helpless and angry. He threw the hammer towards Richter and it missed her by a couple of yards. He watched her shape blur in the area between light and dark then disappear into the night. She was gone.

He turned and looked at Dillon, who'd tried to get onto his knees, his breath still rattling through his injured throat. Hunter kicked him in the gut as hard as he could then stood over the prostrate figure, who started sobbing like a child.

'If that girl lives we might as well dig our own fucking graves and be done with it. I knew it – Pete Handyside should have wasted you a long time ago.' He cleared his nose into his throat and spat a mouthful on Dillon, then kicked him again before he sat down and lit up another cigarette.

About two hundred yards from the *Brighter Dawn* Richter was treading water in the relative safety of the dark night. The boat itself was lit up like a sports stadium so she could see everything that was happening. Most importantly, as she leapt into the water she'd spotted the lights on the horizon that offered the possibility of survival. She was still several miles from safety, but if they couldn't find her then she might have a chance, although she was already suffering from the cold and had to move. The problem was that at some point the boat would get underway and they would guess that she was making for those flickering lights, so against her instincts she swam seawards, putting the boat between herself and the Berwickshire coast. Ingrid Richter hadn't needed religion since she was a child but in that moment she needed God to exist and prayed that they would head for land and not circle the waters looking for her.

Hunter finished his cigarette. They had to get going or the whole thing was going to turn into a massive cluster-fuck – if it wasn't one already. He had to get Gunderson working, look for the girl on the way in and just hope that the bitch couldn't survive the sea temperatures. 'What a fucking mess.' He said it quietly and looked round to see Dillon struggling to sit up. He passed him without a word, stepped into the galley and up three short steps to the bridge. Gunderson was on his feet and took a pace back when Hunter stood face to face with him.

'Did you see what just happened?'

Gunderson knew that whatever answer he gave would be the wrong one and he was drowning in his own fears. In that moment he realised that he knew too much and he couldn't escape the same fate as the men on his boat. Wherever they were going he would carry the same guilt. The reality of the situation steadied him, and he remembered who he was and what he'd once been. 'I didn't see it, but I heard enough,' he said.

Hunter nodded without a word, studying the man opposite him, the near darkness on the bridge accentuating the deep lines that had been hacked into the fisherman's face in his years at sea. Hunter pulled out his cigarettes and offered them to Gunderson, who picked one out of the crumpled pack. They lit up and both sucked in the first lungful as if they hadn't smoked for a month.

'Listen,' Hunter said quietly, all the anger gone from his voice, 'we're fucked, and I don't know if you've worked it out, but when I say "we" I'm including you, my friend.' He dragged deeply on the cigarette, rubbed the back of his neck wearily and wished he was somewhere else. He tried to block out the fact that Ingrid Richter might survive, but it was impossible. They had no option but to finish the job and then lie to Pete Handyside's face. A cold shiver ran the length of his body. He took a deep breath and looked at Gunderson, who was quiet and had nearly finished his smoke; he'd sucked at it greedily and was down to the filter in half the normal time.

'We've killed two women, one made it over the side and there's one still in the cabin. She has to go. There's no other option. There's an armed posse of Scotland's finest waiting for us when we get into Eyemouth so the boat has to be clean when we get in. There's no point in trying to run to another port because they'll track us quite easily and we'd end up with Royal fucking Navy commandos on the case. Do you follow me?'

Gunderson nodded and felt calm. He'd descended into a nightmare and all he could do was deal with it. Hunter explained what they had to do when they got into port, where they'd be lifted by the police. The way out was to stick to the story that they'd hired the boat to pick up a load of counterfeit goods in Holland but it had fallen through. Their lawyers would arrive before they got them to a station, and if they said fuck all apart from the cover story they'd make it out of the mess.

'That's only part of it. If we get through that we've got to convince Pete Handyside. You've heard of him?'

Gunderson nodded. 'Who hasn't?' He'd already worried years off his life that he was owned by some of the worst gangsters in the North-east, but finding out that the man who pulled the strings was Pete Handyside was just more bad news than he needed.

'Can you do this?' Hunter looked Gunderson straight in the eye, demanding the right answer.

'Is there a choice?' Gunderson said, having temporarily rediscovered his balls. All the other options were shit and there looked to be only one way out. What Gunderson wanted was an escape route and then to disappear to a place where these men couldn't find him.

Hunter smiled. 'Either we all spend the rest of our naturals in some Jock prison or my gaffer cuts us up for pig food. Or we get lucky and survive this.'

Gunderson asked for another cigarette. 'Okay. Do what you have to do and let's get ashore or they'll wonder why we're drifting about only a few miles from the harbour.'

Hunter went out onto the afterdeck and resisted the temptation to give Dillon another shot. He needed him to get the job finished. 'Get the girl up here, and don't fuck it up this time or you go in after her.'

Out in the darkness to the east of the *Brighter Dawn*, Richter continued to tread water, waiting for the boat to move. She was cold and beginning to doubt whether she could make it to the lights on the horizon. They looked near enough, but every minute in the numbing temperature of the water would be an ordeal. Over the next few minutes she felt as if she was a spectator to a vile stage show, with the actors playing out the last scene in the glare of the deck lights. She watched the girl she'd only known as Hanna being led onto the deck without protest. Alan Hunter took her life. Richter stared on in horror as they weighted the girl's body and pushed her over the side, into the depths of the sea. She bit into her hand to stop herself screaming, tasting blood, but kept biting till

34

her instincts turned back to hatred for the men on the boat. Even so far from the *Brighter Dawn* she could see that the last girl had been paralysed with fear and went to her death without resistance.

On the bridge Gunderson sobbed quietly as he listened to the sounds of her death – her weighted body hitting the dark waters. His old life was gone and all he felt was self-loathing for what he'd become. Hunter joined him. 'It's done. Let's get the fuck out of here and see if we can get the cops off our backs. Maybe we'll see the girl who went over and finish the job.'

Dillon and Hunter washed the decks down with power hoses and scrubbers till the jets of salt water had removed all trace of the girls. They went down into the cabin and made sure that the few items the girls had brought with them were bagged up, weighted and joined their owners beneath the North Sea.

Gunderson powered up the engines and set a course for Eyemouth as Hunter and Dillon went forward and scanned the waters they sailed through, hoping for a sight of Richter, though her name would have meant nothing to them. Dillon couldn't speak properly – his throat still ached and his gut hurt from Hunter's boots. He promised himself he'd slice the bastard the first chance he got and hoped they could spot the girl so he could stare into her eyes as she died with his hands clasped round her throat.

Meanwhile, on the bridge, Gunderson was wondering what had happened to his life. He felt almost nothing after the shock of what he'd witnessed on the afterdeck of the *Brighter Dawn*. It was as if his soul had died along with the girls who would now be lying at the bottom of the sea. At first he'd felt like throwing himself over the side as he burned with guilt, but here he was, guiding his boat towards the harbour lights. All he wanted to do was live and survive this nightmare. He wondered why he felt so little for the nameless women who'd perished that night.

He was damned, and he knew it.

3

As the *Brighter Dawn* sailed past the treacherous Hurkar Rocks and through the narrow entrance to Eyemouth harbour the call went out to the police team to stand by. DCI Jimmy McGovern had arrived to take control once the boat had been boarded and the men aboard detained. He'd briefed the uniformed inspector in charge of the search team and told him that the information had come from a proven source so it would be on the money. The boat had a consignment of cocaine, amphetamine tablets and women being trafficked into prostitution. The young inspector was excited at the prospect of getting involved in international organised crime, a nice change from breaking down the doors of low-life dealers on Lothian estates.

'Only thing that's bothering us, sir, is that we've got a spotter team up on the cliffs on St Abb's Head to the north of the harbour. They're sure that the *Brighter Dawn* was behind schedule and should have arrived by now. Might be nothing but I thought I'd mention it.'

McGovern smiled. Everyone looked for bad omens on these jobs, but it changed nothing, regardless of what they felt or saw. The job was in place and they had to do what they'd planned. He knew what no one else on the operation did – that the source was an undercover officer risking his life inside a gang to feed them the information. It was part of something bigger, but other than McGovern no one on the Eyemouth operation needed to know. The fewer people who knew about a UC the better. It was one of the cornerstones of good intelligence handling. The more people that knew about a sensitive operation the more likely it was that some bent or dipstick fucker would drop it in the other side's lap.

McGovern was with a young detective constable from his own team, and another half dozen of his guys were well back but available if required. He watched from a distance as, eventually, the *Brighter Dawn* steered into the long narrow harbour then manoeuvred alongside her berth. Two men put ropes ashore and tied the boat safely to the pier. They were joined by a third man from the boat, and they stood on the pier together, smoking and looking around anxiously. McGovern and every other cop there presumed they were holding on for their contacts, but none came. They couldn't know that the targets were waiting for the police team to swarm all over them. After a long half hour McGovern picked up his radio and called the inspector.

'I don't get it. They shouldn't be hanging about with what they have aboard.'

He waited for a few moments then heard the slight hiss on the radio before the inspector replied, his voice flat with the uncertainty of what to do next. 'We're starting to see one or two early workers on the go and we don't need an audience for this, sir.' He'd thrown the ball firmly into McGovern's lap.

'Okay, Inspector, we have a lot of issues here and number one is those women on the boat. We can't wait for the rest of the bandits to arrive.' He remembered the old maxim that more operations fail because of indecision than wrong decisions. He gave the order to the firearms teams to move in and make the arrests. It was all over in two minutes and McGovern watched through his binoculars as the men were restrained and the rest of the team secured the boat. Within five minutes the search team was cleared to go aboard, while McGovern sat massaging the scar tissue above his eyes that he'd earned during his boxing career. He'd suddenly become tired and his gut told him exactly what was going to come back from the search team. He didn't have to wait long before the inspector was back on the air.

'The boat's as clean as a whistle, sir. We'll have to take it apart in case it's a good concealment, but definitely no women on-board. There are three men and they're saying they went to Holland to pick up a load of counterfeit goods, but the deal fell through. They're already shouting for their lawyers.'

McGovern felt it in his water: they could search till Boris Johnson became a member of the Communist Party, but something had gone badly wrong. He got out of the car and tried to think it through. The information was good and had come from the UC. He could have got it wrong but he'd provided information that had taken out two consignments already. The Police Service of Scotland had been working on a joint cross-border operation with the National Crime Agency and it had been going well up to that point. There could have been a transfer at sea, but why go to all that trouble? His head started to ache with the tension but he hardly noticed, and in any case it was just part of being involved in a long-term operation. Headaches, hangovers and heartburn – they all came with the territory.

He snapped his head up and his mind fixed on one other

possibility: they'd known in advance that the police were waiting for them. The inspector had told him the boat was behind schedule. 'What does it mean?' he wondered out loud as the pain in his skull went up another point on the Richter scale. If they suspected something then the UC could be compromised. The problems started to overwhelm his thought processes, and then it came to him – if they knew, were they watching the whole fucked-up operation taking place?

McGovern stepped away from the car and looked round the harbour area. Eyemouth was a busy port, but it was a small place with myriad tight, winding streets in the old town next to the harbour. On all sides it was surrounded by higher ground leading down to the river that gave the ancient port its name. He grabbed the radio and called to his own team, who were all in unmarked cars.

He told them the operation might be compromised and being watched by the bandits. 'Get out of the cars, split up, take a patch each and see if you can sniff anything out.' He carved the surrounding areas into six sections and gave them a patch each. They were already on the move, realising why their DCI was pissed off.

McGovern looked again through his binoculars and saw the three men from the boat being shoved into the back of separate cars to be taken for interview. He went back to his car and pulled out a flask of coffee. It agitated his bladder but it had kept him going through the night at least. He leaned against the car and sipped a mouthful. It lacked quality but gave him the required kick.

'Jesus.'

The detective who was driving him was still in the car and tired. 'What's that, boss?'

McGovern ignored him. He shook his head, trying

to fend off another idea that had come to him. If the information was right about the cargo and the crew had been warned somehow, what had they done? It didn't matter a shit about the cocaine ... but the girls? 'Fuck.' He jumped into the car and called in to get a forensic team there as soon as. He called the inspector and told him to secure the boat and treat it as a crime scene.

McGovern's men trawled their sectors on foot looking for any signs that there were watchers somewhere in the area. Twenty minutes after they started the search, one of the detectives was on the south side of the river but above the harbour and looking down into the basin. He stopped in a doorway and wondered if they were wasting their time. They were getting wet through in the light drizzle that had started to fall as the first dull touch of light started to mark the eastern horizon. He was moving from foot to foot, feeling cold and pissed off when he saw it. Fifty yards ahead of him the tiny but clear glow of a cigarette flared for a second in a parked saloon. He screwed up his eyes and moved closer but kept as much cover as he could. The cigarette glowed again and he could see that there were two people in the dark interior of the car.

The two men were tired as well as bored and thought they'd seen enough for one night. Maxi Turner was the older of the two watchers and had decided there wasn't anything more to see – the boat had arrived, the cavalry had picked them up and the place was swarming with the law.

'Time to get out of here, son; the morning traffic will be picking up so let's get the fuck over the border. Gimme a minute for a hit or a miss.'

He pushed the car door open and saw someone moving into the shadows behind them. He was a pro and didn't panic, opening his flies so he could do what he had to do. As he got back in the car he threw his cigarette onto the pavement. 'Okay, we've got company behind us. Drive off slowly and try to look like an honest citizen. Don't, and I repeat don't, get fucking excited or we'll have these Jock fuckers all over us.'

As they moved away the detective managed to get part of the car number and wrote it on the back of his hand. He pulled out his radio and cursed when he realised the battery had gone down, but that was par for the course. He had his mobile and called McGovern, who was on his phone trying to arrange for SOCOs to attend.

On the outskirts of Eyemouth the Newcastle men stopped the car in a quiet lay-by, opened the boot and changed the number plates. When they'd done that the older man smiled and lit up another cigarette. 'Okay, son, this is the privilege of rank. I'm going to drop you five minutes from here at Ayton near the A1. If they've spotted us they'll be looking for the wrong number plate and two men. You keep your head down and get a bus later. Let's go.'

The younger man shook his head, realising that being a gangster wasn't all glamour, but he knew better than to argue with someone like Turner, who was the closest Pete Handyside had to a trusted lieutenant.

Turner had grown up in North Shields with Handyside and was probably the only person in their world who made sense of the man. They'd screwed the same properties as teenagers, done time together and killed together. Turner had been best man at his wedding. Handyside had the brains and nous for leadership and Turner was a happy second in command. He didn't love his boss, but he trusted him and knew that he would always cover his back. Turner was Mr Ordinary to look at, and he had a remarkably quiet speaking voice, but he was a gangster's gangster: streetwise, suspicious and give him the task and it was done.

When McGovern got the information about the car ten minutes had already passed and it was too late. A message was sent to the control room, but by the time the patrol cars picked it up Handyside's man was heading south on his own.

McGovern headed to where the men had been seen and picked up the detective who'd spotted the watchers. 'Show me exactly where they were parked.' They hurried to the spot and McGovern cursed. It was perfect, and the bastards must have seen it all, including the teams getting into place. He shook his head and looked down.

'Well, well, well – those boys have obviously got some bad habits.' He knelt down and looked at the two clusters of cigarette butts about six feet apart. 'It must have been a long night. Don't let anyone near this. I'll get the SOCOs to bag it all up. Not so fucking smart.'

He stood up, stretched his back and ran the exact amount of time he had left till retirement through his mind, as he did every two or three days. Then he put his hand on the young detective's shoulders. 'That was good work, son; take the weekend off.' It was one of the oldest jokes in the book – the detective was due to be off anyway. But the smile from McGovern was enough. Every man in the team looked up to him. Warm words didn't come often, but they meant everything.

Handyside took the call that his men were clear, one on his way back and the other head down till he could get home by public transport.

'Good work. Go and get some sleep and I'll see you later in the day.'

A weak pink light started to rise above the horizon

as he stared over the River Tyne, watching the early-morning activity starting up around and on the great river. Although he usually kept his tobacco habit to just two or three a day, he'd fired up nearly a whole packet during the night. The smoke and exhaustion irritated the rims of his eyes, but he managed a half-smile that his instinct had been right. About a year earlier he'd agreed to form a business partnership with the top men from Edinburgh and Glasgow. He liked to call it the 'Northern Alliance' and enjoyed reminding everyone that it worked even better without any cockney wankers or Scouse gits to fuck things up. It had performed nicely for a while, but then the problems started. He was sure his team were sound, and he was relieved it wasn't one of them, but in the business of organised crime it was safer to operate without the luxury of trust. Most of his team had been with him since they were in their teens and breaking into warehouses around Newcastle. What had happened in Eyemouth proved the rat was somewhere in the Edinburgh team and his next step was to root out the poisonous little fucker and send out a message to anyone else who wanted to do business with the law.

He lost all sense of time as he stood motionless, running the options and problems through his head. A movement close by snapped him back to reality and he watched a beat cop walk slowly past him. There was something quite reassuring about seeing the policeman there at that time. He said hello to the uniform, who nodded without paying any attention.

For the policeman there was nothing unusual about lonely characters doing their thinking in the middle of the night as they stared out at the river. Sometimes they jumped in, but as far as the cop was concerned that was their business; it wasn't on his agenda to save the sad bastards and risk getting wet. He was on his way back

44

to the station to sign off and get home to his bed. He wasn't to know that he'd just nodded to the man who'd given an order that would fill the front pages for weeks and unleash a chain of events that would reverberate for months, claiming more victims who were safely in their beds at that moment. A different cop might have made a name for him or herself and prevented the consequences of that night, but fate had decreed otherwise.

The bored uniform had failed to recognise Newcastle's most important criminal, who looked round at the river again then beyond to the lighthouse beacons at the entrance to the Tyne. His mouth opened slightly as he watched the morning sky, which seemed to have caught fire, a copper glow melting across his view as if the end of the world had come. It seemed to pour into the calm glass sea, mixing with the greys and blues of the water and turning it to the colour of blood. The spreading fingers of reflected light ran along the surface towards the river – towards him. 'Red sky in the morning, sailor's warning.' He had been taught in school that it was the 'shepherd's warning' and remembered being ticked off by the legions of seamen who inhabited his childhood community. 'There's no bloody shepherds in North Shields, son,' they'd reminded him. He'd felt small and weak for a moment, but it had passed.

He slipped behind the wheel of his Merc and decided that when he was rested up he'd call an urgent meeting. If they didn't turn up, he'd make the journey north and kill them all himself. He was more than capable of doing it, but he was sure none of the Jocks were stupid enough to ignore a call from him. It was business; he'd go home and sleep without any concern about either the order he'd given to his two men or what they might have done to the women whose worst crime had been to be born female and attractive.

As soon as he crossed the threshold of his front door he moved into his other universe. He showered and then slipped beneath the sheets, wrapping his arm round his wife's waist. She moaned quietly and pulled him closer, loving the feel of his cool skin against her. He was asleep within minutes.

Hunter, Dillon and Gunderson sweated their way through the interviews, but with great encouragement from their lawyers they stuck to their scripts and, as McGovern had already worked out, they were going to live to fight another day. They eventually walked free and the detectives who'd hoped for so much the previous night shook their heads in frustration. McGovern spoke to them and all he got back was that Hunter and Dillon were true pros, sneering through their interviews. Gunderson was different: no real form for crime, looking spaced out and saying next to nothing.

The senior interviewing officer summed it up for McGovern. 'I'm no shrink but I'd say that Gunderson's head was fucked up.'

'Put it in your notes and we'll look at it later. I'm going to get my head on the pillow. Goodnight or morning, boys.' McGovern said it wearily and headed home.

4

Handyside looked round the upstairs lounge of a pub he owned near the old fish quays in North Shields, pleased that at least everyone seemed to be arriving on time. The area was a million miles from the one Handyside had inhabited as a kid; the old riverside near the fishing port had been redeveloped and was now full of smart flats and even smarter restaurants. Those days when the area swarmed with fishermen from ports all over the country were gone, but the old men still told stories about the Jungle, one of the most famous boozers in the North-east, where you could buy sex or stolen goods within five minutes of entering the place. In those days the dark streets had echoed with the sounds of men who'd been at sea too long then drank too much, and the occasional mass brawl meant a tough response from the local police force, who treated the area like a war zone. It was just memories now, but Handyside never forgot where he came from – or how hard it had been to climb out of that cesspit. He never wanted to fall back in and he was determined he never would. He saw the world as a bad place full of bad people, including him, and all he wanted was to keep that world away from his family, his only reason for getting out of bed in the morning. What had surprised him was that as he climbed through the social barriers all he found were more bad people. Councillors, lawyers, politicians and detectives – all on the make, and the only difference from his old community was that they needed bigger piles of wonga to keep them happy – or what passed for happiness.

Handyside had only managed a few hours' sleep before he'd told the men from Glasgow and Edinburgh that there was a hitch that required them to get their arses into gear and meet up with him.

The Edinburgh boys walked through the door first, shook his hand then took their seats. They weren't such a problem – easy enough to deal with in normal circumstances – but he knew what was about to be discussed wasn't normal, and he was going to test the level of minerals in their blood.

Eddie and Pat Fleming were twins and hardly old enough to be called men, but they had balls and Handyside had done quite a bit of good business with their old man, Joe, in the past. With his eldest son he'd run almost the whole show in Edinburgh till they were slaughtered by a loyalist team from Belfast who'd tried to take over business in the city. Most of the Belfast boys had died in what had followed. The Fleming twins hadn't been slow to re-establish the family's hold on the capital, and Lothian after that. Eddie was the one with the brains while Pat was all brawn and balls. Handyside liked Eddie – he reminded him of himself a few years earlier, fighting his way through the swamp to get where he was.

The twins were sitting opposite Handyside, their smiles slightly nervous, and ordered beers when they were offered a drink. Given the previous night's events, with the loss of gear and women that had been heading their way, they didn't need to be told there was a problem, though they didn't know it all. Their driver (and muscle when he was required) was shown into a side room with a stocked buffet that would keep him happy while the bosses were in conference. Handyside was fascinated to see how they would react when they realised there was a rat in their team; or, he wondered, was it one of the twins themselves?

The Glasgow contingent arrived ten minutes later, and as always made a fucking racket when they came in the front door. He heard them coming up the stairs, pissing themselves at some in-joke as only the Glasgow gangsters knew how. Handyside didn't like too much joviality and they wouldn't be fucking laughing when he dropped the latest developments on them. If they did, he'd treat it as unprofessional and there'd be consequences. He wondered if he'd made the right choices with the team from the west of Scotland. The problem he'd noticed with them was that they enjoyed playing to their stereotype a bit too much. There was more than a bit of life imitating art and it annoyed him. They thought being born in 'No Mean City' made them fireproof; well, Handyside decided he would burn the bastards if the point needed to be made that they were able to feel pain just like everyone else.

Eddie Fleming sipped his beer and took the chance to peer over the bottle when it was at his lips. He did his best not to stare at Handyside, but the man intrigued him. Like his host, he heard the arrival of the Glasgow gangsters and saw that even at a distance their lack of decorum annoyed Handyside, and whatever he was, he seemed to believe in good manners right up to the point that he killed his enemies.

Eddie just couldn't tie the man he watched to his reputation and remembered the first time he'd met him.

He'd heard all the stories about Handyside's propensity for ruthless behaviour and violence, and shivered at the memory of their first encounter. He'd thought that the North-east's top villain was some poor sod serving food and drink for the congregation of gangsters. When he realised, too late, who he was, the man from North Shields had stared at him as if he was considering flushing a bug down the toilet.

Handyside was a stone lighter than the next smallest guy in the room, with slicked hair and a side parting, and though his suits were expensive they seemed to have been designed for a sixties East End gangster. He always dressed and looked the same, and this get-together was no exception, though Eddie knew that Handyside had been up all night. The man's skin was pale and unnaturally smooth; if there was a line somewhere Eddie couldn't see it. His hair was jet black; his chestnut eyes soft and almost boyish. Whatever it was that frightened people so much was hard to work out, but it was probably the fact that he never became excited – every word was measured and delivered as if he was an old-fashioned hanging judge laying down a death sentence. Nothing seemed to stress or frighten him. He radiated power and it was impossible to ignore it.

Handyside looked up and stared at the doors as they were almost broken open. In common with the attendees from Edinburgh, there were two head honchos from Glasgow and a driver who could have doubled for Frankenstein's monster. The latter was led into the side room with his Edinburgh equivalent and looked as if he was capable of eating and drinking everything in the room, including the Flemings' spare man.

Handyside stood up and strode round the table to shake hands with Bobby 'Crazy Horse' McMartin and his sister Brenda, aka 'The Bitch'. He didn't show it,

50

but he struggled to get his head round a woman being second in charge of a major team, especially in a city like Glasgow. All the evidence suggested she'd earned her position in the criminal hierarchy, but it ran against his belief that women should be in the safe environments of their own homes and protected from the evils that stalked the world he lived in. Not this woman though; not Brenda fucking McMartin, whose ability to hand out and react to violence was as legendary as her inability to complete a sentence without fouling it with brightly coloured language. He shook hands then waved to one of his boys to get them a drink. Bobby asked for a double Bacardi with ginger beer and Brenda went for a pint of lager with a good shot of lime in it. They didn't have an ounce of class, but more importantly they knew it and didn't give a fuck.

'Can you do me a couple of fuckin' packets o' cheese an' onion to go with that, sweetheart?' Brenda said, winking seductively with her good eye to the man serving. He took one look at her and thought it was probably better to get her order right on the money.

Though Eddie had been studying Handyside, his attention swung to the McMartin clan as soon as they walked in. He'd met them a few times before, but like his host he struggled to get his head round the two of them.

Crazy Horse deserved his title, which he'd won in the Paisley drug wars, where he'd come out on top. He'd collected enough scars to impress both friends and enemies, though he'd minced most of the latter on his way up. Knives, sawn-offs or broken bottles, he was good with them all and had even chewed a lump out the throat of one opponent who'd foolishly offered him a square go at closing time. He was a pubic hair off six foot and starting to deserve the description of a bit overweight, though no one but his mad sister would tell him that. He consumed most of his calories from the nearest deep-fry outlet, and for Crazy Horse five a day meant his minimum intake of Bacardi or lager. His hair was thinning and swept back. From a distance he had a bit of the Francis Rossi about him, though the only thing he'd ever achieved with a guitar was doing six months for breaking one over its owner's head. That man's only crime had been to do a gig at a wedding where all hell had broken out when he and his band did a poor impression of the Proclaimers. The battle started between the McMartins and another Paisley family who they'd fought for years, though no one was sure how the original feud had started. Crazy Horse simply attacked anyone in front of him and the guitarist happened to be the last in line.

Brenda McMartin had been as involved as her brother in that melee, and a piece of broken glass had put paid to her left eye. Sometimes she put the glass one in, but on occasions she liked to wear her black eyepatch, which she thought made her look exotic, even a bit mysterious. Most of the people who knew her said covering any part of her face was a bonus and it was just a pity she couldn't do the whole thing. Nobody actually said it to her in person of course.

Handyside had everyone there that he needed. The organisation he'd formed involved the three cities, but in addition they dealt with and supplied a whole range of other teams from Manchester to Belfast. If they didn't get the goods on time and without hassle there was aggravation. Worse still, if word got out that the law was on their backs they'd have a serious credibility problem – and there was very little goodwill in his line of business. Whatever was happening in Edinburgh had to be sorted and tucked away as if it had never happened.

Handyside took his seat and even the mad bastards

from Glasgow knew it was time to be seen and not heard.

'There's a problem. I don't know how much any of you know but it's serious.'

Everyone in the room knew that if the man at the end of the table said it was serious, that meant it was worse than that. Handyside let the words sink in and scanned their faces, looking for the non-verbals that might hint at treachery. He didn't see any and carried on.

'The only person who knows all of what was arranged over the last few days was me. Two of my team knew there was a boat coming into the Tyne, but nothing else. Eddie and Pat knew there was a boat going to Eyemouth, but nothing else. Bobby and Brenda knew there was a boat going into Amble, but nothing else.' He paused again and if it was possible it seemed like someone had pressed the mute button for the room.

Eddie started to see ahead. This was bad – very fucking bad. It involved Edinburgh, or rather the twins, and he was smart enough to know that all was about to be revealed by the devil himself. It occurred to him that he might need a weapon in the next few minutes, but he had nothing available apart from the beer bottle in his hand. It would have to do.

'I've known for some time that there was a problem, or rather that information was leaking from the organisation and that the law was on the case.'

Eddie and every other person there knew that Handyside was delivering a death sentence, but the question was, who was the condemned man? He looked round at his brother, who'd never been gifted with brain power, but even he looked frozen, just waiting for the finger to be pointed.

'I find it hard to believe anyone round this table would have gone to the detectives, other than the bent ones, but that's what seems to have happened. I arranged three boats to arrive at roughly the same time, and I sent a team of spotters to each port to see if there were any signs of our friends in uniform.' He sipped a glass of iced water, looked round the faces again. Nothing showed in them but apprehension.

'There was no sign of them on Tyneside or Amble, but I guess you already know what happened in Eyemouth. What you don't know is that I'd worked out the problem as soon as the cavalry arrived there. The cargo was dumped at sea … and I mean all of it. My men on the boat were detained but did their job and kept quiet. They were released this afternoon. I've spoken to them and they've reassured me that everything that might have been evidence is now at the bottom of the North Sea. What all this means, my friends, if you hadn't worked it out already, is that the problem is in Edinburgh.'

All eyes locked onto the Flemings, and Brenda McMartin snorted something like a laugh. 'Fuckin' Edinburgh wankers. What did I say, Bobby?'

Her brother wasn't impressed. 'Shut the fuck up or I'll slap that ugly puss.'

His sister was equally unimpressed. 'You an' whose fuckin' army?'

For a moment there was a rare flash of impatience on Handyside's face. He put his hand up and two of his men stepped forward in case the Glasgow headcases kicked off. The McMartins shut it for another time.

Eddie hadn't moved a muscle and he wondered when one of Handyside's team was going to pull out a big fat fucking shooter and empty it into him and his brother. He couldn't contain the nervous tension and needed a release, as the pulse in his neck felt like it was about to erupt. What Handyside had just told them was that young women had been tossed into the sea along with the cocaine. If anyone needed further evidence about

54

Handyside's metal, he'd just given them all a perfect demonstration.

'Look, Pete. There's obviously something far fuckin' wrong, but it's not Pat or me, I can tell you that. It looks bad and that the problem's our end, but we'll find the bastard – that's a promise.'

Handyside didn't answer and shifted his gaze to Pat, who didn't need words to get the question. Eddie winced, knowing his brother lacked any form of diplomatic skill, and if ever it was needed, it was in this room and at this moment.

'Don't look at me, pal.' Pat was close to losing it. He could never walk away from a confrontation even when he had no chance of a result. 'I'll ignore that ugly bitch and let her keep her other eye, but we have fuck all to do with grassing to the law. Fuck that. Anyone says different better be able to back it up!'

Pat was threatening the wolf in his den and Eddie put his hand on his brother's arm, squeezed gently and took control before it was all too late. 'Where are we going with this, Pete? Let's stop fucking around and cards on the table.'

Handyside was completely unruffled and carried on as if there had been no insult. 'In a way this is simple. We all agreed that we'd keep the information about these shipments tight, and it was need-to-know only. If you didn't speak to the police, someone else did. So who else knew?' He sat back, sipped his water and waited.

Eddie's mind was racing; he knew their lives might depend on the answers he came up with. There was no way they could fight their way out of the room, but something stank in their team and he had to come up with a body to hang.

'It was tight; it was Pat, me and Tommy Walker, the guy who drove us here, that went down to pick up the gear. We were late and the place was swarming with uniforms when we got to Eyemouth so we fucked off.'

He knew as soon as he said it where the problem lay, and so did his brother. They had told no one about the Eyemouth shipment or anything else. Rip-offs and rats were common, and they ran a tight ship, but they talked in front of Tommy Walker. They always talked in front of him. He was their Baldrick and they tended to forget he was there when they discussed business. He'd always come across as a sound guy. They looked at each other and then to Handyside.

'Tommy is the only other person who knew apart from us.'

Handyside closed his eyes for a moment. He ran the moves through his head before he spoke again. 'So at least we know it's one of three people and you say it's not you. Let's bring Tommy in and see what he has to say. How long have you known him?'

Eddie knew what he was about to say showed they'd fucked up, but there was no way out. 'He's been with us for about a year and was introduced by Ricky Swan, the sauna owner in Edinburgh. I've told you about him – he takes a lot of the girls off our hands.' He lowered his eyes to the table. They'd taken their eye off the ball and he knew it. How many times had his old man told him to trust no one unless he knew everything about them – and particularly their weaknesses?

'You've only known him a year and he came in through an introduction? Poor judgement, my young friend. There isn't a man on my team I haven't known for years, and I know everything about them.' Handyside blinked twice. 'We are where we are, but, depending on what this man is going to tell us, you might need to look closely at this sauna owner.' He nodded towards two of his gorillas standing at the back of the room. 'Bring Tommy in.'

56

Brenda was loving it – the scent of blood quickened her pulse. Walker was pushed into the room, his eyes wide with fear of the unknown. He looked to the Flemings for support, but both of them were eyes down on the table, which made him realise he was in serious trouble – and had good reason to be.

The name Tommy Walker was part of his 'legend', as it was known in the undercover trade. His real name was Rob 'Dixie' Deans and he was a Police Service of Northern Ireland officer with nearly fifteen years in the job. He'd worked undercover for years and was regarded as one of the best in the business. There had been doubts about deploying him into an organisation made up of some of the most violent men and women in the country, but he did it without complaint. The analysts believed that the only part of the criminal association that could be infiltrated was Edinburgh, and they had a CHIS who was willing to make the introduction: a fully qualified slimeball who had taken human form as a sauna manager and knew everyone and their dirty little secrets from the service he provided. He'd worked with the Flemings for years and at one time partnered their old man in running a Leith knocking shop.

Dixie Deans was made to strip then pushed into a wooden seat at the back of the room. Handyside took a long drink of water before rising from his seat. His boys secured Deans to the chair and the audience could see that it was fixed securely to the floor. They could also see in the dim shadows at the back of the room that the floor had been carefully covered with plastic sheeting and then fixed down securely below the chair. The terrified man had already realised what it meant. He could try to survive the pain that was coming his way, but he'd heard stories about the people in this room and what they were capable of. All he could do was try to convince them he was kosher; and if his strength failed just get it over as quickly as possible.

Deans had been worried for weeks that the police team working on Handyside's organisation weren't moving fast enough to take them out. They'd already seized two consignments carried by numpty couriers and he'd seen it all before: they were gathering a nice set of figures in recovered drugs and prevaricating on making a move on the organisation itself. It was the old bullshit story that they still didn't have enough evidence to get the men at the top, while his arse was at risk every minute of every day. He squeezed his eyes shut as his mouth was taped and he struggled to breathe through his nose, which was congested with the after-effects of a bug.

Handyside looked long and hard at the man tied to the chair and saw something in his eyes that told him they had their man. He was the rat, no question about it, but there was something else. He'd gone almost unnoticed by his employers, and Handyside himself had seen him several times, but it was as if he was camouflaged – present but almost invisible. That reeked in his nose, and the fact that he'd been introduced by a third party might mean the worst of all worlds: an undercover cop. If that was the case, there were all sorts of possibilities he had to weigh up. The first priority was to find out if there was any surveillance outside.

Hunter and Dillon came into the room. They looked at the man strapped to the chair and didn't react, apart from Dillon smiling when he realised what was going to happen. They'd both seen other men suffer in this room, it was part of the job, but today was a bit special and they knew Handyside would handle this one himself. They spoke quietly to him, telling him that they'd checked the area and there was no sign of a surveillance team. Dillon knew exactly how it worked and they had enough bent law in the local stations to let them know if there was something going on.

Handyside pulled up a chair in front of Deans and looked at him as if he was concerned about his health. What the enthralled audience never understood was that Handyside got no pleasure from hurting another human being. There was only the cold reality that if action had to be taken then it needed to be decisive, clear and place a gnawing doubt in the minds of anyone who might want to take him on or betray him.

'Try and relax, Tommy. This is going to be hard but we need to do this together.' His words were almost gentle and Deans was mesmerised by the man sitting opposite him. There wasn't the least hint of anger or crude blood-lust in Handyside's expression, and in another situation his eyes might have been described as sad.

'You're going to tell me who you talked to and why. You might think you can hold out, but the man that can keep his mouth shut at the same time he's suffering intense pain is rare. And I confess I haven't met one.'

Deans was a drowning man as he tried to drag air through his choked nasal passages, his lungs heaving with the effort of staying alive. His nose bubbled, spurting snot like a child, and fat tears mixed with the sweat covering his face.

Handyside got to his feet and took up a position behind Deans, who almost broke his neck trying to keep him in view as fear squeezed his heart in the blind panic of what was coming next. If he could have kept his eyes on him, he would have lost control of his bladder two minutes earlier than when it actually happened. His inquisitor had removed his silk tie carefully, folded it, then slowly unbuttoned his shirt as if he was alone in front of his bedroom mirror and lost in mundane thoughts. Handy-side always looked as if he was verging on underweight,

59

but revealing his upper torso showed a man whose physique had all the definition of a body builder with none of the uninhibited vanity. He might not have had the bulk normally characterised in his profession, but his musculature looked like something carved from white marble.

He moved round to face Deans, who made a low moaning sound in his throat just before Handyside ripped the tape from his mouth. Deans gagged noisily; his mouth had stopped producing saliva, and his eyes pleaded hopelessly with Handyside, who ignored the tortured policeman whispering the word 'Please God' over and over again.

'God isn't in this room, my friend.' Handyside said it quietly and watched Deans' eyes drop down to the mash hammer hanging from his right hand.

Eddie Fleming felt like some rancid voyeur at a grubby peep show. It seemed unreal, almost theatrical, but the expression on Deans' face was reality itself. For a moment he pitied the man who'd made him look like some fuckin' amateur in front of these men and the Paisley Bitch. But it passed quickly as the horror show moved on. He felt soiled by the whole thing, and although he wanted to drag his eyes away from it, he knew that would register with the other predators in the room; he couldn't show them another sign of weakness and survive.

What he also realised in that moment was that he wasn't fully equipped to operate in this league. Ever since his old man had been taken out by the psychos from Belfast he'd been forced into dealing with the top men, and well before he was ready. Mistakes were written off as inexperience, but he'd always been sure he could learn on the job. He was as hard as they came, much smarter than the average villain and from good criminal stock. What had just slammed him in the ribs was the understanding

60

that hard wasn't enough on its own. He'd seen it in the late Magic McGinty, his father's main supplier, who'd paid the ultimate price as a gangster, and he saw it now in Handyside, and it was a quality that Eddie knew he lacked. Handyside had one overwhelming drive, which was an absolute determination to enforce his will on other people. There was no management by committee or democracy in his world. Eddie remembered Handyside's words the first time they'd been introduced: 'The only laws in our world, my friend, are the ones we break every day.'

Killing was just another tool to be used when and where it was needed. They did what had to be done then tramped over the bodies towards the next challenger for the title. The thought that jumped into Eddie's brain then was that if he and Pat were going to survive, they needed to bring in someone who had the appropriate minerals, and there weren't many about. But one name did come to mind and that was Billy Drew: ex-soldier, armed robber and all-round murdering bastard. He had the X factor, and if they survived the night Eddie was going to make him a gold-plated offer.

His attention snapped back to the actors in front of him as Handyside suddenly stared ahead, and every person in the room apart from Deans thought he was looking directly at them. Then he turned back to gaze down at the man strapped to the seat.

'I'm going to start with your feet. There's endless ways to cause a man pain and sometimes it seems like a contest in depravity in our game. I find the old ways are best. If you can bear it then I'll move to your hands. This *will* happen and the only person who can stop it is you.' He dropped down on one knee and looked back at Deans, who couldn't drag his eyes from the hammer and the ropes of tight muscle running the length of Handyside's arm.

'I haven't talked to anyone. Please believe me.'

The audience could barely hear what he said, but they didn't need to as Handyside nodded to Hunter, who taped up Deans' mouth again. He didn't hesitate for a moment, swinging the hammer through a wide arc and making an anatomically perfect strike against the metatarsophalangeal joint connecting Deans' big toe to the main part of his right foot. The policeman looked like an electric charge had surged the length of his body as he strained at the leather straps that bound him to the chair. The pain was liquid white heat driving up through his nerves to his brain as bone and flesh were pulped. The veins in his neck ballooned up like they would explode. Handyside didn't wait for effect, and if anything applied even more force, shattering the big toe on Deans' left foot. He stood up calmly and signalled for his iced water. He sipped it slowly as he watched Deans suffer.

Eddie wanted to be somewhere else. He couldn't stop imagining himself strapped to the chair like some Elizabethan heretic who would suffer whether he told the truth or not. He prayed silently that Handyside got his confession from the man in the chair, because he and his brother were fucked if that didn't happen. He pulled out a cigarette and wondered if the tremor in his hand would show when he lit it. He stuck it between his lips and was startled when a flame appeared from the margin of his view. Brenda was holding the light to his cigarette and grinning like Jack Nicholson in the door scene from *The Shining*. He nodded his thanks, wondering if any man had ever been attracted to her then deciding that they would have to have been both blind and insane.

Brenda settled back in her chair and opened a second packet of cheese and onion crisps as if she was just watching the latest edition of *EastEnders*.

Handyside asked the same question again and was impressed when Deans managed to gasp out the same answer. As if with great reluctance, he raised the hammer again… and Deans' resistance broke. He told Handyside everything, though it came out slowly as he tried to speak and manage his agony at the same time.

Eddie cursed and blessed the bastard at the same time. He'd been made to look like a total fuckwit, but he was off the hook as a grass and he knew the sauna owner had to be working for the law. The fact that Fleming did the same thing when it suited him made no difference, and he swore he'd top the bastard when he got his hands on him.

Handyside dipped a cloth in a basin of water and wiped himself down once he had all the answers he needed. Deans was quiet, his head hanging at an angle; Hunter had just squirted a good shot of smack into his arm.

As Handyside pulled on his shirt and knotted his Italian tie he broke into one of his rare smiles and said, 'I forgot to ask you your real name.'

The cop managed to lift his head and looked at Handyside through half-closed eyes. 'It's Rob Deans. People call me Dixie.' He was deathly pale and looked like he was struggling to keep his head up.

'Dixie, I like that. Where are you from originally? I know the accent's Northern Ireland, but where?'

'Downpatrick, near the border.' Then, in no more than a whisper before his head slumped again he added, 'My mother still lives there.' Then he drifted into unconsciousness.

Handyside walked back to the table and sat down. He looked round the faces and tried to read the effects of his actions over the last few minutes. 'This is a mess, but I don't want panic,' he told them. 'We need to clean this thing up, and I want some time to think about a few things along the way.'

'What about him?' Eddie interrupted, nodding towards Deans.

'He'll be removed shortly and no trace of him will ever be found. We can't leave a dead undercover cop at the side of the road like we're sending a warning to the law. If he disappears it's almost impossible for them to build a case.'

He lit up a cigarette, which he normally wouldn't have done at a meeting, but he thought he deserved the break. 'When they realise he's missing you and your brother are bound to be pulled at some stage. They must know we're having a meeting here so admit that it was just business; your story is that when you got home you dropped him off and that's it. I hope the wheels are hired as I instructed.' Eddie nodded and Handyside continued, 'Then there should be no problem with bugs in the car.'

The Fleming brothers weren't about to argue with the man they'd just watched in action, and Eddie knew that they weren't out of the mire yet. Apart from anything else, their credibility was now so low it wouldn't even register as shite and he needed to get back to Edinburgh to work it all out.

'The other problem, or should I say one of the problems, we need to sort is this … what's his name?'

'You mean Ricky Swan?'

'Ricky Swan.' Handyside didn't project any feelings of crisis. He knew that if he didn't control the people in the room they would starburst in all directions, leaving a trail of evidence for whichever police team was on the case.

'I'll sort the bastard, Pete. You can take that from me.'

'No you won't, Eddie. That's exactly what you won't do.' Handyside had leaned forward and there was enough in the non-verbals to say this wasn't up for discussion.

'Whoever it is up there who owns the UC is going to put you down as the top suspect if Swan turns up dead. They don't like losing informants. We'll get him done, but we need to talk to him before we put his lights out. You need to be in the open when he goes so you have a cast-iron alibi. Okay?'

'We're fine with that.' Eddie said it as if they had a choice in the matter, and Pat kept his gob firmly shut.

'I want our friends from Glasgow to take care of this Swan guy.' Handyside nodded to the Glasgow team. 'Can you handle that?'

'With pleasure,' Crazy Horse said – and meant it. His sister looked pleased; she was determined to get involved as well.

Handyside knew he needed to do a lot of thinking and was about to wind it up when Maxi Turner entered the room and came over to whisper in his ear. Apologising as if he were the chairman of a reputable company who had to interrupt a routine board meeting, Handyside left the room with Turner, returning five minutes later to give those assembled another disturbing report. He seemed to gather his thoughts for a moment then looked round the room before speaking. 'It is being reported that a young woman was found barely alive on a beach near Eyemouth earlier today. It seems that our friends in the police are keeping it tight, but the media are speculating it might be related to an earlier operation at the harbour ... There's nothing more we can do at the moment so we need to act carefully and get it right.'

Handyside looked up at Hunter and Dillon, who were at the back of the room and trying not to break for the door. 'How did this happen?'

Hunter did his best but felt like he was attached to a lie detector. 'Don't understand it, boss.' He shrugged.

'Okay, it's just another problem to sort out, and we have enough to do for the moment.' Handyside seemed to let it pass and Hunter looked round at Dillon, who'd developed a twitch at the side of his mouth.

Handyside closed the meeting down and called Turner, Hunter and Dillon into a side room.

'I want you to take the cop out to the moors. He's a brave man and had enough so I want it to be quick. You know the moors so make sure he'll never be found.'

Turner nodded, already knowing exactly what he had to do.

'Get on it then and call me when it's done. The roads are still busy enough so you can get lost in the traffic.'

The dog walker who had spotted Ingrid Richter on the shore reported it to the police as a washed-up corpse. In truth, the young woman was so close to death that it would have been hard to tell the difference, and another hour would have finished her.

About the same time as her eyes first flickered in the intensive care unit, Dillon was moaning again about having to dig the hole that would be the UC's last resting place.

'I'll be saying hello to the fucking kangaroos if we go much deeper. Can we call it a day here?'

They did what had to be done under a moon shimmering against a cloudless sky. The only sounds were the creatures of the night and the rhythmic scrape of the shovel in the damp earth. Turner sat about three feet from the hole, smoking a cigarette as he re-ran Handyside's instructions through his head. The UC was dead and Turner had made it quick, just as he'd been told; the cop hadn't even been conscious when he pulled the trigger. Hunter sat at the other side of the hole, smirking at the bent bastard he despised so much having to sweat for a living. Dillon's head was barely visible above the dark ground; his breathing was heavy and showed all the signs of the forty a day he consumed.

'That should do it.'

Turner flicked the cigarette into the darkness and stood up. In the same motion he pulled out the Glock and double tapped Hunter, who collapsed in a dead heap next to the hole.

'What the fuck?' Dillon screamed, but he already knew the answer as Turner found his way round the edge of the dig and put another one in Hunter's cranium for good measure.

Turner looked down to find Dillon was on his knees and begging for his life in the near darkness of the hole.

'Twat' was the last word Dillon heard before the bullet smashed through the top of his skull. Forty minutes later the three bodies were safely covered up and the gun that had ended their lives was bound for the bottom of the River Tyne by the end of the night.

Turner gave everything the once-over before he left and called Handyside as he headed back to Newcastle. 'It's done, and no problems. I'm going to finish the other job and text you when I'm on the way home.'

The same cop who'd wandered past Handyside on his previous shift pulled up his patrol car in the early hours of the morning. He wasn't that far from the same spot and decided it was time for a smoke. It was quiet – not a soul about apart from the odd drunk trying to get back home to bed without drowning in the river.

He opened his flies and sighed as he relieved his swollen and caffeine-aggravated bladder into the Tyne. He played the stream like a schoolboy then looked down at the river and managed to wet the front of his uniform trousers as he muttered the word 'shit'.

They pulled Eric Gunderson's body from the river under an hour later and didn't need a doctor to tell them that a massive head injury had killed him. The initial assessment was that he was another drunken fisherman who'd fallen in trying to get back aboard his boat. Sadly, it happened too often.

5

Grace Macallan stared out over the cliffs at the breaking waves driven past her view by a cool north-west wind. Despite the breeze, the sun shone through the gaps between the white clouds bouncing across the Antrim coast, dappling the land with light and shade. Her partner, Jack Fraser, had stayed back in their rented holiday cottage, where he was looking after their son, Adam. Jack had read the signs that she needed to clear her head so he made her take a long walk along the cliffs they'd come to love so much.

Macallan had been badly hurt in the Edinburgh operation against the Loyalist Billy Nelson and had gone back to work too soon after her release from hospital, so it had been a real strain trying to get back to her old form. Difficulties with the pregnancy had given her an excuse to go off early after the arrest of 'Elvis' McNally, and she hadn't been back since the birth. The wounds had affected her mind as much as her body, and though she felt physically fit again, she was struggling to work out what it was she wanted to do with her life now that she shared it with Jack and the baby. She thought about the word family every day as she looked into the face of her child, who stared right back at her and gave her part of the answer without saying a word.

Jack had rented the same cottage in Ballycastle where he'd nursed Macallan after the bombing. On a clear day they could stare across the Irish Sea towards the Scottish mainland and the southern edges of the Hebrides. It felt like a different world to the one that had nearly taken her away. The views alone made the rent bearable and there were times when she almost forgot the demons that inhabited her memories. It was as if she had been told a story about another woman, someone whose life seemed more glamorous than the reality that persistently broke into her daydreams and reminded her who she really was.

Macallan sat on a dry tussock, lifted her face to the sky and felt the salt air tingle across her skin in the breeze. She watched the gannets scream and dive vertically into the waves then erupt through the surface of the water with their victims twitching helplessly in their long yellow beaks. She breathed in deeply, filling her lungs, and exhaled slowly, wishing that time would stand still so they could just live there in peace and never grow old. She'd been sleeping like a child, when Adam would let her, and it was the first time in years that her dreams were free of demons. It was deep, easy sleep and they'd put their bedside clock in a drawer with their watches so they could do what they wanted when they wanted. She'd added a few extra pounds to her frame and Jack had given the look his seal of approval. He saw how her skin seemed clearer and, for the most part, she was glowing with good health and contentment. The problem wasn't her skin or her weight though; she was wounded where it didn't show to the human eye, but he was aware of it – and felt helpless. It was as if her soul was covered in scars that hadn't completely faded and he wondered whether they ever would. This was the same woman who he watched putting their child to her breast as if her life had never had a bad moment. Feeding Adam was when she was most contented – where she could forget the creatures she'd spent her life pursuing.

Macallan knew it was time to go back to the job or abandon it altogether and live her life with Jack and the baby. He tried hard to make it easy for her. 'I want whatever you want.' He would say it every couple of days and meant every word. 'The book's going well, and when I finish it I'll get back to work. In fact I miss the court. We could have a good life back here in Northern Ireland.'

She knew they could, and all she had to do was say yes to him. The other possibility was a move to a cushy uniform job somewhere, but she knew she would struggle watching other people deal with the horror stories. It was always that strange drug that she hated and wanted at the same time, and it was these same horrors that she couldn't bring home to the two men who were in her life now. She was lucky in that respect – Jack was far from naive in his life as a criminal barrister.

I'm starving! The thought pounced on Macallan; her current life meant she could enjoy regular meals and her stomach had come to expect fresh food on time every day. Her whole body had welcomed the well-deserved rest from the trials of police canteens and eating on the run.

When she arrived back at the cottage all was quiet and the first thing Macallan did was raid the biscuit tin to keep her hunger pangs at bay. She switched on the kitchen radio and caught the end of the news headlines, which all seemed to be depressing – the sad plight of refugees in the Middle East, more terrorist plots, fewer people able to keep up with their mortgage repayments and a half-dead young woman washed up on a beach somewhere in Berwickshire. She switched the radio off again and went through to the sitting room, where she found Jack spreadeagled and fast asleep on the old settee with Adam, just as sound, lying face down on his father's broad chest. She moved forward as quietly as she could to get a better look, smiled at the synchronised snoring and felt her eyes moisten, wishing again that it could always be like this.

6

Eddie Fleming felt his shirt sticking like adhesive to the plastic seats in their hired car. It was nothing to do with temperature or humidity, just the simple fact that he'd left a meeting where at one point he'd been sure he was going to sleep with the fishes or worms or skip bugs or whatever the fuck. He looked round at his brother, who was driving and had hardly spoken a word since they'd hit the road north, heading for the Scottish border then home. As they drifted past the concrete monster that was Torness nuclear power station (or Tornobyl as it was affectionately known by the locals), Eddie put two cigarettes in his mouth and lit them up with one hand steadying the other. Pat, who'd taken on the pallor of a mortuary escapee, took the proffered cigarette, coughed painfully a couple of times then burnt some rubber pulling onto the grass verge in the nearest lay-by. He bolted from the car and into the darkness.

'What the fuck, brother?' was all Eddie managed to get out as he pushed his door open, stood up and peered across the top of the car towards the sound of Pat heaving his guts up in the bushes. 'Jesus,' he said.

Pat retched then retched again till all he was achieving was noise. Eddie moved in behind him, knowing it wasn't the usual dodgy curry with a lager topping that had caused the problem. It was the same fear that had shattered his own nerves and the awful truth that they were operating in the wrong league. Relegation in this game was permanent and messy. Eddie took out a packet of tissues and handed them over as Pat straightened up, sucking in lungfuls of cool air to clear his nausea.

'What the fuck are we involved in?' Pat looked round, his eyes bulging and pleading with the older twin to reassure him. 'I still can't believe we walked out the door in one piece. Jesus, we brought an undercover into the operation. Do you really think the man down there'll let us live after that?'

'Pat,' was all Eddie got out before he got talked over by his brother again.

'Did you see that mad Weegie bitch sizing us up? This is bad. Very fuckin' bad.'

Pat wasn't ready when his brother lashed the side of his face with an open palm that caught him off guard and dumped him on his arse. Eddie moved in close, ready to belt him again but it wasn't required.

'Now listen to me for once in your life. You better pay attention if you want to survive this. Stop fuckin' about and man up. We have a problem, brother, and we can sort somethin' out or wait for one of Pete Handyside's team to come for us with a meat cleaver or, worse still, get a visit from the Glasgow mob.'

He lit another two cigarettes and handed one over to Pat, who was back in the game after that slap in the puss. He sucked in some poison and blew a cloud up past his brother's face, shook his head and managed a bleak smile. Eddie backed up a step then and offered him his hand for a lift up.

'We have to make this right. First, we get Billy Drew on-board and then we burn that grassing cunt in his sauna. Pete Handyside wants someone else to do it, but if we let these Weegie fuckers do our dirty work we're finished. Look what happened with the Belfast mob – we let someone in the door and the next thing they want the whole fuckin' show. I want the truth from that grassin' bastard before we do 'im. Maybe, just maybe, we get a pass from the man down there and some cred back for cleanin' up the mess. I'm fucked if I know if we can do it, but I don't intend to sit on my arse and wait for the butcher to come for us. We might just square it with Handyside. If he'd been convinced we'd already be in the ground. The big problem we have is with the Glasgow mob. They have an agenda, brother. This fuck-up is their excuse to take us out and run Edinburgh.'

Pat had ignored his brother's hand but listened intently. 'I hear you.' He said it more like the hard case he was. He rolled onto his hands and knees then pushed up onto his feet with the cigarette dangling from his lips. 'Do you fuckin' believe it?'

His face was scrunched up in disgust as he lifted his left hand and Eddie caught the stink as well as the sight of the dog shit that covered Pat's hand. He backed off, revolted and trying to put distance between himself and the offending paw; then his face creased into a broad grin. 'You fuckin' idiot.' In an instant they became boys again and Eddie belly laughed at Pat, who was stumbling about in the moonlight with his hand in the air as if it was on fire.

'You don't get in the car till that's cleaned off.' He jumped in through the driver's door and locked it down. He grinned then waved like the Queen, and for a moment the mood had lifted. He scrolled through the address book on his phone, saw the name he wanted and pressed the call button. It only rang once before it was answered.

'What?'

That was Billy Drew short and to the point. Being an ex-soldier, armed robber, widower and convicted murderer had made him a humourless bastard, but that was exactly what Eddie wanted. He could do humour with his brother, but Drew had the experience he lacked and needed till he learned how to hold his own with the other top men.

'It's Eddie Fleming.'

'And?'

'Have a wee proposition and wanted to meet up.'

'Where and when?'

'As soon as. I'll be back in Edinburgh in an hour.'

'Okay. Come round to my place.'

As soon as they reached Drew's, Eddie told his brother to fuck off and steep his hand in disinfectant for a month. Eddie had all the business acumen and Pat had sweet FA, which the younger twin accepted as a matter of fact. Pat hated the technical side of organised crime but usually enjoyed the violence and fringe benefits.

The moment he was clear of his brother he pulled the wrap of coke from his Ys and snorted the lot before phoning the latest pro he was involved with.

It was the early hours of the morning but that didn't stop Billy pouring out a glass of whisky that would have knocked a Rottweiler out cold. Eddie slugged half the malt in one go – he needed the hit. The heat washed through his veins and calmed his frazzled nerves. He told Drew that he was looking for an experienced and wiser head now that his old man was in heaven. He didn't mention the problem with Handyside right off, wanting to dangle the carrot first. The money he eventually offered was crazy, but it was a case of life or death and he made more than he could spend, so what the fuck? Drew wouldn't have to touch anything at the working end of the business and risk an arrest, which with his record would mean heavy prison time. The forces of law and order hadn't forgiven him from walking away from a lifer on appeal.

Drew threw back his own whisky and gave Eddie the eye.

'What's the catch? There's always a catch. Tell me, because if there is one and you haven't told me then I'm going to be pissed.'

Fleming told him it all, including the sauna owner introducing a UC.

'I always knew Ricky fuckin' Swan was too wide at the mouth and all things to all men, including the law. You did fuck up there, my friend, and I learned the same hard lesson you need to get into your DNA – trust no one. Swan was fuck all till he put his talent as a perv into practice and opened the sauna.' He poured another monster into their glasses and Eddie took it gladly; the expensive Speyside had washed away his worries, at least for the time being.

'Don't I fuckin' know it, but it's done now. What do you think of the show so far?'

Drew sipped from his glass and savoured the whack of spice and slow heat in his mouth. 'The odds are that you're fucked, and if I had any sense I'd tell you to write up your will and pick the hymns. However, I'm gettin' too old for stick-ups and need to work. I'll help you out, but there's something I need in return, my friend. Quid pro quo.'

Eddie nodded slowly and realised he was a bit more than slightly pissed. He'd expended too much nervous energy for one day and needed the release. 'Name it, Billy.'

'I've got scores to settle, but unlike you I don't have a

team and a pocket full of bent bastards all over the shop. I always tended to work on my own or with my mate, Colin Jack – until I made the mistake of taking my idiot brother on-board. Anyway, Colin's inside for a stabbing at the moment and my brother has fucked off because he gobbed to the cops so if he shows his face here I'll take it off.'

Eddie focused on the wall clock, then realised it was 4 a.m. and they were still necking goldies.

'You know the story with my brief Jonathon Barclay? Was my lawyer for years. Top of his profession and turns out he's Mick Harkins' number-one grass. I get life, but when it all comes out I walk on appeal. But ...' He leaned forward just to make sure Eddie got it, 'I don't forgive and forget.' He sat back in his chair and nodded to emphasise the statement.

Eddie knew the whole story already. Everyone in Scotland did, but Billy wanted to tell it again and it was better to let him get it out. With his mate and brother he'd invaded the home of a wealthy Chinese couple in Glasgow to rob them. It had gone badly wrong and they'd tortured and killed the businessman and his wife for nothing. His brother had made enough mistakes to lead the police to them and the jury had no problem bringing in guilty verdicts. The old judge had happily given Billy and co lifers, but luck came his way when his lawyer was exposed as a police informant who had given information about the Drews.

'Help me find Barclay. He must call his wife. Do you have anyone inside the phone companies who can get her call records?'

'No problem. Anything else?'

'After Barclay I want Mick Harkins, and I might need help to make sure he's in the right place at the right time. It should be easy enough – the bastard's lost his mojo since Barclay's boy rearranged his skeleton with the front end of his car.'

Eddie nearly dropped his glass.

'A cop! Mick Harkins?'

'No, Eddie. An ex-cop and pisshead.'

'Are you sure? Mick Harkins is no clown, and the force won't take that one sitting on their arse.'

'That's the deal. Take it or leave it.'

Eddie pictured the UC getting treated with the hammer and he still couldn't get rid of the image of Brenda McMartin grinning as she'd lit his cigarette. It had felt like the condemned man having his last fag in front of the firing squad. He threw back the rest of the whisky.

'Fuck it. You have a deal, but I need some shut-eye. I'll meet you later in the day if that suits you.' He stood up unsteadily as Drew raised his glass. 'Here's to business, and first is Ricky the grass. No way do we let those fuckin' radges from the west clean up the mess. Fuck that.'

7

At the same time as Eddie Fleming was collapsing into his bed, Ricky Swan was waking up to the music of BBC News on the telly and his spoodle licking his face. He was still fully dressed, head pounding and he realised – as he did almost every morning – that he should have given the last couple of vodkas a miss. His stomach burned with the previous night's overindulgence plus years of similar experience. He'd fallen asleep in his favourite chair only a couple of hours after breaking in one of the new girls from his sauna. Swan had sent her on her way when he was done, and like the tight bastard he was he'd let her pay for the taxi back to her flat. It always gave him a real belly laugh when he saw the look of disappointment on a girl's face when she was punted out onto the street in the middle of the night.

He stood up wearily then stretched to his full height of five six. As he yawned noisily his top set of dentures dropped from the roof of his mouth, but he was used to this and left them resting on his bottom teeth till the yawn was complete. He bit the dental plate back into place as he stepped forward to look in the mirror above the Adam fireplace and realised his comb-over was hanging down the side of his head like a decomposed rodent. He trained the strands back into place and admired his reflection. The fact that he used the services of his girls on a regular basis made him believe that he was attractive and had the X Factor in buckets. The small matter that they had little or no choice had never occurred to him.

It was hardly more than a full day since the events at Eyemouth, and the limited press release hadn't quite hit the spot with the public or the news hounds. One reporter, however, had got wind through her police contacts that a major story was brewing and she'd started to harass her best sources. Her name was Jacquie Bell and she'd been a friend of Grace Macallan's since soon after the latter had arrived in Edinburgh. Bell was a relentless investigative journalist, mostly disliked by the police, but only because she did her job so well and regardless of whether it hurt them or not. Although Bell had realised that what was emerging was a major story, she was keeping it under wraps till she'd exhausted all her sources inside Police Scotland. But the police were struggling to make sense of what they knew, and until the girl found on the Berwickshire coast could tell them something, they were toiling to get a major investigation underway. What they did have, though, was a lifebelt with the name *Brighter Dawn* written in big fuck-off red letters, which had been lying next to the girl when she was discovered. This was the clue that had sent the chief into a tailspin. It was the same boat that had been boarded in Eyemouth. The poisoned icing on the cake was that the men who'd been detained in Eyemouth had been released without charge hours before the girl was found. It was a wet dream in the making for the journalists, who loved writing up the constabulary as a bunch of incompetents running around like the extras in an old Benny Hill sketch. Bell was closing in on the problem for the force and she'd also picked up a snippet that a covert officer was missing. She didn't know whether there was a connection but she was pressing all the right buttons to find out if there was. She left Macallan off her call list though. She would still be changing nappies in Northern Ireland and Bell thought too much of her to intrude, especially given how badly she'd been hurt by the events of the bombing in Edinburgh.

Ricky Swan had been so preoccupied with showing his latest recruit what she could expect as one of his employees that he'd missed the breaking news about the 'girl from the sea' as the press had already dubbed her. It probably wouldn't have caused him too much concern, as none of the girls on the boat had been destined for his particular establishment – at least not this time. The only thing that Swan worried about was what kept him happy and his little luxuries, as he liked to call his almost nightly sessions with the staff. What would have raised his blood pressure to dangerous levels, had he known, was that the police were making every effort to contact a missing undercover officer, and the fuck-up at Eyemouth raised the possibility that he'd been exposed.

Swan decided he'd have another couple of hours' kip, though he felt wide awake. His working day never started till mid-afternoon at the earliest so there was no pressure. He slipped out of his clothes and donned his favourite pair of lairy jim-jams before diving under the black silk sheets on the king-size. He switched the telly back on and flicked through to the news channel, which was unusual for him but at that time of the morning there wasn't much else to choose from, and he'd had enough porn to keep him going for the next twenty-four hours. The news was nearly all depressing: the Middle East simmered and the city fat cats just kept swelling. He was feeling for the remote to try to locate some Kyle or Springer reruns when the piece came on about the 'girl from the sea'. He left the remote where it was and followed the report without getting too excited. There wasn't much detail from the 'on-the-spot' hack, who looked miserable on the damp beach and wasn't in a position to say more than the few details that the police had already released. What he did mention, however, was the fact that a police operation had taken place in the early hours, which prompted a very distant bell to start clanging in Swan's noddle. He knew that the team the Flemings were involved with imported their commodities by boat and so it might be that his cooperation with the forces of law and order had brought in the bacon. 'Nice one, Ricky my boy.' He muttered it with a smile, knowing that as a top informant any result meant brownie points for him, and he needed them in case the police decided to change their minds again about their policy on saunas. Since the formation of Police Scotland and the old Strathclyde takeover of the country's moral compass, Edinburgh's previously enlightened stance on Swan's type of establishment was taking a kicking.

Life in recent years had been good to Swan, and as far as he was concerned he deserved the rewards that running prostitutes and a string of saunas had brought him. In his youth he'd left school with few or no prospects and all anyone could remember about him was that he was the creepy runt who used to stare at the girls in the playground. He filled a few dead-end jobs and spent some lonely hours with his favourite porn magazines or, when he could save enough, spent an hour with the cheapest girl he could find on the street. As sometimes happens, however, a life that was destined for obscurity took one of those turns that can happen as easily to the undeserving as to the commendable.

An old aunt, who'd spent more time bringing him up than his parents had, went to her maker and left all she had to him, her only living relative. To his absolute surprise and pleasure his aunt had been careful with her money and had saved what her late husband had left her after a childless but happy marriage. She had no idea about investments but had started to dabble when Maggie Thatcher wanted everyone to worship the religion of greed. Nevertheless, she remained canny, was good at it and reaped the rewards. In fact she spent nothing of the profits on herself, just enjoying the game, and as far as everyone who knew her was concerned she was a nice old lady who just managed to scrape by on her pension. When she made her will she pondered leaving it to good causes, but her sense of duty to her family swayed her into giving it to her nephew. She prayed to the god she'd served faithfully that the money might provide Ricky with a better life than the one he would undoubtedly have had otherwise.

Once Swan had settled down after the shock of this legacy, he knew straightaway where his future lay. He'd spent long lonely hours imagining himself with a string of girls who would do whatever he wanted whenever he wanted, and he dived into the business with relish. He was successful because he knew from his own regular fantasies exactly what the punters wanted. The business expanded, and with it came the discovery that his product attracted all comers, sometimes including the great and good of Scotland's capital city. At the end of the day the customers' fear of exposure was overcome by their desire to take risks with women who made them feel special and weren't shocked by their varying demands. People who would have sneered at Swan in his old life wanted to know him because he held the keys to the product, and they foolishly believed that their friendship bought them a degree of trust with him. They couldn't have been more wrong, and he'd soon realised their weakness had huge value. He'd installed state-of-the-art recording systems in the booths and over the years compiled enough material to bring down, if he chose, some of the very best people from politics, law, entertainment and, of course, the capital's top criminals, who liked the type of women he could provide. The odd cop would turn up supposedly in the course of their job, but there were always one or two who just couldn't resist the offer of a freebie. He welcomed them with open arms and knew the power of having friends in the local station. They were all in his XXX collection.

Nobody actually liked Swan but they put on matey smiles and flattered him because they all believed he wielded power – which he did, through his knowledge of who the clients really were – not the public faces or the doting husbands but the heaving, grunting customers who actually believed the working girls cared about them. They would bare their souls to those women, who hardly understood English, but the audio mics picked up every revelation. Unfortunately for Swan, this meant he'd started to believe he was fireproof, safe from the hazards facing most of the people he knew.

There were only two things in life that Swan really cared about apart from the fringe benefits of his business. The first and most important of these was his daughter, Christine, who was the result of the one relationship that had come close to having any meaning in his life. Her mother had cleared off years before and he'd lost touch with her, which suited him just fine these days. Christine Swan, now grown up, had moved to Dundee to study at the college of art and put distance between herself and his grubby business. He paid her bills and in return she tolerated speaking to him on the phone every couple of weeks. She was happy enough and determined to build a life where she could forget where she came from. Twice a year she would meet him for lunch where they would sit, try to communicate with each other and fail every time. Fortunately, she'd inherited her mother's good looks and very little from her father. Swan really wanted her to have a good life that meant something, and she was the only human being who stirred these emotions in him. He understood her lack of affection, but he was proud of her and what she was becoming. When he was in his cups he'd brag to the escorts about his brilliant daughter, who was destined to become a great artist, even though they were completely uninterested in anything he had to say. The walls of his bedroom were covered with the early drawings and watercolours that had shown such promise. Christine was everything he'd failed to be, and he often worried how he'd cope when a man finally walked into her life. How could she bring someone home to meet the parents when all she had in her family was Ricky the pimp?

His other indulgence away from his business was line dancing – in fact anything to do with the American West. Even when he was on his own at home he would wear his favourite cowboy hat that he'd bought on a holiday to the States. This obsession had even gone as far as naming his house 'The Corral', much to the disdain of his neighbours in one of the best parts of town. His home was in the Ravelston area, only a mile from the city centre. A place in those beautiful tree-lined streets meant you'd arrived. Art galleries, parks and the Water of Leith were the backdrop to beautifully designed homes for some of the city's very best people. These same residents were the pillars of society and having a pimp in their midst who lived somewhere called The Corral was a never-ending subject of local conversation, particularly among the ladies of the house. The irony was that at least two of the husbands were regulars at one of his saunas and, in one case, even Swan thought the punter had bizarre tastes. Those well-respected men tended to say very little when their wives complained about the problem of having a man like Swan contaminating the area.

But the man who'd been the runt at school had started to enjoy playing games and dropping some serious villains in the shit. There were sharp detectives around who saw his vanity for what it was and how it could be exploited. Over a few drinks with these same detectives, he loved to blow about the people he knew – and without realising it he ended up as a CHIS.

DS Mick Harkins had picked up the signals that some of his second-division colleagues had been using the sauna girls and that Swan thought this made him fire-proof. Harkins had then played him to perfection, and when he'd explained to Swan that he had become a fully fledged police source it had come as quite the surprise. It hadn't occurred to him that he'd been grassing up some of the nastiest criminals in the city and what this meant in the real world. The detective had explained there was no going back and that he either played for Harkins or was fed to the associates of the men doing time because of Swan's excellent but ill-judged relationship with the local constabulary.

'You're too fuckin' late pal. You've already helped put two horrible bastards in Saughton. Or did I imagine that?' Harkins had said it with a smile that confirmed he owned Swan lock, stock and barrel.

It was only then that Swan had realised Harkins had never taken anything from him. He was so used to having the goods on other people that he hadn't noticed Harkins revolve the table 360 degrees. In time, he quite enjoyed the role of top grass and liked the feeling that he could help put away punters who in any other arena would eat him for breakfast. It was payback for the type of people who'd shoved him around in his undistinguished youth.

After Harkins was nearly killed by Thomas Barclay and pensioned off, control of Swan had moved over to the Source Unit, who handled all informants for Police Scotland. He got on well enough with the official handlers, but he didn't like the fact that these modern cops were straight pegs and did it all by the book. Harkins hadn't given a rat's arse about the rule book and handled people his way, which was part of the reason that Billy Drew had walked from what should have been a solid murder conviction. Honesty was something that Swan had problems dealing with and he preferred not to have it in his life. He had no leverage with his handlers, which pissed him off at times, but he could live with it. In any case, he always reassured himself that he had his time bomb for a rainy day: the sauna DVDs were safely hidden and no one had seen them, or even knew about them, apart from himself and his spoodle, Gnasher, who wasn't a problem.

When the handlers had asked Swan to introduce someone to the Flemings in order to get to Pete Handyside, he'd been a bit uneasy, but the thought that it might be something tasty had given him a bit of a buzz so he'd gone for it big time. He'd worked out that it was an undercover job and he imagined himself in that role, risking his life and taking on the hard men. He knew Handyside by reputation and had done a bit of business with him through the Flemings, who were trading in working girls. They had a thing going where the girls would work part-time in Newcastle, Belfast, Glasgow and Edinburgh, keeping on the move so the law couldn't get a steady aim on them. Handyside had always been polite and

88

businesslike as far as he knew, but the man's reputation troubled Swan. He'd heard what he was capable of, and while he knew that a lot of reputations in the criminal world were built partly on myth, he had the feeling that was not the case with Handyside. As such Swan was sure it was better not to meet the man personally or have any business problems with him – he was happy to leave that to the Flemings.

The phone startled him; he'd nearly dozed off again with the remote control still clasped in his hand. His heart raced, wondering who would call at that time of the morning. His world tended to operate in the hours of darkness.

'It's Arthur here.'

Arthur wasn't the caller's real name but the one his lead handler used when he needed to communicate with Swan.

'It's been a while, Arthur. How's things?'

'I'm okay, Ricky, you know how it is – crime thriving and all that. Have you seen the news?'

Swan pushed Gnasher off his face. The dog was trying to lick him to death. Gnasher was the one creature on God's earth that actually liked his master, or at least that was how it appeared to Swan. The dog was affectionate and that love was reciprocated with all the luxuries that could be showered on a four-legged friend. The name Gnasher was his little joke, and the irony never ceased to make him laugh when he told people what the bundle of curls was called.

'Not seen too much news, busy looking after the ladies if you know what I mean.' He grinned, suddenly sure that the handler was jealous. In actual fact the man on the end of the line squirmed; he thought Swan was a creep, but a good handler would never let a source see that contempt.

'There's a problem and we need to meet as soon as. It's in your interest so make it happen.'

The handler had his attention and Swan had already made the connection between 'the problem' and the news bulletin about the girl on the beach. 'I can meet you in a couple of hours if it's really necessary,' he replied.

'It's necessary. Better safe than sorry.'

Swan thought that if the handler was trying to give him some form of reassurance then he'd failed miserably. Swan was a double-dyed coward and any hint of trouble got his sweat glands working overtime.

'It really is necessary,' the handler repeated. 'We just want to look after you.' The handler was spooking him deliberately. He could have played the problem down till they met, but he just loved knowing that Swan would be in a panic trying to work out what had happened.

'Arthur' and a second handler met Swan in the café of a small garden centre near Perth. They ordered coffees before they got down to business.

'You look pale,' Arthur said, enjoying every second of the man's discomfort. 'Hope you're not taking too much out of yourself on the job.' He tapped the side of his nose for effect, but it did nothing to calm Swan's growing sense of concern.

'I'm fine. I just want to know what's so important that you have to drag me out of my bed at this time of the day.'

They told him what they could, which wasn't that much, but it was enough to make sure he wouldn't sleep that night. The man he'd introduced to the Flemings hadn't called in when expected and there were fears for his safety.

'We can't be sure what's happened, and we don't know if there's a problem. There's other things on the go and you probably saw the report about the girl on the beach.'

90

Swan nodded weakly as the handler continued. 'Some of our boys turned over a boat in Eyemouth in the early hours that morning so there might be links, but we just don't know yet. We'll keep in touch. There's probably no need to worry.'

Swan found some life. 'No need to fucking worry? Are you serious? The Flemings are one thing, but if these Newcastle lunatics are involved then there's a big need to fucking worry.'

'Just keep your head till the investigation team work it all out, then we'll see from there. You have all the numbers if there's an emergency, and one way or the other we'll get back to you as often as possible till this thing settles down.

'Anything else you want to ask before we shoot off?'

Swan shook his head slowly and tried to run all the possibilities through his head. The handlers stood up and 'Arthur' put his hand on Swan's shoulder.

'Take care, Ricky.' The handler said it like he meant it, but the truth was that they'd loved tormenting him and they pissed themselves all the way back to Edinburgh.

Swan sat for a further half hour and sank another couple of espressos, which achieved nothing more than helping to jangle his already shredded nerves.

'Brilliant – just fucking brilliant.'

The waitress passing at the time asked him if he was okay. He stared at her without saying a word until she became spooked enough to walk away and tell her manager that there was a loony in the restaurant.

Swan drove straight home after that and as soon as he was in the house he pulled all the curtains closed and checked that everything was locked. The Corral was a smart five-bedroom shack, which he loved to show off to anyone who was remotely interested, but for the first time it felt too big – too exposed. He'd have been better off in a flat ten storeys up. He wished he had a gun but knew he was more likely to shoot himself than the enemy if they came to visit. He looked at Gnasher and for the first time felt pissed off at the dog who'd done nothing but love him.

'Why aren't you a fucking Rottweiler?'

The spoodle didn't answer him; he just sensed the tension and tried to lick his master's hand. Swan told the dog to fuck off, stomped into his bedroom and shut the door in Gnasher's sad little face.

8

It was late afternoon and Macallan flicked the switch on the kettle before wandering through to the bedroom to take off her boots. They'd just returned from a walk and the baby was crying, impatient to be fed. Jack could help with that now Adam was taking some solids, so he was busy in the kitchen mashing up some banana to go with the baby rice. The bedside dresser caught her attention and Macallan realised that her mobile phone had been in there for over twenty-four hours without her checking it. She wondered whether she should leave it for another day, but the urge was too much, so she pulled open the drawer and looked at the screen as it filled up with the (mostly useless) apps she was addicted to. She tapped on to her emails and saw that one had recently arrived from Jimmy McGovern. It had to be important; McGovern would never bother her unless it mattered. It was a long message and about halfway through she closed her eyes.

'Jesus Christ.'

She remembered hearing something the previous day about a girl being found on the Berwickshire coast, and the TV news had been suggesting that it might tie in with a police operation earlier that day in Eyemouth. It had the sound of something big but there were few details. In the email McGovern told her that the operation hadn't finished with a result, but the girl might open it up for them. The reason he'd sent the message was that an undercover officer involved in the case was missing. McGovern was aware that Macallan knew the man from her time in Northern Ireland and was giving her a heads-up. In fact she'd worked with his older brother, Tommy, in the Branch, and they'd done some good things together against Republican terrorists. She only remembered Dixie Deans from a couple of training lectures she'd given to the serious crime squad, where he'd been regarded as a natural born detective. He'd asked her a couple of difficult questions but delivered with a smile because he knew she was a friend of his older brother and they both enjoyed the wind-up. Macallan knew nothing but good things about him, and that he'd subsequently gone off the radar to undertake undercover operations; that was the last she'd heard anything about him.

Macallan made some tea, went back into the bedroom and sat in the old chair by the window. The real world was coming for her and there was no way to avoid it.

The door opened and Jack came in carrying their son, who reached out for her. She took him in her arms, still in awe of the look that came over Adam's face whenever he saw his mother.

'Everything okay?' Jack said, stretching the knots out of his muscles.

'Absolutely fine now I've got my two boys.' She smiled at her man and he saw something flicker through her expression. She obviously wasn't fine, but he decided not to push it any further.

'You sit there with our son and heir and I'll rustle us up some grub.'

Later that night Jack had gone to bed and the baby slept as Macallan tried to concentrate on a whodunit, but she was struggling. She wanted to call Tommy Deans, though she knew that with so little information it was better to leave the family alone. Maybe there was a rational explanation for it all and Dixie would turn up. Somehow that seemed like a long shot though.

The phone blinked suddenly on the table next to her – it was John O'Connor.

'Have you heard the news, Grace?'

It had been a long time since O'Connor had used her first name so warmly. He'd been her boss and lover after she'd transferred from the PSNI to the old Lothian and Borders force in Edinburgh. Her life seemed to have changed for the better till the Barclay murder investigation had gone badly wrong and O'Connor had blamed her not only for that but for the subsequent stalling of his career. That was the past though; more recently he'd started to climb again and was now the chief super in charge of the city. She hoped he was leaving their problems behind.

'I got a message from Jimmy.' She wondered for a moment whether to call him sir or John but decided to leave it blank.

'The thing is, there's more to this than you realise. I know you're due back and was thinking about getting you involved. It might be too much too soon but I thought I'd run it past you. I was going to call anyway to see if we could have a sit-down before you start work again.' He was sure she wouldn't say no.

'I've been doing a bit of thinking. I'm not sure about my future in the job any more.' She let it hang there and the long moment of silence confirmed his surprise. 'There's the baby now and maybe I need a break away from it. Anyway, let's sort an appointment and I'll come over as soon as.'

They fixed it up, she put the phone back on the coffee table and then set about gnawing the hard ridge of skin on her forefinger, which was her version of nail biting.

'What do you do now, Grace?' She said it quietly, but Jack had emerged from the bedroom in time to hear her. He leaned over and kissed the top of her head.

'You do what you have to do, detective.'

9

Macallan flew into Edinburgh and then dropped off her case at the late-booked hotel she thought would be more bearable than going to the flat, which these days would feel so empty without Jack and the baby. Not long after, she was sipping black tea in John O'Connor's office, well aware how much his occupation of the smartest room in the house would please him. It was a complete contrast to the farm boxes ninety-five per cent of the force had to endure and had executive written all over it. She smiled, thinking how he could finally look down on the unwashed masses, confident he'd found his rightful place in the world. Her smile broadened at the thought that with the rate Police Scotland were getting rid of staff they might all get an office like his one day. All they had to do was survive the cuts.

Macallan had been ushered in by O'Connor's staff officer, who had the look and speech patterns of a future chief constable, and she wondered, not for the first time, why it was that they all seemed to be the same people in different skins. She thought she was beginning to think like the world's greatest cynic, Mick Harkins, and put her cup back on the desk. O'Connor had been delayed at a meeting but was on his way, and she tried to run the script through her head again. It changed every time she did it; the truth was that she wasn't sure what she would say when he finally looked across the table at her. She still didn't know what she wanted to do and was being pulled in too many directions.

She began to hum the old Bing Crosby song 'Beautiful Dreamer', which had stuck in her head when she was a child and remained there, breaking out occasionally without her thinking about it. She walked over to the window and stared across the playing fields towards the spot where the bomb had exploded, nearly taking her life and the baby she hadn't realised was growing inside her. Then the door opened and startled her out of her memories of those dark winter days. John O'Connor smiled, and for the first time since their relationship had ended there was warmth in the expression.

'Good to see you, Grace. You're looking well; family life seems to agree with you.'

She wondered if there was anything behind those words but thought it was better to give him a chance. And what had she to lose? Time heals – her relationship with Jack Fraser proved that was true.

O'Connor gestured her back to the seat opposite his desk and emptied some papers from his briefcase onto the pile in his in tray. The wall behind him spoke volumes about Chief Superintendent John O'Connor: photographs of the various courses he'd attended and of him shaking the hands of people who seemed to matter were up there with certificates of his academic qualifications, forming the backdrop to a man who just wanted to be one of the stars. Harkins always referred to these displays as ego walls, and she thought he was bang on the money. Mick had his own version of wall decorations – his fifty-yard breast-stroke swimming certificate and the only qualification he'd managed to gain at his secondary school. They'd taken pride of place on the wall behind his desk and he'd enjoyed watching the puzzled expressions of visitors who were normally too confused to ask about the grubby old documents set in Poundstretcher frames. Next to them he'd had a magic wand taped to the wall, and when some visiting senior officer couldn't resist asking what it meant, Harkins would smile kindly as if he was explaining it to a child who just didn't understand the world of big people.

'Well, every month the chief expects me to perform a fucking miracle with shite crime figures. I take the magic wand, wave it about over the figures and guess what? They're still shite!' Harkins had never tired of putting on the same show if someone was daft enough to ask the question. It had sent just as clear a message as O'Connor's wall about who Harkins was.

To be fair, Macallan had to admit that O'Connor had just enough pizzazz for the role he was in, and in the twenty-first century image seemed to matter as much as substance. God, that thought made her feel old.

O'Connor spoke first. 'I thought a lot about our conversation and on reflection, although I was surprised, I suppose I shouldn't have been given what you've been through.'

His words were not what she'd expected; the old bitterness just didn't seem to be there, but she was wise enough to know that he could act with the best of them. She'd promised herself that she would never let her guard down with him again – it had cost too much in the past. There was a pause as Macallan tried to pick her words then threw them out, deciding to say what she felt. She knew there was no point in changing the habits of a lifetime, and she'd never been any good at giving a performance when she didn't mean it.

'I'm just tired, John.' She hadn't used his first name in a long time and it felt strange saying it again. His reaction took her by surprise, and for a fleeting moment she thought there was a hint of sadness in his expression as he flicked his gaze down to the desk.

'It was hard after the bombing, then the baby. The daft thing is I feel really well physically, but I'm only seventy-five per cent clear in my mind. I worry that I could get it wrong in a tight situation.' She shook her head slowly. 'Maybe I've lost a bit of confidence.' She paused again and looked straight at O'Connor. 'Or maybe I just don't care enough any more.'

He saw her strength and weakness in those few words. She cared in a world where few people knew what that meant. He envied her but understood that time and again it had left her exposed then damaged. He got up from his chair and edged round the desk to fill her cup with fresh tea then stood in the same place at the window Macallan had occupied a few minutes earlier. She waited for him to speak and had no idea what else to say.

'I was wrong the way I treated you after the Barclay thing.'

Macallan raised her head in shock; she'd never expected to hear that from him. She had no words, completely lost for a reply that would make any sense.

'I wanted to hurt you; I suspect the truth was that I still cared. Who is it we always hurt?' He turned to look at her. 'Do what's best for you and your family. I'll support you all the way, and you deserve that.'

If O'Connor wanted to throw her off balance, he'd achieved his aim. If it was one of his political schemes then it really made no difference to her. She could say what she wanted and didn't care what the consequences were any more. The job that had been her whole life had been relegated through the love of a man and a child who'd saved her from the demons that had haunted her for so long.

'I'm tired of the politics … fighting people who should have my back. I know that's how the job is, but that's how I feel at the moment.' The comment was aimed at people like him and he knew it.

His phone rang then and broke the moment. He took the call; it was obviously something to do with Dixie Deans and she felt the old instincts rattle her curiosity. It was the familiar craving, her drug of choice just out of reach in the conversation between O'Connor and whoever was on the other end of the line.

O'Connor bent his head and squeezed the bridge of his nose between thumb and forefinger, his eyes closed. He was struggling with whatever he'd been told; she could see the same symptoms she'd suffered so many times in the past. It was there, staring her in the face, the reason why she should walk away and leave her demons behind. He put the phone down and tried to regain his composure.

'Sorry, I have to attend an intelligence briefing as soon as. Had you been planning to stay over?'

'Yes, I've booked into a hotel for tonight. I'm meeting Mick Harkins for a drink later on, and he wouldn't thank me for dashing off for a plane when the evening had barely started.'

'Well, why don't you have a think about the job overnight then let me know what you want to do. We can meet tomorrow if you like.'

She stared for a moment at the man across the desk, trying to understand what had changed him, if anything. 'Fine. Yes, I'll call you tomorrow and we can arrange a where and when. As long as we don't have to eat in the canteen – my organs are only just recovering.' She smiled for the first time.

He managed something near a real smile to match hers. 'Well, if you're meeting Mick give him my regards – and good luck to your liver. While we're on the subject… sources are still reporting that Billy Drew isn't giving up on payback for Jonathon Barclay, which is no worry for us, but Mick is on his to-do list as well. He'll not listen to us but maybe you can get through to him.'

'Get through to Mick Harkins? That'll be a first,' Macallan said and meant it.

They both smiled absolutely genuinely at that one.

She could see that he needed to go and so rose to leave, but she felt the anxiety of not knowing what the story was with Dixie Deans. She'd fought the urge to ask since she'd come into the room and she managed to get to the door before she broke and turned to O'Connor, who looked over his glasses as she paused, still reaching for the handle.

'Have you got five minutes to tell me about Dixie? It would help – his brother is an old friend.'

He didn't have five minutes but picked the phone up in any case.

'Tell them I'm fifteen minutes behind.' When he hung up, O'Connor nodded towards the chair opposite his desk and said, 'Sit down then.'

Then he told her as much as he could.

10

Two hours later Macallan arrived at Harkins' front door, having stopped off on the way to pick up a bottle of his favourite malt. She knew that visiting without alcohol would invite more abuse than it was worth. When he answered the door, the sight of him made her grin. There was just something reassuring about Harkins despite the fact that he had caused so many problems for the force. He looked good, fit and he was standing at the door with no sign of the walking sticks he'd needed the last time they'd met. His recovery was nothing short of miraculous when she remembered the wrecked body left in the road by Thomas Barclay.

'Jesus, you look like a person who's lived a good life!'

'Don't bullshit me, Grace; you know it never works. Getting there though.'

He pulled the door wide open and nodded her in. It hit her right away that the place felt clean and fresh. That just didn't seem to fit Harkins' profile. She pushed open the door to the lounge then realised what had made the difference. Felicity Young appeared from the kitchen area, drying her hands on a towel and smiling at the sight of Macallan.

'Hello, it's wonderful to see you. And you're looking amazing!'

Young had been involved with Harkins before, although it had been an on-off thing. They were complete opposites, but there was no doubting that they cared about each other and Macallan wondered if Harkins had finally been tamed. She'd always hoped it would work out between them because Harkins carried a powerful self-destruct gene, and she wasn't ready for the funeral of yet another friend who meant so much to her.

Macallan could smell the rich tones of coffee and decided to keep the malt in her bag, knowing that Young wasn't much of a drinker. They exchanged the usual catch-up stories before Macallan told them all about the baby and did the required display of smartphone photographs. The coffee had been served on a tray complete with neatly arranged biscuits and napkins, which somehow got to Macallan – she was starting to really miss the old Harkins.

The phone rang and Young took the call.

'That's my lift arriving.' She turned to Macallan. 'Sorry, but this is my badminton night and I know you need some time to exchange detective stories with the boy here. I'll see you the next time you're over. By the way, the force needs you.'

She kissed her man on the top of the head and Macallan could have sworn that his expression turned sheepish. There were times when she was sure there was a marsh-mallow lurking under all that wolf's clothing.

About three seconds after the door closed behind Felicity, Harkins went into the kitchen and came back with two sparkling glasses. 'You'd better have a bottle in that bag or I'm really going to be pissed – that's pissed as in angry. We're only allowed to have a couple of glasses of red French pish with meals now that I'm involved with a fitness fanatic.'

Macallan was relieved to find that there was still some of the old beast left in Harkins as she pulled the firewater out of her bag like a magician. 'Ta-da!'

'That will do nicely, Superintendent.' He nodded happily, wearing the expression of a starving man presented with a steaming plate of fish and chips.

She poured about a quarter glass and Harkins did an up-a-bit sign with his forefinger.

'Jesus, how have you got a functioning liver left in that body?'

'Just pour and leave the sarcasm to a professional.'

They sat down opposite each other and for the first time in a while she felt okay with the decision she'd almost made. It was always the same when she was with Mick; he could be the world's biggest pain in the arse, but there was a certainty about him and a friendship that meant something. They'd spoken a few times on the phone when she'd been off, but Harkins was one of the worst phone conversationalists she'd ever come across and the calls rarely lasted more than a couple of minutes.

He closed his eyes after the first mouthful of whisky, sighed and tilted his head back like the most contented man on earth.

'God, I'll never get tired of this stuff. It's just the dug's baws. Now tell me what the plan is. Anytime we spoke you sounded a bit vague.'

Macallan spluttered midway through sipping the malt. 'A bit vague? Have you heard yourself on the phone? It's like there's no one on the other end.'

It was the usual wind-up, and she loved it; it was as if she'd never been away. She told him it all. The nightmares after the bombing; how she enjoyed loving her new family and that she'd found some form of contentment at last. For the first time in her life she wondered if she wanted to wake up every day as a detective with more questions than answers about what the fuck she was doing. Harkins didn't say much, apart from telling Macallan that he and Young had agreed to keep their separate homes for a bit of space for the time being. He still had commitment issues.

'A true romantic till the end. How does that girl put up with you?'

'Good looks and charm – always been that way,' he replied, then his expression dropped and he became serious. 'Just don't want to piss her about this time.'

The moment passed quickly and they got back to remembering why they were such friends. Harkins would never admit it, especially not to Macallan, but he'd been missing her both as a cop and a far-too-rare human being who'd forgiven him so much. She tried telling him about the conversation with O'Connor, and he leaned forward when the name was mentioned – he'd always worried how she would cope with a man so full of contradictions and so damaged by the woman opposite him.

'By the way,' Macallan said, 'he told me that they keep picking up intel that Billy Drew still wants you, but not in the biblical sense. I know they've already warned you, but you be careful. He's a hard bastard with too many screws loose or missing.'

'Fuck him. If he comes for me I'll be ready.' Harkins necked what was left in his glass and topped up again. She shook her head; she'd already guessed what his response would be before he said it.

'Are you going to invite him out onto the street, Mick – have a gunfight like in a Clint Eastwood film?' The booze was taking effect and she sat back and sniggered at the image of Harkins and Billy Drew dressed up like a couple of cowboys.

'What did you tell him?' Harkins said, getting the conversation back to reality.

'He said I could think about it overnight. I'm going to see him again tomorrow. But I do think I'm going to take this investigation. I'm not sure yet it's time for me to go. There's no way I want to look back and wish I'd given it every chance. It might be just as wrong to stay and risk what I've got now, so let's call it a deferred sentence. I'm going to tell him that I'll make up my mind about the longer term when this one is put to bed. Christ, I don't even know if I've still got it, but I'll soon find out. If I walk away now I know I'll have regrets and never be sure it was the right thing.' She looked down into the glass as Harkins replied.

'It's the right thing. You're not sure; that's not the time to make the big decisions. So go for it, but remember this one is bad from the arse up. The way I see it this can only end up as a mess, but that's never been a reason to walk away from the job. Now let's get pissed and when this bottle is finished I'll get some of that French pish out just to make sure the hangover is as bad as it can get.'

He disappeared into the kitchen, came back with two packets of salt and vinegar crisps and what looked like an expensive bottle of red. The old Harkins would have just thrown the packet at her, but he'd brought a nicely decorated plate. He did his best to arrange the crisps on it, but half of them ended up on the carpet.

'Sorry, my friend, but you just don't do fine dining.' Macallan found herself giggling again, a sure sign she was going under.

Harkins stared at the mess on the floor for a moment and then shrugged. 'Fuck it.'

Macallan woke up in her hotel at 3 a.m. and groaned. She tried to unglue her mouth and headed for the bathroom on tiptoe, her eyes barely open. She stuck her face under the tap so she could slurp as much water as she could take on-board. The reflection in the mirror looked like someone else. Someone who'd been very ill. 'God.' This was the only word she could manage before padding back to her bed, promising herself for the umpteenth time that she would never drink whisky with Harkins again. She fell asleep until the sound of the alarm crashed through her dreams and made her groan again.

She sat on the edge of the bed, taking a long minute to breathe deeply and find the strength to get into her day. About halfway through her shower she felt a rush of energy, the thought that she would soon be back in the game lifting her above her hangover. Then she dressed, did the best she could with her face and headed for her meeting with O'Connor.

11

They'd arranged to meet in Stockbridge at an upmarket café, one of the many smart little places that had opened up over the years and only a few minutes from the old Lothian and Borders HQ at Fettes. The area had fed, watered and provided the boozers for a generation of police staff leading up to the unified Scottish force. Macallan had decided to walk there through the sun-washed trees and grounds of Inverleith Park. She'd done that a few times in the past after a night on the scoosh with Mick Harkins.

As she walked she saw women just like her playing like five-year-olds with their kids and dogs. She was conflicted, wanting to be just like them, but tearing herself away from the job was never going to be easy. The air was menthol cool, the sky a clean empty blue above her as the sun began to stretch its warming hands over the old city. She thought again about that dark winter moment when the bomb had gone off only yards from the park and changed everything for her.

Macallan pulled the phone from her pocket and tapped in a reminder note to catch up with someone when she got time. Lesley Thompson had been her DCI and one of the closest to the bomb when it exploded. She'd survived but there were burns on her arms and body that were for life. Although she'd returned to work she was anchored behind a desk, and it looked like a permanent sentence. When Macallan had first met her she'd been a problem, having been planted in her squad by O'Connor. That had changed as Thompson came to appreciate what it meant to be part of a close team, and she had been developing into a real player before she'd been injured in the blast. Macallan hadn't seen her since she'd left to have Adam.

She smiled as she watched a short, middle-aged guy trying and failing to get a ball back from a nifty-looking boxer who'd stolen it from what she presumed was his little spoodle. (Or was it a cockapoo? And what was the difference? She hadn't a clue but decided she liked the name spoodle better anyway.) The man and dog pursued the beast vainly across the park and the owner's unhindered comb-over flew backwards in the chase like Sir Bobby Charlton in his finest days.

Macallan sucked in a deep breath and headed for the meeting. As she exited the park's west gate she barely noticed a smart-looking but filthy BMW parked nearby that was belching fag smoke from both front windows. She caught a whiff of the blue fumes and as usual she had to remind herself that she was an addict even though she hadn't touched one for long enough. She knew it would take very little encouragement to get her back on the weed. She'd had the occasional lapse but had always managed to struggle back off them again.

The pair in the BMW paid little attention to Macallan; as far as they were concerned she was just another well-heeled yummy mummy taking her early-morning spin round the park, though she didn't have the required sprog or mutt in tow. Brenda McMartin sat in the passenger seat smoking an extra strength and grinding her way through a third packet of cheese and onion crisps. All she was interested in was Ricky Swan, who'd given up on the boxer and was enjoying a cigar as the spoodle tried to work out what to do without his ball.

McMartin and her driver had come through from Glasgow a couple of hours earlier, intending to get an idea of Swan's movements and then lift the grassing little fuck. She'd agreed the job with her brother; the plan was to keep Swan in one piece till they found out what he knew. Once they had the full story, and after a bit of torture, she could let him join his ancestors – which seemed appropriate given the crime. The driver was Jimmy 'Fanny' Adams, who'd worked for the McMartins for years and for their old man before them. He was the wrong side of sixty and relegated from front-line gangster to driver and gofer. As far as The Bitch and her brother were concerned he was a has-been who couldn't shut the fuck up about the old days and the gang wars that had cost so many lives in Glasgow.

Her old man was on his last legs but had always insisted that Adams be kept on for what he'd given back then, when tit-for-tat killings had robbed too many crime families of their sons. He'd been McMartin Senior's top soldier and had the scars to prove it. In his day he had been a feared and respected nutjob who was missing a little finger on each hand. The digits had been taken when he was being tortured by a rival gang who'd abducted him at gunpoint from his beloved mother's graveside. The plan had been to crucify him to even up a score with the McMartins, but they'd made a fatal mistake when they'd left him seemingly unconscious so they could neck a couple of beers before they put the nails in him. Adams was made of the right stuff and had been behind the door when the two men who'd tormented him to the edge of madness came back in to finish him off. Three hours later the CID had broken in after an anonymous call and found the two men nailed to the wooden floor. Adams had added an artistic touch by half stripping them and leaving them in what looked like a very compromising position, one on top of the other. It was the stuff of legend in gangland, and old man McMartin had given him a big fat bonus and private health treatment for his wounds. But when all was said and done Adams was human and now he was nothing more than another old burnout who pissed off his employers just by being around. The Bitch swore that as soon as her father was in his box she'd boot Adams into touch and get a younger model who might even do the business with her as part of the contract.

'I remember when I had to drive your old man through here to do a boy's legs for non-payment.' Adams made the same mistake every time by starting with the words 'I remember'.

'Why don't you shut the fuck up? Who gives one about you and the old man?'

Brenda blew a cloud of smoke into his face and enjoyed his humiliation. He'd no pension so no options. He had to take all the crap they threw at him, but there were times he swore to God he'd cut her throat one day.

'Fuckin' Fanny. Whoever gave you that handle got it absolutely right.' The Bitch sniggered and tiny scraps of cheese and onion crisps spattered out of her nostrils with some snot.

Macallan arrived at the café on time and tried again to fix her face, which still bore small traces of her night with Harkins. Her hangover was almost gone in record time though; she was energised by the thought of what she'd decided and all that it would mean.

O'Connor walked through the door about fifteen minutes late, which was a real change in habit for a man who'd preached punctuality as an unbreakable rule. The pale, worn look on his face explained enough – he was struggling with a problem he wasn't equipped to handle. She'd seen it exposed on the Barclay case and here it was again. She knew he was a man with enough talent to take him most places he wanted to go, but he had difficulty coping with the complexities and uncertainties of serious criminal investigation. He was as good as they came at thinking strategically or being a business leader, but he couldn't handle the crap that most investigators had to wade through to get to the truth.

Harkins used to say that during his service he'd been contaminated with everything that could spurt or pour from the human body or mind and that nine times out of ten he'd received no thanks, or more likely just plain abuse, from whatever family, villains or senior officers were concerned. Only a few were cut out for that level of grief. O'Connor had wanted to wear that badge of honour, and though he'd had real success as a senior detective it had always been where the answers were just waiting to be picked up – the 'gimmes' as they were known affectionately by the more cynical investigators. The Barclay case had shown him for what he was: a talented policeman but a limited detective. It had hurt him badly, but it was the truth, and eventually he'd had to admit it to himself. That had been a hard process, and for a long time after his relationship with Macallan had fallen apart he'd made all the wrong choices. Eventually though he'd realised that he was just like every other human being and was able to move on.

It hadn't been easy but he'd made time to wait on Macallan's decision about coming back to the force. The girl on the beach was still something of a mystery and for the moment the investigation was being handled by local CID. The information about the *Brighter Dawn*'s lifebelt was still being withheld, and the press would love that one when it was leaked or released.

The Dixie Deans problem was being handled internally, and there were some who still hung on to the belief that he'd had a wobbly of some kind or gone over the side with a woman. For the time being they had breathing space, but O'Connor knew that when the dots were finally joined up they had a potential shit storm that crossed an awful lot of borders. The challenge was to decide who was best placed to coordinate the investigation without civil war breaking out among the law-enforcement agencies involved. Deans had been originally deployed in Edinburgh through a local source. If the intelligence was correct, whatever or whoever was cargo on-board the *Brighter Dawn* had been bound for the Flemings in Edinburgh so when the dust settled, all eyes and pointed fingers would be trained on Edinburgh to provide some poor sod to coordinate the whole show. O'Connor wanted Macallan in that role, if it came to it, and was prepared to wait as long as he could for her decision. Bad choices had been made and the order to deploy Deans into the heart of Handyside's organisation could put people face down in the gutter. He wasn't too worried about that though, as it had been pushed by the head of special ops, one of his competitors for higher office.

What did concern O'Connor was what McGovern had told him at a private briefing. McGovern was someone he respected, a man who tended to stick to the facts and never pushed the panic button without good reason. The DCI was sure the original intel had been on the money and that there had been other girls on the *Brighter Dawn* who should have arrived with the boat. As far as McGovern was concerned, the girl on the beach, the spotters who'd been disturbed in Eyemouth plus the missing UC meant only one thing – the operation had been compromised. He believed other young women had been killed at sea and that only the girl found on the beach could confirm the veracity of this horror story. It was better not to think too hard about the UC given Handyside's reputation. The last they'd heard from Deans was that he was driving the Flemings to a meeting of the organisation leaders in North Shields.

O'Connor had stopped sleeping at night. The story just kept festering, and the news that Eric Gunderson had taken a header into the Tyne was the last thing they'd needed. The assessment had been that he was a possible weak link who might be broken if they had some evidence to put to him. But O'Connor wouldn't discuss any of this in a public place, and in any case suspected it might put Macallan off giving him the answer he wanted.

He sat down opposite her to find she'd already worked her way through her first cup of straight black coffee. She saw him hesitate and knew he was trying to work out how to greet her. He did the right thing and left it at a weary smile and 'Hi.' He nodded to the waitress and ordered another two blacks without asking what she wanted. She almost felt sorry for him; she knew better than most how so much responsibility tore lumps out of the men and women who took on the big ones. She wondered what she was letting herself in for, but that was just a light form of self-deception. Macallan wanted it more than anything else at that moment. If she was going out then this was the one to finish on, and if she stayed and it all worked out, she was back in the limelight.

O'Connor put both palms on his face and gave it a rub. There was no disguising his exhaustion.

'You okay there?' she asked.

115

'I'm fine; nothing that a few weeks in the Caribbean with no phone wouldn't cure anyway.' His dull eyes sparked briefly and he looked genuinely pleased to be there. 'How did you get on with Mick?'

'As regards the yellow card re Billy Drew, his exact words were "fuck him". The alcohol bit I think you can guess. It was great to see him though. I can't believe that's the same guy I saw lying on the road that day.'

'Some people just verge on indestructible and Mick is definitely one of them,' O'Connor said ruefully, wishing he had half the man's stamina for what life could throw at its citizens. They sipped their coffees and stayed quiet, trying to see who would get to the point first. Macallan waited him out.

'What did you decide then? I told you either way is fine. This case is starting to burn – the press, and Jacquie Bell in particular, have caught a whiff of the smoke.'

As far back as the Barclay case O'Connor had realised that Macallan and Bell were close. It had infuriated him at the time, but on later reflection he knew she'd only done what so many others had, including him. As far as he knew she used the press more than the press had used her, and not many could claim that virtue. She had her share of vanity like anyone else, but for the most part she'd never let it lead her professional life. He knew that was how she'd become a regular feature with the press; she never overplayed it and had that rare quality of speaking a variety of the Queen's English that the punters understood.

'I want to come back,' Macallan told him, 'and if you can square it I'll take on whatever I'm told to take on. If this thing with the girl on the beach is it then that works, but I want to pick a couple of the team. I don't know where you are with Dixie but the same rules apply.' She waited for a reply and noted that he was relieved so far.

116

'One thing though,' she continued. 'When this is done I might still walk away. I want the job, but it's as much to work out some questions in my own mind as anything else. The last thing is that I've not spoken to Jack about it since I made my decision, and if he asks me not to do it I'll go home and live my life.' She sipped her coffee and waited.

'That's fair enough. It's not much notice but can we say you'll start back on Monday if you're definitely taking this on? That gives you the weekend to mull it over. I've brought a briefing paper for you to look at, which will help you make your decision and bring you up to speed at the same time. You'll probably run a mile when you see what's festering underneath us, but what's new? By the way the MIT you'll manage is based in their own suite in Leith; Fettes is just a building full of ghosts now, including me.'

They finished their coffees, shook hands and went their separate ways. Macallan watched O'Connor head back to Fettes and wondered where they would all be in a few weeks. She was returning to the game and the result was all in the lap of the gods. The sun had warmed the streets, and the early shoppers and coffee drinkers were already on the go. Macallan had always loved this part of town so she lifted her face to the sky and enjoyed the moment.

She walked back to the hotel to pick up her bag for the flight to Belfast. Jack was going to pick her up at the airport, and she ached to have him and Adam close to her again. She sat on the bed and called Jack on his mobile, and he answered on the first ring. Her heart beat that bit harder when she heard how they'd missed her and he asked when was she coming home? She told him what she'd done and there was a pause on the other end.

'That's fine, but if it doesn't work promise me we go to plan B. If it's any help though, I think you've done the right thing. You need to have the answers to all those questions you keep asking yourself on the cliffs.' He paused, then said, 'Anyway, park your arse on that plane and get back here to perform your duties as a wife and mother.'

She put the phone down and wiped the tears from her face.

Before she left for the airport she called Lesley Thompson and promised to meet up with her when she was back in her seat.

'Any chance of a job? They think I'm not fit after the injuries, but the truth is working in intel is driving me up the wall.' There was a genuine plea in the voice on the other end of the phone and Macallan thought she deserved better.

'Leave it with me,' she said. 'I think I have a free hand with the job and could use you. Speak to you later.'

She picked up her case, headed for the airport and smiled at the thought that in a couple of hours she'd have her arms round Jack and their son.

12

A cold north wind had blown down from the Arctic Circle and it felt more like January than early summer. Macallan, Jack and Adam had spent the whole Saturday afternoon along the cliffs and they got back to the cottage chilled but happy. They were starving so Macallan made a deal with Jack that she'd mix up some mush for Adam, cook some grown-up steaks for them and do the washing-up as well if he put Adam to bed after his bath and bedtime feed. She'd started on the briefing paper O'Connor had given her and wanted to finish it the same night. There was only the Sunday left before it was back into the bear pit. The thought of it made her shiver; she was nervous and wondered about her lack of confidence. Jack had told her it was simply a case of being human, no different from an athlete after a long lay-off with injury. Five minutes back and she'd be as right as rain. She wished she could be that sure. What she'd read so far had her interested, but it was enough to prove Harkins right. The case hadn't even started but all the evidence suggested it was a series of booby traps ready to go off under the force. She'd read half the report and so far there hadn't been a sniff of anything positive.

Once they'd eaten and settled the baby down for the night Jack went into the other room to work on his book. The cold weather gave Macallan the excuse to light the fire and she'd stacked it up with logs, pouring herself a small glass of red before settling down with the report. A couple of hours later, and without a break, she finished it, closed the folder and looked into the glowing remains of the fire.

What in the name of God have you let yourself in for? she thought, shaking her head slowly; but she knew that this was what she needed. She dropped the report into her briefcase and wanted to put her arms round Jack to make sure he was real. She knew it would be a while before she had this much peace again so all she wanted to do now was sleep beside Jack with their son nearby.

That same night Ingrid Richter opened her eyes and spoke for the first time since she'd been washed up on the Berwickshire coast. Her memory was nothing more than dense fog inhabited by dark amorphous shapes that might have been human. Those shapes frightened her, and she didn't want to know what they meant. Although Richter had a good command of English, the nurse at her bedside was brought up in North-east Scotland and there were still strong notes of the Doric in her voice. Although it was an effort to try to understand the nurse's words, what comforted Richter in that moment was the woman stroking her brow and soothing her initial panic. The nurse held her gently and helped her sip some water. Almost as soon as she was finished the exhausted young woman fell asleep again, but she knew she was safe.

The nurse closed the door behind her and spoke to the policeman who was on duty. 'Your girl's back with us. She's asleep again, but I think that's her on the mend.'

The nurse phoned the duty doctor, who in turn called their press officer. There was a near frenzy in the media with every journalist trying to find out what had happened to the girl from the sea, and the hospital administrators wanted to keep the waiting hacks as calm as possible. They were in the awkward position of not wanting to upset the media on one side or the police on the other.

Within an hour the press officer had alerted his masters that they needed someone to start talking to the cameras. His last call was to Jacquie Bell to give her a heads-up on the story. Bell was nearly undressed, the worse for drink and having just spent an exhausting night in a bar with an MSP who thought he was interesting. It had taken a lot of gin and all of her womanly charms to get him to give her the goods on a small but interesting scandal that was about to erupt in the Justice Directorate. The call from the press officer had her attention immediately though – Bell just couldn't resist a good story. She knew in her gut this one had legs and enough potential to ruffle a few official feathers, and there was nothing she liked better. The bonus was that the girl probably wouldn't be able to speak yet, which meant she could grab some sleep and recover from her night on the piss.

The press officer agreed to meet her for coffee before work, and when he put the phone down he wondered again whether he had any chance of a relationship with the reporter. He was sure she had feelings for him, but they never seemed to get to the next level and he wondered what he was doing wrong.

Bell desperately wanted to turn the light off but made a last call to one of her contacts, a young flyer doing a stint in the Chief's office. He didn't drink and had gone straight to bed after his Pilates class, and although he was a boring bastard, he hadn't realised it yet. Unfortunately for him, like the press officer, he had hopeless designs on Bell and the sound of her voice so late at night gave him a brief moment of hope that she might finally want to be with him. Bell never wasted time on small talk unless she needed to so she just asked who would run the investigation into the girl on the beach. Normally he wouldn't dream of discussing sensitive issues with anyone outside the job, but he wanted to impress Bell almost as much as he wanted to be chief constable one day. In his ideal world he'd have both.

'I shouldn't tell you this, Jacquie,' he said, 'but they're tying several cases together and it involves drugs, people trafficking and a number of murders.' He felt a twinge of panic, recognising that what he was disclosing could cost him his job. But she was worth it.

'What about the UC officer?'

'How did you know about that?'

'Because I'm a reporter.'

'They're all connected.' His panic increased with that admission, but he trusted her.

'So who's going to run it then?'

'All I can tell you is that I heard the chief speaking to John O'Connor and it looks like Superintendent Macallan is taking it on. Can't confirm it, but that's what I heard.' He asked her if she wanted to have dinner one night and closed his eyes while he waited for her answer.

'I'll let you know.' Bell put down the phone. Her head had cleared enough to decide that she was going to put everything else on hold and get her face into this story. 'Grace.' She said it quietly and with a smile. She set the alarm for abnormally early, switched off the lights and was asleep almost immediately.

13

Across the city Brenda McMartin watched the last of the punters leave Swan's most popular sauna and the one that he tended to use as a base. About half an hour later Swan left with a short-arsed guy and locked up the premises. She nodded; it had gone much as expected. She'd been told Swan was a creature of habit, and so it seemed from what they'd learned by watching him.

'Looks good. I'll get one of the boys to come through tomorrow and lift the grassin' bastard when he locks up. The daft fuck parks his car in the quietest bit of the street and that'll do nicely for us, Fanny boy.'

'You want me on this?' Adams would have loved to get in on the physical end of the job, and the guy didn't look more than a lightweight so shouldn't have been any trouble.

'You can drive. Stay the fuck away from the lift. No way I'm riskin' you havin' a fuckin' heart attack when we're stuffin' that wee cunt in the boot.'

Adams started up the car and thought again about slicing the fat cow beside him as they headed back to Glasgow.

The man who'd left the sauna with Swan had barely registered with McMartin because he was a short-arse. If she'd realised who it was it might have given her pause for thought, but The Bitch came from the 'I don't give a fuck' school of philosophy and had never worried in the past about men half her substantial size.

Short-arse had been working as a minder at the sauna for nine months, and as far as Swan was concerned he was the right man for the job. Size had hee-haw to do with it in this particular case. The minder was Andy 'Cue Ball' Ross, a man every villain and cop in the city with half a brain knew was seriously off his trolley. The problem for anyone mad enough to take him on was that no matter how many times you put him on the deck, he just got up again then came back twice as hard. He was a one-man pain dispenser who'd earned his living dealing street quantities of dope, which gave him a wage, but he was always pissed off at having to serve the losers who appeared at his door like the Legion of the Damned. He was careful in his own habits, never touched the stuff himself and a few pints at the weekend was all the social life he needed. Most nights he liked to sit at home and watch cookery programmes. Apart from that he would nip into the saunas occasionally for a bit of light relief, which was where he'd started to chew the fat with Swan.

One of Swan's minders had gone on the run after the local gendarmerie had kicked his door in and found the half-kilo of coke he'd been holding for a mate. Swan liked Cue Ball, or, more accurately, liked the fearsome reputation the little man had built up over the years, so he'd offered the man decent money to mind for him and a freebie every week with the girl of his choice, as long as it was outside working hours. As far as Cue Ball was concerned Swan was a twat, but a twat with money and the job was a dream. It meant he didn't have to sit in his flat every night and hand over gear to the stream of fucked-up losers who thought he was their friend. He'd also recognised that every one of the junkies who turned up at the flat was a potential grass, and he'd been lucky to survive this long without the pigs handing him a long holiday in HMP Saughton.

The thing that had surprised Swan was that the girls loved Cue Ball. Always polite, he treated every one of them with respect – which was more than they got on an average week, and certainly not from their employer. When he took advantage of the freebies he never messed the girls about and always dropped a few notes in their pocket for a drink. All in all, Swan liked having him around, and he knew that if there was a problem that required an extreme and violent response then he had the right man for the job. Like all weak cowards Swan admired the men of violence, fascinated by what they had that he clearly lacked, and if McMartin had researched her job properly then she might have avoided meeting Cue Ball the following evening.

14

As the hospital stirred with the early-morning business of cleaning and feeding the customers, Ingrid Richter opened her eyes again and wanted to stay awake. She'd dreamt since the nurse had let her sip some water during the night. The dark shapes in the fog were beginning to take form and they terrified her, but she still couldn't remember why.

A different nurse came into the room and smiled broadly. 'Look at you!'

Richter understood her and smiled back. She was hungry, alive and her body had made a good recovery, though her mind would take time to accept the horror it had locked away. What she had that would save her was that special elixir of youth and a fierce desire to live.

The doctor came in, examined her and the smile on his face said all she needed to know. He ordered her to eat, drink, sleep and she would be well again. The doctor suspected that was only partly true though: her body would recover, but her memories might disturb her for a long time.

Richter gave her name and where she came from to the

police officer on duty and within an hour the information had been relayed to the British office in Europol in The Hague. In less than two hours Richter's frantic parents had been contacted and were making arrangements to fly to Edinburgh.

McGovern was at home eating his favourite breakfast of fried everything with toast and reading the paper without rushing, which he considered one of life's little luxuries. Even though it was a Sunday this was a rare day off; he felt weary and kept thinking about the anniversary holiday he'd booked to prove to his wife that they actually had a life. When his phone went off on the table next to him he tried to think of a reason to ignore it but caved after the fifth ring. His office gave him the news that Ingrid Richter was back in the land of the living and seemed ready to talk. McGovern's wife came through to the lounge to pour him more tea and he looked up while he was still speaking and gave her the hangdog eyes. She shrugged and cancelled all their plans for the day; she'd been there too many times before.

McGovern RV'd with a young female detective, Pam Fitzgerald. She'd just joined his team and couldn't believe her luck at having her day off cancelled to get in on the case about the girl on the beach. McGovern saw her raw enthusiasm and remembered he'd been the same before the hard years and the bogeymen had replaced it with a healthy dose of cynicism.

When they arrived at the hospital the duty consultant was friendly enough but insisted that they kept it short because the girl's memory of whatever had happened needed to be recovered slowly and very carefully. The doctor could only guess what she'd experienced out there in the cold water, but there had been a massive shock to her system and he'd arranged for psychiatric backup as part of her recovery. McGovern's instinct was to plough on, but he was pretty sure he knew what she'd been through and wasn't surprised that her memories were buried for the time being. If what he suspected was correct, she'd survived a living nightmare that would haunt her for the rest of her life once she remembered what had taken place on the *Brighter Dawn*. McGovern had a daughter and when she came into his mind he shivered at the thought of something like this happening to her. It was the same thought that every detective experienced when they stared at the human wreckage left by the scum they pursued.

Richter looked tired but well enough when they spoke to her. She'd eaten some food and swallowed the hospital coffee as if it was the best she'd ever tasted. She smiled at the two police officers, and before they could ask her anything further she wanted to know if her parents had been informed.

'They'll be here soon, Ingrid, don't worry. And they're so happy you're safe and well.' McGovern said it as softly as he could, as tears of relief flowed down her cheeks.

'Where am I?' She knew she was in the UK but was not sure where.

'You're in Edinburgh. It's a beautiful city, and you'll love seeing it.'

She repeated the word Edinburgh once and closed her eyes for a moment. They managed to get a brief story from her before she fell asleep mid-sentence and the staff nurse moved between them like a boxing referee demanding a break.

Richter had told them she could remember being abducted and was sure that along with some other girls they been loaded onto a fishing boat in Scheveningen. That was as far as they got, but McGovern thought it would do for the time being. He wanted a steer on where to go with it, and although Macallan wasn't due in till the following morning he called her. He was glad to have an excuse to speak to her; he hadn't shown it in front of the troops but he was a happy detective knowing that she was back in the game. Even the sound of her voice on the phone gave him confidence that they might just get answers to the puzzles that were erupting all over the case. He told her what they had and that it wasn't much so far.

'No problem, and there's no way we can force her. Christ, it's hard to get your head round what might have happened to her out there. You keep thinking you've heard it all and the next case proves you wrong.'

He could hear her scribbling notes as she spoke.

'I'll be there early doors and sit down with you to get a full briefing. No doubt I'll have to spend the whole morning speaking to everyone in the building before I can get on with the job. We'll want to get these guys from the boat back in again as soon as. Do we know where they are or should be?'

'Don't know about the other two but guess you've read the report that they fished Eric Gunderson out of the Tyne with the side of his skull caved in. They think he took a header into the river when he was pissed, and he certainly had a bucket of alcohol in his blood. Apparently it's not unusual for deep-sea fishermen to say au revoir to the world like this. Who knows?'

'First thing, Jimmy, is to get a hold of the other two and get them in. They're going to say nothing, but it gives us a look at them. The other priority is to set up a meet for us with the investigation team in Newcastle. That'll do for now. By the way, how's the family?'

'Pissed off at me for never being home, but what's new?'

'That's what I like to hear – everything normal. We're being punished for something we did in a different life – I'm convinced of it. One last thing. Make an arrangement for us to see Ricky Swan before we do anything. There might be something he can help us with, and we need to make sure he doesn't become the next corpse.'

Macallan put her phone down and watched Jack lay out the table as if they were celebrating something special; he'd done the whole bit with flowers and wine as well. She smiled to herself, thinking how good they were together, and promised she'd let nothing take that away. Jack and the baby were going to follow her over to Edinburgh later in the week and settle back into the flat, where she'd be waiting for them.

15

Swan had calmed down since his handler had broken the news to him about the problems with their missing UC. He'd come up with a good cover story for the Flemings: the UC had been introduced to him by a Northern Ireland businessman who used the sauna on trips to Edinburgh. The Flemings would be reluctant to fuck about with anyone over the water and Swan would stick to the story that the businessman hadn't been back over for months. If they wanted to start poking their noses about in Belfast then that was probably their funeral.

He'd spent most of the day in the sauna after giving Gnasher a run around in the park. That was about the only exercise Swan ever got apart from his sessions with the girls in his business. Cue Ball had arrived around six and they'd had a good night with a regular stream of punters who just wanted what they came for – no drunks or bother. A senior police officers' conference on ethics was being held in Edinburgh and Swan smiled behind the backs of a couple of the punters who were probably high flyers in their day jobs. They almost sprinted out of the door when they'd finished their sessions. Business always picked up for working girls in the capital when there was any professional convention taking place.

'God gave us all the same working equipment.' Swan laughed at his own wit and Cue Ball thought again that the man was a twat, but he was the twat who paid his wages and took care of his other needs so he did a pretend chuckle.

'Amen to that, and the more the merrier with these guys. They look terrified when they come in and last about two minutes. My kind of punters.'

Swan wouldn't have been in such a positive mood if he'd realised who was sitting watching the sauna no more than a hundred yards from the door.

Brenda sat in the darkened Beamer with Fanny Adams at the wheel and one of the McMartins' terminators brought in for the lift. His name was Joe Baker and he'd worked for them on and off since they were teenagers. Baker had done a lot of time inside and nearly all of it for extreme violence, some of it football related when he wasn't assaulting punters for the McMartins. He was barred from most of the grounds in Scotland but still managed to find a pub where even the dullest game would set him off and cause some poor citizen to end up in casualty. McMartin knew they couldn't trust him with anything complicated because basically he had shit for brains, but the kind of job they had with the sauna owner was tailor-made for him. He had tremendous physical strength, and if there were any unforeseen interventions by concerned citizens or pigs then he would take them on without a second thought.

The Bitch lit up another cigarette. The inside of the car stank to high heaven. They'd been there for hours and the combination of tobacco fumes and McMartin's hygiene problem made Adams feel like gagging up the pepperoni pizza he'd consumed at tea time. It was a cool, damp evening and she'd warned him about opening the windows and the risk of getting a chill.

'For fuck's sake, can we not get some air in here? I'm dyin'.' He wouldn't normally risk pushing her buttons so far but he was revolted to the point where he just didn't care any more.

'You been takin' brave pills again? Shut the fuck up or we'll put you in the same hole as Ricky Short-arse.'

She sniggered at her very own brand of humour and turned to Baker, who hadn't even twitched in the previous hour. 'What says you?'

After a five-second pause, Baker turned towards her and grunted without actually forming a word. McMartin shook her head slowly and wondered where they found their staff.

'Fuckin' Dumb and Dumber. The long winter nights must fly past in your front rooms.' She lit another cigarette off the last one and gave Adams a look that said 'open that window and I break the offendin' fuckin' arm'.

She looked at her watch and saw it was pushing towards eleven. When she raised her head again she saw the door of the sauna open and a couple of the girls come out. They'd counted four girls in earlier, and two had left at nine, so these had to be the last of the workers. She was sure that only left Swan and whoever the other midget was inside.

About ten minutes later the door opened again and Swan came out with Cue Ball. After he'd locked up they went their separate ways, with Cue Ball heading for Leith Walk (or, more accurately, the chippie) as Swan wandered down towards where his car was parked on an old piece of waste ground that was near perfect and dark enough for what McMartin had planned. He had to pass their car on the way and she felt the rush of excitement she always had just before she frightened the crap out of some poor soul.

Swan wandered past the car and never gave them a second look.

'Let's do this, boys, and give the grassin' wee fuck some good old Glasgow medicine.'

Even the command for action didn't overexcite Baker. In fact, apart from football there wasn't much that bothered him, and it was as if he had the ability to let his mind hibernate when there was nothing else to do. He shook his head a couple of times to break out of the near trance he'd been resting in and cracked his knuckles, as he did before every action.

Swan speeded up in the direction of his car; the cold drizzle was chilling him through his thin cotton jacket and between his lifestyle and his consumption of spirits and cigars, he fought a constant battle to keep warm in the ever-changing Scottish climate. With his right hand in his trouser pocket, he clicked the remote button on his car key and watched the headlights flare up when the car lock clunked open. The big Merc stood out in the line of parked cars like a Tory peer at a TUC conference. Swan liked to change his car every year just to make sure he always had the current plate to say 'fuck you' to anyone who cared. Since the day he'd bought his first new car his belief had been that the wheels were a statement that this particular owner had class, style and money. When Swan drove the Merc through the Edinburgh streets in daylight hours, he liked to plant a couple of the best-looking girls in beside him so he could watch for the odd citizen's envious stare. He reminded himself every day of his life that they were the same kind of people who had made his days at school a reclusive misery.

Swan's bladder was swollen to explosion point and he re-enacted the strange ritual he performed every night.

Instead of pissing in the sauna toilet, as any sensible person would have done, he always waited till he got to the car. It made him feel like he was a 'don't give a shit' kind of a guy, which was nothing more than self-delusion, and the three cups of black coffee and two large vodkas he'd had made him ache for release as he unbuttoned his flies.

As far as Swan was concerned, Cue Ball was heading for the lights on Leith Walk to graze on his favourite supper of deep fried haggis with chips awash in brown sauce. He was wrong; Cue Ball had walked no more than fifty yards from the door of the sauna when he'd hooked up with one of Swan's best earners, who was waiting for him in the dimly lit entrance of a payday loan shop. Unbeknown to Swan, Cue Ball met the girl called Li most nights in the same place. She was Chinese by birth, had only been in Scotland for three years and, although her command of English was passable, she still had problems with the Scottish version of the language.

The problem was that Swan liked her as well, at least as far as he was capable of liking any woman for something other than sex. She depended on the work in the sauna and didn't want to end up freezing her arse off on the street trying to wave down punters in cars, not least because the thought of ending up as a corpse butchered by some predatory weirdo haunted her imagination. The previous murders in Edinburgh were the stuff of dark legend among the working girls and, like many others, she had tried to find somewhere slightly safer to trade. Cue Ball didn't give a fuck about what his employer thought about their relationship and wanted to get it in the open, but Li wanted to be sure that he meant it first. In her world it was hard to trust the word of any man, even him, and while she wanted it to work, there were obvious doubts. Cue Ball didn't steal for a living but his two professional skills were drug dealing and violence. Every morning when she woke up beside him she tried to see a joint future and couldn't come up with the answer to the question of who would pay the bills.

On the other hand, since he'd started to take his free-bies from the girls they'd quickly become attracted, the difference between them being that Cue Ball just enjoyed the new emotions without question and let them run. A man like him never looked too far into the future – no matter how good you were, when you led a violent life there was always someone waiting out there who was that bit better or would just carry luck on the day.

Li's flat was the other side of Swan's Merc and they were waiting for him to drive off so they could go and settle in for the night. They watched his dark silhouette briefly illuminate as he unlocked the car door. Li covered her mouth and giggled as a cloud of urine-based vapour seemed to envelop her employer, who whistled a form-less tune in his moment of relief. Cue Ball shook his head slowly in disbelief that this event took place every night at the exact same time and place.

'He's just left the sauna where there's a perfectly good cludgie an' pisses in the street like some daft jakey.' Cue Ball was helping Li with her English and she'd already learned what a cludgie was but couldn't remember jakey.

'Jakey?' She frowned and looked to Cue Ball for guid-ance.

'Like those drunk men you see on Leith Walk every night. Pish heids.'

'Pish heids?' Li repeated it as best she could and Cue Ball smiled broadly; he loved her serious attempts to learn the street lingo.

Cue Ball was still smiling when he noticed movement in the street opposite Swan, who still seemed distracted by his call from nature. He saw the door of a darkened Beamer open and close noiselessly, which sparked his senses onto full beam. Why would a law-abiding citizen worry about the noise of a door? Cue Ball instinctively knew it was trouble before he could see who'd stepped out of the car. Whoever it was had picked the right spot so they were streetwise, no doubt about it.

He screwed his eyes up as Li was about to ask him what was wrong, raised his hand towards her palm outwards and put two stiff forefingers from his other hand to his lips. There were two of them out of the Beamer, and it was too dark to see if anyone else was still inside, but they came from the passenger side front and back, which meant there was probably a driver. If they had a driver they must be pros.

'Big bastards.' He said it quietly, but size didn't frighten him – it was just something he needed to feed into his battle plan. Although he was a wild fucker he'd learned every trick in the book over the years, which was how he'd survived so many skirmishes without ending up in the mortuary fridge. Being his size meant he had to use his brain as well as speed and a refusal to give in even when he seemed beaten.

He turned quickly to Li and put his hand on her shoulder. 'Go to Leith Walk and take the long way round to the flat. I'll see you there later.'

Li knew the signs and was frightened. He saw it, smiled and decided in that moment that he was getting soft: worrying himself about his lemon before he went into action. 'No worries, darlin', it's just work. Cook us up some supper when you get in.'

He winked and nodded towards the lights at the junction with Leith Walk. Li knew better than to argue and that whatever he was going to do she'd be in the way and a distraction if she stayed. She told him to be careful, which would make no difference but was all she could think to say before heading for the Walk.

The two figures who had stepped out of the car had stopped for a moment, but Cue Ball knew they were ready to move.

What the fuck have you been up to, Ricky my boy? he thought. He'd already identified one of the figures as Brenda McMartin, and whatever trouble Swan had got himself into, the presence of the Glasgow woman meant they were at DEFCON fucking 1. It was pretty obvious they hadn't turned up for a chat about the weather, but he had to wait and see before he went nuclear. There was always the chance that it was some kind of final warning, but as far as he knew McMartin only made an appearance for wet work. His instinct was that this wouldn't end with handshakes all round and a promise to meet for cocktails. Saving Swan's skinny little arse wasn't the perfect end to the night for him, but it was his job and he'd demand a fat bonus for this one if they survived it.

There was of course an additional problem in that as soon as he weighed in he was at war with the McMartins, and not many people in the game would give a big thumbs-up to that particular idea. He paused for a moment before he came to his usual conclusion about whether to fight or retreat.

'Fuck it, Andy, you can only die once, boy.' He said it quietly and calm settled over him.

He opened up the olive-green combat jacket he was wearing, pulled out his brass knuckleduster and a short wooden baton weighted at the end with lead. Zipping up his jacket again he pushed the brass onto the fingers of his right hand, pulled the leather thong of the baton over his left wrist, sucked in a few deep breaths and tried to roll the tension out of his shoulders. He watched intently as McMartin and the other pile of muscle took off and

138

moved quickly towards Swan, who had just done up his flies, oblivious to what was coming at his back.

The drizzle was cold and steady as Swan tugged his collar up then pulled the car door open, promising himself a few vodkas over ice when he got home. A contact from Amsterdam had e-mailed him some XXX porn and he'd take it in with Gnasher, who always seemed interested in human adult entertainment.

'How's it hangin', Ricky?'

The voice startled Swan, and when he turned round something grabbed his balls and squeezed till the pain drove all the air out of his lungs, leaving him helpless and frightened. He'd needed glasses for years but had always been too vain to actually wear them, and the fact that he rarely read anything on paper meant it wasn't a priority for him. What street lighting there was blurred his vision and was behind whoever or whatever gripped him where he lived. He managed to squeeze out the word 'please' between clenched false teeth as his legs gave way beneath him. There were two of them and they were big fuckers, but then again most people were bigger than him. A ham-sized paw closed round his throat, pulling him up then forcing him back, arching his spine over the Merc.

'Take my wallet. That's all I've got.' He prayed it was a mugging but had already worked out that his connection to the problems with the missing UC meant he was probably being a bit optimistic.

Whoever was crushing his windpipe laughed and Swan realised that the laugh was female – rough but definitely what should have been the gentler sex. Brenda McMartin pushed her face about six inches from her victim and grinned. Her breath reeked with the stink of cigarettes, the beginnings of serious gum disease and several packets of cheese and onion crisps. It revolted him even with the excruciating pain he was suffering. That was the least of his worries because, like Cue Ball, he recognised her. Everyone knew 'The Bitch', even if they hadn't met her personally. The tabloids had run a few stories about her over the years; she made such excellent copy.

'Do I look like I'm a fuckin' mugger?' She turned to Baker and smiled, enjoying what she did best, but he just stared blankly and waited. She shook her head again, wondering why she bothered trying gallows humour on someone who was only part human.

'It's a bit more serious than that, Ricky, and we're taking you for a wee run. Hope you don't mind.' She was going to turn to Baker with a smart one-liner then remembered the cunt was brain damaged in some way and just didn't get involved in funnies. She nodded to him and he pulled a black canvas bag over Swan's head. He'd gone limp in McMartin's hold and she realised that he'd passed out cold.

'Keeps him quiet, I suppose,' she said, but she was disappointed at not being able to string it out a bit and enjoy the wee man's terror.

The word 'suppose' had just left her mouth when Baker groaned and slumped down beside the car, gripping his right knee and ear at the same time. Blood poured through the fingers covering his ear; he was hurt and out of the game. If she'd had the time to think about it, she would have picked up something like a dull cracking sound a moment before he was on his way to the deck.

An old woman high up in the flats opposite Swan's car had seen exactly what had happened. Well into her eighties, her only pleasure was sitting at her window watching the drunks and bampots heading home from the Leith end of her street. Swan pissing against his car was a regular occurrence, and she shook her head and tutted to no one but herself, though the truth was she was fascinated with the bizarre show every time it happened. It gave her something to moan about when her daughter visited her at the weekends. She always managed to make Swan's little antisocial habit sound like a mad pervert exposing himself on the street. The daughter didn't really care and wished her mother would hurry up and die so they could sell her flat and knock a few holidays out of the proceeds. The old woman had watched intently as the two figures left the Beamer and headed for the other side of the road. Her blood pressure rose at the possibility that the two citizens were outraged by what was happening across the street and thought that with a bit of luck they'd kick ten bells out of the pervert with the flash set of wheels. That would be enough to make her night – her week even – but there was better to come and that would keep her going for months.

The two figures had already started on the pervert when she saw something moving at speed from the right side of her view. At first she thought it was a large dog because of the speed it moved across the half-lit street towards the drama taking place at the door of the Merc. It was too much excitement so she poured a stiff brandy from the bottle next to her. She'd already had one but thought that under the circumstances the occasion deserved a bit more lubrication. She raised the glass to her lips and realised what she'd thought was a dog was in fact a man tearing into the people at the car, despite being only half their size.

'Get intae the bastards, son.' She was on her feet, having decided to change allegiances and support the wee man. The old woman hadn't had so much entertainment since she'd witnessed a guy beating his wife unconscious the previous Christmas Eve.

By the time Cue Ball reached Brenda McMartin and the

ape who was with her, he'd already worked out that the size difference meant there was no way he could win a wrestling match with the two of them. That meant he had to get one of them out of the game as quickly as possible. The Bitch was too involved to notice his approach, and his initial plan was to take her out first, but as he closed in Baker turned slightly towards him, having picked up the sound of the rubber trainers bouncing across the cobbles. He was side-on so Cue Ball changed plan when he saw that the moment had exposed the side of Baker's right knee and swung the weighted baton back. Cue Ball was already within striking distance when Baker snapped his head round, but it was too late: Cue Ball lashed the baton through a wide roundhouse action and when it hit Baker's shinbone below the knee the sound told him he'd done enough to break it. The big man gasped with shock, and Cue Ball followed up by burying his knuckleduster into Baker's ear. That put him out of the tussle while he took on McMartin, who'd spun round and let go of Swan. The sauna owner was on the deck and barely conscious.

'What the fuck?' Saliva splattered from her mouth with the oath. She lunged at Cue Ball, whose idea was to back off and use his speed to counteract her size and body weight. For a moment his luck deserted him and as he stepped back he caught Baker's outstretched leg, losing his balance and hitting the cobbles face up. McMartin was too good an operator to miss her chance – she was on him like flies on shit and tried to force her thumbs into Cue Ball's eyes, growling like an animal that had just made a kill. All he could do was screw them up as tightly as possible to buy a couple of seconds, but it felt like they were being pushed into his brain. Her mistake was in concentrating on blinding him; she hadn't real-ised he'd come well armed for the job. Cue Ball drove

142

the baton point forward up under her breastbone with all the force he could muster, which caused her to roll off him, grasping her gut and choking as if her throat had closed off. Cue Ball tried to open his eyes but they burned and ached from her assault and tears streamed down his cheeks as he pulled himself up with the car door handle. He wasn't prepared for McMartin getting back on her feet so quickly. In next to no time she was on him again, taking him in a bear hug from behind and, just to prove she was a savage bastard, she bit down on Cue Ball's left ear and gnawed like a dog. He yelped at the excruciating pain as she lifted him clear of the ground.

The old woman opposite decided she needed a third brandy – what she was witnessing in the street was better than a holiday in the sun, and she prayed that the local polis wouldn't wander past and spoil the whole thing.

Cue Ball thought he was going to pass out when McMartin finally separated half his ear and spat it onto the pavement. She had a brief moment of triumph and felt her attacker weaken through the pain he was suffering as she squeezed even tighter. There was a six-inch blade in her belt and she decided that's how she'd do it – squeeze a bit more breath from the little fucker then slice him up right there on the pavement. If she'd known the reputation of the man she'd gripped in her massive arms she might have squeezed a bit longer and harder before starting with the blade.

Cue Ball knew he only had one chance left; though he was weak he wasn't yet beaten. He couldn't believe the strength of the woman and he went for playing dead, letting the top half of his body drop forward as if he'd passed out like Swan, who was coming round but unaware of the battle taking place near him.

McMartin felt Cue Ball's body appear to relax and made her next mistake of thinking that it was all over apart from the butcher work. She loosened her hold on him slightly; Cue Ball felt it and took his final shot at the title. He swung the top half of his body backwards with all he could get into the movement, and she had no time to react before the back of his head smashed into her mouth, breaking three teeth and bursting her top and bottom lips. She tried to curse, but there was too much blood bubbling over her tongue. She let go of Cue Ball, clasped both hands to her face and bent over double as he leaned back against the car, his chest heaving with the effort of staying upright. He felt wet at the back of his head and knew it wasn't just her blood.

'You're a fuckin' dead man and so's that grassin' bastard,' Baker spat at Cue Ball. He was still on the deck and propped against the car but unable to make any movement without setting off fireworks in his smashed leg. The Edinburgh man looked down at him and smiled, and Baker realised that while he might be a short-arse, this man was also a grade 1 fucking psycho.

Cue Ball, keeping eye contact with Baker, took the two steps he required to stand over McMartin, who'd dropped onto her hands and knees, pieces of broken tooth mixing with the blood that dribbled from her shattered mouth onto the pavement. In one sharp movement he raised his knee as high as he could get it and brought the heel of his foot down onto McMartin's right hand. His eyes never left Baker's. McMartin screamed like an animal as she felt the bones give way, and lights started to go on all over the street.

'Fuckin' hell,' was all Baker could manage before Cue Ball put him out of his misery for the night. He should have cleared up the grass reference first, but he'd needed to hurt someone. His temper was cooling now though, and he knew what that might mean.

'It's time we fucked off out of it,' he said as he helped

144

Swan to his feet, pulling the bag off his head at the same time. The sauna manager, who was starting to take in the scene around him, whimpered like a beaten dog and had to be led round to the passenger side, where he was pushed roughly into the seat. Cue Ball stood up and stretched his back, trying to ignore his injuries and the worry surrounding the word 'grass'. He felt weak but this business still wasn't finished. He ran his fingers over the knuckleduster, gripped the baton and strode back across the road to the Beamer, which hadn't moved.

Fanny Adams knew it was time to either fuck off or fight – and after what he'd just witnessed he knew he was simply too old to take this one on. In his day he wouldn't have given it a second thought, but not this night and not for the crazy bitch who was lying in the road. If he just ran, her brother would top him, so the only chance he had was the mental case coming to beat his brains in. Adams opened the door and stood with the car between him and Cue Ball, who was covered in blood and looked like he'd just climbed out of a meat grinder.

'I'm just the fuckin' driver here, chief. Any chance of a break?'

Cue Ball spat a wad of blood and saliva onto the road. 'Do I look like I'm involved in charity work here?'

'Look, I hate that horrible fucker – as far as I'm concerned she's a disgrace. The other boy's just brain dead and does what he's told. I need to go back injured though or her daft brother'll waste me. Just gimme a break and don't make it permanent.'

Cue Ball thought for a moment and decided the guy might just be straight up, but to be fair he looked about 150 years old and clapped out. 'I'm really gettin' soft these days. One thing – your pal over the road mentioned the words "grassin' bastard". What's he talkin' about?'

'That's why we're here, pal. That man you're backin'

up there stuck an undercover into a Newcastle team the McMartins are involved with.'

'A Newcastle team?' The alarm bells were going off in Cue Ball's head.

'Pete Handyside.'

Cue Ball cursed. He'd just walked into the wrong fight and was definitely on the side destined to lose heavily. To be identified with a police informant would fuck his reputation and probably mean a death sentence if it was Handyside. The McMartins and Handyside were a nightmare scenario, and he'd just minced Brenda and her gorilla. They had big armies so he was fucked, no doubt about it.

He shook his head, slid the knuckleduster from his fingers and put it back in his pocket with the baton as Adams walked round the car towards Cue Ball. He could see the man had balls – and just how badly he needed Cue Ball to do the business.

Adams never even saw the first blow coming it was so quick, and it stunned him for what came next. By the time Cue Ball was finished Adams was a hospital case, but he'd recover and could tell whatever story he liked to Crazy Horse McMartin.

Afterwards Cue Ball was exhausted; all he wanted was to go home and be with Li, but he needed to unload Swan first.

'One last thing,' Cue Ball muttered to himself. Knowing that there was no going back he needed to get all his retaliation in there and then. The McMartins weren't going to forgive him, and he was streetwise enough to make sure there was one fewer able to come for him. He was going to pull Brenda McMartin by the legs till her feet were just under the front offside wheel of the Merc. But he was done-in and hadn't the strength to do what he wanted so he gave up and was about to pull himself into the driver's seat when he realised there was something else he needed.

'I'm fuckin' ugly enough. Need the ear.' He picked up the part of his ear that McMartin had bitten off and looked at the woman moaning weakly beside the car, wondering what kind of woman could have spawned someone like The Bitch? He pulled himself stiffly into the Merc, gunned the engine then moved slowly away from the three casualties left in the street.

'What happened?' Swan asked weakly.

Cue Ball looked round at him and shook his head slowly, trying to come up with the right answer. 'I think we just started World War III, that's all. By the way, I'm bleeding all over your car.'

The old lady at the window stared open-mouthed at the three casualties lying in the road, and could hardly wait to call her friends and daughter about what she'd seen. It never occurred to her that an ambulance and the police might have been an option.

'Where're we headed?' Swan was coming to life and trying to understand what had just happened. Cue Ball looked round at him and wondered why he'd even bothered helping. The man was incapable of defending himself, and there was no way he wanted to be in the front line of a war with the teams from Glasgow and Newcastle.

'Look, I think we need to talk. One thing you can put your wages on is that it's barely started – that woman only appears for serious business. I want to know why, then I'm taking what's left of my ear to A&E.'

Swan noticed for the first time that part of Cue Ball's ear was gone and realised at the same time that the wet thing lying on the dashboard was the rest of it. 'Stop the fuckin' car,' he said.

Swan heaved his guts up onto the pavement at the top of Leith Walk but no one took much notice; it was a common-enough sight to see some punter laying down a pavement pizza after a night of excess. He climbed wearily back into the car and tried not to look at the ear again. Cue Ball switched off the engine.

'Why? I need to know what the fuck this thing is. Two of the workers back there told me it's because you're – and I quote – a "grassin' bastard". Tell me they're wrong. Please tell me it's all shite.'

Swan couldn't look him in the eye. Cue Ball's instincts were nearly always on the money, which was why he'd survived such a long time. Swan didn't have to say anything – he'd just confirmed that he was a police informant, and that Cue Ball had just mangled three of the opposition.

'Fuck!' Cue Ball thumped the dashboard with the heel of his hand and left a bloody mark there. He put his head down on the wheel for a moment and tried to think. Swan kept quiet as it dawned on him that he was about to lose it all – everything he'd built up over the years – and now he'd be hunted by beasts who'd enjoy killing him slowly.

Cue Ball lifted his head. 'Here's what's happening. We're going to your place and you'll give me the documents to your car. You just sold it to me for fuck all. I know you stash readies there and I need money because I'm off. You owe me all that. If I'd known what you were I would have let them bury you, and you'd have deserved it. Don't speak till we're done or I'll finish what they came to do.'

Cue Ball pulled out his mobile and called Li. 'Pack a bag; we're leaving. Don't argue – I'll explain later.' Li knew enough not to ask questions and did what she was told.

Cue Ball took Swan home then picked up the documents for the Merc and a few grand from the wall safe.

The remnants of his ear went into a plastic Tupperware box filled with ice. He hardly spoke a word to Swan, who prayed the hard man wouldn't hurt him.

Just before he left, Cue Ball stopped at the door and turned to Swan, who was sitting like a child on the sofa with Gnasher beside him, the dog sensing his distress. 'One more thing. If you report the car stolen or anything about me to your CID friends then I'll come back for you and finish the job. And that includes your stupid fuckin' mutt – though at least you'd die together.' He still had his sense of humour.

As soon as Cue Ball left, Swan called his handler. 'Arthur' tried his best to calm the man down, but his informant was in a blind panic at what might come after him, so the handler and co-handler arrived at Swan's place within the hour.

'We checked with the locals and apparently it's like a fucking war zone near the sauna. Three casualties in A&E and the woman is in a bad way. What the hell happened? They'll want someone locked up for this carnage.'

Swan had worked out that he was in a vice but the last thing he needed was to add to the pressure. He'd calmed down and knew he had to act carefully if he was to have any chance of survival.

'All I know is that someone attacked me. A punter jumped in when I was on the deck and the two of us did the business on them. No idea who it was, but he was a fuckin' hero. I knew this would happen, and you did nothing to help, did you? Well you better start taking better care of me, boys.'

The handler snorted a laugh. 'You must have had a fucking dream when you were unconscious. You and some caped crusader wiped out the Glasgow professionals – is that the best you can do?'

Swan realised he'd maybe gone too far, but it was unlikely that Cue Ball was going to walk into a station and give a witness statement because he was a good citizen. There was even less chance of Brenda McMartin cooperating with the bizzies, so he could probably spin it any way he liked. He had to use every tool in the box to keep his head attached to his neck. 'Tell whoever your boss is that I've got enough muck to ruin half the top men in this city, and that includes police. Tell them that, and tell them I'll use it with the press if I end up with problems over the foreign pros. Know what I mean, Arthur?'

The handler wanted to strangle Swan, but if his threats were true he needed to get it up the line to someone who gave a fuck. It was obvious this situation was going to cause waves for the foreseeable and he really wanted to be somewhere else.

16

In the early hours of Monday morning the hospital began to wake up to a new day. There was nothing too unusual about this Monday; two patients had died during the night and in both cases it had been expected. One of the deceased had passed on with his family at his bedside – they loved him and he'd loved them back. The other man was a chronic alcoholic and not a soul in the world had cared for him apart from the nurses who'd helped the broken man through his final hours. Take away the deaths and nothing too interesting had happened, apart from the woman and two men who'd been brought in to A&E after meeting Cue Ball Ross, his knuckleduster and his lead-weighted baton. The nurses and doctors didn't get too excited – street battles and the resulting casualties were common enough, though seeing a woman that messed up was one for the memories. She had difficulty speaking through her broken teeth and split lips but kept mumbling that she was going to kill some bastard. One of the young doctors thought that might be difficult for her given the state she was in, but even badly injured she frightened the medical staff who had to care for her.

In a different ward in the same hospital Ingrid Richter had slept soundly, experiencing a vivid dream in which it was spring, warm, and she was a child again with her mother and father in Prague. The world in her dream was a good place.

She gradually surfaced, realised she was safe and then slept and dreamed again. It was a different and more threatening world this time: she was standing by the sea, which was pitch black against a white sky. The deep orange sun sitting just above the horizon seemed to bleed a dark reflection onto the water and streamed towards where she stood on a vast empty beach. She turned her head for a moment to look behind her and found nothing but a barren desert.

She waded into the flat, calm water even though she was frightened. For some reason she couldn't stop what she was doing; it was as if someone else was controlling her. When she was waist deep the seabed disappeared from under her feet and she was dragged into the depths by something gripping her ankles – it was the women who'd been on the *Brighter Dawn*, pulling her down to be with them. Their faces were bleached white, the eye sockets empty and dark, and their hair was woven with strands of seaweed that undulated with the movement of the deep waters. She tried to cry out and water flooded into her lungs as she glided up towards the sweet air. She woke gasping for breath. The memories of the events on the *Brighter Dawn* downloaded and flooded into her conscious mind. A nurse heard her crying and held the girl till she calmed down.

'It was just a dream. You're okay. You're safe.' She gave Richter some water and smiled reassuringly at her, wondering again what could have frightened the young woman to a state that she'd buried her memories so deeply.

'I remember what happened; I remember it all. Please don't leave me.'

The nurse stayed and held her hand up to attract the attention of the bored policewoman standing outside. About fifteen minutes later the uniform was on the phone to let the local factory know that Ingrid Richter wanted to talk.

Macallan headed along the road for her appointment with McGovern, her stomach churning with nervous tension. Although their team was based in the Leith station she'd arranged to meet him in Fettes as the rest of her day would be tied up there reintroducing herself to the job and all the senior people who wanted to see her first. It was a certainty that as the morning wore on she'd be trapped by a range of desk pilots who would demand her attention across the day. It seemed like a good idea to settle herself with a walk from her flat, where she'd dropped off her cases. The early flight from Belfast had got her in on time and she was missing Jack and Adam already. Doubts had started to gnaw at her again. Their weeks and months together had sealed her relationship with Jack, and their baby's arrival had given her what she thought of as a real family for the first time in her life. Not having had a happy childhood, the police had filled that role for her in some ways, but she'd eventually realised that her life before had been nothing more than a stage play and when the curtain came down she had always been alone.

The morning sun had started to dry up the overnight rain and the birds were starting to make the streets buzz before the lines of rush-hour traffic clogged up the far-too-narrow arteries that fed into the city centre. The car park in Fettes was still quiet enough though as she headed for the back door of the old HQ.

McGovern was standing at the broad office windows drinking his first brew of the day when he saw Macallan cross the car park and enter the building. He felt a huge sense of relief that she was back. They'd need her, but he worried that what she'd been through might have taken her edge away.

His phone rang and the caller told him that Ingrid Richter had recovered her memory – someone needed to decide what to do with her.

'One of our DOs will be there as soon as. If she says anything at all before that, make a note and tell the detective who attends.'

As soon as that conversation had ended McGovern called Pam Fitzgerald, who was just finishing off her morning session in the gym. 'The super's arriving in the next few minutes and I'll need to brief her. She'll be swamped for the rest of the day so get straight to the hospital and make a start with Ingrid Richter. We need what she's got as soon as. I'll get over there and join you when I'm done with the boss.'

He put the phone back in its cradle and worried about an earlier call from the informant handler who needed to see him urgently. He'd agreed but made it clear the meeting would have to be after he was finished with Macallan. The handler had said enough for him to worry but not enough to understand.

'Did you hear about the battle last night? Looks like Brenda McMartin won't be playing netball again.' This type of comment would have caused an attack of the vapours for the majority of modern police leaders, but the handler and McGovern were products of a different age and appreciated the odd dig at a career bastard's misfortune.

154

McGovern had some of the details but he already knew the McMartins were in bed with Pete Handyside. It hadn't taken a wild guess to realise that the dots were all starting to join up. 'This sounds like you have bad news for me. Correct?' he'd said.

'Correct. Look, I think the super needs to hear this as well. I know she's just back in the door, but let's label what I'm going to tell you as a potential clusterfuck.'

McGovern knew the handler wasn't prone to over-dramatizing these things so it was probably best to take it as fair warning. 'Okay,' he'd agreed. 'I think there's a shitload of problems developing on all this so we might as well start dealing with them now.'

Swan woke after a few hours of restless sleep, his brain thudding against his skull with the effects of the excessive amount of vodka he'd consumed trying to dull the fear that had gripped him since he'd been attacked. Gnasher was beside him on the bed because, like all good dogs, he sensed his master's pain. He followed his natural inclination and licked Swan's face, then seemed hurt when the man he loved told him to fuck off.

Swan tottered to the en suite and threw a couple of aspirin down his neck with a half pint of water. The events of the previous night lit up in his addled brain and he groaned as his heart began to pound, quite certain that his blood pressure must be soaring. It was all bad.

He sat back on the bed and looked into Gnasher's sad eyes. 'I'm fucked. That means you're fucked as well.' The dog couldn't understand the words of course, but it was clear he knew something was wrong.

Swan leaned over and buried his face in his hands. There was no way a man with such limited bottle could deal with the fiends who wanted to do him harm. There was a fresh bottle of vodka on the bedside cabinet and he necked a good whack in one go before falling back onto the bed into something between sleep and a coma. Gnasher hadn't been out for far too long and the mutt's bladder couldn't stretch any further. Increasingly nervous and stressed, he emptied the contents all over Swan's black silk bedsheets.

17

Crazy Horse McMartin took the call from the hospital and blew a fuse, which was his normal reaction to a crisis anyway, but this was family. It meant nothing but grief for his team, who tried to keep him stable – or what passed as stable for someone with his particular handle. It wasn't that he was at all touchy-feely with Brenda; it was just that ancient instinct that the family name counted for something. As far as he was concerned it was similar to the NATO charter – an attack on one McMartin was an attack on all and should generate a response.

He blew his top at those assembled in the room: 'Find out what the fuck happened through there and what went wrong. I thought the cunt was supposed to be a ringer for Jimmy fuckin' Krankie?' His team looked at each other and collectively shrugged. No one wanted to make a response because they'd seen his reaction before and it usually ended up with one of his own team needing stitches. 'Get the fuck through there. Speak to Brenda and the boys and get me some answers. Or do I have to do the whole fuckin' action on my own?'

Twenty minutes later he was raging down the phone to Handyside, promising to put it all right. Handyside let him talk, knowing that there would have to be a divorce from the Scottish teams because they were just too fucking unpredictable and the definition of business meant something different to them. He would have to try to take charge of a situation that might spin out of control, taking them all with it. He let the Glasgow man rant till he started to run out of steam.

'Listen carefully to me, Bobby,' he said finally. 'We need to step back and find out what the situation is. Our friends in the constabulary will be taking a great interest in this, and we need to let the smoke clear. I've got a bent one here so I'll see what I can dig up from him. I'm sure you have your own up there so get digging and then we'll speak again. I'll talk to the Flemings too and get their take on it. This is their territory so they might know a bit more than we do.'

'Fuckin' wankers,' was all McMartin got out before Handyside interrupted him.

'Listen to me. We have more than enough to deal with at the moment, and the Flemings are part of our organisation for the time being.' The inference was enough to satisfy McMartin that they might be able to take action against the Edinburgh team in time. 'Just concentrate on what happened last night and then we'll get to the next problem.'

McMartin had gone quiet and Handyside was probably the only man on God's earth who could achieve that with the Glasgow headcase. After a pause, he got his reply: 'We're good. Just leave it with me and I'll be back to you as soon as I can.'

Handyside put down the phone and sighed as he turned to Maxi Turner. 'Fancy a drink, Max?' He was the only man who shortened Turner's first name that way, and it was a small but important sign of the bond between the two men.

'A bit early for you?' Turner knew this offer was a sign of stress in a man who was almost always in command of a situation.

Dark rum, being a popular drink with seamen, had always been Handyside's poison of choice, and these days it was also a nod to their younger, wilder days on the shores of the Tyne. Handyside measured some out, threw the neat double shot down his throat and rolled his neck, trying to ease the knots of tension that were spreading to the back of his head.

'This situation could get badly out of control. We need to make sure we have all bases covered or these crazies north of the border will pull us down. I wonder if we should have taken out the Flemings when we had the chance? I thought we should find out what this Ricky Swan knew. Any thoughts?'

Asking Turner's opinion was another mark of respect; he was the only man in Handyside's world who received this tribute. Turner knew he was close to the man, but he also accepted that Handyside was not as other men and that for all the years they'd been risking their necks together he would cut him adrift without a second thought if it made business sense to him – or, more importantly, if it meant defending his family. He would always pick his words carefully, but he knew there was something that needed to be said, surprised as he was by Handyside's doubts about letting the Flemings live. He couldn't remember the man ever hesitating when something needed to be done, and for a moment Handyside looked human – and that sent something crawling up Turner's spine. Their lives depended on the boss's strength and will to outdo all others.

'Look, we've taken care of the rough edges down here

159

and we should survive any aggro from the law. The evidence is safely tucked away at the bottom of the North Sea and under the moors. The girl in Edinburgh doesn't know anything at all about us, and I'm not sure what this fucker Ricky Swan has that could hurt us. He can probably damage the Flemings, but can he do the same to us? What I'm saying is – do we need to start these combat operations up there? Shouldn't we sit tight, take a few holidays in the sun and wait for it to settle down again, call off the dogs for the time being? I'm telling you the McMartins are fucking aliens and can't be trusted to do what they're told.'

While Turner was speaking Handyside's mind drifted to the time they were boys living on the edge of the great river, when the quayside had been their playground and more of an education than school. As kids they'd seen drunken sailors beat each other senseless, sniggered as they watched the local pros service their clients in the alleys round the fish quay and had become cynics long before they were adults. He remembered the games of dare that had taken them to their limits and the night the boys had decided to prove themselves by climbing down the iron ladders that hung precariously on the quays to let the fishermen climb down to their boats. The dare was complete when their feet were just above the river. They'd had to hang on till the other boys counted a hundred. He remembered his arms aching, but he was Pete Handyside and wouldn't give in for anything. That was until he'd realised what was living in the darkness under the old piers. His friends had counted about halfway through the challenge when he'd noticed dozens of dark shapes scuttling across the boulders and rubbish strewn under the pier. Rats – one of the only things in the world that terrified him. They had been everywhere, and some of them had stopped and stared, their eyes glinting like small specks of hell. His throat had closed up and all his strength had left his arms. He had been lucky that Turner had dived in and saved his unconscious friend from floating down the river. He'd never told anyone what he'd seen or why he'd passed out and it was left at that. In his darkest moments he remembered those rats staring out at the vulnerable skinny kid hanging onto the ladders. He was there again now, staring into the dark where the rats watched and waited for a fall.

Handyside shoved the glass forward, nodded for a refill, and that really was proof that he was feeling the strain. 'It's the big picture. You're the best at what you do, but you don't see the whole battlefield, my friend.' There was no tension in the voice but the rebuke was there. Turner got it immediately and poured three shots into his own glass.

'The girl who survived can identify Dillon and Hunter, though only a miracle could raise them from the dead. She really makes no difference to us alive or dead so there's no need to take risks getting to her. The police already know about Dillon, Hunter and Gunderson so nothing we can do about that either. They probably know they worked for us, so we'll get a visit at some point, but if we say nothing they're beat. The problem is that we've done one of theirs, and they'll want to even that score, which means we need to think carefully before we act. What if the Flemings go down, turn on us? And don't tell me the cops up there don't have something running on the McMartins – take that as read. It can all fall like a pack of cards, Max. And last but not least there's credibility.'

Turner knew what was coming – it was always the dilemma in their business.

Handyside shook his head at the problems swirling round his mind as he tried to make sure he'd covered all the permutations. He looked up at Turner and tried to make his right-hand man see it all. 'You know what I'm going to say. We can't keep what happened here a complete secret. The undercover and now this fiasco in Edinburgh means that we look like we've lost our edge or control, call it whatever you want. We've taken care of all the opposition over the years, but there's always someone else coming of age. The Scousers would love to piss on our dead bodies, and they'll already have heard what's happened. If we can't sort it we look weak, and they start to claw us. You see that, don't you?'

Turner saw it but wished it wasn't the truth. They had to remain stronger than the other guys, but he'd enjoyed the peace when it had arrived. He liked living on the profits of their trade. But there was always another battle to take part in and he was tired of it. He'd committed so many crimes, dished out so much pain and it had never bothered him in the past when they were climbing. Now it did, and it kept him awake at night wondering when he'd be able to sit down in the Med getting fat and tanned like so many of the East End tossers they'd come across in the business. Turner had worked out that it would take a major event to get Handyside to that point. He had to keep proving all over again that he was the man to listen to, the man to go to and the man to fear like no other, and Turner nodded wearily. 'I know it – just wish to fuck it didn't have to always be that way. What do we need to do?'

Handyside looked at him long and hard. 'If Crazy Horse can't sort it this time then we need to go up there and do it ourselves. We'll give them one last chance and then take over. Last thing – get in touch with our bent friend in criminal intelligence and squeeze him. I want to find out everything I can about this Ricky Swan. And I mean everything. Give him a bonus if he produces the goods.'

'Consider it done.' Turner sat down heavily, full of nagging doubts. Killing the women on the *Brighter Dawn* had been too much and they were going to pay; he knew it in his gut. The ability to use violence when it was required was the mark of the top men in the game, but drowning those young women had marked them forever even among their own kind, including the bent cops who kept them safe.

18

When Fitzgerald arrived at the hospital she was surprised to see Richter sitting in a chair at the side of her bed. She still looked tired but she was making a remarkable recovery. Fitzgerald spoke to her doctor first, who told her that the girl would be fine with another few days' rest and observation.

'She's young, strong and determined, Miss Fitzgerald. No medical intervention tops that. Her parents have arrived and she'll soon be ready to try to get her life back. Not sure what psychological problems her experience will leave but that's for others to take care of.'

Fitzgerald sat down with Richter, and if anyone else had told her the story that she listened to over the next hour she'd have been sure they were making it up. She watched as the girl flinched from her memories of the *Brighter Dawn*. The truth was exposed as much in her pained facial expressions as it was in her words and tears, evocative as they were. Her story had been created in a nightmare world and Fitzgerald was barely equipped to deal with the job she'd been given. McGovern had warned her of that when she'd joined the team.

'You might think you've heard it all on the beat and CID but no matter how experienced you are we have to listen to stories that almost beat us. When that happens, remember that this is why we're here. You have to get the job done, otherwise order another uniform.'

Fitzgerald did the job, but she would remember her time with Ingrid Richter for the rest of her life.

The briefing with McGovern was straightforward enough and Macallan felt that very human moment of panic, having gone from months of living without external pressure to the mass problems that face a senior detective every day. There was never the luxury of dealing with one issue or one case at a time; there was always a mass of paper and problems hurtling in every direction. Over the previous week she and Jack had watched a late-night repeat of a detective series where the grim-faced lead hunted the killer without ever putting a word on paper or trying to whip up the energy to write a staff appraisal. It was nonsense.

McGovern saw the tension in her eyes and knew she was going to find it hard to get back into the chaotic and dysfunctional but very real world they inhabited. She needed reassurance, something that made her feel she was welcome back and that she still had the equipment to face whatever came at her.

'It's good to have you back,' he told her. 'If it means anything, the troops all feel the same. This thing with the UC and all the attached shit is going to take lumps out of us, but we've a great team out there. A few changes since you were last here, but they're all good material and ready for anything.'

Macallan sat forward, ready to start assimilating new names and facts. 'Who's dealing with Ingrid Richter?'

'Pam Fitzgerald; she's not been in the team that long,

still got a lot to learn, but keen as and we can trust her. She's probably a bit like you two thousand years ago; just loves doing it and would work for nothing. Remember that time?' He smiled warmly.

She did remember it. Sometimes she was sure it had all been a dream or her imagination, but the scars were real enough to remind her of what had passed over the years. She smiled back, thankful she had someone like McGovern at her side.

His next words brought her quickly back to reality though.

'Now, unfortunately that might all have sounded like difficult stuff, but you know that you wade through one pile of crap only to find another one in this job. Ricky Swan's handlers are outside and they want to brief us on the situation, and I don't know what they're going to hit us with, but they said enough for me to know it's just more grief.'

McGovern had hit the right spots on her ego; Macallan sensed her tension receding as her quick mind started lining up the issues and how she'd deal with them. There were plenty, and she still had a day of parading before her own bosses, who'd all say basically the same things then probably ask her to write a report on something they didn't actually need. While McGovern was briefing her she kept looking at her desk and the heap of paper and sealed envelopes that awaited her attention. She groaned inwardly. If she was lucky there might be one piece of paper that was worth further action or a reply – most of the rest just fed the bureaucracy machine lurking behind the scenes of any modern organisation.

The two handlers shuffled in and although Macallan recognised them she didn't know them personally. She felt the slight buzz she usually did talking to people who did what she'd done for so many years in Belfast.

McGovern had told her they were good men and that was enough for her. They both looked tired and that was a positive sign in her book – as far as she was concerned a good handler should look permanently knackered. They sat round the table, did the niceties and some old police leg-pulling with McGovern. Macallan let it happen, knowing it was a necessary warm-up for these types of men.

Once the piss-taking was roughly a score draw she steered it back towards the business of the day. 'Okay, guys, Jimmy tells me you have bad news and more bad news. Let's have it.'

The lead handler pulled out his notes though he didn't really need them. They were a prop so he could pick his words carefully. He'd been around a long time and could smell a bear trap a mile away. The Ricky Swan situation was toxic, and he wanted to deliver the message then get the fuck out of it. He was three days from a Med cruise that he'd been promising his wife for years and knew he was getting out of the path of the shit storm at exactly the right time. If bets were allowed on the situation, he'd put a wodge on heavy casualties both sides of the fence. He told her what Swan had said.

'Do you think he means it?'

The handler looked at Macallan. He could see why so many people wanted to work for her. Within five minutes of being in the room he trusted her, and that was no mean feat. He would have been the first to admit that he was a truly cynical bastard.

'Can I speak freely?'

'If there's bad news then I'd be annoyed with anything else.' There was enough in her expression to tell the handler that she meant exactly what she'd said.

'Ricky Swan is a creepy little bastard, and he lacks just about everything he needs to survive on the dark side of

167

life in this city. However, his form of defence is that he's devious and clever and that's let him survive so far. He knew that someday it might all go belly up. I think we can safely say that has come to pass and the evidence is lying in the hospital looking like they've had a square go with the SAS.

'We've picked up source intelligence in the past from girls who worked for him that suggested he might be recording some of his more important customers in their slightly more exposed moments. Nothing much was made of it because, at the end of the day, who's making a complaint? I know the man pretty well now and my guess is that he has got material, but how much, how bad and who the stars are is only guesswork. Let's be honest, there's bound to be a cop or three involved because there always is where there are working girls going for free. That's certainly how Ricky would get our boys on camera – just offer them something for fuck all and Bob's your Aunty. The problem is that Ricky knows if you start digging into foreign women being trafficked into the city then his name is going to come up. He wants us to look the other way for all his public-spirited service in the past. It's simple: we drop him in it, he drops us in it.'

Macallan looked round at McGovern, who was shaking his head, partly in disbelief and partly at the thought that some numb-brained cops might be hanging over the edge of their careers and families for taking a gift from Swan. Macallan would have guessed without any help that there would be police in the sewer – there always were. She knew enough to work out that if Swan was the man described then he could probably squeeze hard on the balls of people who mattered, and those same people would start calling in their own favours until it all crashed onto her desk. There had been a similar situation in Northern Ireland where a paramilitary team had worked out that blackmailing a dignitary was a lot easier than shoot-outs with the police or army. It got you points. And of course, points mean prizes.

'What do you think, Jimmy?' She sighed just before saying it, knowing she shared the same sense of frustration he did that a hard investigation had just been elevated to a complete pain-in-the-arse investigation.

'I think it's a headache we don't need.' McGovern gave the handlers the nod to head for the door. He and Macallan needed privacy. They were happy to oblige, relieved that the time bomb they were sitting on could go off now under the arse of a higher rank.

'Fire away,' Macallan said as soon as the door closed, intrigued to hear what McGovern obviously thought was so sensitive it was for her ears only.

'Thought you might be interested to know how we originally signed on Ricky Swan as a source. You know well enough what happened to Harkins on the Barclay case – Mick saved the bastard's skin after he messed up an escort and that was how he turned the mighty QC into a top grass…'

'How can I ever erase that one?' She would never forget the revelation that Harkins had been running the advocate for years as an unofficial source. Barclay had been wrongly convicted of murder and Macallan had worked out it had actually been his son who'd been responsible for a string of attacks on prostitutes. Before he was arrested, Thomas Barclay had discovered his father's relationship with Harkins and nearly killed the detective with his car.

'What you probably don't know is that the woman Barclay assaulted was one of Swan's, and that's how Mick got the call that night.' He paused and waited for a reaction but Macallan hadn't yet joined it all up.

'Swan was Mick's informant as well. Mick was the man

who first recruited him and ran him for years before the new dedicated units came in and took over the handling of all sources. Unfortunately for all concerned, Mick handed over Swan but didn't mention Barclay.' Macallan shook her head but wasn't surprised. Although she had been responsible for arresting Barclay she hadn't been told about Swan's previous relationship with Harkins. The rubber-heel squad had run that part of the investigation, and this form of sensitive information was need-to-know only.

'How do you know all this? I'm friendly with Mick and that never came up.'

McGovern shrugged. 'Why would it? When it came to his sources Mick kept it all close to his chest.'

Macallan had to nod, because she knew better than anyone that it was true. The DCI stuck an indigestion tablet into his mouth and continued.

'I know because I was a much younger detective working with Mick at the time. When I say working, I mean I was his gofer and driver. Mick did the detecting, and I was there to watch and learn. I knew about Ricky because I would drive Mick to the meets and he was usually half-pissed if it was quiet. He was one of those detectives who seemed to be able to operate even with a skinful, but to be fair, when a job went live he was the most focused DO I ever met. You know how it was back then – one-to-one and nothing written down. Eventually I was able to work out who it was he was speaking to and saw him a couple of times with Ricky.'

'Jesus, I never cease to be amazed at how much ground Mick covered in his career. Anyway, let's set up a meeting with Swan and see what he's got to say. As far as I'm concerned, if I find evidence to connect Swan to trafficking or harming women then he'll go in the same shithole as the rest of them; it makes no difference to me what he holds. After that, I want to meet whoever it is that's handling things down in Newcastle, then we can see where we're going. You get up to the hospital and let me know as soon as what Ingrid has to say while I spend most of the rest of the day talking to my betters, probably achieving sweet FA. I should be clear by mid–late afternoon, and I want to really get moving on this by morning at the latest. On second thoughts, if we can see Swan today, so much the better.'

McGovern already had his jacket on and was heading for the door as Macallan went to the office window and looked out over the green playing fields that surrounded the old headquarters building. She knew there was no going back, and whether she'd made the right decision or not she had to see the case through to success or failure. She grinned tightly, thinking that just occasionally they fizzled out to a kind of score draw. 'Don't think you'll get off that easily on this one, Grace,' she said to her reflection in the window.

'Pardon, ma'am?'

Macallan spun round and saw that one of her team had brought in a mug of coffee and an intelligence report.

'Sorry, I was talking to myself. The first signs of old age!' She didn't recognise the young detective but thought that he looked about fourteen and she knew exactly what that meant – the years were passing.

'Please tell everyone I'll be out in a minute. I haven't met some of you yet. Sorry.'

'I'm Alan, ma'am, only been in the team a couple of months.' He smiled broadly; it was an easy, relaxed expression and she thought that he looked like one of the good ones.

He closed the door behind him and she called Jack's number. It rang onto voicemail and she left a message telling him she loved and missed him. She asked him to kiss Adam, and shivered even though the room was warm.

As she took her first sip of coffee Macallan screwed her nose up and promised to stop drinking the bilge concocted in the office. She looked more closely at the cup, which was stained, like it had been dipped in wood tar. Some things never changed. For some reason, that thought cheered her up.

Macallan had got as far as turning the handle on her office door when she remembered the intelligence report that had been dropped on her desk. She went back to pick it up, scanned the sanitised information and sat down.

'Mick.' She said it quietly and chewed the hard skin on her forefinger. A human source had called in with information that Billy Drew had teamed up with the Flemings and that he was still making noises about doing Harkins. She sighed. Mick would laugh it off, but she understood what Drew was capable of. If he'd made up his mind then the threat was serious. She would see Harkins about Swan but she had to get acquainted with her team again first.

McGovern called Swan's home number but he was still unconscious and unaware that his bed was soaked in Gnasher's urine. He snored like a pig as the dog hid under the bed trembling, the animal's instincts telling him that something was very wrong.

The seeds of a perfect storm had been sown and the players all knew it. Only some of them had met, but they realised that they were locked into a conflict that would bring casualties. They all wanted it to be someone else and would do whatever it took to make sure that was the case. In the end, it would come down to survival of the fittest.

19

Handyside had been unable to sleep so he'd risen at 5 a.m. and run a few miles before showering, getting into his car and driving down to the fish quays at North Shields. He ignored the sign warning that the fish market and harbour were a restricted area with no access to Mr and Mrs Joe Public and walked past it, nodding to the security men, who knew who he was. The minimum wage was not enough of an incentive to order the celebrity gangster off the premises and he always slipped them a few notes on the way out.

He sucked in air all mixed up with the smells that hang over a fishing port and market. The stink of diesel always hit the olfactory receptors first then cocktailed it with fresh fish, rotten fish and tar, all chilled by the salt air blowing off the North Sea. The wind had turned to the north and brought the cool arctic air that can freeze the skin of the east-coast natives even on the sunniest day. The place took him back to his early days, and he always went back there to work through his tangled thoughts.

Handyside was probably incapable of caring deeply about anything, any place or anyone apart from his wife and children, but the old harbour came close. As a boy he'd loved to watch the deep-sea fishermen unload their catches as the air rang with the voices of salesmen rattling off words in a language no one but they understood.

He stood on the edge of the pier, watching a trawler's fisherman cast off the ropes that had held the boat safely to land and head down the river towards the open sea. There had been so many times he'd wished he'd chosen a life at sea, and even though he knew it was foolish, he still liked to imagine the simplicity of that existence compared with the one he'd chosen. He couldn't know it but his yearnings were not that far removed from Grace Macallan's.

He lit up a cigarette and blew the smoke into the wind, which wafted it back onto his face. He looked up to the sky, closed his eyes and tried to forget just for a moment who he was and what his existence meant. The breeze whipped up off the deep waters and cooled his face. There was a storm coming, he was sure of it and he needed to be prepared.

He turned away from the pier and headed home, where he gave his wife some instructions. He'd avoided it before but had planned what to say if the situation arose. She squeezed his hand and her frightened look made him choke.

'It might never happen. Just be sure you know what you're doing if it does.'

She nodded and bit her lip till it hurt. She didn't want her man to see her tears.

20

By halfway through the afternoon Macallan would have struggled to recall all the meetings she'd attended during the previous few hours. It was always the same so she knew what to expect: everyone who was senior in rank wanted to prove they were senior in rank, and the scripts were almost identical. She'd been in the game long enough to know it had to be endured to keep them happy and so she smiled at the right times in case she had to call in a favour at some point in the future.

O'Connor saw her first and she was pleased that at least he'd kept it short and sweet. All he'd asked was to be kept in the loop. 'This one has sensitive written all over it. It's a miracle that the press aren't on top of it already – a missing UC and trafficked women drowned like nineteenth-century slaves. I think we need to put something out to them before they start giving us a kicking. What do you think?'

'I agree,' Macallan had said, knowing the papers would create havoc for the investigation by sensationalising the story. Why not? It *was* sensational. 'We have to give them something, and I guess a few of them will have picked up parts of the story from the usual sources.'

There'd been a brief pause that hinted at embarrassment for both of them. The usual source was everyday code for leaks from inside the job. When Macallan had been involved in the Barclay murder case she'd leaked information to Jacquie Bell; O'Connor had found out and seen it as a betrayal, though it was his realisation that Macallan was a more talented detective than he could ever be that had made him try to destroy her career.

At least until he'd received a call from Harkins, not long before the Loyalist Billy Nelson had nearly killed her in the bomb blast near Fettes. Harkins had rarely given rank much respect when he was in the job and post retirement he could say what he liked to whoever he liked. O'Connor owed him from the past (and, truth be told, he'd always respected and to a certain extent envied Harkins) so he'd agreed to go to Harkins' home, and almost as soon as he'd set foot in the place he'd been ordered to 'shut the fuck up and listen'. Harkins had proceeded to explain to him, not at all tactfully, that he was a fool and that Macallan had never set out to hurt him; that it was his vanity that had stalled his career and broken a relationship that she had wanted more than anything. He'd reminded O'Connor that he was a talented cop, just not a talented detective, and to think about that.

'Don't you think she's had enough for one life?' he'd said. 'You've just lost the opportunity to be with someone special. I warned her about you, that ego that fills every fuckin' room you step into.'

O'Connor had got the message, thought about it and realised he still loved Macallan. But it was too late, and he'd have to carry that loss for the rest of his life.

'John?'

He'd blinked and apologised, realising that his thoughts had drifted. 'Leave it with me; I'll get some form of words out and run it past you first. They'll be hammering on the door soon enough.'

He'd smiled as he'd stood up to shake her hand warmly and Macallan had puzzled again at what could have changed the man from bitter enemy back to something like the person she'd first known and then loved when she'd joined the old Lothian and Borders force.

All her meetings over, she flopped into the chair in her office and toed the shoes from her aching feet, sighing with relief that at least the formalities of starting again were over and the real work could now kick in. She picked up the phone to track down McGovern and he told her he was on his way back from the hospital where he'd been involved in a second session with Ingrid Richter. Fitzgerald was with him and Macallan asked him to bring her in for a meet when he got back.

She put the phone down, resisting the urge to try to speak to Jack because too many calls would sound like she was struggling and all that would do was make him worry unnecessarily. He could cope with what he had to do, and the break away from criminal work had worked wonders on him both mentally and physically. There was no doubt he was starting to get the urge to return to his practice as a barrister and the break had given him new drive. Macallan had thought that his attempt at writing was an indulgence, but it still made her proud of him. What had come as a surprise was that there was real interest in the book, and it looked like he was going to get a deal that might let them buy the cottage rather than having to rent it. She thought about all those good days on the Antrim shores when they were concentrating on no one but themselves, just being happy, and smiled.

The knock at the door as McGovern came in startled

her from her daydream. He tried a smile, but it was tense and she guessed it had been hard going with the interview. Listening to what other human beings were capable of could still shock the toughest detectives. The girl who came into the room behind him looked drawn and seemed unsure at what to do in the company of her new boss. Macallan remembered that feeling and tried her best to put the young detective at ease.

'Sit down. I hope Jimmy hasn't been working you too hard,' Macallan said, nodding to McGovern to take a pew. She thought it would be easy to like Fitzgerald. It was enough to have McGovern's recommendation but she noticed another plus: the girl had an open face that had still to be lined by the constant strain of investigating other people's secrets. She was tall and had hardly a spare ounce from what McGovern had told her was a fanatical appetite for a range of sports – including those of the extreme variety. Her straw-coloured hair was pulled back into a ponytail, she wore no make-up and her clothes were casual enough to show Macallan that fashion and appearances didn't concern her too much. McGovern had been right; there was a lot in the young woman that reminded Macallan of herself years before – though she certainly hadn't been as fit at that age.

'Okay, tell me what you have and what you think. No holds barred in this room, Pam, and I guess Jimmy will have already told you that I like to hear it as it is. Never what you think I want to hear.'

They gave her it all and occasionally pulled out their notes to make sure they hadn't missed anything. They'd had to make a huge effort to hide their emotions as they'd listened to Richter describe the horrors she'd witnessed in sight of the Berwickshire coast.

McGovern had heard so many terrible stories in his career that he wondered why anything bothered him any more, but listening to the girl had made him want to kill the men who'd committed such an atrocity. Macallan hardly spoke and didn't need to – there was enough information for her brain to start forming images of young women being beaten to death and thrown into the sea like so much garbage.

McGovern watched her clench her fist repeatedly, although her expression rarely changed and she never touched the brew she'd poured for herself. Fitzgerald had left it to McGovern initially but she needed to unload and eventually joined in, filling in the blanks when he missed some fact or just to put her slant on it.

When they were finished Macallan asked Fitzgerald to get the statement typed up as soon as and watched her leave the room, reassured that McGovern had been on the money with his assessment of the young officer. When they were alone she tried to gather her thoughts, get the priorities in some kind of order, but there were stacks of them jostling for attention and she knew there were more to come. It was difficult trying to focus and block out what had happened on the *Brighter Dawn* at the same time. It was terrible, but her job was to deal with it and every day that passed would make it that bit harder to get a result.

'You okay?' she asked McGovern. 'You look tired.' It was an obvious question, but she knew that these events sucked the life out of the officers who listened to the victims recount what they'd seen.

'I'm fine. To be honest, I was amazed how calm and collected Ingrid was. Maybe it was the sedatives but she looked dreamy when she was telling the story. God knows how she came through all that and lived. She must be made of the right stuff to do what she did to survive.' He shook his head wearily and promised to tell his wife and children that he loved them when he was finished for the day, whenever that was.

Macallan wanted to send him home to get some rest, but it would have been foolish to even suggest it at this stage of a case, and anyway, he'd just find some way of politely refusing. Men like McGovern put their own comfort way down their list of priorities, and he was one of the lucky ones in that his wife actually understood and let it be. She was happy just to have the bits of him that the job hadn't chewed off over the years. Ruined marriages were accepted as routine collateral damage in investigation work, but McGovern was an exception to that rule and he thanked his lucky stars every day for it.

'First things first,' Macallan said, trying to get them back on track and work the lines of enquiry. 'It was good work sealing off the *Brighter Dawn* as a crime scene so quickly. Make sure all the samples are taken to the lab for profiling.'

McGovern nodded and started to make notes as he got back into gear.

'Concentrate on samples from the bunks where the girls slept; that's our best chance. Next thing is that we need to contact the British office in Europol and try to see if they can get us possible missing persons who match the descriptions Ingrid has given us. How long is it taking to profile DNA samples at the moment?'

McGovern shook his head. 'This is Police Scotland – even urgent is going to take two to three weeks.'

She wanted to say fuck it, but it was what it was. 'Okay, let's get on with it. We've got Ingrid and the first thing is to get her DNA matched to a sample on the boat, but the lifebelt tells us what we know already. Did she describe what bunk she was sleeping in?'

'We've got it in the statement.'

'And where's the boat now?'

'Still in Eyemouth. Two uniforms are guarding it 24/7 till we decide what we're going to do. All the investigations are being run by separate teams at the moment. Any steer yet on our role?'

She nodded and gave him the answer he wanted, although it would strip a few more years off his life. 'As of now we combine them all under my command: Dixie Deans, Ingrid and Ricky Swan. We'll need to get a few more staff on-board; and if you could get hold of Felicity Young and Lesley Thompson in the morning and make arrangements to second them to the team, that will help tremendously.'

McGovern grunted an acknowledgement.

'Good. Right, the next thing is to get the Newcastle team to find out where Alan Hunter and Frankie Dillon can be located. Unfortunately we know where Eric Gunderson is. Once we meet the guys down there we can arrange to have them lifted at some stage and, depending on Ingrid, get an ID parade set up. If she does the business we've got enough to at least see them locked up. We should be able to confirm her DNA from the boat.' She stood up and walked over to the window, stared across the city and thought for a moment that it just couldn't be that simple.

'These two men who were watching it all – you sure about that?'

'No question. They were spotters, has to be and it fits. The cigarette ends are already lodged for examination.'

'So we need to get the DNA results from those fag ends and ID the spotters then we can really stir the bastards up.' She felt her mobile tremble and clicked on the screen. It was a close-up selfie of Jack and Adam with some kisses. She put it away quickly; she would stare at it later when she was alone. Its arrival had distracted her slightly but gave her a warm feeling that cheered her, and she felt a familiar rush of energy as the wheels started to turn.

'Last thing for now is to get a team started on getting

the Flemings lifted. Dixie Deans was working for them, we know they were going to Newcastle for a meet and then he goes off the radar. They have to know something. Okay they'll probably say nothing, but let's get in their face.'

McGovern felt his mood lift at the thought of some action coming up.

Macallan stood. 'Now let's go and get my car. I want to see Ricky Swan and hear what he has to say.'

21

Less than an hour later Gnasher barked loudly enough to wake his master, who'd slept through the doorbell ringing for the third time. He'd been woken twenty minutes earlier by a call from his handler that some big fucking cheese was on the way to see him, but he felt like shit and just wanted to lie perfectly still till his hangover had passed. He'd fallen asleep again almost immediately. When he resurfaced it dawned on him that the bed was soaked and he thought at first that he'd pished himself again. It happened occasionally and he never really bothered, because that's what he paid his Polish cleaner less than the minimum wage for. The realisation that it was the bedclothes rather than his jim-jams that were wet led to him promising Gnasher that he would kick fuck out of him when he got his head together. The dog still hadn't learned English but his instincts told him that something was definitely very wrong so he stayed on his belly under the bed. If that wasn't enough, the dog was hungry; Swan had forgotten that the beast needed fed occasionally.

When the door opened after the fourth ring Macallan's

first impression was that Swan looked exactly like what he was. His foot-long comb-over was hanging limply over his ear and he looked as bad as he felt. McGovern made the introduction and was in mid-flow when Swan turned and padded back towards his lounge, leaving the door open.

McGovern smiled. 'I think that means come in, Superintendent.'

'Have a seat for a minute and I'll just get a wash,' Swan said. 'It's been a funny old night. Do you want a drink or something?'

McGovern and Macallan had already picked up an overpowering smell of pish and politely declined. Swan washed himself as best he could, put on some clothes and filled a glass half and half with ice and orange juice. For a small man he had a jumbo-sized capacity for drink and his tolerance meant he recovered quickly. When he sat down he took in the woman and was impressed. A bit older than the twenty-somethings he preferred, but he thought that he'd definitely give her a turn if she was up for it. She saw the look in his eye, knew exactly what it meant and felt decidedly queasy for a couple of moments.

'We know about the attack last night and understand that you're upset. They also told us that you made some threat of disclosing information about some people who may have used your facilities.' Macallan let it hang there, waited for a response as Swan slugged back the juice. She was fascinated by his Adam's apple, which seemed to have a life of its own. He drew his pyjama sleeve across his mouth and burped wetly before patting his mouth politely and saying 'excuse me' as if he meant it.

'Upset. Did you say fuckin' upset, Inspector?'

'Superintendent, Ricky,' McGovern interrupted, but Swan ignored the prompt.

'I'm attacked outside my own business by these fuckin'

184

nutjobs, nearly killed and you think I might be upset!' He took another drink and the detectives waited. 'One of your boys is missing and my prints are all over it as far as the fuckin' gangsters are concerned, so you could say that I'm upset, yeah. That would definitely be a fair description.'

The door to the bedroom swung open and Gnasher padded into the room with his head down as if he'd already been beaten. The need to eat was overwhelming for the dog and Macallan saw the animal was shaking uncontrollably. She'd never had a dog, but it was obvious something was wrong.

McGovern had always had them as pets, so he knew exactly what he was seeing. 'When did you last feed that thing?' he said, failing to cover the anger in his voice.

Swan looked at Gnasher and for a moment thought about dispensing the beating he'd promised the dog earlier, but when he saw the look on McGovern's face he decided that might be a bad idea.

'Just all this aggravation, must have forgotten.'

'Tell me where the dog food is and I'll fix it.' McGovern got up and made for the kitchen, scooping Gnasher up on the way.

Macallan was losing patience but tried her best to keep it professional considering the idiot opposite her might be capable of blowing up reputations in the middle of one of the most complicated operations she could imagine. 'Can we get on with it?' She gave him a hard look and he shrugged.

'I'm not going to tell you what I have and who it concerns. Not at the moment anyway. Just believe me when I say that I have it and they're all in there: politicians, judges, some of your lot and a few footballers – although what's new there? I've got them with the girls, some of them very young, snorting lines of coke and a couple I've hooked up with boys. The papers would fuckin' love it, Superintendent.' He smiled, though it was more of a self-satisfied leer, and she shifted uncomfortably in her seat as he played what he thought was his ace. 'I'm no fool and realise that some of the crap regarding these women on the boat might land at my door. Let's just say I've given a few foreign tarts some work over the years. If anything comes up that might mean charges, I want assurances that I'll be left alone.'

Macallan tried to control the anger constricting her throat and she felt her face heat up from a rush of blood. McGovern came back into the room, glaring at the man for his offences against dogs. Then he saw Macallan's face and knew there was a problem.

'So what is it you want from us? And can I add that I won't let whatever it is that you have interfere with my investigation. If I find evidence then I go with it; if it's criminal, it'll be investigated. Understand?'

They both knew it was never that simple and that disturbing the great and good of the city would cause ripples. Phone calls would be made to call in favours and so it would go on. But Macallan didn't care about that, and she hoped they'd find something that would bring her back to Swan's door. That would be a bonus.

'What do you want from us, Mr Swan, and are you asking for protection?'

'Protection.' Swan leered again and Macallan planned to take a shower as soon as she got back to the flat. 'If you put protection round me you might as well shove up a sign at my front door with the word "grass" in big fuck-off letters. I want you to put these lunatics inside. I can stick to the story that the undercover was introduced to me over in Belfast and had fuck all to do with yours truly. But the McMartins will come back for more after what happened to The Bitch. I can explain it to the Flemings but not to Glasgow or Newcastle.'

Macallan raised her eyebrows. 'The bitch? Who's a bitch?'

'It's what they call Brenda McMartin, and it's well deserved in her case,' McGovern said, still angry at Swan's treatment of his dog.

She shook her head impatiently. 'Look, we're on this already but we can't do it overnight so bear with us. Are you prepared to give evidence against the people who attacked you last night?'

'You're doing it again.' As Swan said it she saw a vein pump frantically in his neck and the combination of alcohol and rising anger turned his face crimson going on purple. 'If I step into the witness box I'm fucked again. You don't give evidence against people like them and keep breathing. Just make sure there are some cops in the area if needs be and get those bastards locked up for something else. I saw the headlines about that girl found near Eyemouth. Do the fuckin' maths.'

'That's enough; you'll give yourself a coronary.' McGovern leaned forward when he said it; he wanted Swan to give him some excuse to clobber him.

'You need to watch it, Mr Swan,' Macallan said, her face tight with the strain of fighting her instincts to kick the greasy little bastard in the nuts. 'We will be looking at women trafficked for sex so there's every chance we might end up back at your door.'

Swan leaned back in the chair and chuckled. 'Don't give me any of that crap about sex workers. Your lot haven't been able to make up their minds for years whether it's right or wrong to protect the women on the game.' Macallan had thrown the dig in without anything to back it up and Swan did a good job at not reacting, even though she was closer to the truth than she realised. He was up to his eyes in taking trafficked women from the Flemings and it had been good business. What worried him more was that he'd pointed the Flemings

187

at one or two gold-plated contacts who were looking for women to keep for themselves. He hoped that particular sewer didn't erupt in his face.

Macallan stood up; she could see the conversation was going nowhere, though that would make no difference to her investigation. 'If you want protection then ask for it, but you need to give us some information or you can take a fuck as far as I'm concerned. I'll make sure there are extra patrols in the area but that's all you get unless you want to cooperate as a witness. I'm sure there's a lot you could tell us if you wanted. Other than that, I can't stop you disclosing to the press.' She turned to go.

'It'll stay safe for now, Superintendent, as long as none of your lot start throwing charges at me. Any problems then I feed it to the dogs and the first ones to go will be from your job.' He looked like he'd already made up his mind to do it anyway.

When they got to the car, McGovern patted his pockets. 'Sorry, left my notebook in there. Jump in and I'll be back in a sec.'

He knocked at the door, told Swan the lie about the notebook and followed him back into the living room. When Swan turned round his balls were crushed for the second time in twenty-four hours and he really wished he hadn't pissed off the Chief Inspector whose face was about three inches from his own contorted phizog.

'If I come back here and see the dog in that state again,' McGovern said, 'your shagging days are over, my friend. Nod if you understood that.'

Swan nodded weakly as McGovern let his knackers go then slid to the floor, where he lay for at least ten minutes after McGovern slipped into the car and pushed the key into the ignition.

'Is that a creep or what?' Macallan asked as she stared out of the driver's window.

'You're not wrong, Superintendent. He's got some balls on him.'

Macallan didn't get it and didn't ask for clarification, but McGovern felt a whole lot better about his day.

It was still quite early, but Macallan knew there were hard days ahead and that the real work would start in the morning, so she insisted McGovern head for home and get some rest. He looked at his watch and tried to put up some resistance: 'Are you trying to turn me into a nine-to-five office worker?'

'I'm pulling rank on this one. Go home and talk to your wife. All I want to do is meet Ingrid for myself. Ten minutes is all I want with her and then I'm for home. The girl's probably had enough for one day, but I need to get a feel for her.'

McGovern knew it was pointless to argue, and anyway, this was too good an offer to refuse. He'd been working flat out for weeks on end before Macallan had come back to the team and he was weary in the core of his bones.

'Okay, you're the boss, and to tell the truth I've hardly seen my family over the last few weeks. One thing though: something's bothering me about Ingrid. I can't put my finger on it, but see what you think. I told you she looked a bit dreamy or spaced out. Maybe something they've given her. Could you check with the medics just in case? It worried me a bit.'

Macallan pulled up outside McGovern's home then watched his wife open the door and wave. She saw the look on her face, the genuine pleasure at seeing her husband back home. Macallan knew what that meant now. In the past going home to be on her own wouldn't have bothered her too much, but without Jack and Adam there the rooms would feel empty. There was good reason to go and meet Richter, but part of it was to avoid going back to the flat and spending the night wishing Jack was beside her. During their time together Macallan had made a great discovery: it seemed ridiculously simple, but Jack had become her best friend as well as her partner, and it was a revelation. She'd leaned so heavily in the past on Bill Kelly, and to a lesser extent on Mick Harkins, that she'd never realised the role they filled in her life, but Bill had stood by her through all her problems in Belfast, which had proved his loyalty and sealed his place in her heart. Their relationship had been very deep and on his death she had mourned for him more as a daughter than a friend.

From Macallan's earliest memories of childhood her father had treated her like a stranger, and she had never been able to work out why he seemed to want to punish her by never showing any form of affection. It was only very recently, and almost by chance, that she'd discovered the answer. Her mother had died barely two months after Adam was born, and the day before the funeral she'd fallen into conversation with her only aunt, Jean, a woman she'd hardly ever met. Jean had spent most of her life in London and had barely been on speaking terms with her sister or brother-in-law. They'd started chatting and Macallan had quickly warmed to her, wishing that she'd known her better. On impulse, after Jean had commented on how totally besotted Jack looked with his baby son, she'd asked whether her aunt knew why she had been so unloved. Jean had paused for a moment and given her a searching look before deciding that Macallan had grown into a strong and intelligent woman who needed to understand – and who deserved to know the truth.

The revelation that her mother had conceived her through an affair and that her father had known had been shocking. In a way it was a simple explanation, and she wondered why she hadn't figured it out before. Her father had then inflicted the worst of all punishments – he'd stayed with his wife but never forgave her.

There was more: unknown to Macallan she'd had an elder sister who'd died before she was two. Jean had told her that her father had been a decent man but this event had nearly broken him; finding out about his wife's later infidelity had then destroyed what was left of his dreams and turned him into the cold, unsympathetic character Macallan had grown up with.

Later that night Macallan had sobbed like a child and barely slept, but by morning she'd felt that years of guilt had been lifted from her. Like so many children she'd been convinced that somehow or other she was to blame for the way her father had treated her. When he had died all those years ago, and her mother more recently, she'd felt the same old guilt and wished she could feel the pain of loss, but there had been none. Now, though, she had Jack, and she swore that their son would have all the love he needed to take his place in the world. It was a strange feeling, but when it was her time she wanted Adam to grieve for his mother in a way that she couldn't for hers.

22

When Macallan arrived at the hospital she wondered how much time she'd spent over the years in these places. Detectives return again and again to those sterile rooms trying to find answers from the broken victims who meet the wrong people at the wrong time. She asked to see a doctor, who told her that Richter was responding to treatment but they were concerned about her mental health. McGovern had been right; the nursing staff were reporting some unusual detached behaviour and the consultant had asked for a specialist assessment as soon as possible. The doctor told her that Richter was showing a variety of symptoms for post-traumatic stress.

'There are long periods of emotional detachment, and I think this is her way of avoiding what's happened. Then there will be periods of anxiety, and the nurses tell me she wakes every night shaking and in tears. The dreams aren't necessarily of the event but true nightmares that leave her exhausted. Hardly surprising given what the girl's seen and experienced. People who suffer such severe trauma, coming so close to death, can spend all their time reworking the event and imagining they'd died. It seems more logical – makes more sense than surviving against such odds.'

Macallan had seen this condition in Belfast where people had been close to bomb blasts and somehow or other made it out when others had been killed. She'd even felt something like it herself when Nelson's booby-trapped car had nearly wiped her out.

'What's the prognosis for her?'

'It's not my field, but we need to be careful.' His phone beeped. He apologised, read the message and continued. 'It's very common for people to feel guilt at surviving. There are almost bound to be some long-term effects; however, she's an intelligent woman who'll realise that in some ways she is damaged for life even though there isn't a mark on her body. I'll keep in touch, but if you'll excuse me ...' He hurried off and Macallan felt like a lead weight hung in her chest. She wanted to go home but pushed the thought from her mind.

She spoke briefly to the uniform on duty outside Richter's room. He seemed to know how important it was to protect the girl even if it was boring the arse off him. They'd had one massive fuck-up on the Barclay case where the idiot guarding Pauline Johansson had decided it was more interesting to chat up the night shift than look after the victim and that wasn't going to happen this time.

Macallan looked through the glass windows to the single room Richter was occupying. McGovern had managed to talk the administrators into giving her the room after intensive care because they needed to control access till she recovered enough to tell her story about what had left her fighting for survival on that beach. McGovern and Fitzgerald had done a good job, but Richter would be revisited to the point where she'd be sick of the sight of those hunting the men who'd tried so hard to kill her. It had to be done though. Time and time again witnesses would give several statements then come up with the gem that detectives pray for.

Richter seemed to be sleeping but the sound of conversation outside her quiet room made her roll her head on the pillow and open her eyes. She stared, expressionless, in the direction of the police officers. Macallan could see she was a beautiful young woman and that there was no obvious sign of physical damage. She thought again about how often she'd had to visit broken faces and bodies, struggling to get their owners to recount the horrors they'd endured.

She stepped into the room, smiled and introduced herself. 'Can I call you Ingrid?'

The girl nodded and pulled herself up on the bed. 'I'm sorry but I was very tired after your colleagues left today. I don't seem to have much energy. I hope my English is okay for you?'

'Your English is excellent so don't worry about that. It's remarkable you've made so much progress. Chief Inspector McGovern told me your story and even for us it's hard to understand why men do these things.'

Macallan sat down and asked Richter about her home and family. She'd done more than enough for one day with McGovern and Fitzgerald and forcing her back to the events on the *Brighter Dawn* could do more damage than good for the next interview.

Macallan liked Richter immediately and thought that in another life she would have been a good person to know. She kept their meeting short but told her she would come back and that there would always be a liaison officer available till she left for home.

'Home?' She said it as a question.

'Of course. When you're well enough and we've finished with your statements then you can go home and be with your family. You understand when we arrest whoever is responsible there might be a trial?' Ingrid seemed to ignore the question; her mind was drifting.

'I have these dreams, every time I fall asleep and I'm frightened to think what they mean. It is strange because I realise it is ...' she searched for the word and muttered, 'zlý sen,' trying to trace the English equivalent. Macallan knew she was trying to find the word nightmare. She'd had enough of her own over the years and they still came to visit, though not as often as they had during the Troubles.

'I understand what you mean: it's a frightening dream.'

She nodded. 'I try to find my way home but I don't know where it is. When I wake up it is as though home and my past was just in my imagination and there is no way to go back there.' She looked at Macallan for an answer, but there was nothing the detective could say that would give Richter some form of explanation. She knew the young woman was struggling against the demons given birth since she'd been washed ashore. Her survival was nothing short of a miracle, but she was fighting with something left inside her mind like a parasite by what she'd witnessed under the stars that night. Macallan knew, and Richter was coming to realise, that it would occupy part of her mind for the rest of her life. There was no surgery or medical intervention that could remove the invader, and it terrified her.

'Are you going to be okay?' It was all Macallan could think to say. She felt helpless witnessing the girl's struggle against an enemy she could only see lurking at the edges of her imagination.

'I'm tired, just very tired and the dreams won't let me rest.'

'Your family are here now and they'll look after you. It's early days and you'll get much better, I promise you.'

She knew the words meant nothing but goodwill on her part. They were always so helpless in these cases and she'd seen the effect in McGovern's eyes earlier on. She would have been as well to apologise for a human race that could give birth and life to people capable of such barbarity.

Macallan stopped off in the hospital café, bought a strong black coffee and felt her shoulders ache. Aching shoulders – that proved she was back in the game and all the health benefits she'd gained in the last few months would be washed away over the course of the investigation. She said a quiet prayer that it wouldn't be a long haul, but given what they'd learned so far it could be as short as it liked and it would still be a bastard of a case.

She sipped the last of the coffee and wondered whether to increase the ache in her shoulders by going to take a quick look at the woman she had been intrigued to hear was called The Bitch. It had to be worth the pain. Apparently the CID had tried to speak to Brenda McMartin and her answer had been to gob blood on a detective sergeant's brand new suit. The other two Weegies scraped off the road in Leith with her wouldn't even give their names. There was no chance of McMartin speaking to her, but it would be interesting and would fill in the picture of who they were dealing with.

She didn't have to travel far because McMartin was in the same hospital. Macallan spoke to the nurses, who'd lost any sympathy for McMartin about five minutes after she'd been admitted, when she'd tried to whack one of the junior doctors in A&E. The staff nurse on the ward described her as the worst patient she'd ever dealt with in twenty years in the job. Apparently McMartin had been visited by a couple of hard cases earlier in the day; the nurse reckoned it was a serious powwow and they'd had to sedate her after the men, or what passed for men, had gone. Another nurse had told her that she heard an order to kill some poor bastard although it was difficult to make out what McMartin was saying through her shredded lips.

'Christ, I'd hate to get the wrong side of that one,' the nurse muttered, and everyone on the ward would have agreed with her.

'She's a piece of work alright, and what you've told me matches the descriptions I've been given.' Macallan could do nothing but sympathise with the nurses who had to try to heal the McMartins of this world and wondered how anyone could do their job and remain calm in the face of so much abuse. She decided that it would be enough to see McMartin and that the men who'd been with her could wait for another day.

Local CID were still handling the rammy in Leith, trying to work out who they were going to charge with what. They'd been unable to work out who'd done the business on McMartin and her team, apart from the fact that it definitely wasn't Swan, who couldn't punch his way out of the proverbial paper bag. He was sticking to his story that it had been a passing Good Samaritan who'd downed the three Weegies, but the DOs knew that had to be shite.

They had a statement from an old woman who'd witnessed the whole thing, although apart from describing Swan's rescuer as a 'handy wee bastard' she hadn't been a great deal of help, though she'd clearly enjoyed every blow delivered in the street battle. Criminal intelligence reckoned it had to be Cue Ball Ross, who worked for Swan and was definitely capable of the level of carnage the uniforms had found at the locus. But Cue Ball seemed to have disappeared off the radar, and in any event no one was making a complaint, and certainly not Brenda

McMartin, who would have poked her good eye out before cooperating with the bizzies. They'd transferred her to a single room to prevent her causing any more disruption on the ward where she'd already threatened two elderly patients for snoring during the night.

The staff nurse showed Macallan to the room. 'I'll leave you here, Superintendent, if you don't mind. If you're not out in ten minutes I'll send in special forces.' She winked and set off to care for some patients who appreciated what she did.

Macallan opened the door and saw that McMartin had certainly come off second best to whoever had rescued Ricky Swan. Her face was still swollen; her lips were burst and looked like a collagen injection had gone horribly wrong. McMartin had a pair of earphones on but Macallan could hear that she was blasting heavy metal. She stood a safe distance from the bed, remembering the story about the detective sergeant's new suit, until McMartin eventually realised there was someone in the room and looked round slowly to face her.

'Who the huck are you?' She had problems forming words with her swollen mouth and missing teeth, but it wasn't going to stop her swearing.

'I'm Superintendent Grace Macallan; I just wanted a quick word.'

'Huck och.' She pushed herself up and clenched her remaining teeth as the movement generated a pain that would have rendered a lesser mortal unconscious. Macallan had met some terrifying women in her time in Northern Ireland but this one took first prize. The eyepatch only added to the image of a truly frightening human being.

'The local guys are dealing with you, McMartin.' She used the surname as part of the wind-up. 'I'm dealing with something more serious. Some girls murdered and a missing policeman, but you wouldn't know anything about that?'

The Bitch tried uttering some other expletive-ridden abuse, but this time the lack of front teeth made it completely unintelligible. She was losing it – she just hated any pig in plain clothes. To make it worse for her the visitor was a good-looking female specimen, which was like rubbing sandpaper across her already stretched nerves. If she was fighting fit she would have already had Macallan by the throat, but when she tried to get out of the bed her broken ribs reminded her of her limitations. Cue Ball had done a professional job on her.

'It's alright, McMartin, I'm going. Just wanted to see why they call you The Bitch. And now I know.' She took two steps towards the bed and decided to risk a spit job.

'I just want you to know that if you have anything to do with the cases I'm looking at I'll make it my business to see you away for a long time.' Macallan saw she was grinding the woman's nerve ends as she looked round then lowered her voice to make sure no one else heard. 'You make me sick to my stomach, and if they ever find the man who rearranged your face I'll shake him by the fucking hand. Trust me; I'll be watching you from now till I come to lift you.'

The McMartin temper was legendary in Glasgow gangland and Big Brenda rose beautifully to the bait as Macallan stepped back to the door and smiled broadly. No one dared speak to a McMartin like that and she lost it completely. She tried to rise out of bed with the intention of strangling Macallan, but the searing pain lacerating her chest injuries took her breath away and she rolled out of the bed, hitting the floor like a ton of bricks. She lay face down, moaning for help, and Macallan changed her smile to a look of concern as she called the nurses.

'I don't know what happened but she got upset and landed on the floor. It must be the stress of it all.'

The staff nurse nodded then winked and whispered 'nice one' on the way past.

Like McGovern's treatment of Swan's balls, the visit hadn't really achieved anything, but it had made Macallan and most of the nursing staff feel a bit better.

23

Macallan walked out of the hospital entrance and sucked in the cooling early-evening air. Every corner of the access area held a patient or visitor inhaling the tobacco fumes that had landed half of them there in the first place. She headed across the car park as a twin-prop aeroplane moaned across the sky above her and she wondered where it was heading. It could have been the Belfast connection.

A wave of tiredness washed over and through her, and she just wanted to get back to the flat, empty or not, then sink into a hot bath with something to drink on the side. The months away from the job meant she wasn't match fit. It was just a question of getting back into the grind, trying to stay alert enough so that she didn't miss the clues when they were staring back at her.

The streets were quiet enough and she turned on some forgettable music to distract her mind from the images of those young women and what had been done to them on the *Brighter Dawn*. She wanted to see the boat and treat it the same as any other crime scene. It was good that McGovern had realised its potential importance at the time and ensured it had been secured and kept under guard since it was seized in Eyemouth. They were getting the usual hassle from the uniformed commanders because men and women were being tied up keeping watch on Richter and the boat round the clock, but that was par for the course and a friendly 'fuck off and chase some motorists' usually did the trick.

Macallan pulled up near Leith Police Station, switched off the ignition and thankfully put an end to a song by Peter Andre. She closed her eyes, leaned her head back on the rest, just wanting to stay there for a while, and fell asleep almost immediately. She woke again after only about three minutes, the ringtone on her phone pulling her out of a warm darkness. It took her a few seconds to fumble through her pockets for the mobile and felt that ridiculous moment of panic that she might actually miss a call.

'How's it going? Have you solved it yet and put Big Brenda where she belongs?' Macallan would probably have been pissed off to hear the wind-up from any other reporter, but Jacquie Bell was a friend and that strange breed of hack she could trust.

'How do you know about Brenda? And you know I can't comment about ongoing investigations.' She wasn't surprised that Bell had picked up some of the story: she'd cultivated sources all through the force and the judiciary and had a few politicians eating out of her hand. What really set her apart was that the bigger the beast the more determined she was to pull them down, especially if they held an office of trust.

'You know I'm all-seeing in these matters, Grace, and a relentless pursuer of the truth. Fancy some French red? Got this really expensive stuff from a very old judge who fancies me something rotten.'

'Actually I'm knackered – heard too much bad stuff

today. Anyone else and I'd have said Foxtrot Oscar, but it would be good to catch up. Jack and the wean won't be coming till later in the week so it's just me in the big flat with the forces of darkness closing in. Half an hour, but let's meet in a bar; I could do with some background noise and Edinburgh bar prices to distract me from the job.'

'Right, see you in the Ship on the Shore and we can share a plate of seafood at the same time. It's only ten minutes' walk from the station.'

They met in the old bar next to the dark waters of Leith and hugged like people who'd really missed each other. Bell saw the troubled look in Macallan's eyes but decided not to ask. There had to be a good reason given what had been leaked to her so far. The pub oozed warm atmosphere from every corner and it was as if it was welcoming them in. At one time The Shore had been a roughhouse inhabited by only the brave or demented, but now it was a row of beautifully restored old dens that fed and watered the tourists or citizens who could afford the prices. They ordered up a plate of seafood that would have been too much for an average family and washed it down with some decent beer.

'This is on me. I've hit a few good stories recently and can afford to splash it.'

'No way. You know the deal – Leveson and all that. We split it just to make me happy. Don't want the rubber heels taking me away in a dawn raid.'

'Jesus, is there no way to corrupt you? I've tried, God knows I've tried.' She was harking back to the night they'd slept together and smirked at Macallan's slight moment of discomfort. It had been a troubled time for Macallan. She'd never been able to explain why it had happened and it still puzzled her. It didn't bother Bell in the least, and she loved to press Macallan's Presbyterian buttons whenever she had the chance. Jacquie Bell would have been the first to describe herself as a bit on the hard and cynical side of the female population, but for Macallan she made an exception. She just liked her company – the honesty and combination of strength and vulnerability that made her so engaging. The reporter only heard from other people about Grace Macallan the detective, driven and almost impossible to pull away from a case that she believed could be solved. But she liked the Grace sitting across the table from her now, clumsily trying to crack open a crab claw and failing miserably. She pouted like a small child before she moved onto a langoustine carcass that made for easier extraction. That's when Bell told her what she knew, which was a lot, and Macallan decided it was time to stop battling with the seafood.

'How the hell do you get so much of this?' For a moment she was annoyed with her friend, but she knew the reporter was just doing what she was paid to, and could Macallan really complain given the information she'd leaked herself in the past?

'Look, a missing UC, a young woman abducted and trafficked from Eastern Europe and mixed up with some of the most horrible bastards in the country. Mix that in with the street battle in Leith and you have a huge story. I'm running out of time, Grace, but I thought I'd speak to you before I put it in front of my editor.'

Macallan realised that Bell hadn't mentioned the *Brighter Dawn* so she didn't know it all – just enough to set the public's imagination on fire. It was the old problem of how to handle the press, and in this case her friend, without alerting the men she wanted to put away. It had cost her dearly in the past and she wasn't going to run off with this one on her own. 'Look, there's more to this than you might imagine, so give me a minute.'

Bell nodded and threw back half a glass of her Belgian lager in one go.

Macallan stepped out onto the street and called O'Connor. He sounded tired when he answered but his voice lifted when he heard hers. The case had already cost lives and she wanted to play it straight. The wrong decision on this one would end careers, which she didn't want for herself and in this case O'Connor didn't deserve it either. After all that had happened he'd supported her and she wasn't going to betray that investment. She told him exactly what had been said, and his answer surprised her, proving something really had changed within him.

'Christ, if the press get this wrong we could be in all sorts of trouble and the targets will clean up and take a holiday.' There was a pause and she expected him to tell her to say nothing till he'd taken silk on it. 'We shouldn't be surprised; there was no way someone like Jacquie Bell wasn't going to pick up a bit of this story. She's your friend, tell her the score and if she plays ball with us we'll feed her the inside developments as they happen. But this stays between us.'

She thought for a moment, trying to weigh it up and shrugged to no one but herself. 'You sure? Okay by me, but I want to know that you're sure.'

'Go ahead. Come and see me in the morning before you go to Newcastle.'

Macallan sat down opposite the reporter again, sipped the fresh beer that Bell had got in while she'd been on the phone and proceeded to tell her what had happened on the *Brighter Dawn*. Even though she knew it was true, it was still hard to hear her own words and believe it could have happened.

Bell sat back in the chair and put her hands palm down on the table as if she was trying to steady herself. 'It's one of those rare occasions where I haven't a fucking clue what to say. Is there any doubt about any of this?'

Macallan shook her head.

'What do you want me to do?'

'The story about Ingrid is going to leak out eventually and we need to control it for the moment till we grab some people down in Newcastle. What you could do is say the police are linking the woman washed up to a trafficking ring, with a report that some Eastern European women are missing and there are concerns for their safety. Lay it on thick that they may have come to harm. We haven't a clue who the other women are and probably won't, depending on where they came from originally. They made a mistake taking Ingrid though: educated, a family who reported her missing and one tough specimen who wasn't going to go easy. Put something in that we're following definite leads on who the other women are and that might spook the bastards into making a mistake.'

'I can maybe squeeze it in tonight if I get my arse in gear.' Bell looked twitchy, as if she was about to get up and leave immediately, but her expression changed and she leaned forward in her seat. 'What about the missing UC?' she asked, still trying to get her head round the thought of the frightened young women being killed then dumped into the cold dark waters so far from home.

'Leave that for the following day – we'll drip-feed it so the taxpayers don't go into lynch mode. These bastards know we're on the case and during the next few days we're going to be knocking some doors down.'

Bell always looked like she'd just stepped out of a beauty salon, which for someone with her lifestyle was a remarkable feat, but it was as if she'd just woken up with a hangover. Her face had turned unusually pale and she looked perturbed with whatever was on her mind. Macallan thought it was time to go and get some rest, but Bell put her hand over the table and held Macallan's lightly. 'Wait. Quid pro quo. I never reveal sources,

206

but this is about more than the two of us and so-called careers.'

Macallan smiled for a moment. 'Don't tell me you're getting soft. What's happening to us? I'm a shadow of my former self and Jacquie Bell is warm and caring.'

Bell got the piss-take and straightened up. 'Look, just so you know that fucking creep Ricky Swan feeds me the occasional corpse and a lurid story to go with it. He's told me about the recordings he's got, and for a reporter it could be gold dust, but as I say, the man's a creep and up to his eyes in the hooker business. I'll play him along for the moment and run anything past you first if he starts to spew the stuff up. I know he must be looking for some favour from you after the incident in Leith, and he's obviously upset some serious people.'

'Serious is an understatement. I can't tell you why he's in bother because it really could put people at risk.'

'That's not a problem, and just let me know what you need when you need it.'

'Thanks, that could be a big help.' She gripped her friend's hand that bit tighter and told her it was time to go. They shared a taxi but didn't say much till they arrived outside Macallan's flat, where Bell gave Macallan a hug and told her to be careful. As the taxi pulled away she turned and waved from the rear window.

Once she was inside Macallan pulled her clothes off and threw them in a pile on the chair next to her bed. It was way before her usual bedtime but she was out cold about thirty seconds after her head hit the pillow. She hadn't even noticed the text from Jack saying that he loved her and they were both missing her.

While Macallan slept, Richter tried to stay awake. Her parents had been with her most of the day and she'd endeavoured to explain to them what she was feeling.

When she'd got the news that they were coming to Scotland she'd ached to be close to them and tell them how frightened she'd been. The reality had been difficult; she almost felt anger at their confusion, shock and inability to accept that such things could happen to their child. When they left she'd felt that something precious had been broken with the people she loved most in the world. She was drained and exhausted but didn't want to sleep, to be visited by the terrible dreams that haunted her every night. The doctor had agreed that she could be discharged after another few days' assessment and the thought of facing the world terrified her. She sat up in the bed hoping she could stay awake, but it was impossible to keep her eyes open, and she gradually drifted off into her waiting dreams.

She was back on the long empty beach and the heat was unbearable. This time the sun filled half the sky and blazed red, its surface crawling with fire as it hung just above the horizon. It was as if her skin was burning.

She turned away from it and stared at the vast empty desert behind her. It was always empty – nothing more than a rock-strewn wasteland – but there was a change. The whole length of the horizon was topped by a pitch-black line of cloud moving slowly towards her.

She turned round again; although the sea frightened her she walked towards the water's edge and noticed the small single-mast boat waiting a few yards from the shore. Richter groaned when she saw the two men sitting front and aft on the boat, staring towards her. They were motionless; lidless eyes bulging from the dull grey pallor of their faces; their clothes were rancid and too big for their frames.

She tried to scream for help but although her mouth stretched wide nothing came out. There wasn't a sound from the approaching storm behind her or the sea in front of her. It was a world of utter silence. She tried to run along the beach to escape but the sand sucked her legs up to the knees and she could barely move.

Pulling her legs free, she kneeled and gasped for breath, dreading what was coming for her. When she'd struggled to her feet she looked around, and once more uttered a soundless scream as she realised the small boat was now on the beach. The two men hadn't moved and she saw they were in decay. She realised it was the two men from the *Brighter Dawn*.

24

Crazy Horse McMartin was fucked if he was going to let the situation lie. Two of his team had been through to see Brenda, who told them what had happened but added the lie that the bastard who'd attacked her got her from behind. She warned them to wait till she was back in the game and she'd take care of the situation herself.

'Is she fuckin' mental?' he asked the boys who'd spoken to her and dreaded giving her brother the feedback. It was a daft question because Brenda could be described as nothing but mental, but there was no way they could say that to her brother. 'How the fuck can we wait? That bastard down in Newcastle thinks we're fuckin' amateurs; well we'll show him how we do it in Glasgow. Then it's the malky for these Edinburgh cunts. Do you hear me?' Crazy Horse was starting to froth at the mouth and that meant nothing but bad news. They knew that it was all going tits-up, but who the fuck could they complain to? 'I'll do the pimp. Then I'll do the Flemings, and then I'll gob in Handyside's fuckin' eye. What do you think, boys?'

'Nice one. That'll show the cunts.' They said it but really thought it was a shite idea.

'Do you realise the boy we took on after your recommendation was an undercover?'

Swan was so barely awake he wasn't even conscious of having picked up his mobile when it rang, which meant he was a bit thrown by the angry voice in his ear, and it took him more than a few moments to work out who was on the other end. When, at last, the neurons in his brain started to communicate properly and he worked out it was Eddie Fleming his system went into overdrive and he started gabbling. All he wanted to do was give him the line that the man had been introduced by a Belfast punter, who seemed to have disappeared off the radar, and hope Eddie would be satisfied and leave him alone.

'You know me – what the fuck would I do with that shite?' he said. 'I was nearly killed by the fuckin' Weegies, so that explains it. You need to square it with them, for old times' sake. I'll make it worth your while. I've had to hire a couple of fuckin' minders to look after me.'

'No worries,' Eddie replied. 'I knew there had to be an explanation and you go a long way back with this family. Leave it with me and I'll get back to you once I've squared it up.'

Eddie put the phone down and decided he was going to kill Swan as soon as possible – he knew he was lying through his teeth. There might be a couple of heavies but they'd find a way. He called his brother Pat and Billy Drew and told them to put the job together. Later the same day they'd action a couple of boys from their team to watch the grass and find the best time and place to get to him.

They weren't to know that McMartin had exactly the same idea and intention, and that he planned to take

211

care of the twins. Glasgow was carved up, but he'd seen weakness in the Flemings. All the McMartins had to do was burn them out and then they would have the whole market on the east side of the country.

Eddie felt they were about to get back on course and that taking Swan out would send everyone the message that they'd cleaned up their own mess and the McMartins could stay in their own shithole. The twins kept repeating the same mistake though and had missed something important, which meant they were at risk from more than the McMartins.

Swan shook his head and wondered whether Fleming had bought it. He checked his reflection in the en suite mirror, thought he still looked like shit and wondered whether he should invest in a toupee. Gnasher padded in behind him and nuzzled his master's leg.

'Let's go and see the gorillas.' Swan opened the front door and beckoned them in.

They were an unusual pair – identical twins – and Swan wondered what their mother had done to deserve not one but two ugly-looking bastards. Tam and Stan Bonnar were a year off thirty, born and brought up in Granton and made their living as bouncers and through a bit of crime. They still lived with their mother, who saw nothing but good in her boys, and were always available if someone needed a debt collected or some revenge dished out. The mother had given her all to bring them up after their old man had been killed in a factory accident when they were still in primary school, and they adored her for that effort. School had been a waste of taxpayers' money, but what they did like was boxing and martial arts. They were under six foot, but layers of hard muscle made them seem bigger. No one could ever remember either of them being involved with a woman, but then no one cared to question their sexuality, at least to their faces. Swan was paying them top dollar, but with his problems getting out of hand he needed this level of protection. If the McMartins came back they'd need a fucking bazooka to get through the Bonnar boys.

'How're we doing today, guys?' Swan said it cheerfully; he liked the idea of giving orders to a pair of violent bastards.

'Good,' Stan answered (he tended to do all the talking, which wasn't much). The twins loved dogs and Gnasher had taken to them big time. The spoodle was staring plaintively up at the twins hoping for some attention. Stan got down on one knee and let Gnasher lick his face for a minute, which annoyed Swan.

'Let's get down to the sauna. Need to get things up and running or I'll lose some of the regulars.'

On the way he stopped to buy the paper he bought every day but barely read and twenty cigarettes to make absolutely sure he'd never reach old age. His body was already there. When he saw the story about Richter and the suggestion that there might be other women involved he knew a bad situation was getting out of hand. He called Eddie back.

'Have you seen the headlines?'

'Nothing to worry about, Ricky.' He still sounded like Swan's best pal. 'There's hee-haw to find and we're sound.'

'Did you manage to speak to the man through the west?' Swan squeezed his eyes shut waiting for the answer.

'I've set up a meeting with him. It sounds like we can work it out.' Eddie smiled at his brother and Drew as he gave out the lie.

Swan breathed a sigh; he might just get through the crisis. 'What about his fuckin' sister though?'

'Why don't you put out a contract on Cue Ball as a gesture of goodwill? That should do it, and if they find him she can go and finish the job herself if it makes her happy.'

Eddie put the phone down and slapped a high five with his brother, oblivious to the fact that they were in as much danger as the man on the other end of the phone. Drew didn't see anything funny. As far as he was concerned he was working with two young men who were good, but maybe not good enough for the top league.

'Let's get down to it, boys, and take care of Ricky Swan.' Drew had a plan, and if it worked it would clear up all their problems and unfinished business. He explained that trying to get through the Bonnars during business hours would be messy at best.

'We need to get the wee bastard when he's on his own. When the boys have checked his routine for a couple of days we'll go for it. My idea is to let him get back to his place at night and then make sure the Bonnars are off home. The story is that Ricky's place is alarmed with cameras outside, but he's pissed most nights so by the time he gets home he forgets to switch the thing on.'

'It's dodgy trying to do him in his place then, Billy?'

Drew nodded. 'We do him in the sauna. It's simple: let him get back to his place, see the Bonnars home and then Ricky boy gets a call from the cops that the alarm's gone off at the sauna and he's the key holder. For one night, and one night only ... we're the cops. He has to come.'

'It might just work!' Eddie liked the simplicity of the plan – the simple ones were always the best.

'All we need to do is wait and grab him when he arrives. If there's any problem we stay back and find another way. We need to get it done pronto and then you can make your peace with the man down the road. That doesn't apply to the McMartins; once Ricky is off the programme then we need to sort them out. They want your business, it's as simple as that.'

The Flemings saw the logic and agreed. They would push their boys to get the homework done on Swan and then take their shot at the grassin' wee bastard who'd nearly got them killed.

'Any progress with your contacts in the phone companies to try and track Barclay?'

Eddie could have done without the hassle, but he needed Drew and had invested in getting him the information he wanted.

'Better than that, Billy. Got a bent private detective on it. Ex-CID and doing the work on the phones. Signs are that Barclay still calls his wife from time to time so you might get a shot at him after all.'

'I need this; don't let me down.' He said it like he meant it. Drew tended to only do serious statements; he'd stopped doing humour a long time ago when there was still something to laugh at. Eddie was paying Drew's wages but he wondered if the man realised who the boss was.

25

Macallan was in O'Connor's office by 7.30 a.m. and was anxious to get to the meeting with Northumbria Police in their HQ at Ponteland. McGovern had booked a car for that morning, but she wanted to welcome Thompson and Young to the team before they set off. Young wasn't known as 'The Brain' for nothing, and they were going to need her in the hunt for an answer to the question of what had happened to Dixie Deans and the young women who'd died on the *Brighter Dawn*. Macallan explained to O'Connor that she'd taken full control as the coordinator for the incident on the boat, the missing UC and the attack on Ricky Swan.

'It's a lot to ask, Grace, I know, but we can't separate the problems and no doubt they're all linked. This threat from Ricky Swan – what do you think?'

'It's straightforward as far as the investigation is concerned. Whether he dishes some dirt on people who asked for it or not won't make any difference to what I do. I'm no politician and won't be distracted by it unless people make it a problem for me. If I find evidence that Swan has been involved in trafficking women then he gets a pull ... same rules apply.' Macallan knew that was probably too simplistic a statement because in the real world of rolling news, scandal could and did destabilise investigations. Swan was a registered informant so it didn't take a lot of imagination to see the headlines if a source was up to his arse in the same sewer as the people they were chasing. The Met alone was sinking under the weight of enquiries into their dealings with the press, phone hacking, institutional racism and anything else the politicians could throw at it. Plebgate must have made the Commissioner want to bury his head under a pillow and weep, and the police were now available for a kicking 24/7, which was something O'Connor knew better than Macallan. That was her weakness (or strength, depending on how people looked at it): she lacked a political radar – or refused to have one. In the modern police force senior officers couldn't work in isolation – the taxpayer demanded cooperation among the public agencies.

'You have full control of the investigation, but if there's fallout from Swan let me help you. You do what you do and I'll deal with the wolves at the door.' He grinned and told her he had to go to the morning meet with senior staff, who probably had one or two wolves in their ranks.

She stood up and thanked him, and she meant it. It was a bonus if he took that weight off her shoulders, leaving her to try to find the answers to the real problems she was handling.

'One thing...' He'd picked up his papers, ready to go. 'Everything okay with Jacquie? I see she's started to run the stories.'

'Ah, she did manage to get her copy submitted in time last night then. It's sorted and we'll drop it in gradually; she's going to ramp it up tomorrow about the other girls. We have Ingrid's statement and no reason to disbelieve her account.'

Young and Thompson were waiting, and as Macallan passed McGovern he tapped his watch, knowing she always had a problem with punctuality through spinning too many plates at the same time. She shook their hands, resisting the temptation to give them a hug, but she was very glad to see them arrive. Young was going to Ponteland with them and Macallan asked her for a quiet minute with Thompson. She closed the door behind the analyst and looked round at the young woman who'd caused her a problem when she'd first arrived but had learned the hard way where her priorities lay.

'Are you okay being here? I know you asked for a move but this is going to be tough and probably more than a bit messy.'

'I'm happy, honestly; just tell me what you want me to do.'

'Jimmy is going to set up some surveillance operations on the Flemings when we get back up the road. The field intelligence officers are out working on getting the job started and we should be ready in a day or two. I want you fully involved in the investigations and surveillance; if you're up for it you can head one of the teams. How does that sound?' She didn't need to ask that last question – Thompson's expression gave Macallan all the answer she needed.

'That's great,' Macallan said. 'We need to go. Get over to Leith. Start reading the files and get yourself up to speed with the case. There's a lot to do, and I want the team properly briefed and ready to go when we push the button.'

Macallan headed for the door, hoping she'd made the right decision bringing in Thompson after what had happened. She'd been seriously burned, but if there was a positive it was that apart from some signs on her lower neck the damage was to her body and not her face.

Mindful of the time, the two police officers plus analyst hurried to the car for the drive down to Ponteland: territory of footballers and fat cats, home to the Northumbria force HQ and a safe distance from unwanted attention and the good people of Newcastle.

Macallan was quiet on the journey as she sat spinning all the problems and options through her head. She was still annoyed at herself for missing the text the previous night and the chance to call Jack before she'd gone to bed. The busy day followed by drinks with Bell, even though they'd only been in the early evening, was too close to the life she thought she'd left behind and she promised herself to be careful. Her life had proved how easy it was to lose something precious and she wasn't going to let that happen with Jack.

Before she'd left for her meeting with O'Connor she'd sent a text telling him she was counting down the days till they were together again. Living with her when she was in the middle of an investigation was going to test them, but there was no going back now.

26

When they arrived at Ponteland they were welcomed by DS Tony Harrison, who with his unmistakable London East End accent was clearly a long way from home.

'Did ten years in the Met, came up here to arrest some villains when I was in the Regional Crime Squad and met this local lady who asked me to marry her. I've spent all my time trying to civilise the local natives, but it's not easy.'

Harrison was a bear of a man who seemed to smile and laugh easily. It was hard not to like him and Macallan relaxed. The reception they'd receive from other forces was always a lottery. The police service is made up of human beings and you could never be sure which kind would be your host for the day. There was no doubt from the off though that Harrison was onside and there to do the job.

He introduced his senior analyst, who was the equivalent of Felicity Young and a DI from criminal intelligence, and then they squeezed themselves into a room that just about held them all. Harrison apologised, but they all knew that there was never enough space in any police building and it was a permanent battle trying to find a room for any private business.

They did the small talk and introductions as their host poured tea into a collection of seriously chipped mugs then Harrison got down to the real business of the day. 'First things first: as you know, we've already been providing intelligence in response to the requests from your guys investigating the girl on the beach and the missing UC. We'll give you every assistance because at the root of this is Pete Handyside, and we want him as much as you do.'

'Thanks, and if it's okay with you, I'll give you a rundown on what we have so far.' Macallan pulled out her file; she'd made copies of the briefing notes for Harrison and his team. The atmosphere in the room was confident and there already seemed to be a mood for cooperation at all levels.

Before Macallan continued Harrison broke in again and she saw the smile had dropped from his face. 'One thing I need to tell you: what's said in here stays in here. We have a problem. As you know, Frankie Dillon, who was on the *Brighter Dawn* that night, was an ex-detective and a disgrace to the job. He was eventually locked up and I was involved in that particular case. But when he was released he spent time and a lot of Handyside's money on recruiting other bent officers. As we speak, I can tell you that Handyside has someone else inside this force who has access to criminal intelligence.'

Macallan sat back and, although she didn't need the news, it never came as too much of a surprise. The top tier of criminals couldn't compete unless they invested heavily in corrupting officials, whether it was local politicians, civil servants or, increasingly, sources inside the telecommunications companies. Bent lawyers and accountants were normally easy enough to find, but the most successful organised crime teams always had a broad range of paid sources. Someone inside law enforcement was an absolute priority, and from a business point of view was invariably cost-efficient. Drug raids were a nuisance, and it was always better to know when they were coming. Just toss the friendly cop the odd low-level twat dealer plus a fat envelope and everyone was a winner – apart from the twat.

'Does it compromise this case?' Macallan prayed he'd give her some hope.

'The problem is that we have no idea at the moment who it is, but there is an operation in place to try to identify the source. However, what I propose is that any sensitive request you have is channelled through the people in this room. Handyside will know we're looking at his operation so we keep general enquiries going through the main system and that way we don't spook them unnecessarily. Whoever is leaking will expect to see enquiries from your end to us and vice versa.'

'That sounds good to me,' Macallan said, figuring it might work to their advantage. She kept her thoughts to herself but knew that feeding what was known in the trade as disinformation into the system could be a useful tactic. Slightly on the edge, legally, but always worth considering.

She looked round the table. There was general agreement, and they decided that the two senior analysts would have direct contact during the life of the operation. All correspondence between any of them would be copied into Harrison and Macallan.

Macallan spoke again and felt the anticipation of an arrest stir the old instincts. 'The other issue that we need to get underway is to find Alan Hunter and Frankie Dillon and bring them in again when we're ready. I anticipate that we'll soon have enough evidence with Ingrid Richter's statement and, hopefully, some DNA from the boat. If we can confirm the presence of the other girls it adds to the evidence chain.'

'Have you found out any more about the other girls on the boat?' Harrison asked.

'We're trying through Europol but the truth is that depending on where they came from and what their backgrounds were, we might never find out. They picked the wrong one with Ingrid. She comes from a middle-class family and had already been reported missing.'

Harrison took a moment and looked at his colleagues before answering. 'We anticipated that you would want to see Hunter and Dillon, but they're off the radar. Gone. There's no sign of them at their home or usual haunts. No phone traffic and we've tasked our sources to report sightings, but zilch coming back.'

'What's your guess?' Macallan said, feeling her optimism dipping again.

'I know Pete Handyside and have taken him on numerous times over the years. You have to respect him – he's smart and a real professional. What marks him out is his business acumen, and he never hesitates when something has to be done. The man doesn't flinch. Given what happened on the boat and the fact that a girl survived … my guess is that he got rid of them. They fucked up. That's how he works. The only people he trusts are his wife and his right-hand man, Maxi Turner. Anyone else is disposable if there's a business case.'

Young listened intently to Harrison and, as always, she doodled and made notes. It occurred to her that Harrison seemed to have made the classic mistake she'd seen committed so often by senior detectives: he couldn't let go. A world full of problems and they obsessed about the one man they couldn't put away. The personal references to Handyside, the years of failing to take him: that had the potential to burn out the best detectives once they lost focus. She scribbled 'too close to the problem' on her pad.

Macallan shook her head, realising they'd just taken several steps backwards. 'Eric Gunderson?' She knew the answer before it was given.

'It was initially treated as an accident because that's not an unknown end for deep-sea fishermen. However he turned up in the river at the same time they disappeared so we have to presume it's connected. I've asked the CID to make fresh enquiries.' Harrison sat back, knowing that what he'd disclosed so far was a body blow to the Scottish team. Dead and, worse still, missing-presumed-dead suspects were a nightmare for an investigation team.

'Not sure where this leaves us and we'll have to think it through. I know it won't do any good, but if we wanted to see Handyside do you think he'd go for it? We know they worked for him and there'd be nothing wrong with approaching him as a voluntary witness.' Macallan thought there might be a problem with the proposal as they were on Harrison's ground. Senior detectives could be sensitive about foreigners trampling all over their patch and upsetting their criminals, but he looked like he'd expected the request.

'He would, in the same way you want to see what you're dealing with. It's the same for him. Most of them at that level will tell you to fuck off if you don't have a warrant. Not Pete – he's polite, and you'll think you're with the wrong person. He doesn't fit the usual profiles – looks a bit of a throwback to another age and would be more at home working in the City or behind a desk.'

She turned to McGovern, who shrugged, knowing what the question was.

'Let's do it then and see if we can get him today. Felicity, why don't you go through what you've got here and see if there's anything we can take back up the road? Is that okay with you, Tony?'

His warm smile came back. 'They did one of ours and, trust me – you'll get whatever you need from this force. I'll make the call to Handyside and see if I can set it up. Anything else?'

Macallan explained that they were sure there had been spotters and that the cigarette ends McGovern had noticed should give them a DNA profile.

'Good enough, and might be a break for you.'

Given what they'd learned at the meeting, that was probably more optimistic than realistic. Whoever had watched the events at Eyemouth Harbour were up to their necks, no doubt, but proving they had committed any crime was near impossible. If they were pros they just needed to sit tight and wait on their lawyer doing his or her job.

As Harrison and his team left the room, Macallan's phone came to life. It was a Fettes number, and when she answered it turned out to be O'Connor. 'Just a heads-up. Ingrid insisted on discharging herself today and booked into a hotel with her parents. They have a family suite so she'll not be on her own, and she's agreed to attend as a day patient for her psychological assessment and treatment. They don't want a cop sitting on their door – they think it'll just attract attention and the press. There's nothing we can do to stop her, but the docs are very concerned about her ability to cope with her memories.'

'I don't like it, but I agree that we can't force her. Can we stick a couple of uniforms near the hotel just in case?'

'It's taken care of – they're already in place. Do you want anything else done?'

'Not at the moment; we'll be back up the road tonight and I might go and see her in the morning, although I want to get the Flemings in.' She put the phone down and felt a knot of worry squeeze her gut as she told McGovern what had happened.

Harrison came back into the room fifteen minutes later and sat opposite Macallan. 'He's up for it and, as always, couldn't be more polite. Quote: "I'll do anything to help the police." He's suggested you see him at home, and at the end of the day if we're not detaining him we might as well go along with that, but be careful what you say. Most of our modern gangsters like to bug their homes as much as we do. Do you want a couple of our local boys to stay close to you?'

'It's fine. Jimmy here is Scotland's answer to Rocky Balboa and I don't intend to have more than a short meet with the man.' She shook hands with Tony Harrison, feeling that at least they had an ally on Handyside's home turf. That couldn't do any harm.

27

As Macallan walked between the manicured lawns to the door of Handyside's home, she had to admit it had style. Understated, and the beautiful twenty-five-year-old Jag parked outside looked perfectly at home. Handyside answered the door dressed in a sparkling white shirt, open at the neck, and chinos that had been perfectly tailored. It was supposed to be a casual look, but it showed a great deal of care and he was groomed perfectly. He apologised that his wife had to go out earlier on, which wasn't quite the truth. She knew how he worked; he'd told her to go to their gym and he'd meet her there in an hour. His wife never questioned him, but he saw the worried lines round her eyes and had drawn her close to him before she'd left the house.

'I've told you what to do if needs be, now stop worrying and go work up a sweat. I've arranged a babysitter and we're going out for dinner tonight.'

It wasn't up for argument, but she'd sensed that their life was about to change and that there was nothing she could do about it. She just had to trust that whatever happened, he would do everything in his power to protect her and their infant children, and if it came to it, she was certain that he would sacrifice himself if he was forced into a decision on their future.

The interior of the house had the same feel as the outside. Tasteful but spare, and the balance was perfect. For a moment Macallan imagined she might live in something like this some day with Jack and Adam. She allowed herself a hint of a smile, thinking that at least it proved Handyside had good taste. She got what Harrison had told them – it simply didn't feel like they were in the company of a man with such a fearsome criminal reputation. He was polite, and it was obvious that he would be easy to underestimate without prior knowledge. He was just as courteous with McGovern as he was with Macallan, although he couldn't have missed the ice-cold non-verbals McGovern was dripping all over the carpet.

Handyside showed the detectives into a spacious lounge furnished with an unusual mix of old and new pieces. It took a real eye to make it work and Macallan had the feeling that this was down to the imagination of this unusual man rather than his wife, unless it was a well-paid interior designer. Something about the layout and care for space and light matched up with Handyside, who smiled warmly at the two detectives. The fact that he knew they suspected him of being involved in the murders of the women on the *Brighter Dawn* and the UC didn't raise his blood pressure by a single notch. This was his way of life: confrontations with the law had to be dealt with as part of the business, and as long as he'd done his job, the odds were that he'd survive to see his old age. It was all about staying focused and having a plan B – and plan C if necessary. He had nothing but contempt for most of the criminal bosses he encountered, who were no more than aggressive animals that acted on instinct. Eventually most of them paid a heavy price for their stupidity and greed. The ones he'd cleared from his path to take his place at the top of the hill certainly fell into that category. There was always the chance of sheer bad luck wrecking what he'd built up, but he'd even factored that into what he liked to think of as his war plans.

In any case, for Pete Handyside there was no point in worrying about something he couldn't control. He put out his hand to Macallan, who wasn't expecting the gesture; it was soft yet seemed to hold back on a deep reserve of physical power.

McGovern hesitated when it was offered his way, but gave it a try and thought he could mash the gangster's knuckles a bit then enjoy watching him twitch. Handyside looked a good couple of stone lighter than the detective and McGovern waited for a reaction. It never came, and he was thrown when the pressure he applied was equalled by Handyside, who stared intently at the surprise in the detective's eyes. McGovern realised that if Handyside wanted to, he could go all the way till his fingers broke under the strain. It was as if the man was enjoying a sport where the opposition just wasn't in the game. Handyside's expression was like a curious predator playing with a catch that wasn't even worth eating, and in that crude moment, Handyside taught McGovern that he was a man who might not deserve his affection but certainly deserved his respect.

Macallan saw it and felt a moment of pity for her DCI, who wasn't used to being on the wrong end of a physical challenge. McGovern's face had paled and the contrast with Handyside's cool demeanour was stark as they unlocked their hands.

Macallan thought again how accurate Harrison had been with his assessment of Handyside. He acted the perfect gentleman, the soft voice warm and the North-east tones restrained, and every part of the lounge held expensively framed photographs of a petite, attractive woman side by side with Handyside through a range of ages all the way up from the smiling young couple who'd just been married. Pride of place above the fireplace was a silver-framed picture of two laughing infant boys. It was impossible not to react to the feeling that a family who cared for each other lived in this house and without thinking Macallan picked up the photograph of the boys and tried to imagine Adam in a few short years.

'Handsome boys. You must be very proud.'

She noticed the space between McGovern's eyes scrunch in a 'what the fuck are you doing?' look. Macallan ignored it, knowing that acting the officious bastard just wouldn't work with a gangster who controlled the whole of the North-east through a potent mix of will and intelligence. They were there to spar, Handyside knew it, and he accepted that anything that happened on both sides was an act, at least for the time being. This was all about feeling each other out and deciding what tactics they'd pick before the real fight.

'I am, Superintendent. A few years ago I would have laughed at the idea that I would end up the doting father, but that's exactly what's happened. In those days I went off the rails a bit, but you know that already. What about you?'

'Baby boy. Same for me – sometimes I have to pinch myself that it actually happened.'

McGovern realised what was going on and eased back into his seat. He'd seen her do this thing before. Some people would have sneered at this form of verbal intimacy with a man like Handyside, but Macallan worked her designs instinctively. It hadn't been taught in detective training because there was no way to teach it. She reacted to deep instincts and she'd once told him that

230

it was as if she needed to communicate with the killers on more than one wavelength, to feel where they really lived and breathed. Harkins used to joke that it was her equivalent of Spock's Vulcan mind probe. Whatever it was though, McGovern knew he couldn't tap into the unspoken conversation that was taking place at the same time as the polite exchanges about their offspring.

Although McGovern had already dropped into a seat without asking, Macallan waited for an invitation to sit; she wanted to match her host in courtesy. He smiled again and stretched his hand palm up towards an antique chair. Handyside took the seat opposite her, side on to McGovern, who now had a ringside view of the exchanges between the detective and the man who (legend had it) could take the decision to kill as if he were ordering a coffee; the same man who smiled warmly from the family pictures spread all over the room.

'Now tell me, Superintendent, what is it I can do for you? I appreciate it has to be about Alan and Frankie. I read the papers; this thing with the girl on the beach is hard to take in. The fact that they occasionally did some work for me is upsetting to say the least.'

'Do you know where they are?' Macallan asked the question, but she knew they were still circling, probing for weak spots, and that the answers she wanted would not come at this meeting. It didn't matter; she was just using every sense in her body and mind to assess Handyside's reactions.

'I wish I knew, and if I did I'd make sure you had access to them. Is there any way I can help you?' He looked every inch the concerned citizen and it started to chew on Macallan's nerve ends.

'When did you last see them? That could be important for us. As far as we know they disappeared the evening after they were detained in Eyemouth. No one appears to have confirmed a sighting of them since then.' Macallan was certain that they had died the same night that Gunderson had taken a header into the Tyne. Young had confirmed that their registered phones had stopped functioning about the same time.

She waited for a response and began to wish that they'd left this meeting for another day. Handyside was playing it like a trained actor and they weren't going to achieve what they'd come for. She couldn't read him, and they certainly couldn't put fear in him. It was written all over McGovern; he was a picture of discomfort and clearly just wanted to get out of there.

'The last time I saw them was the day after the incident on the boat. As I mentioned, they do some part-time work for me, mainly a bit of driving and delivery. I heard what had happened and was furious with them. I have a number of businesses in Tyneside and can do without this kind of thing. You must know that the press have given me a hard enough time in the past with allegations that have never been proved. The bottom line is that I told them they were finished working for me. Frankie Dillon was the one that really got to me – an ex-policeman who no one wanted when he came out of prison and I gave him a chance – but there you go, Superintendent, we all live and learn.'

He sat back in his chair; he'd delivered his lines perfectly. Macallan looked towards McGovern, reminding herself that they'd promised this meeting would be short and they had to be careful to avoid treating him as a suspect. If they did, a lawyer would rip into them at any trial. That had been her intention, but she was disturbed by the whole act in these tasteful surroundings all paid for in other people's misery.

There was also the small humiliation of having McGovern in front of her as Handyside handed out his lesson to both of them. They were being played; Macallan had a nagging feeling that he was too well prepared and had known all about them before they arrived. Her thoughts strayed to what Richter had described and the likelihood that the man opposite was responsible in some way. At the very least he'd probably given the order to kill the young women on the boat. If Dixie Deans had been exposed then he was already dead and Handyside must have at least some knowledge of what had happened to the missing officer. And if that was the case then the UC's body was lying unmarked and a long way from home. His distraught mother might spend the rest of her life wondering what had happened to her youngest son. It was too much for Macallan to continue the play-acting and her patience drained away as if a tap had been turned on all the way.

'When we find them the likelihood is that they'll be charged with multiple homicides. They're only part of it. Eric Gunderson died near enough the same time they went missing. Do you think that's coincidence?'

For a moment something dark touched Handyside's expression and his smile faded before he straightened his back and nodded. He looked at McGovern, who stared back, conveying nothing but barely concealed contempt.

'I'm not the detective, but I wonder what you're implying, Superintendent. Am I a suspect?' He'd regained his composure, but just for a moment he'd exposed the man she was looking for. It was almost nothing, but it proved he was human, and although he might be careful, somewhere along the line there would be something she could exploit. Taking Pete Handyside head-on was going to be a waste of time; it was the men around him who would give up the answers that would lead right back to his door. There was no reason to be confident, but Macallan felt in her gut that he would fall;

233

what he'd done required an answer, and she wanted to deliver it in person.

'You don't look that worried, Mr Handyside, but maybe you should be.'

McGovern shifted in his chair, knowing Macallan was going too far. She'd lost her script and had shown her hand far too early. It was time to back off; Handyside had scored his second small victory by making her deviate from her plan.

Macallan saw McGovern's disapproving look, knew exactly what it meant and cursed herself for giving in to her base instincts. Handyside had taken control of the situation from the moment they'd walked into his home and she hadn't known it till they'd been outmanoeuvred.

'I just wanted to make sure that you know that we want them for murder and that I could count on your help if needs be. I'm sure we'll meet again, Mr Handyside. Hopefully sooner rather than later.' She managed to slip back into character, although the damage had been done. If he was recording then it would be thrown at her in court that there had been a suggestion that he was a suspect without any form of caution. What seemed such a trivial matter on the surface could be a powerful technical point for a defence advocate.

'I expect we will; perhaps when you have some answers to this puzzle. I hope you don't mind, but before you came into my home I thought I'd Google your name. Quite impressive. I said to one of my guys that I think whoever you're after should be worried.'

He gave her full eye contact and Macallan decided that he was one of the most convincing liars she'd ever come across. Somehow or other he was able to control his non-verbals in a way that made him almost impossible to read, which meant he was special – no doubt about it – and she wouldn't forget it, no matter what happened during the rest of the investigation. She saw a man who probably knew most of their moves already. That he had someone at the heart of criminal intelligence just made it worse.

The friendly smile was back in place now he was satisfied that he'd shown his visitors he was no ordinary villain and they would need to think carefully if they hoped to take him out of the game. There was enough in what had been said for him to know that he was safe for the time being, and if there had been any problems she would have dropped it on him by now. The senior detective had lost her cool for a moment and that usually meant they were a long way short on evidence. In one way though it didn't make any difference because he saw something in Macallan that concerned him, and he had the feeling that they were tied into a conflict with each other where one of them was going to lose badly. She'd displayed some special qualities in Northern Ireland, and he knew that only a fool would think there was a possibility of buying her off.

When they got back in the car Macallan turned to McGovern and put her hand on his forearm. 'Sorry about that. I know he's our man and I went too far so he won that little round, but no real damage done. The problem is that he's not going to come easy and somehow we have to find where he's made his mistake. They all do. If not him then one of his team. Trust me.'

'Okay – you're the boss, thank God. That bastard gives me the creeps.' McGovern shook his head; the admission was rare and he couldn't remember another man having that effect on him before. Handyside should never have been a match physically, but he was and had proven that with a simple handshake. Then there was the way he'd stared into the detective's eyes … there was something deep and poisonous there. McGovern couldn't touch it or see what it was, but Pete Handyside frightened him.

'Never thought I'd hear Jimmy McGovern admit that one.' She saw the troubled confusion in his eyes and knew that a man who'd never backed off in his life had just faced his moment of truth.

'Neither did I.' He tried to remember again, as he turned the ignition key, how long he had to go to retirement. It was nonsense, because McGovern loved the job, but the retirement date always provided a moment of comfort when things went wrong.

'Well we'll go back and see Harrison and pretend that we actually achieved something today, pick up Felicity and have a meal down here before we head up the road. First thing in the morning we pick up the Flemings, but this time as suspects and give them the full bhoona. How does that sound?'

Macallan was doing her best to lighten the mood, but the meeting with Handyside had been sobering and they were both going to spend too many of what should have been their sleeping hours thinking about him.

Handyside stood at the bay window with the phone to his ear and watched the car carrying the two detectives drive off. 'I want to know every move she makes against me.'

'Of course; she's easily handled, and the day we can't take care of a few Jock cops then there's something wrong.' The voice on the other end of the line tried to sound confident, but they were trying to fool the wrong man. Handyside rarely swore, but he didn't need to put up any act with the man on the other end of the line whose house in Italy and very comfortable lifestyle he had been financing for years. It was payback time.

'Listen to me, you fucking idiot. I own you, your house, your wife, your family and your police career. Do your

236

job or you go to jail or in the ground. Either way, you're fucked if I decide you're fucked. You obviously haven't even taken the time to research this one. Have you seen her record? Unlike you, my friend, it's real. Get to it.'

He cut the call without waiting for an answer, picked up his bag and headed for the gym to be with his wife.

Later on that evening they sat in a decent Indian restaurant and managed to neck a few beers, which brought some relief from the job and thoughts of the hard days to come. Macallan was beginning to look forward to getting the Flemings hauled in for interview. There was always the possibility of a break. Sometimes it happened that way; just when you thought there was no way ahead, a wee lucky fell into your lap. They couldn't know as they ate and drank that events in Edinburgh were spinning out of control and the first winds in a perfect storm of events were whipping through the streets of the capital.

28

As Macallan finished off her meal she felt as if the damp mood left from their meeting with Handyside had been washed away with the beer. It was, however, mostly down to Young, who was ever the optimist and buzzing with ideas after talking with her equivalent number from Northumbria Police. McGovern prayed that she wouldn't start talking hypotheses, because her brain worked on a different level to the detectives who sweated at the front end of the line.

Macallan suddenly felt waves of tiredness flood her and wished they didn't have the drive back up to Edinburgh in front of them. Any other time they would have stayed the night, but there was too much to be done. They had to get the Flemings in, even if all they achieved was giving them a hard time and searching their homes before kicking them back onto the street. If nothing else it would be a starting point for the surveillance op on the twins, which was almost ready to go. To add to the hassle, the journey back up to Edinburgh wouldn't be quick. The analyst had offered to stay off the booze and drive, but she was possibly the slowest and worst driver in the world. Harkins refused to ever let her have the wheel, even though they were in a relationship and a result of his injuries was that he still found driving difficult.

Young had started to work on the phone analysis and it was revealing an interesting pattern of contacts. Despite Eddie Fleming having been warned by Handyside about the need for clean phones before the job, he hadn't been quite careful enough. He'd got hold of a fresh one but made a call to Swan, who was a lynchpin for the trafficking of women into and through Scotland. Swan knew the police loved up-to-date info on gangsters' numbers and his handlers had been complaining about his lack of effort recently. Fleming's number was a nice little titbit that would keep them off his back for a while. It would never have occurred to him that further down the line that small piece of intelligence would be seized on by an analyst and contribute to a chain of events that would tear down a number of lives, including his own. Like so many things in Swan's life, he'd managed another massive fuck-up by playing a game he'd never really understood.

Young had picked up Fleming's new number on an intelligence report and spotted that it wasn't registered to him. That had interested her, and she'd used it as a starting point for one of her many lines of analysis. She'd noticed that he continued to make his normal stream of calls from his registered phone and only the occasional one from the number that had come from Swan's handlers. When she'd seen the pattern of calls before and after the Eyemouth incident it had brought a smile to her face. She'd dug into the numbers Fleming had called and noticed one that had no trace on a subscriber. The resulting tremor in her gut was the excitement of realising that she'd hit on something and just needed to methodically follow the trail of calls. One of the phones he'd contacted had been in the Newcastle area at the time they were all interested in so she'd followed the trail from that phone and identified calls to unregistered numbers that had been in the Eyemouth area on the night the *Brighter Dawn* had sailed into the harbour.

She knew she was onto something but wasn't quite ready to tell Macallan yet. It was vital to be sure and not give the detectives false trails and equally false hope. None of it would put Pete Handyside in the dock, but Macallan was right, there was always an opening somewhere and you just had to find it, rip the bastard open and dig about in the entrails.

Handyside's team were professional and took precautions like exchanging their mobiles with each other on a regular basis because they knew that would completely distort the picture the police thought they were looking at. They knew the major crime teams would be looking at their call traffic as a matter of routine intelligence gathering. That was why, when Handyside had critical business going on, he made it a three-line whip that all his team had clean phones that couldn't be traced back to them. As soon as the job was finished he would send out an order that all the phones should be binned. Like DNA, communications had become one of the cornerstones of modern investigation, but the problem for the police was that any criminal with more than two brain cells knew it.

The saving grace was that even though every criminal in the world was convinced the law was listening to them, they still made mistakes on the phone. It was the old 'failure to shut your gob' syndrome that affected the best of them from time to time. Eddie Fleming was smart, tough and extremely talented, but in his business that wasn't enough. He lacked the iron discipline and focus that men like Handyside relied on to keep them alive and at the top of their game.

Macallan nodded for the bill and went outside the restaurant to call Jack, who'd be back in Edinburgh in just a couple of days. He answered after the second ring, the sound of his voice making her squeeze her eyes tight for a moment and she felt stuck, wanting to say too many things at the same time.

He did it for her. 'Hello there. Hope you're not in the pub with that Mick Harkins.'

She smiled and relaxed. It was as if she still couldn't believe that she was part of the same family as Jack and Adam. Despite the headlines and her reputation as a relentless detective, Macallan lacked confidence in her ability to be wanted by another human being. She often wondered why and guessed it must have grown out of being an only child, plus the sterile relationship she'd had with her father. 'I miss you,' she told him. 'It seems like weeks rather than a few days.' She should have said something more but just left it there and let the line go quiet.

Jack knew how it worked and that for Macallan loneliness was like a physical disease that she would always struggle with. She lived a life surrounded by people who loved and admired her but she could never quite accept it as fact. She needed to be told over and over again; he was fine with that, and it was no more than she deserved for what she gave away in wrecked emotions. He knew, however, that humour worked for her and some piss-taking was required, which was why Harkins never failed to bring her back to life – although the price was usually a hangover. 'I miss you even more than you miss me, honeybunny.'

She snorted down the phone and he laughed with her. 'I'm a lot of things, but definitely no honeybunny. How's our son and heir?'

'Great, I swear to God I can see that boy grow every

241

day, and no wonder with the amount of food he packs away.'

Macallan squeezed her eyes again and wished she didn't have to miss a minute of his life. Every day was precious, and she couldn't bring any of it back. She thought about Ingrid Richter's parents and how they'd probably felt the same emotions when she was a child. Now that girl who they'd nurtured and loved was like a lost soul wandering among the living.

'Kiss him for me, and I'll see you both in a couple of days. By the way, how's the book?'

'Great. And not only am I going back to being a stupendous barrister, but I'm going to be a famous author to boot! You must be so proud of me.' He was on a roll with the wind-ups so she thought it must be time to go.

'Pull your head in, Fraser. Take care and I'll see you soon.' She stuffed the phone into her bag and went back to the restaurant, where she found Young explaining advanced analytical techniques to a bewildered McGovern, who looked to Macallan for salvation.

'Okay, guys. One more drink and then we're off up the road.'

Jack hadn't asked her how the case was going; he didn't need to, as it was all there in her voice. He knew her problem was overthinking the investigations. Although it often produced brilliant results, the process sucked the life out of her, leaving her drained and empty at the end of each major case she had to deal with. He would let this one run its course but promised himself that he'd try to talk her into leaving the job before it either killed her or robbed her of the ability to ever be happy again.

The signs were already there: her suspicion that all the world was bad or a threat, that every shadow hid something terrible. He'd prosecuted some of the worst cases imaginable in Northern Ireland but still managed to leave his demons in the files piled up in his chambers. He'd watched her in the months they'd spent together after Adam was born; they'd both been so happy on the Antrim cliffs, away from the world they normally inhabited, and he was sure part of it was the distance afforded by the Irish Sea – a protective barrier keeping her safe from those horrors she witnessed in the job. He only hoped she would listen to him.

29

Back in Edinburgh, the Fleming twins were having a drink at the foot of Leith Walk. It was their territory and the old pub was safe ground for them. Everyone knew everyone, and if you supported anyone but the Hibees then you could fuck right off, and you didn't mention the Jambos unless it was to slag the bastards off. There was something almost poetic that the great Edinburgh rivals were relegated together, but the supporters didn't quite see it that way. Pat Fleming was still shaken up by the events on Tyneside and he was convinced that either Crazy Horse or the Newcastle team were coming for them. His marginally older sibling tried hard to lighten the conversation, with no success. Pat looked like he was starting to lose it.

'Well it can't be fuckin' Brenda, the state she's in.' Eddie had tried for a bit of humour but it dropped like a lead weight.

Pat looked sideways at his brother and threw back his third pint of the night. He'd always admired Eddie as the one with the brains and the answers, but the elder twin was coming up with fuck all but stupid cracks about The Bitch when some nutter might burst through the door at any minute and shotgun their brains over the walls. 'I'm tellin' you we need to act, brother, or we're fucked.'

Although Eddie didn't like to admit it, Pat was probably right for once.

The pub door opened and they both spun round, but it let in nothing worse than a wave of fresh air mixed with car fumes, plus Drew, who they'd arranged to meet so they could talk over their options. He ordered a round for the three of them, knowing they were under strain, and as far as he was concerned they had every right to be. In military terms they were caught between horrible bastards on all sides and were making the worst mistake of all – endless talk but no moves – because they just didn't know whether to escalate or hold the line. That kind of inaction could cost a life or two.

'The worst thing you can do is nothing.' Drew paused and sipped his Guinness for dramatic effect. 'Any action is better than no action in this particular case.'

Eddie took a moment and sucked up a mouthful of his fresh pint. He was nervous and admitted to himself that he'd wobbled on what the fuck to do next. Drew was absolutely right, and he was pleased he'd brought the older head into the team, although he'd had his doubts along the way.

He banged the base of his pint glass onto the bar, slopping some of the lager onto the stained surface, which was no big deal in this place.

'You're right, and we've already worked out a plan to take that grassin' wee cunt, so why not now?' He looked to his brother first, who shrugged and nodded in agreement.

'I'm in. Billy's absofuckinlutely right, we can fanny around forever, wait for somebody else to make the moves or man up and get into the bastards. Let's fuckin' do it.'

'What about you, Billy? We ready to go tonight?' Eddie was energised by the thought of action, and if the plan worked they would at least have some cred back in the bank.

Drew took a moment, pleased the twins had taken his suggestion. It was exactly what he'd wanted from them and he'd been ready to go before he'd even entered the boozer. 'Good for me, and I say we stick to the original plan?' He threw the ball back to Eddie, who thought he was in charge.

'Absolutely. We'll run through it one more time, right? Billy and me do the eyes on the sauna. Pat, you go up and watch for the bastard gettin' back home. We'll give you plenty warning when he locks up and is on his way there. When he arrives and the Bonnars fuck off home to the zoo, you give us a call. Right so far?' They nodded; they had the plan off by heart. 'We give him ten minutes then Billy makes the call that he's local polis and the sauna's alarm's gone off. He thinks it's been screwed. Ricky's the key holder and has to come down to check. Pat, you follow him back and when he gets there we nab the bastard, tape him up and stick him in the boot of the car.' He saw the look on their faces; the scent of blood always got them high and the thought of torturing Swan tickled their nerve endings. The sauna owner was a bottler and they guessed that he'd scream like a fuckin' cat when they started to cut him up. It just didn't get better than that.

'We got all the tools ready for the job?' Eddie asked the question but there was no need. They'd prepared it well and were ready apart from the fact that Pat might have gone a bit easier on the booze, but that was nothing new.

'The sawn-off's ready to go, the boiler suits and other gear's all checked and bagged.' Drew said it like the professional he was, all calm and matter of fact as if they were going out to pick up some females for a party.

'You sure we need a shooter? I mean, it's fuckin' Ricky Swan we're talkin' about here.

'Always have a backup plan. We shouldn't need it, but just in case ...' Drew tapped the side of his nose and hoped the twins didn't make an issue with the sawn-off. He needed it for the job.

Eddie shrugged and let it be. 'Right, there's time yet. He never leaves the sauna till eleven at the earliest so let's finish up here and meet up again at half ten down at The Shore.'

When they stepped out of the boozer Pat headed for his flat to change clothes and his brother took the chance to pull Drew aside. 'Wee bonus for you. My ex-CID rat who's been doing the phones has come up with an answer. Barclay does call and though he had the mobile it wasn't tying the bastard down. Turns out he gets pissed almost every other night and a few of the calls come from a pub near Inverness. The rat took it further, travelled up there and eyeballed the bastard. Says he looks a fucking mess, but there's an address for you.'

Eddie handed the scrap of paper to Drew, who stared at it as if he'd just won the lottery. He looked back up at Eddie and grinned – but there was something in his expression that the twin really didn't like. 'Cheers. I won't forget this one.' He put his hand on the younger man's shoulder and squeezed his thanks.

'One last thing, Billy. Story is that his daughter's topped herself. Even though she couldn't stand her old man the whole mess was too much and she strung herself up, poor cow. Anyway give him a dig for me when the time comes, and I'll see you on The Shore before we cover the sauna.'

Eddie walked away from the pub and felt a brief moment of pity for Jonathon Barclay, who was going to meet his worst nightmare in the form of mad Billy Drew.

30

Ingrid Richter's parents had booked them all into a hotel suite with a panoramic view over the city and castle. She'd refused food, had hardly spoken a word since they'd arrived, but had promised that she was okay and they were not to worry. When they were in the restaurant having dinner she sat at the window of their sitting room and stared over the city nightscape. There was a full moon hanging over the castle, bathing the old fortress and town in cold white light that made the city seem to glow with dark energy. She was in a trance; it was as if she was back in her native Prague and childhood, where she'd loved her father to read about old castles and faraway places where fairy tales actually happened.

When her parents returned she hadn't moved from the chair and didn't even turn when they came into the room. Her mother put her hand on Richter's shoulder and bit her lip when she saw the expression on her daughter's face. She was smiling, but her eyes were looking at something only she could see. Her father said her name softly and knelt down in front of his daughter. After a few moments she broke out of her thoughts and noticed her parents were in the room with her. She told them she was fine – she just wanted peace. They decided to call the hospital first thing in the morning, recognising that her recovery was a long way off.

They helped her undress and put her into the bedroom next to theirs, where she fell asleep in moments. Her father told his wife to go to bed; he would join her when he'd finished the nightcap he'd ordered from room service.

He stared out of the window, watching the traffic flow past and wondering what the future held for the daughter who meant so much to him.

One of the cars that glided past Mr Richter's view was driven by Billy Drew, who'd picked up the sawn-off and gear for the job from a storage unit on the west side of the city. Things were moving fast and he was happy with that – he'd hated inaction since he'd lost his wife to cancer, and as far as possible he avoided sitting on his arse and thinking about what his life meant.

For the best part of half an hour before he picked the gear up he checked his rear view for a follow. He was methodical about making sure he wasn't the subject of some pig's surveillance operation and knew that the day he didn't check would be the day the bastards were up his arse. He was sure he was clean and had gone through his full repertoire of manoeuvres to try to draw out any watchers. What they had planned was a tricky job, and there was always the chance of some nosey fucking plod wandering past when he should have been mumping a free drink off one of the local taxpayers.

The Flemings had tasked some of the best men in their team to get out on the street and create a bit of havoc to keep the pigs occupied while they were kidnapping Ricky the Rat. During the late evening the crew set off fires at a couple of good schools and paid a dozen junkies in the powder of their choice to set off alarms, steal cars and basically run amok, which included committing a series of unprovoked assaults on whoever happened to be in reach at the time. Anonymous calls were made to stick it in some dealers who were moving gear the same night. As the chaos and pressure mounted, Police Scotland in Edinburgh were run ragged and had to call in assistance from other parts of the force.

Drew watched the blue lights flashing past him every few minutes on the way back to Leith; the diversion was working almost perfectly and his lips briefly formed a satisfied smile – a rare event for a man who struggled to find anything pleasurable these days. Crime was all he had left, everything else of meaning in his life having long disappeared. He'd lost his army career and his wife, there were no kids, and his idiot brother had taken off because Drew would have killed him for fucking up on a job that nearly cost them a lifer. The only thing that still gave him a buzz was violent crime, which was a major high, but like any other drug there was always the crash on the other side of the hill. He'd worked for years on his own or with a small team, but that meant he'd never made the big bucks that the organised gangsters raked up in shitloads. Drew had seen the opportunity that Eddie Fleming had offered him as soon as it was dangled under his nose, only he saw a slightly different deal to the one that Fleming thought he was laying on the table.

He looked in the mirror and thought he looked not too bad for his years and exactly what he was – a right hard bastard.

'It's all good, Billy. It's all fucking good.' He said it quietly and felt the buzz hitting his system at the thought of what was about to happen.

*

250

Drew met the twins down at The Shore as the late drinkers started to drift off into the night shadows. 'We all good then?' Eddie said, rubbing his hands together to ease the nervous tension he always felt before a job. He had as much bottle as any other villain but he always felt a rush of adrenalin before a piece of work that involved violence. The fact that Drew seemed completely chilled worried him – it just didn't seem natural – but then the man was a killer, so maybe he was just plain fucking mad.

Drew and Pat nodded; they'd rehearsed it over and over again and there was no need for a rerun.

'You get up to his place, Pat, and make sure you have a good view of his front door. Stay as far back as you can and there's no way he should tipple you. Gimme a shout when you're in place.' He slapped the open palm of his brother's hand and headed for his car.

Drew jumped into the driver's seat of the stolen car he'd rigged up with plates that would pass muster for the few hours they needed. Eddie climbed in beside him and they headed for the sauna. They parked in almost the same spot Brenda McMartin had occupied before her failed attempt on Swan. It was a natural vantage point for a watch, tucked nicely into the shadows, and gave a perfect view of the front door to the sauna.

The old lady who'd enjoyed Big Brenda's attack on Swan so much was back at her window and had enjoyed her second medicinal brandy of the evening. The battle she'd witnessed between Cue Ball and the Glasgow crew had been one of the best nights she'd had in years, and like an addictive drug she wanted more, so she made sure she was in her window seat every night, just in case. She didn't think it could happen again, but she lived in hope. If things had turned out just a bit differently that night she would have had her wish; events, however, were running out of control, though none of the players had realised it yet ...

The lights were on in the sauna and they watched a couple of punters exit the place, collars up, moving quickly to get away from the evidence of their sin and head home for a late cup of tea or a blether with the wife. Pat had texted that he was in place at Swan's and the house was in darkness, as it should have been.

Eddie slid down in the passenger seat, feeling a bit more relaxed now that they were in place and the job was running. Drew offered a cigarette and he nodded. They lit up and sat quietly, both imagining a variety of scenarios for what might happen next. Neither of them got it right.

About halfway through the smoke Eddie's phone buzzed.

'Pat, I thought I said no calls from you till we give you the word he's on his way.' He was fucking annoyed and wished Pat had avoided the extra drink he'd guzzled in the boozer earlier on.

'You won't believe who's here.'

'What the fuck you on about? We don't have time for this.'

'It's Crazy Horse! He's here, and he's only fuckin' creepin' round Swanny's place.'

Eddie pulled up out of his slouch and pressed the phone closer to his ear. 'Say it again, Pat, and this better be fuckin' right.' He snarled it through clenched teeth, sure that Pat was just hyper or had stuffed some powder up his hooter.

'You heard it right the first time. That mad cunt is here and must have the same idea as us. What do we do now?'

Eddie told him to put the phone down and he'd call him

back. He clicked the phone off and looked at Drew for a moment or two before telling him what had happened. There was no plan for this. Drew calmly took an extra long draw on his smoke as he realised this wasn't a crisis – it was an opportunity that had fallen right into his lap.

'We change course but stay on the job. We're not letting that psycho operate in our territory. If he does the business with Ricky then you're a dead man walking, credibility down the swanny. He's mad but he can't take the Bonnars on as well without making a fucking racket. He must be planning to wait till they wave ta-ta and then make his move. We'll follow Ricky up there and see what happens next.'

After another fifteen minutes Swan left the sauna with the Bonnars and locked up before heading for his wheels. He drove off with his minders in the car behind him.

'That's him on his way, Pat,' Eddie said into the phone. 'Hopefully no detours and he goes straight home. Can you still see Crazy Horse?'

'He's settled down in some shrubs a few feet from the door so he must be going to take Swanny there.' There was tension in Pat's voice, but Eddie knew that if there was going to be a violent situation then his brother was reliable. They'd need to be on their game if they were going to take on Crazy Horse, but there was no option, and having Drew and his sawn-off suddenly seemed like a blessing.

They waited till they saw the lights of the Bonnars' car turn left into Leith Walk then pulled away from the kerb to follow them. There wasn't too much traffic apart from blue lights steaming past them or in the opposite direction every couple of minutes.

The old lady at the window was disappointed once again as Swan got into his car and drove away without incident. Another car pulled out of the shadows a minute later but she made no connection. She sighed, feeling a deep sense of depression that this was all her life amounted to, finished her drink and went to bed to dream about better days.

When Pat called to say that Swan and the Bonnars had just passed him and parked up outside The Corral, Drew pulled over into a side street to wait.

'We'll leave the car here and come to you. Let us know when the Godzilla brothers are on the way towards us so we can get our heads down.'

Pat was in a good position with a clear view of Swan's door and garden. He was well back in a small cul-de-sac that looked across the road to the front of The Corral and there was little chance of being spotted by any nosey neighbours. He watched Swan lean in the window of the Bonnars' car then straighten up, giving them a wave as they pulled away slowly. They passed Pat's line of vision and he made the call, his brother and Drew slipping behind a garden wall till the lights of the minders' car drifted past them and out of sight. When they were clear, they jogged the short distance to get to The Corral where they could find out what the fuck Crazy Horse was up to.

Swan, remarkably sober, felt a real thrill of pleasure at the thought of getting into a fresh bottle of vodka and maybe a bit of late-night porn. He was knackered and had good reason to be. Things had been bad, but he was sure they couldn't get any worse, and he was going to figure out a plan to dig himself out of the problems he faced. Thankfully, more by luck than anything else, he hadn't been due to take any of the women who were being brought in by the *Brighter Dawn* so there was no reason he should take a hit from the police on that one. What nagged at him was that he was up to his arse in other deals that involved trafficked women, and he was one of the main fixers in

Scotland for the trade. It was a rare stroke of good fortune that he hadn't needed or had one on order from the last *Brighter Dawn* shipment. All he could do was hope that the threat of disclosing the dirt he'd recorded would keep the forces of law and order at bay. That had seemed reasonable till Macallan had arrived at his door. He just didn't like the way the detective did business. As far as he was concerned she had no idea how mutual backscratching worked. What the fuck did they expect putting women in these positions anyway? He muttered the word 'bitch', pulled the keys out of his pocket and was pushing them in the direction of the lock when the voice behind him made him whimper with fright. He froze and dropped his keys onto the step.

'Aren't you going to ask me in, Ricky?'

He couldn't believe it was happening again and he turned to face Crazy Horse, who was dressed in a combat jacket and woollen hat and carrying the biggest hunting knife he'd ever seen. The serrated edge on the knife mesmerised him, and he tried not to think what it might be used for. Although he attempted to say something, the words just wouldn't form; it was as if a numbing agent had been squirted directly into his throat. He did manage something like a squeak, but as it wasn't a social visit Crazy Horse wasn't too offended – in fact he liked that look of fear that came from him being the guy with the big fuck-off knife in his hand. The Glasgow man stooped down, picked up the keys and stuck them in the door because Swan was shaking so violently there was no chance he could manage that simple task himself. Crazy Horse then spun him round and, scrunching up the back of his jacket collar to control him, pushed the quivering heap face first through the door.

Eddie and Drew arrived on the scene just as the door closed behind Crazy Horse. They jumped into Pat's car and listened to what he'd seen, but Eddie felt there was way too much tension in his voice.

'Take it easy. Cool it, for fuck's sake.' Eddie tried to sound calmer than he felt. McMartin was a class-A nutter, and if they fucked up with him then it was all over.

'What do you think, Billy?' Eddie looked at the older man, who seemed almost dreamlike as he ran through the options.

'He's either going to do Ricky or take him away some-where, but if that was the case he'd have brought some of his team with him ... He's on his own so that means he's going to do him in there. You sure he just had a blade?'

'That's all I saw, but fuck knows what's under the jacket.'

'Stay in the car; I'll take care of him when he leaves. Just have the motor running when I pull the trigger and get me back to the other wheels pronto.' He loaded the shotgun and opened the door of the car.

'You sure you want to do this on your own?' Eddie didn't like it but Drew was ex-military, and if he needed backup they could be out of the car and with him in seconds. Drew shook his head but didn't speak. He got out of the car and skirted round the edge of the street walls into Swan's garden, keeping close to a boundary wall, and took up a position near the door, covered by some shrubs.

When Crazy Horse drew the door behind him he left it unlocked and handy for a quick getaway when he was done. He held the hunting knife against Swan's skinny little throat and pushed him towards a leather seat before he turned him round and without too much force punched him in the gut to make him sit quietly. There was no need for more than that because he was dealing with a physically weak man who wouldn't be a problem.

256

Swan was winded and slumped back into the chair. He held his gut and wondered how he'd managed to be the subject of yet another visit from a McMartin and whether he'd survive this one. There was no Cue Ball and the Bonnars were out of range. He wheezed with fear, and the dig to his gut area hurt like a bastard, but adrenalin was flooding his system. He might have been the worst form of coward but he still had the instinct to survive and tried to think of a way out, because without a shadow of a doubt he was about to be killed by a fucking maniac.

Crazy Horse launched into a short speech. 'I'm no here tae fuck around, wee man. Yer a grassin' cunt, and Brenda's a fuckin' mess – well I suppose I should say a worse mess than usual.' His face broke into a kind of lopsided grin. 'I'm just here tae say cheerio, so any last words?'

For the first time in his life Swan did something that required balls. Crazy Horse had done what so many other bastards had done and had only seen the runt in front of him. The Glasgow gangster had seen it as all too easy and had taken his eye off the ball when he was gloating at the other man's fear. Swan picked up a glass paperweight from the coffee table beside him and with all the force he could muster he pushed up from the seat and swung it against the side of his tormentor's head. Crazy Horse was stunned, but only for a moment as he had the advantage of having taken a lifetime of blows to various parts of his body. He took a step back and shook his head, spraying the blood pishing from the two-inch gash at the side of his eye. Swan froze as he watched Crazy Horse swipe at the wound before staring at his blood-covered hand. The lopsided grin returned.

'Ya wee bastard,' was all he said as he grabbed Swan by the throat and tried to make up his mind where to stick the knife first. Swan's painful attempt at defence meant that he was going to get a series of stab wounds

257

before he died rather than one big one through the heart.

That's when the tables turned in Swan's favour. Gnasher hadn't been sleeping when his master had arrived at the door. The sound of another voice hadn't excited the dog too much but he'd been curious and padded to the lounge door, pushing it open with his nose. The spoodle stared at the scene just as the paperweight opened up the side of the stranger's head, and when the man grabbed his master by the throat the dog's instincts to protect boiled over. He wasn't bred like his devil-dog cousins, but there were still traces of his ancestors' hunting and pack instincts in his genes. Those instincts took control as he launched himself at the Crazy Horse's back leg. His left trouser leg had ridden up and Gnasher saw the lower part of the man's calf muscle exposed and bulging with the effort to position himself for the blow. The faithful dog sunk his small but very sharp teeth into the fleshiest part of the muscle and the reaction was instantaneous.

'What the fuck?' Crazy Horse could take pain, and though on the grand scale of things the bite wasn't the worst he'd had, it came with the element of surprise, which always added to the effect. It was only a momentary distraction, but it ruined what he'd planned to do, and it was about to change his life completely. Crazy Horse let go of Swan and spun round to face whoever or whatever was attacking him from behind. The dog had let go but was still defending his master as Crazy Horse lashed out with his boot.

That was all the distraction Swan needed, and he was already off for the door and out into the garden by the time Crazy Horse realised it was all going badly wrong. Swan knew the narrow tree-lined path at the side of his home was unlit and would give him cover to get the fuck out of it so he flew out of the door like an Olympic athlete, turned sharp left along the front of the house then jumped over a low wall into the protection of the deep shadows.

Drew was on his feet on the other side of the door, and though his instinct was to stop Swan there was a bigger problem inside the house. He had to wait and see where that problem was because he didn't want him at his back so Drew held his nerve; Crazy Horse was the priority, and he could hear the commotion happening inside. The barking dog gave him some idea of what might be going on, but it was all or nothing and whoever came off second best in the next few seconds would be dead.

The twins had seen Swan legging it and that Drew was at the side of the door with the sawn-off ready and waiting. It was obvious to them what he was doing and why he was holding back.

Inside the house, Gnasher had worked out that he was on a loser and that the man he'd defended so bravely had legged it. The dog made for the door and followed his master into the safety of the night.

'Fuck it.' It was a mess and Crazy Horse wondered what Handyside would make of it.

The Fleming twins were at the entrance to the garden when Crazy Horse stepped outside, wondering which way to turn and whether it was even worth trying to find Swan in the dark. That was when he saw the two Edinburgh boys and their pickaxe handles.

Crazy Horse was still raging and decided that if he couldn't have Swan then they'd do for the time being. He raised the knife in front of him and was getting ready for the charge when he heard the crunch of gravel behind and to the side of him. He turned to face Drew, who had the sawn-off pointed at him. For most men being on the wrong end of a gun is a totally disabling and terrifying experience, in contrast to the film heroes who calmly face down the working end of those machines. That course of action wasn't for Crazy Horse, an animal bred for violence, and the moment he looked into Drew's eyes he saw a man like himself who would pull the trigger without a moment's hesitation. He was fucked and he knew it, so he decided he might as well try to malky the bastard as a final gesture.

He snarled and tried to rush Drew, who pulled the trigger when they were no more than four feet apart. It was as if Crazy Horse had run into a rubber wall then bounced backwards. He was already dead when he hit the ground. Drew studied him for a moment and was satisfied that the gaping hole in his chest had done the job; there was no need to put another one in him. He'd been too close though, and he was covered with some of the material that had made up the recently deceased gangster. That was evidence, which meant it was time for them to go. Swan could wait.

'Get in the car!' he barked at the twins, who were already heading in the direction of their wheels. He noticed that a couple of lights had clicked on in other houses but he still had work to do. He took a couple of deep lungfuls of air and walked back towards the car when he heard Pat starting up the motor. In no rush, he reloaded the sawn-off and wiped droplets of sweat from his eyes with the back of his hand. He stopped at the open passenger window and stared down at Eddie, who looked up at him and understood at last why he'd had those niggling doubts.

Drew saw the question in the young man's eyes. 'You just weren't ready for the big seat, son.'

He pulled the trigger again and blasted most of Eddie's upper chest and neck into a pulp, filling the car with a red mist that blotted all the windows. Pat was covered in the mess from his brother, his hearing shattered, and he was halfway to madness when Drew pulled the trigger again and finished him.

Drew was already in his car and driving when the first call was made to the police about some kind of disturbance in the Ravelston area. The police assistant who took the call was having one of the busiest night shifts ever and decided that a disturbance in Ravelston could wait.

'Toffee-nosed gits,' was her reaction when she put the phone down and took the next call about a serious assault on the Royal Mile. The phone operator was so busy that she forgot about the Ravelston job till a second call came in from an elderly female resident who said that her husband had been walking the dog and had seen something awful near the bottom of their drive. The unfortunate gentleman had passed out and split his head open. The cavalry was dispatched but they were far too late to catch Billy Drew.

31

Drew headed towards Cramond, the lovely old village nestling at the mouth of the River Almond where it runs quietly into the Forth estuary. It wasn't far from the Ravelston area and he'd already rehearsed his next moves. Killing Crazy Horse hadn't been in the plan, but it didn't cause him any real problems – he'd just moved the timetable a bit. Swan would be taken care of in due course.

As he swung the car into the parking area near the beach he breathed a sigh of relief that no one else was there. There was always the chance of a couple playing away from home or a pack of doggers enjoying their fantasies and spreading a few STDs.

He took a petrol can from the boot and soaked the inside of the car, letting it puddle in the front and back seats. There was a full moon, but it was dark enough for his purposes; he stripped off till he was naked, piled the bloodstained clothes into the passenger seat and put the sawn-off on top of enough evidence to make sure he died in the pokey.

He stepped back to make sure he hadn't missed

anything and took a few seconds again to steady his breathing. The rucksack he'd made up for the job held the running shorts, trainers and top he needed for the road home. He tipped the last of the petrol onto the clothes and took another few seconds to run through the checklist he'd memorised to avoid fucks-ups. Mistakes were easy when this level of stress was involved. He was sure he'd missed nothing, pulled on the running gear and was ready to go. Just to be sure, he'd put three lighters in the rucksack, but there was no need as the first one lit easily enough.

He cupped his hand round the sputtering flame and stared for a few seconds before holding the lighter under a rag he'd soaked and stuck into the filler. There was going to be an almighty blaze, and he ran to make sure he didn't go up with the car.

He heard the first whoosh as the heatwave ran over him and pounded towards the path along the seafront that would take him back to Silverknowes, home and safety. Eventually he slowed to a steady jog and kept looking to his left where the moonlight sparkled across the calm waters of the Forth. The exertion helped to calm him as he ran through his mind what was still to be done. The air was cool, and he promised himself a large whisky when he was back home and cleaned up.

Thirty minutes later Drew arrived at his door and stopped for a moment to check for watchers. Once he was satisfied that the street was quiet and there was no sign of the law or any nosey bastards behind their curtains, he went to the back gate and pulled another bag from his shed. He stripped off again, hung the garden hose from the six-foot fence that he'd built round the perimeter of the garden to ensure privacy and turned on the outside tap to get a fine spray. The cold water took his breath away but he forced himself to stay under the cleansing water. He rubbed his body, hair and hands to wash away as much of the night's events as possible. His teeth were chattering and when he'd had enough he grabbed a large soft towel from the bag to rub himself dry. After a couple of minutes there was a wonderful tingling sensation all over his skin, as if a surge of youthful energy was charging his body.

He changed into a pair of jeans, a sweatshirt and slip-on shoes. The running gear he stuffed into the bag with the wet towel before he walked three streets away to where he could shove the bag into a bin that would be collected that same morning. Exhaustion from the high-octane mixture of danger, stress and physical effort pounced on him, but that was okay, and he reduced his pace as he headed back home.

The difference between the Flemings and Drew was that he was always prepared to go the extra mile to avoid a fuck-up so he wasn't finished; he peeled off for a third time and stood under a hot shower till his skin was red and he looked like he'd been in the sun too long. He cut his finger- and toenails then scrubbed again with a hard brush, and when he was finished he poured half a bottle of bleach round the shower basin and sink in his bathroom.

Drew had copped a lifer because his halfwit brother had failed to take care of gear that had his DNA all over it. It was only because Harkins had worked outside of the legal process that he'd walked out on a technical appeal. He was sure that his last change of clothes were clean, but he bagged them anyway, and just to be sure walked a half-mile from his house to dump them in a skip. He was nearly done, and confident that he was as clean as he could be and ready for any unforeseen visits from the suits.

The scent of booze hit the back of his nose when he

opened the fresh bottle and filled his glass halfway up. He slumped into a seat, took a sip and felt the warm rush wash through his veins, then he lifted the clean phone to make the only call he needed to that night before he swallowed the rest of the drink. He closed his eyes, listened to it ring and heard it picked up, but the person at the other end didn't speak, which was what had been arranged – Handyside was waiting for Drew to talk in case something had gone wrong.

'Didn't go strictly to plan but the twins are gone,' he said.

'Good work.' That was all Handyside said in reply as he waited for the rest of the update.

'Crazy H turned up unexpectedly at the pimp's so I took care of him as well. Only problem is that the pimp got away but that's no real problem.'

Handyside took a moment to run it through his head. 'Okay, McMartin was going anyway so that's a major problem out of the way. Tell you the truth, I thought I'd have to take care of it myself.'

'What do you want me to do as regards the pimp?' Drew asked, happy enough to find and gut the bastard if required.

'You go about your business like a good citizen and stay normal till this dies down. There's always the chance they have some intel on you working for the twins. We'll take care of him ourselves. Once that's done we're more or less cleaned up apart from Brenda, but she can be controlled with her brother out of the way. In fact I think she can be used to our advantage, and she might just like taking over the manager's job.' Handyside felt it had all gone reasonably well and he was pleased that he was doing business with a man who understood the need for clarity and sense of purpose.

'Ricky will know it was Crazy H but I'm pretty sure he

never saw me or the twins. He was going like a fuckin' greyhound when he left the house. I'll call you later.'

'Take care now and get some sleep.' Handyside pushed the red button and promptly called Maxi Turner; there was still some work to do.

32

On the night Eddie Fleming and his brother had witnessed the UC being slaughtered by Handyside, their subsequent decision to call Drew had turned out to be a fatal mistake. When Fleming had arrived at his door in the middle of the night and spilled his guts about the events in Tyneside, it had taken about five minutes for Drew to realise that this was a business opportunity he couldn't refuse. What the young man hadn't recognised was that part of the price of that opportunity was his neck. Drew had listened, unlocking Eddie's thoughts and fears with a bottle of good whisky and then told him to trust no one. It was good advice, but Eddie hadn't listened to the man who would eventually take his life. What he'd said in the early hours of that morning had convinced Drew that the Fleming twins had committed the ultimate sin by introducing a UC into an unforgiving organisation, and that could only mean one thing. In Handyside's world, ignorance of the crime was no defence. Credibility was everything, and the wonder of it all was that the Flemings hadn't been composted much earlier. On top of all that it was clear that the McMartins had all the excuses they'd needed to move on the Edinburgh business and take over.

Drew hadn't known Handyside personally, but he'd known all about the man's CV. Drew had pulled a couple of home invasions in Northumberland and had shifted some jewellery through local contacts who spoke about the top man as if he was some sort of dark spirit feeding off the blood of ordinary mortals. Drew knew that Newcastle was a hard man's city so anyone who'd made it to the top had to be a bit special and an absolutely pitiless bastard when required. Eddie's proposal to Drew had been almost laughable, and to even consider fucking about such a man had proven the young gangster wasn't fit for purpose. There was nothing to worry about with his brother: all he was ever going to be was the late Joe Fleming's hard son. Pat was nothing without his brother and the family name, and he had shit for brains up to the point Drew had atomised that particular organ.

Drew had thrown the dice and made contact with Handyside via one of his old contacts in Newcastle. He'd known the risks, but for a man who'd considered suicide too often it was worth a gamble to change from what he was into a big-game player and perhaps find a reason to go on living. He could offer Handyside the opportunity to get rid of the twins who'd put him in so much danger and planned to undermine him at the first opportunity. They'd planned to take Swan despite what Handyside had ordered, and he'd hoped all of that would be enough to get a seat at the table with the Newcastle kingpin. Betraying the Flemings meant nothing to him; they'd deserved to go under as far as he was concerned, and if that was all it would take to get him into a position of status in the game then it would be worth the risk. He could offer a clean-up of the Edinburgh mess and get the business under control, which would make sense to Handyside if he was indeed the smart character of legend.

He'd agreed to a meeting on neutral territory and booked a hotel room where Handyside had turned up with Maxi Turner. They'd listened to him, and though at one point Drew had felt they were measuring him up for a coffin, they'd said almost nothing, only asking for a half-hour break to talk it over. Drew had gone to the bar, where he'd sunk three drinks to stop the tremor in his hands, but when they'd met again Handyside had offered his hand and invited Drew to sit down.

'We ran over the options. One of them was to take you out; Maxi was all for that and offered to do it himself.' Drew had looked at Turner, who'd smiled and winked like an old friend before Handyside continued, 'I think there was sense in that, and in some circumstances you would have been dead already.'

Drew hadn't moved a muscle; he was a hard ruthless bastard, but the man opposite hadn't been putting on some show to impress – he'd just been stating what he thought was obvious. 'The fact is that there's a mess in Edinburgh, the Flemings were prepared to betray me and you're a godless criminal who could probably get things back in order for us all. Here's what I propose. And betray who you like, but never betray me.'

Drew had realised in that moment that, true to his reputation, Handyside had all the compassion of a bed bug just before it bites you on the arse, and while Drew was a gold-standard bastard, he'd promised himself never to cross the man unless it was to fulfil his occasional reflections on the benefits of suicide.

Handyside had let Drew live and they'd agreed what they would do to create a firebreak around them as far as the events on the *Brighter Dawn* were concerned. They'd cleaned up part of the problem already, but Handyside had decided that the Flemings had to go next and Crazy Horse in due course. His sister had failed in her attempt on Swan, and for Handyside that meant Crazy Horse was responsible, being the man who gave the orders.

Swan was another problem, and Handyside wanted him taken but squeezed dry to see exactly what he knew in case they were vulnerable in ways they hadn't yet recognised. No one could tell him what exactly Swan was up to or knew, but he was a major player in moving women in Scotland, and the Newcastle man couldn't help wondering why he wasn't involved with the *Brighter Dawn* cargo. It could have been a coincidence, but there was only one way to tie up that particular loose end.

Eddie had put his trust in a man who he thought would save him from the devil, but the moment that Drew had smiled and said yes to his offer, he'd signed his own death warrant. When Drew pulled the trigger and blew away Pat, he'd brought to an end the family who'd controlled the Edinburgh drugs market for over a decade – and that left a gaping void. Drew thought all he had to do was step in and take over. What he hadn't realised was that this kind of void would be filled by chaos before stability.

33

Gazing blankly out of the car window, all Macallan could think about was hitting the pillow and getting in a few hours' sleep before her next round with the Flemings. They were on the bypass and just about to take the exit to head into the city when her phone came to life. She screwed up her eyes and tried to focus on the screen, hoping it was Jack, but she didn't recognise the number. McGovern reminded her again that she probably needed glasses, and she was reluctantly coming to the conclusion that it was inevitable – another of those small markers to remind her that her life was passing while she wallowed in the same cesspit as men like Pete Handyside and Ricky Swan.

'Jesus – glasses and grey hairs making an appearance. Is this the beginning of the end?' she said to him.

'It was always the beginning of the end. Live with it – I do.' McGovern grinned and thought about calling his wife to tell her he'd soon be there.

Macallan sighed before lifting the phone to her ear. She listened and felt her heart start pounding with growing anger as she realised the day was now far from over. She said yes and okay a few times.

McGovern knew exactly what those lifeless answers from Macallan meant, and he was just as pissed off as she was. All he wanted was to go home and crawl into bed beside his wife.

Young felt the tension in the car and a tremor of anticipation ran through her as she sensed she was actually going to be around during a situation. For an analyst this was a small taste of the front line. So much of her work was in a closed room with only a computer screen to play with, and the nearest she got to the real deal was intelligence reports. Her circuits hadn't been burned out by experience like her two companions and she hoped that whatever was happening, it was serious and she could see it for herself.

'Head for the Ravelston area,' Macallan said when she hung up. 'There's some kind of major incident at Ricky Swan's place. When I say major incident, that includes bodies.' She tried to avoid grinding her teeth at the thought that sleep had just moved off into the distance and she wished sincerely that she hadn't been drinking.

'You did say bodies? That's plural?' McGovern asked as his headache increased to nuclear proportions.

'If what they've said is true, there are three who departed this life in and around The Corral.'

'Christ,' was all McGovern could be bothered saying before he seemed to sink down into his jacket.

Fifteen minutes later they saw the blue lights dotting the streets on their approach to the locus. A fresh-faced rookie, who looked no more than fifteen, stopped them and Macallan watched his Adam's apple bounce when they told him who they were.

'They must be getting them straight from school,' McGovern said, attempting to lighten the mood, but they were beyond that possibility.

'Just us all getting older. You probably looked like him at some point.'

A perimeter had been put in place around the locus and the uniforms were directing new arrivals to an area of grass verge where they could park. By mid-morning, it was worth a small wager that there would be angry residents complaining that the plods had messed up their lovely streets and caused a lot of unnecessary noise for the genteel inhabitants, who weren't used to being visited by the dark side of the old city. They left the car and asked one of the older uniforms who was in charge. He told them with a barely disguised smirk that the senior officer at the scene was Superintendent Elaine Tenant.

'For fuck's sake!' McGovern said in front of the old PC, who shrugged and said, 'You know her then, sir.'

'Tell me?' Macallan asked, knowing already she wasn't going to like the answer.

McGovern shook his head wearily. 'They call her Ice Cold Tenant. Another fucking genius from the Met come north to show us how it's done. It's all by the book, no imagination, no humour and there's a story that she gets a daily Botox injection to stop her smiling.'

Macallan hoped that it was just the age-old detectives' rant against anyone who wasn't on their team, but McGovern was a top man and usually gave people the benefit of the doubt. She turned to the PC again.

'What about CID senior officers?'

'There's DI Ronnie Slade and DS Martin Bowman with their team. They're here but the SOCOs are all over it at the moment so you'll find them at the incident caravan.'

Macallan nodded and walked over to the CID team, who were in discussion and all making notes on clipboards. She turned to McGovern.

'You know these guys?'

'The best. Worked with both of them and they're the business.'

When the suits recognised Macallan and McGovern they stopped their briefing. Slade shook McGovern's hand and there was obvious warmth between the two men. The DI turned to Macallan.

'Superintendent, are we glad to see you here.' Slade was a good-looking man in his late thirties, not a pound overweight and with the look of a gym fiend. He had an easy smile and she could see that it wasn't just his rank – there was no doubt who the leader was in the team round about him.

'What have we got, Ronnie?'

'What we have is a mess. Three dead. One lying in Ricky Swan's garden. Looks like a shotgun blast did him. No positive ID but one of my team reckons it's Crazy Horse McMartin.' He waited for a response.

'Go on.'

'Two dead in a car not too far from the garden. Driver and passenger and looks like a shotgun, again at close range. You can imagine. The driver is missing most of his head but we've had a look at the passenger and even with the damage I'm sure it's Eddie Fleming. I worked Leith for years and knew them all.'

'All we need.' She turned to McGovern, whose colour had drained at Slade's revelations, then told the DI she'd have a word with Superintendent Tenant and get back to him. The detectives had enough to do taking initial statements from neighbours and the old man who, before he'd collapsed in shock, had been the first to see the mess in the car.

'Anything else before I speak to her?'

'Nothing, apart from the comics in uniform are already calling it the Gunfight at Ricky's Corral. You can bet the contents of your wallet that's what it'll be known as from now on.'

274

She wanted to say the word fuck a few times but she had to maintain the dignity of her office in front of the team. She compromised by saying it just the once. 'Fuck.'

'Amen to that, Superintendent. The press will love that one as a headline,' Bowman chipped in with a wide-toothed grin. He was the oldest of the team and had CID stamped into his soul. She knew these were men who could get something done and thanked God for that. She'd need them the way things were going.

'What about Ricky Swan?' she asked, and despite what she thought of the man, she hoped he'd survived because they were running out of live suspects.

'No sign of him so far unless he's lying in a bush,' Bowman chipped in again. It was obvious that he did most of the cynical funnies; those tended to be the gift of the elder detectives who'd never quite achieved senior rank.

Macallan headed off to find Tenant. What had already been a shit day was going downhill fast.

She found Tenant ripping a strip off a young cop who'd removed his hat while helping move equipment onto the site. She waited till the humiliation was over then watched the uniform walk away with his shoulders slumped. Superintendent Tenant was obviously a master in the art of motivating her troops.

Tenant turned to Macallan, who realised that the Botox reference wasn't much of an exaggeration: this woman didn't do smiley faces.

'Can I help you?' she asked.

Her demeanour was cool verging on freezing, but held back just enough in case Macallan was someone important or a rank above her. Her face was unusually pale, with pinched features, and looked worn though she was probably no more than mid-thirties. Macallan explained who she was and saw Tenant's eyebrows twitch just a fraction as she told her that the events here would probably end up as one of the investigations she was coordinating.

'The decision will have to be made in the morning, and to be honest I have enough on my plate, but I'm sure I'll land this one as well. It'll stay firmly with a dedicated team, but there are a number of related problems I'm trying to keep on track.' She waited for an answer but Tenant continued to eyeball her as if she had a personal hygiene problem. Macallan tried to prompt a bit more of a response. 'We've been in Newcastle since early yesterday and were on the way back when we got the call that this was on. I don't want to get in the road at the moment so I thought I'd touch base with you first.'

Tenant turned to face Macallan full-on. 'I have a lot to do, Superintendent, and unless you have a role here I suggest you keep well back from the locus.'

'Sorry, I thought I'd explained that there are a number of related cases and it's likely this one will fall into the same category. I'll head off and get a couple of hours sleep and pick it up first thing, but do you mind if I have a look around before we head off?' Macallan was struggling to keep the tension out of her voice and wished she hadn't taken the call.

'You say you've been in Newcastle all day.' Tenant said it already loaded with a punchline. 'Does that include drinking time? I can smell it from here. If that's the case you are going nowhere near the locus, suited up or not. Is that understood?'

Tenant almost smiled. The only thing that mattered in her life was her march to the top, plus her absolute dislike of just about anyone who didn't matter, and particularly her competitors. She knew all about Macallan, and just reading about the media's favourite detective made her angry. Turning up stinking of garlic and lager was a gift that was just far too good to ignore, and there was no way she would miss the chance to stick it to a senior detective with so much going for her.

Macallan cringed and cursed herself because there was no credible defence if the woman opposite wanted to make an issue of it. In practical terms they'd done nothing wrong, but in the modern police world it was simple enough to turn practical into neglect of duty. The best she could do was a tactical withdrawal, but everything about the case seemed corrupted and sometimes she wondered if there was indeed such a thing as karma. She had a trail of dead suspects and now she had this unhappy piece of humanity on her case. The worst thing she could do was overreact and make a bad situation worse. Hopefully she could explain it to O'Connor and if he really had changed then perhaps he could hose the whole thing down. It made her want to weep that she was trying to corner one of the most dangerous criminals in the country at the same time someone was trying to attach a question mark to her sense of duty.

'We had a long hard day, were off duty and needed to eat so we had a beer with the meal. I can assure you that the driver had nothing to drink so please don't go in that particular direction. We'll get out of your way, and as I said I may well pick this up in the morning once I've spoken to Mr O'Connor.'

'Very well, but you of all people should know that if you want to examine the locus then that means you're back on duty.' Tenant turned her back on Macallan, who felt her face glow red as she headed back to find McGovern and Young. She spoke briefly to Slade and tried to act as if nothing had happened, but the tension in her expression confirmed that Tenant had acted true to form.

'We'll head off, Ronnie, and get our heads down for a couple of hours,' Macallan said. 'It's going to be a long day tomorrow. You'll probably get a break so I'll see you when you're back on. It looks like you'll be working with us. I know you don't know what's going on, but Jimmy will brief you later.' The DI nodded. He knew what Tenant did to people's nerve ends, but he didn't want to get caught in the crossfire between two senior ranks while he was still working at the locus.

When they got in the car McGovern looked round at Macallan in the back seat. 'What happened back there? We should have had the sterile suits on by now.'

'That fucking woman just laid into me because we smell of drink. Can you believe it?' She shook her head, but more in annoyance at herself because Tenant was clearly one of life's awkward bastards, and if she took it any further she'd be on solid ground. So much of rank politics worked this way that Macallan would bet her salary that this trivial matter would end up dropped in all the right places.

'Just what we need in the middle of all this, a zealot on our case.' McGovern felt genuinely depressed at the thought; worse still his headache had turned into a general feeling of nausea and he was sure he was going to regret going anywhere near the Newcastle curry. He knew Macallan was right and that if push came to shove they were in the wrong. 'What the fuck's happened to my beloved police force? I saw it coming when they closed the bar at Fettes all those years ago.'

Macallan put her hand on Young's shoulder as she started the car and headed back to Leith. 'If anyone asks you, no self-sacrificing loyalty. Tell them the truth and keep yourself away from any allegations.'

The analyst's earlier enthusiasm to be at the locus had evaporated under the reality of modern police politics. She nodded but said nothing.

*

278

Macallan was in bed in less than an hour but knew there was little or no chance of her sleeping. Her mind swirled with the problems that she faced and the speed that events were moving had overtaken anything she could achieve by way of investigation. She was way behind the ball and wondered how she could get the operation moving while the lines of investigation were being burned all around Pete Handyside. The Flemings would have been next on her agenda, but where could she steer the operation after tonight's events? The thought that she might not have an answer to her own questions – well that made her sweat. It could make her appear inadequate for the job she'd been handed.

If there was a weak link it certainly wasn't in Newcastle and her gut feeling had always been that the Fleming brothers offered the best chance to get at Handyside's organisation. She decided that perhaps they'd neglected Ricky Swan. From a distance he didn't give off the aura of a big-time criminal, and because he was a high-value source who'd provided so much intel in the past, he'd never come close to being considered a viable target in his own right. Maybe it was time to really find out what his role was. Perhaps he was another route to Handyside. She wouldn't know till she'd pushed his buttons. The fact that he'd introduced the UC into the Flemings' organisation meant the links were there. He ran knocking shops and escorts all over the city and beyond, mostly staffed by foreign women and so little was known about them or where they ended up after they left Edinburgh. She'd read the reports on Swan and they were always vague, lacking in detail about what he was actually up to. In other words, no hard intelligence – and that should have rung bells earlier.

Macallan's laptop was next to her bed; she sat up and emailed Thompson, instructing her to get a specialist team organised first thing to start digging into Swan's finances. As far as she was concerned they should go as far back as possible. Trafficking women made her sick to her stomach and there was no way she could ignore Swan – the murders were a priority for her.

When the message was on its way she lay back on the bed and tried to focus on the fact that in the late afternoon Jack and Adam would walk through the exit doors at Edinburgh Airport. She needed to be with them to remember what mattered in her life. Her old demons were trying to force their way back into her mind and that frightened her as never before.

She forced herself to imagine them taking a long, warm holiday when it was all over, somewhere far away. Eventually her eyes flickered and she settled into a restless sleep.

34

While Macallan slept uneasily, Richter sat up in bed, listening to make sure her parents were not awake. She'd slept lightly for less than an hour and was now determined to keep her eyes open to prevent herself re-entering her terrifying dream world. She could find no way to explain what it was that had crawled into her thoughts and squatted there like a venomous toad inhabiting the dark recesses of her mind. Whenever she'd tried to look into the future it seemed to hold nothing for her but endless years of fear, but now, for the first time in days, her mind was clear and settled. It felt as if she'd been inhabiting two parallel worlds: the conscious, where she was racked with guilt, and her dreams, where she was haunted by memories of the women who'd died for reasons she still didn't understand. This survivor guilt had been recognised by her medical team, but for Richter it was like a physical pain she suffered every minute of her waking day. It was almost a feeling of shame – what right had she to survive when the other girls had perished that night? There was a natural order to things; she believed that she'd gone outside that order and that the dreams were her deserved punishment for avoiding her fate.

She dressed quietly, not wanting to disturb her parents, who she loved so much but who seemed like strangers now. There were no wounds or scars to show them, and she didn't want them to even imagine what she'd witnessed – or the ghosts who visited her every night.

Her father's wallet and some small coins lay on the table inside the suite door. Richter took the notes, stuffed them into her jacket pocket and closed the door quietly behind her.

The city was quiet as she stepped onto the edge of the pavement, taking in the strange environment. Seeing the beauty of Edinburgh's silhouette sketched against the moonlit sky made her pause. She'd read about the old town with its ancient castle, graceful architecture and dark underbelly that had spawned literature both terrifying and entertaining. It was one of the places she'd dreamed of visiting when she eventually finished university.

There had been so many dreams and hopes before her life had been torn apart by the men with no soul. She wasn't frightened any more though; sometimes life was what it was and you just had to accept it.

Richter noticed the small yellow 'for hire' glow above the windscreens of a line of taxis not far from the hotel, dug her hands into her pockets and walked slowly towards them while trying to work out what to say. The weather had changed and fat clouds seemed to bounce across the sky as the wind picked up, and Richter smiled for the first time in days at feeling the night air on her face.

The taxi driver was leaning against the first car in the line enjoying a cigarette. He looked up as she approached him. 'Where to, love?'

'I want to go to the beach please.'

'There's a few beaches to choose from, honey, just tell me where.' He was used to tourists with vague requests, especially the Americans with Scottish ancestry who trawled the city looking for links to their forebears.

Richter was embarrassed when she realised that of course there had to be more than one beach so near to a coastline. 'I just want to go for a walk on a beach.' She was almost pleading with him and the driver wondered if the girl was okay, though as far as possible he tried to avoid other people's problems. He'd seen it all in the back of his cab at one time or another and a foreigner wanting to look at a beach in the middle of the night was purely routine.

'I can take you to Portobello, that's not too far. There's a decent prom there. Can't sleep?'

Richter didn't completely understand what the driver had said so instead of answering she simply smiled and reached for the car door, which was fine for him. He scrunched the fag end out under his shoe and climbed into the driver's seat. The young woman had no idea where Portobello was but it didn't matter as long as there was a beach and the sea. She jumped in the back of the cab and watched the city lights blur across her vision while she thought about her parents sleeping soundly in the hotel. It made her sad, and she wished it had been possible to explain to them what she was feeling – but how could she? What right had she to bring her nightmares to them, and how could she tell anyone she loved what she saw in that other world?

The Flemings' and Drew's plan to cause major disruption in the city and draw the police away from Swan's place had unforeseen consequences for Ingrid Richter. Two uniforms had been deployed 24/7 to stay close to the hotel and the Richter family, just in case, but the chaos that had resulted from the actions of the Flemings' team and the twins' deaths meant that every spare cop in the city had been drawn away from other duties to try to hold the line against the mayhem on the streets. Hardly anyone apart from some uninterested night staff had noticed Richter walk away from the hotel and off into the night.

The taxi drew in at the bottom of King's Road on the west end of Portobello promenade. The driver swung round in his seat and smiled at the sad-looking girl in the back who seemed completely lost. 'This is it, honey, and if you head along the prom it should give you a nice walk and help you to sleep.'

When he told her how much the fare was, she pulled out all the notes from her pocket and handed them over without checking the amount. The denominations would have meant nothing to her anyway. The driver pulled the notes apart and frowned. 'That's far too much, honey.' He handed her half the cash back, but she put her palm up to him.

'Please take it. It's okay, I promise.' She said it with as much of a smile as she could muster and he looked at her with more interest, feeling a twinge of concern. There was no word he could find to describe what he saw, but the girl was troubled, no doubt about it. He remembered his golden rule never to get involved and stuck the money in his pocket.

'You take care, honey.' He waited till she was out of the car, gave her a short wave and drove away slowly, still unsure why he was so worried.

Richter headed slowly along the prom, past what had once been the site of the Fun City amusement park, when Porty, as it was better known, had been a popular destination for day trippers. There was no sign of anyone else, and she was glad that she seemed to be the only person there. The clouds had started to cover the sky and though the temperature had dropped she was unaware of the chilled air. She felt warm and relaxed for the first time in days because she had accepted what her life now was and why she was in this strange place in the early hours of the morning. Coming from a landlocked country, she had always been fascinated by the sea, and on coastal holidays she'd spent hours doing nothing but staring out over the endless waters, dreaming of what might be beyond the faraway horizon.

She leaned on the prom railings and tried to imagine what this place would be like with the sun shining on the people who used the beach. She remembered her first holiday by the sea, the excitement of playing in sand; her father laughing and helping her to mould castles then dig moats to keep imaginary attackers at bay. It was so real she could almost feel the heat of those warm days on her face.

Stepping down onto the sand, Richter abandoned her shoes and padded to the water's edge where she sat down, crossed her legs and listened to the waves lapping, almost reaching her then retreating as she stretched out her hand to feel the cold tingle of the salt water. It was summertime and the first hint of the new day started to touch the deep inky blue of the night. Time stopped for Richter and the colours of the eastern sky intrigued her.

Some streaks of red started to appear on the skyline, becoming angry slivers of fire that seemed to arc towards the city. She gasped when it seemed as if a switch had been pulled and the world changed again; the deep colours departed, replaced by the monochrome world of her nightmares. The dark sun rose out of the sea and she felt her skin burning as if she was on fire. It was unbearable and she needed the feel of the chill water to ease the heat that was eating into her.

She stood up, dropped her clothes and slipped into

the water, finding there the relief that eased and cooled her flesh. The water was energising. When she felt her feet lose hold of the bottom she started to swim a steady stroke, breathing easily, and the terrifying black sun disappeared. The early morning half-light and the streaks of red were in front of her as she aimed towards those far-off horizons and what lay beyond.

35

The taxi driver had reached Princes Street when he said 'fuck it' and banged his fist on the steering wheel. He couldn't get the foreign girl out of his head and was annoyed at himself for breaking his own 'I don't give a fuck' rule. He wheeled the cab round and headed back to Portobello. The streets were empty so he was there in fifteen minutes and parked at almost the same spot where he'd left the girl earlier on.

Lines of grey and blue cut by great streaks of fiery red lay along the horizon as the new dawn made its appearance. There was no sign of the girl, and he hurried along the prom, not quite sure what he would do if he actually saw her. What worried him more was what he would do if he couldn't see her. For a man who stayed out of other people's business it was a difficult problem to resolve.

By the time he'd reached the east end of the promenade he had done his best to convince himself that he was overreacting. He was due to finish his shift, and he wasn't sure how his wife would react to a claim that he'd suddenly become a concerned citizen. She never really believed half his stories and any mention of a foreign girl would just add to her suspicions that he was playing away. The driver compromised, telling himself that he'd walk back to the cab along the water's edge and if there was still no sign of the girl he'd forget all about her and go home.

About halfway along the beach he stopped again and looked up at the dawn light: a whole range of blues and reds had mixed together to create an impression that the sky was raging at the world. It was beautiful, almost desolate, and it looked like it was approaching the old city to engulf it in its flames. He lit a cigarette and smiled at the thought that he'd got himself carried away by the sight of an attractive young woman who looked like she had problems.

'The story of my fuckin' life,' he said and tossed his cigarette into the receding tide – and that's when he saw the discarded clothes in the sand. He felt his heart thump in his chest and hoped that it was debris from the previous day's visitors.

He picked up the jacket and recognised the floral design on the collar. His instincts had been correct, but he had a problem convincing the police of that when they finally responded to his call and he couldn't quite explain why he'd been so worried or why he'd turned back. The two uniforms had just spent one of their worst nights in months answering calls in a city that seemed to have gone mad. They were both knackered and the taxi driver's story just didn't make sense. It was smelly enough for them to think he might have tried to get his leg over a reluctant passenger and it had all gone horribly wrong. The younger of the two uniforms wanted to make it into CID and had already decided that the increasingly nervous driver was a murdering bastard.

'I'm tellin' you, Charlie. The guy's at it,' he said to

his partner. 'I'll phone the CID and see what they say. Suppose we'd better leave the girl's stuff in situ.'

'*In situ!*' the older and wiser cop said with a tired smirk. 'I think you'll make it right to the top of the CID using words like that, son.'

They called for another uniform to stay with the clothes and took the blubbering driver to a station, where he would be given a hard time before his story was finally believed.

The chaos that had engulfed the city had nearly passed. As the night-shift officers signed off and ached to get home, the sky seethed angrily above their heads and the wind picked up, driving cold rain into the faces of the men and women entering and leaving the stations around the old city. It was unseasonal weather, but it was Scotland and unseasonal was normal.

36

Macallan had struggled all night to get anything resembling rest. There had been a brief period where she'd hung somewhere between the conscious world and sleep, but she hadn't been able to take that final dive; there was simply too much to think about. Eventually she gave up trying and swung her legs over the side of the bed. It was pointless to spend any more time trying to rest, despite how tired she was, and she decided she might as well take the day on, whether she was knackered or not. It would look like she'd lost the plot if she was spotted going into the office this early so she decided to relax for half an hour with coffee and out-of-date bread that would do the job once it had been carbonised in the toaster.

Her new power shower was a godsend and she let it blast her skin red before doing a minute under the cold till she couldn't stand it any longer. She dried off quickly, brewed the coffee, lay back on the bed and devoured her jam-covered toast. Once she was fully awake the anxieties of the night drifted away as she put things back in perspective. Jack and Adam would be with her by the evening, and she was sure that alone would lift her spirits.

The main problem of the day would be making the right decision on where she steered the investigation now that the Flemings were off to join their old man and brother. She thought digging deep into Swan's life was the right call, and it might throw up some unexpected leads to Handyside. Even if it didn't, he would take a serious hit if he was trafficking women. The challenge was to work out how he'd reacted to the previous night's havoc at The Corral or – perhaps more importantly – simply to find him. As it stood, Swan was the main witness for a triple homicide and the investigation team needed to get hold of him as soon as. There was still the possibility that he'd been taken out as well and his skinny little carcass just hadn't been found yet. She still didn't know why the shootings had happened the way they had and untangling the whole mess was going to be a nightmare.

Once she was dressed, Macallan decided to walk to the office, needing the air and a stretch to untangle the knots in her mind and body. The one thing she was sure of was that Pete Handyside was part of the answer, and she'd have to rethink how to get him cornered.

When she'd been making her coffee earlier it had been raining and the wind had been blowing hard through the city streets, but by the time she left the flat it had cleared again and the sky was ablaze with a swirling palette of reds, purples and blues. She thought it might have been an angry reflection of the night's events and prayed that she could find an answer, a chink to squeeze open … just something to motivate the troops into digging up the evidence that would put someone away for the horrors that had taken place.

The traffic was still light as she strolled along Constitution Street, and it was quiet enough to catch some of the dawn chorus still being belted out over the old port. Macallan couldn't remember having to face a situation where the main target was killing the witnesses and suspects quicker than she could get to them. Smiling grimly she decided that at least it couldn't get any worse. She was wrong though – she hadn't yet heard about the latest tragedy.

Another torrent of rain and wind crashed into the city just as she entered the front door of the station. Thankfully the office itself was quiet. The rain thumped at the windows like an angry man, the sky had turned dark grey again and the clouds dropped to blot out the tops of high buildings. The old station was getting a bit worse for wear, and the gaps in the windows and doors led to an almost permanent low howling sound throughout the building. There was no one else in the office and even the cleaners hadn't shown up yet. It was just the way she wanted it, because she needed some time in the working environment to get her head back into place.

She booted up her PC and paged through the information system, shaking her head at what must have been a bastard of a time for almost everyone who had been on during the night shift. It started to niggle – all that mayhem that seemed to be well away from the Ravelston area of the city. Macallan knew better than most how diversions worked, the paramilitaries having been masters of the art during the Troubles. This had the same smell. Coincidences could happen, but this was too conspicuous. She made a note on her scribble pad to see who, if anyone, had been arrested and get them seen by her own team. She wanted to know if there had been any coordination in what had taken place on the streets of the capital.

She read an email saying that there would be an early briefing on the situation at The Corral and she replied that she'd be there with McGovern.

The list of incidents seemed to go on and on and she'd already flicked past the report of a possible MISPER down at Portobello. It didn't sound that unusual, probably just one of those events where too much drink was involved and the locals would resolve it when the girl had sobered up wherever she'd passed out. Macallan only glanced at the details and she was three entries further on when an alarm went off in the back of her mind. She scrolled back up and felt the skin on her back tingle when she found the entry on the MISPER. Her heart sank as she went backwards through the information. It wasn't the taxi driver or the clothes that had caught her attention, but where the driver claimed to have picked up the attractive foreign girl.

'Please, no,' Macallan said to the empty room around her.

The taxi stand was close to the hotel where Ingrid Richter was staying with her parents. It could have been another coincidence, but Macallan knew that wouldn't be the case. That wasn't how Sod's law worked, and it felt as if the investigation and everything that it touched was cursed.

She flicked back through the information log and stopped at the point where the beat officers had described the pile of clothing on the beach. Maybe it was an omen, but she realised that they were the same uniforms who'd found the Fleming twins' mother in a gibbering heap after she'd been abducted by Billy Nelson's Loyalist team. It had been just before the bombing that had nearly killed her.

Macallan shivered; being back in this building kept resurrecting the memory that Jack had been trying so hard to erase. She dragged herself back to the present.

The medical staff at the hospital had told Macallan that Richter was being haunted by nightmares involving visions of beaches and the sea. It all made terrible sense to her.

As she sat back in her seat and closed her eyes to digest what she'd read, a text came up on her mobile to call one of the area inspectors. Macallan stared at the message, knowing what she was about to be told.

She leaned forward, held the top of her head with both hands and tried not to break down. Her heart thumped against her rib cage as she tried to calm herself. It was too much to cope with and her thoughts started swirling again as she began to panic at the scale of the problems she was being expected to handle.

She stood up and walked over to the window and concentrated on Jack and Adam for a few minutes till her heart slowed enough for her to make the call without the tremor in her voice that would expose her uncertainty.

The inspector, sounding like she was dead on her feet, confirmed that Richter was the missing person. Her father had woken early and discovered that his daughter was gone. They'd no idea when she might have left and CID were still interviewing the driver, though it looked like he was in the clear for any assault on Richter.

Macallan explained some of the background and that Richter was the girl found near Eyemouth. There was a pause as the voice on the other end of the phone digested what this meant. Macallan gave as little away as possible while still trying to sound supportive to the exhausted uniform.

'Thanks, Inspector. All you can do is give it the full treatment as a MISPER and possible suicide. I'll get someone from my team with a bit of background knowledge to liaise with whoever is handling it at your end. She was an important witness for us, but we'll let the CID handle it. I know she hasn't been found but I can't see this ending well given what she's been through.'

Macallan sat back in front of the computer and stared at the screen without seeing a word. If Richter was dead, Pete Handyside would never stand trial for killing her, even though he was the killer as far as Macallan was concerned. She felt rising anger displace the seething doubts of the night; it burned through her and she decided it was time to get back in the game.

'Fuck them all,' she snarled into the silence of the office.

'Beg your pardon, miss?' The old cleaner almost whispered it – as if she'd done something wrong.

Macallan swung round in surprise and smiled broadly. 'Winnie, you're a sight for sore eyes. Let me make you a cuppa.'

Winnie felt like royalty as a senior police officer made her coffee, fed her biscuits and asked about her family. Most of the cops she saw treated her as if she was invisible and unimportant. When she got home at the end of her shift she called her sister and told her all about it.

McGovern still didn't feel that well; nevertheless he was in the office sharp and not surprised to find Macallan already at her desk. What did surprise him was that she seemed to have found new energy; he'd been worried that she was going to be overwhelmed given everything that had happened.

'Good morning!' she said to him. 'You look like shit, but then so do I. Take it you didn't sleep either?'

'It must have been the curry but I'll survive. What's doing?'

She hit him first with the news about Richter and he sank into a seat opposite her. She knew the girl's story had been hard to listen to – the look she'd seen in his eyes when he'd recounted the young woman's statement had made that perfectly clear.

'I just checked again and there's no sign of her yet.

There's a team out searching the beaches down to Musselburgh and a chopper is in the air as we speak. Not much we can do, but could you get Pam Fitzgerald to liaise with them as she knows as much as anyone about the girl. Make sure she's briefed not to discuss any of the investigation side of it, and particularly not Handyside.'

'What's the plan for us now the Fleming boys are no more?'

'First things first. We have to attend a briefing at Fettes on the incident at Swan's and then we'll stay there for a closed session with Felicity to see what we've got and what we do with it. One thing is for sure – I had my doubts over the last few days but I'm certain now we'll nail the bastards who've done all this.' She slapped McGovern on the arm, and as they headed for the murder briefing McGovern took a call that Swan had been in touch with his handlers. Apparently he was in complete meltdown so they were on their way to see him and would call in as soon as they had more information.

'At least he's not dead.' Macallan felt the tide had turned with Richter's disappearance. If there had been any reason for the detective to wallow in self-pity then it had vanished with news of the night's events, and if it all turned out to be part of some master plan then she was going to make sure whoever was responsible paid a suitable price.

Ronnie Slade arrived at the conference room and looked like he hadn't slept in a week though it was only just over twenty-four hours. His smile was present though, and it was genuine, and Macallan thought there was a bit of a young Harkins about him – with a dash more dress sense. She hadn't known Harkins when he was younger but she'd always had an image of what he must have been like before he decided to rebel and do it all his way.

Young was already there along with the usual reps from specialist departments. Macallan didn't notice any surprise guests as she scanned the room until Tenant strode in with O'Connor. She swore to herself – that could only mean a problem she didn't need. It made no difference though; a day earlier it would have concerned her, but since the news had come in about Richter she was prepared to take it on the chin. She'd promised herself that she'd left her self-doubt behind – that it was probably just a consequence of getting back into the game. Though it was going to take time, whatever the future held she was going to do her best for the girls who'd died needlessly on the *Brighter Dawn*, and that included Ingrid Richter.

She tried a quick smile to O'Connor but received no more than a nod back her way, which told her that Tenant had already stuck her oar in. She felt a moment of juvenile self-satisfaction when she looked at Tenant, who looked like a bag of old mince, and on a good day wouldn't look any better. The phrase 'a face only a mother could love' occurred to her and she could barely restrain a tight grin. It was wrong to judge people on looks, and she would have ripped up anyone else for doing it, but she thought she deserved a small moment of indulgence.

Tenant saw it and her already grey complexion deepened by another tone.

O'Connor opened the meeting and asked for the lights to be put on. Outside the storm pounded the city and water zigzagged down the edges of windows that should have been replaced years before. Then O'Connor handed over to Slade, who told the meeting more or less what they all knew already. This, however, didn't stop Young scribbling endless notes, which was reassuring in its own way. No matter what anyone else ever thought, Young always believed the answers were there somewhere, waiting to be connected.

Slade told the meeting that they'd confirmed the identity of the first deceased and that as far as they could work it out, Crazy Horse had been shot at close range and probably died immediately. There were footprints in the grass and soil heading away from the body in the general direction of the car where the Flemings were killed. It was impossible to confirm till all the tests had been carried out but it looked like the Flemings had known their killer. The position of the car meant they must have seen whoever it was walking away from The Corral towards them.

Slade paused and let it all sink in, watching as they worked through the flood of images forming in their minds. 'Whoever it was must have been a cool bastard because this all took serious balls.'

There was a deep sigh from Tenant's direction as she folded her arms tightly across her chest. She clearly disapproved of the word balls, but the rest of the room ignored her as best they could.

Slade flicked through some of his notes, looking for anything else he could tell the meeting that was confirmed as fact. 'A witness has been spoken to on the door-to-door enquiries,' he added. 'They were a bit further away and looked out of the window when they heard the shots. They describe a figure in dark clothing get into what they thought was a BMW and head off. That's as good as it gets from them. The intelligence team have let me know that such a car was found burned out down at Cramond. Can't confirm it's the one just yet but the team at the locus reckon there's the remains of a sawn-off there. The car and contents are completely toasted so it's unlikely we'll get any forensics.' He waited for questions and Macallan asked him if Brenda McMartin had been told yet.

'Yes. She went radio rental and tried to sink her teeth into the detectives who told her. Luckily she's still not recovered from her injuries and they managed to restrain her. God knows what'll happen when that woman gets out of hospital and back on the street.' Slade felt weary; he just wanted to get the briefing over, stand in the shower and sleep for a few hours – but there was still a bit to do.

'The other priority is that we need to get Ricky Swan. Crazy Horse was found on his lawn, the front door wide open and Ricky and his dog gone. Given this is the second incident involving a McMartin, we can assume that Swan is in a bad place. I mean, these fuckers are mental.' Slade realised he'd just used tut-tut language in the wrong place and blushed.

Tenant looked like she would explode; she clearly thought O'Connor should rip him up but that didn't happen so he crashed on. 'I believe Superintendent Macallan has got some info.' He sank back and let her take over. His face was burning, and he tried to avoid eye contact with Tenant in case she turned him into a pillar of salt.

'Jimmy got a call when we were on the way here.' Macallan left out the reference to handlers because it was need-to-know that Swan was a source. 'Swan's at a flat used by one of his escort girls. We should get a call back shortly and I'll brief Ronnie before he goes off for some well-deserved sleep.' She nodded over at the DI then looked round the table before she broke her main news.

'I'm not sure who knows here but Ingrid Richter, the girl found on the beach at Eyemouth, is a MISPER and I'm afraid the signs are not good. The locals are handling the search and liaison with the family but obviously I'll be kept in the loop. There's no reason to suspect anything suspicious at the moment, but she was our one and only witness for the *Brighter Dawn* and it looks like we've lost her. Apart from anything else it's a tragedy for the family. The girl made it to the shore but didn't really survive what happened on that boat.'

'The press are going to combust over all this, Grace, but we are where we are, I suppose.' O'Connor looked flat when he said it.

They ran over some of the routine matters and O'Connor made the formal decision that the shootings would be included in the cases being coordinated by Macallan. A team including Slade would be free to investigate but everything had to be run past Macallan, and she would have the final say on the direction of the various linked investigations.

O'Connor then closed the meeting and asked to see Macallan before her meeting with Young. She nodded to McGovern, who still looked sick, and told him she'd be there as soon as she was clear of O'Connor. His office was close to their meeting room and she followed him in and closed the door behind her. She knew exactly what was coming, but she was prepared.

'I had Elaine Tenant in here first thing. She's a hard woman to like.'

Macallan hadn't expected this level of honesty about a senior officer. Considering O'Connor was ever the politician, this suggested he really had changed. 'You probably know what she's said and you're too smart a detective to be surprised by this. Did you have a drink last night?'

'I had more than one. It was a hard day and we were tired and hungry so we had a meal and two or three beers. Just for the record, Felicity volunteered to drive back so had nothing more than water. On the way up we were called about the shooting and I decided to have a look. That's all that happened. Superintendent Tenant made an issue of it and I left. I was wrong if it's any help, but if you want an apology it's not coming. Do what you want.' She felt strong again; her edge was back and the uncertainty gone. Whatever happened she was going to do this investigation so if they sidelined her she was finished with the job.

'Look, I don't expect an apology because you are what you are. That's why you have this case. It's a bigger mess than I realised, and we're going to be hung out to dry in the press. I'm the one who had the vanity problem but there are times you're too stubborn for your own good. We don't need distractions, and you would have been furious if one of your team had given a woman like that an open goal. Let's just make out that you've had some kind of arse-kicking from me then I can throw cold water all over this one. Please, Grace, I do not need this hassle and you certainly don't. Accept it for old times' sake and let's get on and do the job.'

He'd thrown her, but she saw the desperation in his eyes and decided to jump off her high horse before saying anything else she might regret. To most people the drink issue would have seemed trivial, but Macallan knew how much mileage Tenant could make out of it if she wanted. O'Connor was trying to help, and it was a good offer. She relaxed back into her seat.

'Okay, for the record I've had my arse kicked. I can take it. Can I go and get on with the job, sir?'

'Okay. Just do what you do and till this is finished I'll do everything I can to cover for you.'

Macallan stood up and made for the door but couldn't resist asking, 'What happened? We were so involved, then you turned on me and now this. I wish I understood...'

'Not now. Just accept it, and when this is finished I'll buy you lunch and explain. I have to put Tenant back in her coffin during the hours of daylight.'

Macallan saw the look in his eye and left it there. She

headed for the closed meeting with Young. On the way she picked up a call from the handlers – Swan was close to a nervous breakdown, and in a way she could hardly blame him. Having the McMartin clan on your case was enough to terrify the strongest character, never mind the original eight-stone weakling. She told them to stay with him and she'd come over once she'd finished her meeting.

37

When Macallan entered the room she found Young already waiting for her with McGovern and Lesley Thompson had joined them. She tried to sound as upbeat as possible but she was distracted by McGovern, who was clearly suffering in silence. She didn't need a quack to tell her something was wrong so she eventually offered to let him go home and sleep off the bug. As always though it was a waste of time trying to get him off the job and he insisted he'd be fine.

Time was passing and she was due to meet Jack and Adam at the airport in the late afternoon. There was no way she could miss that, and as there weren't enough hours left in the day to do what she wanted, she pushed them on.

'Tell me what we've got, Felicity, and by the end of this meeting we'll decide where we go from here. It's getting harder by the day and we're running short of options but we aren't quite out of them yet. We've been slow to get going and part of that's my fault, so let's change all that. You've been looking at the call patterns and we have a criminal intelligence and forensic report, some of which

I'm seeing for the first time, on what we have so far, but I'll go over that.' She nodded at the analyst, who ran into her usual preamble about her methods and cautions where the analysts' work had produced a hypothesis only.

'I looked at all the phones we'd known about from criminal intelligence and though that was valuable it didn't take us anywhere near the incident on the *Brighter Dawn*. There *were* calls between the Flemings, Handyside and the McMartins but all on their regular phones, and as we know they would normally use clean phones for a significant job that didn't give us anything. They did made one mistake though – or rather Eddie Fleming made a mistake. He called Ricky Swan on what I now believe was his clean phone and Ricky passed the number to his handler as a routine piece of info.'

It was that moment; Macallan felt her pulse pick up another twenty beats a minute at the word 'mistake'. As an investigation it had been nothing but endless bad news and there was the one simple word that could change the whole game.

'We followed the trail from that number and I'm certain we've identified the chain of clean phones used for the *Brighter Dawn* job. Of course it's clear that they were all disposed of at some point after the UC went missing. However from that traffic I'm able to say that there was an exchange of calls between Edinburgh, Tyneside and Eyemouth on the night we're interested in.'

'What about Glasgow?' Macallan asked.

'Not that night, but the days before and after so they're all there. It looks like they used these phones to call the meeting they had the night the UC went missing. He'd reported that he was driving the Flemings down there that night, so we can be certain of that particular fact. That's the last point that we know the UC was in contact, or alive for that matter.'

Macallan felt there might be a bit of an anticlimax because it gave them a picture that confirmed what they'd suspected already, but the phones were gone and so it was nothing on its own. In a chain of evidence it could help, but they needed more than that. She was about to take over when Young said there was more – much more.

'There is something else. I've checked it several times because I really thought it was wrong.' Macallan felt her heartbeat thumping even faster. 'I've put the phone that appears at the centre of the web up on the whiteboard so you can see the pattern of calls. We can be pretty sure it's Pete Handyside, or at the very least someone he trusts completely, and from what we've been told that can only be one other person – Maxi Turner. However my view is it has to be Handyside.'

Macallan loved Young but she could be frustrating in the time it took her to get to the point. She did it every time, always forgetting that the detectives were like drowning people who just needed a lifeline.

'Whoever was using that phone made one call to a number that only appears once and that was on the night of the events in Eyemouth.' The analyst seemed reluctant to carry on and Macallan was sure she saw Young's hand tremble as she clutched her notes too tightly.

'Who was it?' Macallan asked, intuitively knowing the analyst was unsure how to report what she'd proved.

'My team have been working half the night on this, tested it and we're as sure as we can be ... It's Tony Harrison.' She looked round the faces in the room and said the name again. She paused for a moment, watching their reactions. 'You could say they made a mistake, but they'd no reason to think that call would ever mean anything. The phone was and would have stayed clean if Fleming hadn't called a source who passed us his number. That was the mistake on their part that led me to the Newcastle connection.'

'A big thanks to them then.' Macallan did her best not to show too much emotion, but it was difficult and the room was quiet till she broke the spell. 'Jesus, are you absolutely sure?' Despite Macallan knowing the answer, she wanted to buy a bit more time to gather her thoughts. Young nodded and waited for some response.

'Anything else?' Macallan asked. 'There could be an explanation for one call. Harrison said they've crossed swords before. Anything to back it up?'

'There is. While my team were looking at the phone calls I decided to get one of my researchers to look back at his career and see if anything looked out of place. We found it. When he was in the Met he was seconded to the Regional Crime Squad and there were a lot of integrity questions round them at the time. Mostly around corrupt payments, tipping off criminals and stealing drugs. I found a report about Handyside being arrested when he went down to meet an East End team for a cocaine deal. There were several arrests at the time and for some reason Handyside was released without charge. When I dug into it, I found that Tony Harrison was the arresting officer. There were subsequent internal investigations and it looks like Harrison left the Regional Crime Squad under a cloud but nothing could be proved against him. He did another spell in the Met and then transferred to Newcastle. On paper, an impressive career – until you look deep under the surface. He's had quite a number of headline arrests, all competitors of Handyside when he was on the rise, but of course nothing against the man himself. One last point is that Harrison has quite a life-style: second home in the country and a place in Tuscany. Maybe a coincidence ...' Young let her words hang, put her papers down on the table and waited for Macallan.

'I'll see that bastard locked up; trust me. Okay, we need to think about this, but I can tell you now that the call from that phone would have to have come from Handyside. If you look at the forensic report we've been given, the cigarette ends found where the watchers' car was spotted by Jimmy's boys in Eyemouth have been DNA'd and we have names. One of them is Maxi Turner, who we know about, and the other is a young tearaway called Geordie Simms, who's fairly new to Handyside's team.'

Macallan sat back feeling relieved and seriously angry at the same time. They'd just found an opening and what she did next would be crucial to the outcome of the investigation. She needed to think before deciding what they would do and knew she needed to let her anger subside before taking any action.

'We'll meet again after I've seen Swan and we'll decide who we move against and how. There's other crime intel in the report, and the main thing is that several sources on the periphery of the Flemings' team report that Billy Drew was working closely with them. No one's exactly sure what his role was, but he was there, and without jumping to conclusions he would have been capable of what happened at The Corral. But why?'

No one had an answer so she brought the meeting to a close. She noticed a text and when she opened it up she found it was from O'Connor, saying that he'd bribed Tenant with a plum training course being run at Bramshill. It was the International Women's Leadership Programme and would keep her out of harm's way for five weeks. O'Connor finished the text with 'everyone's a winner'. Macallan nodded, though the spat with Tenant had slipped well down her list of problems given what she'd just been told.

McGovern headed straight for the bog and threw up,

retching in an attempt to relieve his discomfort. Macallan had been planning to take him with her to see Swan, but one look at him told her that wasn't happening. 'You have to go home,' she insisted. 'I'm not taking you like this. Don't make me order you.'

It was a rare occasion where McGovern gave in, but he had to because his legs felt like they were about to give way under him. Macallan got one of the team to run him home, guessing it had to be the curry, though she'd eaten the same and was okay...

Thompson did her best not to show it but she almost grabbed Macallan when the detective asked her to come with her to see Swan, and together they drove along roads snarled with traffic, the streets awash after the storm, hoping this might be the break they needed.

38

The handlers were with Swan when Macallan and Thompson arrived at the small flat in Causewayside rented by one of his escorts. The girl was pure Glasgow and wanted hee-haw to do with the police, so after Swan had swallowed all the booze she had in the house she'd packed her few belongings into a bag and took off to catch the first train back to Glasgow. She'd already made up her mind that Edinburgh was going off its fucking head and life was safer back in the west.

When Macallan walked into the flat, Swan groaned; he'd decided at their previous meeting that she wasn't his favourite detective. He looked a mess on his good days but the added toxins of fear and the escort's cheap booze made him look even worse, if that were possible. Gnasher lay quietly under an old chair, looking pissed off. Macallan stroked the dog's head and watched the poor beast's eyes lift in a 'get me out of here' expression.

'What the fuck are you going to do about all this shit? This is completely out of order, and remember what I still have stashed away if you don't get the finger out.' He was just under half-pissed and Macallan knew there was little chance of getting sense out of him, but he was their star witness so he needed to give a statement before they could do anything more with him.

'How much do you know about what happened at your house last night?' Macallan said as calmly as she could. He looked bewildered and the handler known as Arthur stepped in.

'Ricky told us that Crazy Horse got him at the door of the house, forced him inside and was about to gut him, when, according to Ricky, he fought him off and escaped. Now call me an old cynic, but we're taking that one with a bucketful of salt. He legged it and we've told him nothing about events after his daring escape. Right so far, Ricky?'

They all looked at the dishevelled man in the corner for an acknowledgement.

'I don't give a rubber duck if you believe it or not but that's what happened. Now will someone tell me what the fuck is goin' on?' Even through his scrambled brain Swan realised that something very serious was taking place. Two handlers plus madam God All-Fucking Mighty arriving on the scene meant things were taking a definite turn for the worse.

'Tell him, Lesley. Ricky doesn't like me so you can have the pleasure.' Macallan sat down in a chair and waited for Swan's reaction to the news that his home was now an infamous landmark.

'I'm DCI Lesley Thompson, Ricky. We're here to tell you that, after you got away from your home last night, someone killed Bobby McMartin on your front lawn.' Thompson thought it was best to give the deceased his proper name in the circumstances. Swan made a small whimpering noise like a cat and Macallan enjoyed watching him suffer.

'About the same time, Eddie and Pat Fleming were

killed in a car parked not far from your home. It looks like they were all shot. As it stands, we don't have anyone in custody.' She stopped for a moment as Swan went to pieces. He tried to light up a fag but couldn't get his hand to stop shaking, and the involuntary whimpering noises he'd been making went up a few decibels.

'Someone will need to take a statement from you, but what we need to know is – did you see any of this or do you know who could have killed them?'

Swan bolted for the kitchen but failed to reach the sink before spewing up what little was in his stomach. He collapsed to his knees and started saying 'Oh God' over and over again. Gnasher stayed where he was, watching the proceedings from his comfortable spot under the chair.

Macallan stood up, went to the sink and filled what passed for a clean glass with cold water.

'Here, Ricky, drink this and you'll feel a whole lot better.' She helped him up and back into his chair where he wiped his mouth with the dish towel from the kitchen. The spew seemed to have calmed him down, and as he sipped the water and finally managed to get a cigarette into his mouth, he looked back towards Macallan.

'I'm dead if I stay here. You know that?' It was directed at her as a question with an obvious answer.

'There have been two attempts so far by the McMartins; one of them is now dead but the other is well on the way to recovery in hospital. You do the maths: you say you have nothing to give us as evidence, don't want to be a witness – and that means if you tell us nothing the taxpayer can't finance a protection team for you. Why would they?'

Swan knew he was in the worst of places. Of course he had information on trafficking, because he was the fucking man who made the moves when the girls were brought into the country. He did good business with the Flemings, they dealt with Newcastle and Glasgow, so he could put a shitload of evidence on the table – but not without exposing himself. He'd been the middleman for years in Scotland, but what really worried him was that some girls had been handed over to wealthy businessmen or criminals and never seen again. If the detectives worked it all out then the only deal he would get was a couple of years off a big one inside. Inside. The word terrified him – the thought of being locked up with men of violence was his idea of hell on earth.

'I don't know anything, Superintendent; I'm just a businessman.' He'd calmed down, understanding that his only chance of survival was to get out of the city and hope the police could take out the main men. Crazy Horse and the Flemings were dead, that was a good start, but there was that fucking nightmare down in Newcastle … and he didn't want to even think about The Bitch making a recovery. The other question was: who killed the Flemings and why the fuck were they hanging around his place? Someone else was out there in the city and maybe the plan had been to kill him as well.

'I'll give a statement about Crazy Horse, that's all. Then I'm out of it. You can't stop me unless you intend to charge me with something.' He wanted to see if Macallan had anything.

'Not at the moment, we're too busy picking up all the bodies. But don't worry, we'll get round to you eventually.'

She had an idea and decided to play it there and then. There was no time to wait. 'We won't stop you going, but let us know where, so if anything happens we can get someone to you quickly. Other than that we'll keep in touch and let you know how things are progressing.'

312

She'd taken a more conciliatory tone; everyone noticed it and wondered why.

'Okay, I've got an old cottage up near Loch Melfort, south of Oban. Just use it a few times a year if I want to take a couple of girls away for a party.' He managed one of his leers and Thompson swallowed hard, trying to erase the image from her mind. 'I'll go there for as long as it takes to sell up. I'm not short and maybe it's time to live the dream in the sun, get myself out of this shithole.'

Macallan ignored him and phoned the office, telling them to leave a message for Slade and his DS that Swan was available for interview when they were.

She turned back to Swan. 'That's agreed then, Ricky. When you're finished with the investigation team we'll sort out a plan to get you home, pack up what you need and get you out of the city. After that we'll rig up a system where we can keep in touch whenever we need you or vice versa. How does that sound?'

Swan decided he was prepared to work with Macallan now she seemed to have changed her attitude. He supposed she must have been at a bad time of the month on their first meeting.

Macallan and Thompson had another meeting to attend before they went back to the office. The post-mortem on Crazy Horse and the two Flemings was scheduled and Macallan had arranged to attend with Slade. When they parked the car she turned to her DCI.

'I'm fine if you'd rather give this a miss. As long as Ronnie's there with the SOCOs, it's enough. I just always feel I have to go whether I like it or not.' Knowing that Thompson had suffered a lot with her injuries, Macallan wanted to be careful with her and tried her best to sound reassuring. Some of the toughest detectives struggled at PMs and there was no shame in not wanting to be there.

'No, don't even suggest that. We know what these men did and I want to see it all so I can do my job. People have been treating me with kid gloves since the explosion; please don't you do it as well.' There was anger as well as frustration in her voice and expression. Macallan realised that Thompson was right to be angry and that what had happened was something the DCI would deal with herself.

'I'm sorry, I do understand, and I won't do that again. Let's stick some Vicks up our hooters and get in there.' She put her hand on Thompson's arm and gave it a squeeze.

The post-mortem was messy but unremarkable apart from the revelation that Crazy Horse had some prior damage to his brain which the pathologist guessed must have come from his exploits as a battler. No one was surprised. Because of the nature of the injuries to the three men, it was a slow process and the mess that had been Pat Fleming's head took some time to satisfy the pathologist. The end result was another non-surprise: the three of them had died from gunshot wounds at close range. Macallan looked round at Thompson a couple of times but saw nothing but resolve; if she wasn't mistaken a real detective was taking shape in her DCI.

As Thompson drove them back to the office, Macallan said very little, preoccupied with trying to work out the next play. They had a chance – it wasn't going to be easy and they would need a slice of luck, but it was there if she had the nerve to play it.

Immediately on their return to Fettes, Macallan went to O'Connor and ran the meeting with Swan and Harrison past him. She presented him with the kind of news no senior officer wants to hear, far less make a decision on. No one knew Macallan's track record better than him and she wouldn't settle for prevarication – she was about to make him back her or take control himself, and he knew what she was going to say before she spoke again.

'I trust you to keep this to yourself at the moment – we don't want the rubber heels sticking their oar in yet. If this is going to work you need to back me here and now. If you can't do that then please say so. It could go wrong, but at the moment we're losing anyway – so what the fuck?'

O'Connor was floored by the revelation about the Newcastle detective. Corruption happened, but this was a senior detective conspiring with one of the worst criminals in the country. On top of all that, Harrison was making it look as if he was leading the hunt for the leak in his force. It was the sort of headline the police didn't need when they were being slaughtered almost daily in the media. He stood up and paced backwards and forwards in front of the window a couple of times.

'One last thing. If we don't report this then we've already crossed a line.' She watched O'Connor's eyes as she spoke.

'I know that, and I'm with you.'

'If we're going to use Harrison we might as well go all the way. I'm not sure that we can get to Handyside by any conventional means. The next time I meet Harrison I want to confirm to him that Swan is a source and that he was working for us when he introduced the UC to the Flemings. Then the lie ...'

'Go on.'

'I tell Harrison that Swan has information on financial transactions and trafficked women that can put Handyside away.' She sat back and waited.

'This breaches Swan's human rights, our duty of care goes in the toilet ... and if it comes out or, worse still, he gets killed, it's over for the both of us,' O'Connor mused, staring across the playing fields. This went hard against the grain for him; O'Connor always played safe because nobody got to the top posts by acting like Mick Harkins.

'I'm sick of these bastards,' Macallan replied. 'I don't know if I can do this job much longer, but I don't want to walk away and see them get away with what happened to Ingrid and those other girls. I didn't need to tell you this, John, but I promised I wouldn't bypass you again.'

He turned round and nodded, his face set. 'Okay. Let's do this. I agree with you. Do you have everything you need in resources?'

'We're okay, and if I want anything I know I can ask you. Thanks.'

She headed back to her office in Leith and called in Young and Thompson. 'I want you to get some things started and then I need to go to the airport to pick up my beloveds. Lesley, I want you to make a call to Harrison, give him my apologies and explain that we need a meeting with him tomorrow because there have been developments.'

'Tony Harrison?' Thompson couldn't resist asking.

'Pete Handyside isn't going to put his hands up for us. If Harrison is the corrupt bastard that we think then we'll use Swan to draw him to us.' She tapped the desk with the end of her pen and the answer was enough for Thompson as Macallan pushed on. 'At the same time we need to make arrangements with them to have Maxi Turner and Geordie Simms lifted so we can interview them. Turner will say nothing, but who knows with the apprentice? Felicity, I want you to press on with the phone analysis and the financial investigation on Swan. There's an application for an authority to intercept his phone and it's a priority to be able to bring him in if we need to. What I really mean is bring him in and keep him. Lesley, I want you to pull all the stops out on this one and I'll sign it as soon as it's ready. The bastard's been free to run this trafficking game for years and given too much room because he's a source. As well as all that, I want a completely up-to-date pen picture on Billy Drew – anything and everything.'

She stood up and pulled on her coat. 'Right, I'm off to the airport; I'll phone Jimmy on the way to see how he is.' She picked up her briefcase and made for the door. 'If there's anything at all, call me. Anything.'

39

Macallan jumped in the car, feeling like a young girl again at the thought of having Jack and Adam back in her arms. She was so excited she forgot to call McGovern, who was on his way to A&E with a suspected heart attack.

As soon as she'd parked the car at Edinburgh Airport, Macallan found herself almost running to the terminal even though she was on time. She scanned the arrivals board and saw there was a delay of about forty minutes. The past few days had been chaotic so she decided to indulge herself with one of her favourite pastimes and drink some coffee while she people-watched. There was something about airports, watching the excited tension on the faces of the waiting friends, lovers and children. That moment when someone dragging a trolley bag walked into view and all the love spilled over.

She sat down with her coffee and watched a twenty-something walk through the gates to be devoured by the guy waiting for her. Macallan couldn't suppress her smile as the couple went into complete lockdown mode and refused to let each other go. An old man sitting at the next table to Macallan chuckled. 'Think they'll have to get a jemmy to separate that pair,' he said.

Macallan nodded in agreement, the moment adding to her change in mood, and she felt the tension easing out of her neck. She'd had terrible doubts since she'd arrived back in Edinburgh, but no matter what happened she wasn't going to let them distract her again. She would see this case through, and now that she had her family again that would be her priority.

She ended up having her own moment when Jack struggled through the gates with Adam and a pile of luggage. It was impossible to hold it back and tears streamed down her face. She didn't bother speaking and just held and kissed them, not wanting to move because it felt so good. The old man who'd joked with Macallan watched them, remembering all those moments he'd had himself and wishing he could do them again.

'You're such a girl, all that blubbing! What happened to the big-time detective?' Jack pushed her back gently and handed Adam over. What surprised and shocked him was the strain cut into her face already. If he'd needed evidence of what the job could do to her in a very short time then the proof stood in front of him.

'You look great.' Even though she looked shattered he meant it, and exhausted or not he was glad they were back together.

'No I don't; I look like shit,' she replied before pressing her face against Adam's and sucking in the sweet scent of her son. He gurgled and wriggled his arms about while Jack grabbed the trolley then steered them towards the car park.

With all three of them back together in the flat it felt like home again. They unpacked, fed Adam then put him down and, thankfully, he was asleep in minutes.

319

'You go and have a bath and I'll cook. How does that sound?'

'Good deal for me, and any chance of an early night if Adam lets us?'

'It's fine by me, detective.'

Macallan soaked properly for the first time in days and she had to fight the urge to fall asleep in the bath. The investigation had been put away for a few hours and all she wanted to do was sit and talk to Jack about nothing in particular and enjoy their meal together. He was a much better cook than she was – though she would never admit it – and while she tended to be careful with her intake of food, always mindful that she'd had a weight problem at one time, this wasn't a night for restraint.

She smiled at the man opposite her when she put down her fork. 'No more, but thanks – that's the best meal I've had all week. Let's just vegetate a bit in front of the box. I think *MasterChef* is on so you might get even more great ideas.'

They settled down on the sofa and within five minutes Macallan was sound asleep on Jack's shoulder. He let her be – talking about her future could come later. He knew she was in the middle of something bad and that would be the worst time to muddle her with questions about their future.

Jack's voice woke her but she didn't want to move, didn't even want to open her eyes. She was so relaxed she felt almost drunk.

'It's Lesley from the office.' Jack had been tempted to let it ring if she would stay asleep, but he knew what she was like and if it was something important she'd beat herself up for days. She took the phone and tried to sound wide awake.

'Hi, Grace. Look I hate doing this on the phone but it's

more bad news. It's Jimmy – he's had a heart attack.'

Macallan grabbed her brow and it hit her that she'd forgotten to call on her way to the airport. 'Jimmy. Are you sure?' She knew it was a stupid question but couldn't think of anything else to say.

Thompson knew how close they were: McGovern and Macallan had become real friends, not just colleagues. The news from the hospital was that the heart attack wasn't likely to prove fatal. Apparently he'd been having symptoms for weeks but had done the man thing and ignored them. The doctors had assured his wife that it was mainly a warning and he'd be fine with a few life changes. McGovern was an enormously fit and strong man, and that had made a difference when things had started to go wrong.

'Are you sure?'

'Of course I'm sure. Apparently he said to his wife that you shouldn't be told till the morning because Jack and Adam have just arrived.'

Ten minutes later Macallan was in the car and on her way to the hospital. When she arrived on the ward Sheena McGovern was on the way out to grab a coffee.

'Grace, you didn't need to come,' she said, but the expression on her face mixed relief with the gentle reproach, and the moment Macallan reached out to give her a hug Sheena broke down, needing to unload her worries after spending the last few hours pretending to her husband that she was fine.

They went for a coffee together and Macallan just listened. What Thompson had told her was near spot on – the consultant was sure that McGovern would be fine and the event had been mild as these things go. That he'd been ignoring the symptoms could have been costly if he hadn't kept to such a strict fitness regime over the years.

'I'm just worried what this might mean for his job. He hasn't got long to go for his pension but that's not the problem. You know what he's like, and I don't know how he can go back to what he's been doing. The job's everything to him, you know that.'

Macallan put her hand over the table and held Sheena's as she started sobbing again.

'We'll do whatever's best for him, that's a promise,' Macallan said. 'If he can't go on the front line we can get him into criminal intelligence. It's a good job, and he'd be ideal for it. Anyway that's for later. Let me have five minutes with him and I'll see you back here.'

McGovern looked almost embarrassed when Macallan arrived at the side of the bed. If she hadn't been told he was ill she wouldn't have known. In fact she thought he looked better than he'd done for the last few days.

'What people will do for some time off! How you doing, big man?'

She saw his eyes fill and was glad he managed to control it. McGovern would hate to blub in front of her over a small matter like his health. He was old school to his core and public blubbing was regarded as a sin. She kissed the top of his head and sat down. 'What are we going to do with you now?' She forced a smile; she couldn't imagine not having this tough joint of a man at her side.

'That's what's worrying me. The quacks keep saying I just need to take it easy. A DCI doing what we do – how does that work?' McGovern was in turmoil, the life he'd known and loved seeming to have disappeared in a moment. And how could he be a proper man again with this weakness in him? No one could see it, but it was there and he knew it would influence every decision he'd make for the rest of his life.

'Look, you know this wasn't the big one. You look good and probably just need a bit of a rest, but that doesn't mean the job's finished for you. You're still harder than most of the men in the service and you can stay on the team. This is probably not the time, but I know what you're like so let's get it out of the way rather than you lying in here worrying all night.'

'What's the deal?'

'Willie Rafferty retires from criminal intelligence soon so there's a DCI's job up for grabs next month. Just think – nine to five and not having to get in spitting distance of these men we take on.'

'That's the point: the front end is all I've ever wanted to do. Can you see me sitting at a desk all day? I don't even like paperwork.'

'Let's get you back on your feet, a bit of a rest and then we'll see. Just for the time being, please do this for Sheena.' She stood up. 'I have to get back to Jack. Quality time and all that bollocks.' She dropped another kiss on the top of his head and left her friend trying to imagine the future away from the sharp end.

Macallan told Sheena it would all be okay and that McGovern would have a cushy number waiting when he was ready to come back, then added, 'For God's sake just don't let anyone tell him that or he'll have another attack.'

They embraced and Macallan left, longing to get home for a few hours. The days to come would be tough and she'd just lost her right hand, but McGovern hadn't done anything wrong. What he *had* done was remind Macallan that they were all human.

When she got back to the flat Adam was awake so they sat on the floor and fell into happy-families mode. It was enough for Macallan. By midnight she was in a deep sleep with Jack's arm slung round her, while in the half-lit ward McGovern stared at the ceiling, trying to come to terms with the fact that he was mortal. Although he'd accepted that he'd been lucky, it would take some time to fully appreciate the gift he'd been given.

40

Billy Drew sat in front of the TV watching one of his favourite old black-and-white gangster films. He was pleased with the way things had gone and was convinced that at last he was on the up. For the first time in his life he'd paid sixty notes for quality malt and thought he deserved every drop. He drank it slowly, savouring the feeling that he'd gambled with his life and come out on top. And then there was that bonus waiting for him down the line. Once Handyside had sent Ricky Swan to meet his ancestors and the turmoil had subsided, he'd take care of Jonathon Barclay first and follow up with Mick Harkins. He was going to spend a bit of time with both of them, making every minute count before he opened them up. It would be his little treat, to spoil himself a little watching them suffer. That was about as good as it got in Drew's world.

Handyside switched out the light, but he was wide awake. When his wife fell asleep he slipped out of bed, dressed and headed down to the riverside at North Shields where he wandered along the quayside to do his thinking. The storm had passed and calm had settled over the city streets again. He knew what had to be done, but his instincts filled him with doubt about his future. For the first time he realised that his order to kill the girls on the *Brighter Dawn* had set off a chain of events he couldn't control any more.

There was a line of fishing boats unloading their catches and he wondered again what life might have been like if he'd gone to sea.

The night air was still and surprisingly warm now. He paused to light up a cigarette and began to blow smoke rings above his head like a kid showing off to his mates. The old Tyneside was disappearing; soon all that would be left were his memories of those days as a child and then his fight to the top. Maxi Turner had been right – they should have taken some time off to enjoy what they'd earned, but it was a bit too late for that. He decided that if they survived the next few days he'd make sure that Turner got his wish: he could go and develop skin cancer in the south of Spain. He was clear in his mind what needed to be done and how things could go wrong.

The other problem was Grace Macallan. When she'd come to his home he felt he'd won a small victory, but that was all. Somewhere along the line, one side would lose the game – or maybe they both would.

'Everything alright there, sir?'

The voice startled him. He turned to find a young policeman, who looked like a teenager and too thin to be wearing the uniform, standing behind him.

'I'm fine, officer. Bad case of insomnia, and I always come down here when I can't sleep. Grew up round here.'

'No problem, sir.' The uniform walked off into the darkness, his heart thumping hard in his chest. He'd just spoken to Pete Handyside, who he'd recognised from the information bulletins. He made a note to pass the details

326

on to criminal intelligence – doubtless he'd get a pat on the back from his shift sergeant for being on the ball in the middle of the night.

Handyside smoked the rest of the cigarette and ambled round to have a look at the fish being landed. This was the place he loved, where most of his memories were formed. It was a place haunted by ghosts from the past, but he knew that under his feet the rats scuttled about below the old piers, watching and waiting. The thought that this might be the last time that he'd take the walk round the old harbour nagged at him, but he accepted it was a possibility. It always had been, but something had changed.

He got back into his Jag, stared at the black waters of the Tyne for a few minutes then headed home. He slipped back into bed and kissed his wife, who pretended she was still asleep. He felt better having made the visit to the harbour and it was all in the lap of the gods now. He was asleep in minutes.

Few citizens of Edinburgh would recognise the address 297 Cowgate, and yet so many of them ended up as short-term guests there at some point. The dark corner of the old town held the city mortuary, whose bland and uninspiring architecture meant most people walked past in blissful ignorance of this reminder of the fragility of life.

Crazy Horse lay quietly beside his former enemies Eddie and Pat Fleming on three matching trays in the chilled darkness of the fridges. They were missing their brains, and in Pat Fleming's case his head, so they didn't feel any discomfort. There was no sound apart from the quiet hum of the power units keeping the guests nice and cool. An audience of detectives and the Procurator Fiscal had watched the pathologist display his skills in forensic examination and sophisticated butchery in the penultimate big event of the men's physical existence. A place in the fridges meant that they'd failed in their chosen career, but at least they'd get the regulation top gangsters' send-off when the detectives were finished with their remains.

As the clock touched midnight Ricky Swan was escorted to The Corral, where he packed some cases, loaded up his car and, with Gnasher staring out of the back window, headed for Loch Melfort.

The winds that had swept over Edinburgh headed north. The sky cleared above the old city and the wet streets reflected the gleaming reflections from a shimmering full moon. The city was quiet again after what had been a perfect storm.

41

It was a brilliant clear morning, the sky was an endless blue from horizon to horizon and it was as if normal services had been resumed after the storm. Macallan woke before the alarm did its job and blinked at the light streaming in through the space between the bedroom curtains. She swung out of bed, padded over to the window and peered out at the world to find summer was back in place and the streets were drying, though there were still puddles that couldn't find a way into the choked drains. Having Jack and Adam back with her had given her the boost she needed and a shower finished the job before she stuffed bread into the toaster. Jack hadn't stirred at all when she got up but came through rubbing his tangled hair, having reacted to the smell of coffee and singed bread.

'I don't know how you're going to get back to full-time work, Jack Fraser; you just can't get out of your bed any more.' She kissed him and put a thick layer of marmalade on her toast. She was desperate to get going but forced herself to take a bit of time over breakfast with her man.

'I was thinking. I had an idea last night, but you were either snoring or rushing off to see Jimmy.'

She said, 'Mmmm,' as she flicked through the routine messages on her phone.

'I was thinking maybe we should get married when you're through this case. Nothing fancy: a few friends, a few drinks and a bit of a party.'

She looked up from the phone and blinked, nearly choking on the piece of toast she was trying to chew. The remains of it dropped from her hand back onto the plate and she stared at him, struggling to find a response. In the end, all she could manage was, 'Why?'

'Why not?' He picked up her toast and chomped a huge bite out of it.

'Okay, but I keep my name.' She tried in vain to hide the tremor in her voice.

'That's it done then. You'd better get off to work. I can see you're a bit agitated.' There was the hint of a boyish grin on his face as he watched her surprise, and that's just how he'd planned it. He loved seeing Macallan caught off guard – those moments when the vulnerable girl was exposed and human.

Macallan sat in her car for a few minutes but didn't start it. She stared in the mirror and realised that marriage had hardly crossed her mind. 'What have you just done?' Her face broke into a grin and she did a silent scream before turning the key and heading for the office.

When Macallan and Thompson arrived in Newcastle, Tony Harrison treated them like old friends. She had to admit that the man knew how to lie, which probably explained why he'd survived so long.

'We've arranged to get Maxi Turner and Geordie

Simms brought in and thought we'd have a briefing before we get going with that.'

'If it's okay, I wouldn't mind a one-to-one before we start briefing you about the shootings in Edinburgh. There are some sensitive issues I need to run past you and we have to keep them watertight.' Macallan's act was flawless and Harrison looked pleased that he was invited to join the inner loop.

The real reason she wanted to see him alone was that their next move required lying skills on a par with Harrison's and Macallan was concerned that Thompson might give something away if she was there when the story was being delivered. For better or worse, lying wasn't one of Thompson's talents, but Macallan's time in Northern Ireland had taught her how to look into the eyes of the hard men and make them believe in her. She could handle Harrison and her old instincts were back in play. He took her into his office and she noted the hint of greed in his eyes. The bastard was sniffing the bait she'd just dangled in front of his nose so Macallan started to play her game.

'It's a mess up there and I was beginning to think that we were going to lose it.' She saw that glint again and it sickened her that the man across the table could betray the job and, more importantly, people like Ingrid Richter. She was walking on the thinnest ice herself by handing over information on Swan, but she and O'Connor had agreed this course of action, and despite her own history of whistleblowing she couldn't bring herself to feel bad about breaching Swan's rights given his background. It would only ever be Harrison's word against hers anyway, and he was a rat, so she told him exactly where to find the pimp, laying it on thick about Swan being a police source who'd agreed to introduce the UC to the Flemings.

'We're sure he can provide evidence that will wrap up a number of major targets,' she concluded, 'including Handyside if he was prepared to cooperate. The attempts on his life have wrecked him so he's definitely ready to turn.'

Harrison felt it was his lucky day. He told Macallan that it would go no further, all the while thinking he'd struck a little nugget of gold. Handyside would find this level of inside info irresistible.

'He's taken off to a holiday cottage he has somewhere in the wilds of Scotland, but we know where it is so we'll keep working on him. He's scared to death so I'm sure we'll get him on-board. It looks like he has all the goods on discs and he did a lot of business for the Flemings so has dates, times and money transfers as well – and, just as importantly, the names of women brought into the country and where they ended up.'

'So he's not protected?'

'Won't have it, and we can hardly provide it for a pimp who'll probably turn out to be the major trafficker in Scotland. We're working on his financial history and if we get a case together then he gets his turn fair and square. As it currently stands, he's going to spend some time selling up his businesses then head off for retirement in the sun with the only company he has at the moment, which is his daft spoodle. We don't have enough to arrest him for anything yet and can't tie him to the *Brighter Dawn*. I'll keep you in the loop, but remember this is strictly need-to-know. I'm going to have a couple of meets with him and try to talk him over to our side.'

'You've got it, and anything you need down here … just let me know.'

Macallan was satisfied that he'd bitten and she'd given him enough bait for now. If he'd taken it and he was working for Handyside then they'd want more. They left it there and joined Thompson and some of Harrison's team for the briefing on the situation in Edinburgh.

It was the start of a long day and two hours later Macallan and Thompson were sitting across the table from Maxi Turner, who was as relaxed as Macallan had expected him to be. Men like Turner didn't have to be dragged in screaming for an interview – they took a professional pride in facing up to it and being able to take whatever the pigs threw at them, so he'd already told his lawyer not to interrupt unless he needed his advice.

Macallan had expected nothing else, but she wanted Handyside to know that she hadn't gone away; there was a message to deliver and she wanted to make sure he got it. She pounded Turner with questions for over two hours and he took it in his stride.

'There's no crime I'm aware of in sitting smoking in Eyemouth, Superintendent. Maybe you can charge us with a litter offence for dropping a pile of fag ends, but that's about it unless you can come up with something better. We just went there for some fishing and enjoyed the view. Anything else?'

'You did know Frankie Dillon and Alan Hunter though?' If Turner thought he was pissing Macallan off, he had it all wrong. She knew exactly how the script would pan out and she'd played the same game many times in Northern Ireland.

'They were a couple of wasters and Pete gave them the odd driving job, but nothing more than that. Whatever they were doing in Eyemouth was nothing to do with us. They were freelancing and I take it they legged it after your boys let them go? I haven't seen them since well before the Eyemouth thing.' He sat back, looking satisfied with the way it was all going.

Turner stuck to his script and repeated the same lines over a dozen times during the interview. Macallan

333

thought he would have made an excellent politician, the way he could spin round the questions and avoid getting to the point. He was good and she respected that, but after two hours she decided they'd all had enough play-acting. Thompson had enjoyed her supporting role, and at one point almost managed to wind him up when she described him as Handyside's pet dog. It had hit a chord and Macallan had realised that Thompson's experience had started to give her a hard edge. It was good to see given how hard it must have been for her to fight her way back after the explosion.

'Okay, Maxi, that'll do for me,' Macallan told him. 'One last thing ... We're building this case despite what you might think. Tell Handyside that it's only a matter of time. I don't think you believe that, but tell him anyway. He'll get it, trust me.'

Geordie Simms had a long way to go to emulate Turner. He was a young and hard criminal, which was why Handyside had agreed to take on his cousin's oldest son, but while he'd always regarded himself as a rising star, he'd soon realised that he'd just been promoted to the position of occasional gofer. As so many before him had discovered, being top of the pile as a local hood and working for the top man were entirely different worlds, and most of the other gangsters had treated him like shit. When he'd complained about that to Turner he'd ended up flat on his back, convinced his jaw had been broken.

'Man up or fuck off out of it,' Turner had told him. 'In this game you earn your way to the top, and if I hear any more from you I'll put you in the fucking hospital.'

That was the moment Simms had realised he was out of his depth, and this lack of experience in the big leagues meant he was nervous to the point of coming apart in the interview room when Macallan brought him in. On the night he'd watched the *Brighter Dawn* sail in to Eyemouth harbour he could have no idea what exactly had taken place out at sea. It hadn't been explained to him because he didn't need to know, but when he saw the headlines on TV and remembered Turner's phone conversations that night, it became clear to him what he'd got himself into.

It made no difference though because when he sat in the interview room with Macallan, Handyside's favourite bent solicitor was by his side, and Simms knew that any slip he made would be reported back to the main man. It hadn't escaped him that Hunter and Dillon hadn't turned up for work for a while, and it didn't take a genius to work out what had happened to them.

Macallan saw it all and understood exactly what was going on – she'd seen it often enough in Belfast. It was clear that Simms would break without the lawyer in the room, but that wasn't going to happen. In any case, it would be almost impossible to prove they were doing anything wrong in Eyemouth that night. Macallan gave the pointless interview just over an hour to make it look real, but she was glad when it was over. She'd dropped the lure for Harrison so it was time to back off and wait for a reaction. She'd give him a couple of days to fester, after which she'd call him and tell him that Swan wanted to talk.

There was, however, one more surprise to drop on Harrison before they headed back to Edinburgh, and Thompson was going to deliver it. Young had been too busy to come with them to Newcastle but it had been arranged that Thompson would have an hour with their intelligence officer and analyst before they headed back up the road. Macallan would keep Harrison occupied over a late pub lunch to give her time and space, and during the exchange Thompson would drop into the conversation the information that they'd picked up a number used by the Flemings around the time of the *Brighter Dawn* incident, mentioning that it looked like a clean phone and that they would continue to develop that line of enquiry. It would get back to Harrison pretty quickly, and he was smart enough to see there might be a problem for him once he worked out the implications of what Thompson had said.

Macallan kept their pub conversation away from the job; she could see he was twitching for more information so she played the 'walls have ears' card. 'Better not to discuss anything here, you never know who's listening. Tell me a bit about your time in the Met.' She gave him the full-on 'you're a really interesting person' face and he lapped it up.

Macallan had arranged with Thompson to text her when she'd planted the phone story with the analyst. As soon as that was done the DCI would make the excuse that there was an urgent development in Edinburgh and pick Macallan up from the pub.

'Sorry about this,' Macallan said as she read the message on her phone. 'Need to get back to Edinburgh. The Fiscal wants to see me urgently as there are some developments.'

She could have sworn that a tiny bead of sweat popped out above his right eye.

'How did it go in there?' Thompson asked Macallan as she snapped the seat belt on and the car pulled away from the pavement.

'He's biting, no doubt about it. Our Tony is dirty, and no matter what happens we'll put the bastard away.'

'Amen to that.' Thompson pressed the accelerator and they left the smell of corruption behind them.

Harrison headed back to his office, thinking that Macallan might be worth a pull. She was uncomplicated yet eye-catching and it intrigued him. Few women held any attraction for him these days – it was normally whatever spare Tom he could rent out from his favourite escort service. He didn't quite know what to make of her, but he'd definitely try and have her out for dinner with a couple of drinks the next time she was back in Newcastle. He thought he might go up to Edinburgh and find out what exactly the Sweaties were up to with the shootings. Once he was back in the office he sat down with the intelligence officer and the analyst. There had been an exchange of bits of intelligence and some requests for data searches. It was all routine until the analyst brought up the information Thompson had provided about Eddie Fleming's number.

'Say again.' He tried not to show too much interest.

The analyst repeated what she'd said and Harrison searched his memory for signs of a problem. He coughed nervously as he tried to remember whether he could be somewhere in the pattern of calls. He'd spoken to Handyside on a couple of occasions around the time of the *Brighter Dawn* incident but was fucked if he could remember if there had been a call between the clean phone and his number. He dismissed his team, and when the door closed behind them he stood at his office window flicking through his call lists.

'Fuck.' It was there – one single call. He stared out of the window and tried to work out what this meant.

Harrison was no fool, and though he was a bent bastard, he was also a talented detective. There was a problem in the information about the clean phones, but the maximum they could prove was that there had been a call from one of them to his number. They couldn't get a subscriber from a clean phone, but if they identified them all they could tie down Handyside's to the Newcastle area. Macallan's team would find it eventually, but they

337

were swamped with lines of investigation and research so it might take a bit of time. He was glad he'd mentioned that he'd had a few run-ins over the years with Handyside so he could pin it on a threatening call from the man. It was weak but it would hold if he stayed tight. He knew someone like Macallan might see through it eventually, but suspicions and proof were different things. There was also the outside possibility that they could miss it, though he wouldn't rely on that one. They couldn't prove a thing – and he'd survived worse in the Met and the RCS. He decided not to alert Handyside to the fact that the Scottish team might dig up their relationship through the phone analysis, but he did need to know about Ricky Swan, so he picked up a set of car keys and headed for the nearest call box.

'Fuck.' He muttered it again in frustration at the small slip that was going to cause him a bit of stress. Despite always being careful about phone contact they had somehow slipped up, but it was what it was.

When he got to the call box, which looked and stank like a sewer, he held the receiver a couple of inches away from his face as he dialled the number.

'We need a meet about the game north of the border.' He waited for a reply.

'I'll see you near the river.' The phone clicked off. They had a series of meeting places that changed month by month. 'Near the river' was an old industrial site close to the mouth of the Tyne.

Handyside turned back to Turner, who'd just arrived at his home. They were in the study and his wife had taken the children to the park to soak up the glorious sunshine that had followed the storm. 'Tell me again what she said.'

Turner repeated the message Macallan had given to

him at the end of the interview. What worried him was that Handyside's face seemed to harden, so whatever it meant, the message had hit home. 'What did she mean?'

'Nothing. The woman's a class act and she's trying to play mind games. Ex-RUC Special Branch, so she'll know all the moves. Forget it.'

Turner wouldn't mention it again, but he saw that it had touched something in his friend.

'How did Geordie stand up?'

'According to our legal friend he didn't do that well, but he kept to the script. Not much choice, has he?'

Handyside ran his hand over his face and smiled grimly. 'Tough game this, Max, and it's just about to get tougher. I asked you to get as much as possible on this Ricky Swan. Tell me about him – everything.'

Harrison had given them everything he could on Swan, and Drew had filled in any gaps. Handyside listened without interruption, trying to put a picture together of the man who'd caused them all so much grief. Turner went through every detail he'd been given, knowing that the top man hated anything being missed out. He was a details junkie and that was part of his talent.

When he was finished, Handyside stood up and took the keys for the Jag from his desk. 'Let's go and see our man from the constabulary.'

It took about thirty minutes to get to the meet with Harrison and during the drive Handyside made up his mind about what had to be done. Unless the detective dropped something new on them, he needed to act fast and hard. In a way the plan was simple enough: he would get the job done north of the border, Drew could get the Edinburgh side of the business back in working order and he would talk Brenda McMartin back on-board. There was no way she could work out who'd pulled the trigger on her insane brother, and for the time being that would suit his purposes. It might all be simple, but perhaps it was also a bit on the ambitious side – the feeling in his gut still told him that he needed his plan B, which was more likely to succeed.

When he stepped out of the car he could smell a problem on Harrison. The detective was wound up tight and normally he was an arrogant shit who'd never quite worked out where he sat in the food chain. Self-delusion was a powerful drug when it was administered with the help of envelopes stuffed with hard, tax-free cash.

'What's up?' Handyside asked him. 'Got a cold or something?'

'I'm brand new, just up to my eyes in work.' It was a lie, but it didn't matter to Handyside who watched it drip from Harrison's lips.

He told them about his meeting with Macallan; how she'd told him Swan was a top grass and confirmed that he'd stuck the undercover into the Flemings.

'The problem is that it looks like this fucking slag has information that can hurt a lot of people. He's frantic after the two shots at taking him out and is considering his position with the law, if you know what I mean?'

'No, I don't know what you mean. Tell me in English and not Met wankspeak.' There was no rise in tone when he said it; Handyside remained calm, but Harrison knew he could see through him and it chewed his nerve ends.

'That's all I know. The slag ... Sorry, this Ricky Swan has information on a number of people and they're trying to turn him. He's not gone over yet, but they think they can get him into the witness box eventually, and he's sitting on records of all our dealings north of the border, courtesy of the Flemings. Laundered money, girls' details, that kind of thing. He's headed for some place in the wilds till he sells up his businesses, then it's

340

off to the sun for a spot of retirement. There's no police protection, not at the moment.'

'Does this affect me, Tony?'

'So she says.'

'Is there anything else I need to know?'

'Nothing, that's it all, but I'm there if anything develops.'

Handyside watched the lies drip from his mouth again, but they were sins that would have to wait for another day. He needed Harrison for the time being. The one thing he'd learned about bent detectives was that they had a limited shelf life and when the time came they had to be cut adrift.

'How's that wonderful home in Italy?'

'It's the bollocks. Going to retire there in a couple of years.'

'Good for you.' Handyside turned and headed back to the car with Turner, who'd kept quiet through the meet.

'The man's a cunt, Pete.'

'I know that; that's why he works for us.'

On the way home, Handyside ran his decision past Turner. 'We do this job ourselves and no slip-ups allowed. There's no time to wait – Ricky Swan needs to go. You mentioned that he has a daughter who he hardly sees but who's still the proverbial apple. We need to get her to get to him. Do we know where she is?'

Turner nodded; he was good at looking ahead.

'If all this falls apart then there's no parole for us, my friend,' Handyside said.

Turner didn't like it, but they'd been together too long and he was in, whatever he thought. The whole thing was a mess, but if they came out the other side he was going to retire, regardless of what Handyside wanted. He'd squirreled away a small fortune so he could easily stretch out in the sun, drink with the Cockney wankers and exchange war stories about the good old days for the rest of his life.

'Okay, we do this together,' he replied. 'I'll get a team together pronto. We'll need a few of the boys for this kind of job.'

Handyside took his right hand off the steering wheel and offered it to Turner, who gripped it tight. 'We've come a long way; who'd have believed it?'

Later that night Handyside lay in bed with his wife and felt her tears run onto his chest. She'd had her arms wrapped round him since he'd told her what she needed to do. 'Are you sure? It scares me.' She dug her nails into his skin and he kissed her forehead gently.

'It was always a possibility, girl, you know that. I just need you to promise that you won't hesitate. Do exactly as I've shown you and we'll be fine. I just need to know that you can do it.'

'Of course. I trust you and always have.'

42

Macallan was up at the crack of dawn, but Jack didn't wake this early even with the smell of coffee wafting through the open doors of the flat. She went through to check Adam and found he was still out for the count. It was unusual for him to wake in the night, but she'd almost welcomed it in the early hours as it had given her some time to catch up on holding him close. Jack hadn't argued when she'd said it was her turn to see to Adam and he'd been snoring again almost before she'd left the room.

Adam hadn't really cried much, just enough to get someone's attention; he'd just made up his young mind that he was going to be awake for a couple of hours and that he'd decide when it was time to go back under the covers. Watching the summer light rise up over the city while she was holding him had made Macallan's heart beat faster – it was going to be a beautiful day and she'd stood there, looking down at her baby and thinking about their future.

Jack would soon be going back to work but he'd loved all this time with Adam, though he had a tendency to

343

spoil the boy. Though maybe it wasn't possible to spoil them at that age? That kind of attention had been missing from her own unhappy childhood.

Adam had fallen asleep again in her arms and she'd decided that there was too big a day in front of her to try and sleep again. There was no point in worrying about lack of rest or stress; she was in it now till the case was resolved one way or another. The thought that she was going to marry Jack had given her extra strength, so she would do whatever it took to make someone pay for what had happened on the *Brighter Dawn* and then concentrate on what really mattered to her. She would be in the office by seven and had arranged to see O'Connor before she had a full briefing with all the heads of the investigations she was coordinating.

On her way to Fettes Macallan stopped off at a small café in Stockbridge, thinking she'd treat herself to a coffee and a read of the paper before she kicked off the day's work. Jacquie Bell called her when she was halfway through reading about some senior politician's latest PR gaff.

'How's my favourite detective?'

'Same as always,' Macallan replied. 'Up to my armpits in alligators. How's you?'

'I'd like to see you, but I guess you must be snowed with all this mayhem. Have you time to talk?'

Macallan sipped her coffee as Bell explained that the papers were going to war with the police over Ingrid Richter, the *Brighter Dawn* and the Gunfight at Ricky's Corral.

'My God, are you going to use that?'

'Too late, my friend – two of the red tops have done it already this morning. They're going to slaughter the handling of the cases and I've no option but to follow the editorial line. You know I wouldn't do anything to harm you, and I've told them I'm fucked if I'll put your name up – but you, O'Connor and anyone connected with this are going to get caught in the shit storm. I'm really sorry but I've no control on this one.'

Bell wasn't sure how her friend would react; she was prepared for anger, and half expected it given what she'd been through, but Macallan's answer took her by surprise.

'It's fine. Go for it; I want it to happen. Do your job and I won't hold it against you. To tell you the truth, I'm tired of trying to take these men on with one hand tied behind my back. We know who's behind all of this and I want you to print that. Big letters, Jacquie. By the way, I'm getting married and you're invited.'

'Why?' was all Bell could manage to say.

'Jack said, "Why not?" to that question. Look, can I see you later for a drink? I think we're close with this one and I'll give you the inside track when it's done.' Bell agreed and Macallan put the phone down, realising it was time to head to work.

'Fuck me.' Bell leaned back in her chair and shook her head. 'Good for you, Grace,' she murmured then turned back to her laptop and started typing up the story.

O'Connor was sitting behind his desk and looked tired, the well-defined features that had made him so attractive a little blurred. Macallan wasn't sure whether it was strain, drink or both, but since she'd come back to the force she'd been struck by the impression that he was a man carrying a heavy load. He was on the phone when she stepped into his office and he pointed at the seat opposite his desk. It was pretty obvious from the side of the conversation she could hear that he was on the receiving end of some flak for the mass of incidents hitting Edinburgh. She guessed, rightly, that it was an executive-level twat making sure the shit ran downhill, as always.

He put the phone back on the desk and tilted his head back in a gesture of exasperation.

'Sorry, you could probably write that script without any clues. To think that's the job I used to dream about.' He smiled wearily, lifted a pile of paper and dropped it in an untidy heap into his pending tray. The statement puzzled her and she couldn't remember his desk trays ever overflowing the way they were now. He was a careful man by nature and hated missing any note that might need a response or report of some kind.

He broke through her thoughts and got straight to business. 'Okay, where are we with this thing?'

Macallan took her time and explained everything that had happened in Newcastle.

'Christ, what happens to a man like Tony Harrison?' O'Connor asked, knowing there was no answer that would ever make sense.

'I gave up trying to understand them a long time ago. They happen, that's it and we have to clean it all up.' She shook her head; she didn't waste time trying to find answers where there were none. 'All in all, it seemed to go well and I thought we'd give it a day or two and then feed Harrison the story that Ricky might be coming round. I think we have to presume that they'll already be considering making sure he's taken out this time, but we've no way of knowing what their plans might be. We can't expect to get anything reliable from Harrison.'

'Okay, I want you to keep in touch all the way on this. There are going to be some tough decisions here, and I think however this turns out we get flak – too much has happened. Anything else?'

'I could do with the intercept going on Ricky's phone,' she replied. 'Any progress?'

'Yes, I think we might have it up and running by tomorrow. I had to call in some favours on that one. There's so much pressure on the lines for the counter-terrorist stuff that you need influence to get an urgent one, and everybody's case is urgent now, which is a sign of the times.'

Macallan stood up and was halfway through her excuses for leaving when O'Connor told her to sit down again. 'I want you to know first. I intend to resign in a few weeks.'

Her mouth dropped open an inch and she was going to ask why, but he decided to answer all her questions in one go. 'It's okay – I'm not dying with some terrible disease or in trouble. I've just had enough. I used to want nothing but the top seat; you know that as well as anyone. Since I came back from the German post, so much has happened and I made some mistakes, my priorities all went to rat shit and, well, I suppose you know that too. Whatever it was that was driving me that way is gone, and I get almost nothing out of the job now. It's pretty simple really.' He stopped, looked down at the table and seemed to drift off as if he was pondering a memory.

'I'm sorry, John, and despite what happened …' Macallan couldn't think how to finish the sentence and he took over again.

'Honestly, it's fine. In a way I'm relieved I've made the decision, and it's the right one.' He smiled again and looked more like the man she first knew. 'I've been approached to go for a job with the UN. You know that's what I always wanted anyway. The big stage, travelling the world and talking about drugs even though it doesn't make a bit of difference to the reality of the situation. They pay you a fortune for talking bollocks while you guys are struggling in the real world. I was born for it.' His smile broadened and it was as if a weight had been lifted from his shoulders with that declaration. She got it and returned the smile because he was right.

'Thing is, yes, you'll be good at it. You'll probably end up with a knighthood.'

'The least I can expect. Now go and get 'em; I want to have a drink with the boys when you clear this lot up.'

The men and women attending the briefing had already arrived when Macallan got to Leith, and she asked them to give her a minute so she could go and call Sheena McGovern. Forgetting about her friend was not an option. It was a safe bet he'd feel lost, and being cut off from his beloved team in the middle of an investigation would chew him up.

The phone was picked up immediately and Macallan realised that McGovern's wife would probably panic every time she received a call now.

'How's our boy, Sheena?' she asked.

'He's good, and your visit was a big help. It'll take time, but I think he's coming round to the idea that criminal intelligence isn't the worst option in the world given what's happened. The docs are happy and reckon he'll be out in a couple of days.' Her voice was strong and Macallan was glad that at least McGovern's wife was looking at a good future for them.

'Just think, you have him all to yourself for the next two or three weeks while he's recuperating.'

'That's what worries me – Jimmy is useless in the house so I'm guessing he'll just sit there with the remote ordering tea and biscuits. Such is life.' There was a hint of humour in Sheena's voice, as well as relief. It made Macallan smile, considering how bleak things had seemed less than forty-eight hours earlier.

'Tell him I'll see him soon and give him an update on

348

the job. I know his nose'll be twitching.' She put down the phone, feeling relieved. McGovern was going to be okay, and though she'd miss him by her side he'd still be in the job he loved.

The team at the briefing were in babble mode when she came back into the room and apologised for being late. Macallan opened it up, gave as concise an introduction as she could then handed over to Young, who knew that the information about Harrison was not for the ears of that particular audience. Instead she ran through the rest of the phone analysis, pointing out that even though they couldn't confirm the clean phone users it might still be useful in a circumstantial case.

'There are a couple of good little developments. We've picked up a report from a source to his handler that early on the night of the shooting he was in the pub and saw Billy Drew come in and join the Flemings. This source has nothing to do with them but knows them all by sight.'

She finished giving her update and looked at Macallan, who was rhythmically tapping her fingers on the table as she gathered her thoughts. When she started to speak she did so quietly, as if she was still considering the options.

'We know from other sources that Drew seemed to come on-board with the Flemings just after the *Brighter Dawn* incident. It's a strange one because he always operated on his own or with a very small team. He avoided anyone else. What we do know is that he's proved that he'd be more than capable of the level of violence we've seen at The Corral.' Macallan scanned the room and could see Slade making notes.

'I think that the timing of Drew joining the Flemings is the significant point. We're pretty well agreed that the undercover officer must have been exposed at the meeting in Newcastle, as that's the last time he made contact with us. We know how Handyside reacts to failure and Hunter and Dillon's disappearance is probably testament to that. The Flemings must have explained how we'd managed to infiltrate their organisation. And that brings us to Ricky Swan. Since old Joe Fleming was taken out by the Belfast team and the twins inherited the business they've made costly mistakes, but this little error was the cherry on the cake. We can only speculate how they managed to stay alive after what happened and I think they wanted an old pro to steady them up. Felicity has confirmed that late on the night the UC went missing Eddie Fleming made a call to Billy Drew. There was no intelligence of them working together before this call. Correct, Felicity?' She glanced over to the analyst, who was, as usual, covering sheets of A4 with notes.

'I agree with the superintendent – it seems to be a reasonable proposition. What I can't work out is – if Drew is the killer – why? The only reason I can see is that he wanted to take over the business, but historically it's not his game.'

Macallan would have to rein herself in from getting too focused on Drew. He'd walked away from a life sentence because Harkins had fucked up on procedure, but that was in the past. Nevertheless, she would love to see payback for Drew, an animal that had killed for pleasure.

She looked towards Slade. 'Ronnie, I honestly think things are coming to a head in this case, which might surprise some of you, but we have to be ready for anything and get ahead of the game. I want you and your team to crawl all over Drew. I mean get right in his face. There'll be nothing to find in his house, but take it apart anyway and get him lifted. When he's released we follow him so he can see us, and find any excuse anytime to bring him in again. If he drops a fag end I want him harassed. Is that clear?'

'You're talking my language, Superintendent.' Slade had just been given a ticket to do what he enjoyed most – hassle the bastards.

'Felicity, you said there was something else…'

'Yes, just to say that the financial investigation on Ricky Swan is in the early stages but going better than we anticipated. I think we'll get there because he got sloppy and thought he couldn't be touched. It's a mountain of work, but we're pushing hard with it.'

She pulled her glasses off and chewed the ends, which meant she was finished.

'Excellent. The only other thing I can say is that you will all have guessed that there are other strands of sensitive work going on, but as always it's need-to-know only. As soon as I can share anything, I will.'

They carried on round the table with the progress on forensics, and information from witnesses was pouring into the Home Office Large Major Enquiry System where it could be stored and analysed. HOLMES, to give it its much more manageable and sexy acronym, was the engine room of modern serious-crime investigation, and dozens of highly trained operators made sure that what came in one end was processed and logged properly. It wasn't the glamorous side of crime investigation, but in the real world detectives didn't just stare plaintively into the distance and come up with the answers. It had been created to make sure the mistakes of the seventies and eighties could not be repeated: the Yorkshire Ripper investigation had proved that the old systems of detection just could not cope with the information generated in the media age, and particularly where a serial killer was involved. There was an outpouring over the story developing around Ingrid Richter and the result was that calls from the public were almost overwhelming the team dealing with the investigation.

'Last thing I have before we close this off is that Pam Fitzgerald has been assisting the team looking for Ingrid Richter. Pam?'

Fitzgerald was clearly nervous, but it was the high-end company that was frazzling her, and once she got into her stride the tension dropped from her voice and she got on with it. It wasn't positive but no one expected anything else. There was still no trace of Richter – the weather and unusually high tides hadn't helped, and from what the experts said, she could wash up miles down the coast – if she was found at all.

Macallan saw that this item above all others had everyone's full and undivided attention.

'Thanks, Pam, and please keep us informed.' She wanted to bring the meeting to a close but she needed to add something to the report on Richter. 'If anything can keep us going when it gets hard it's what happened to Ingrid and those other girls on the boat. Please remember that until we wrap this investigation up.'

She looked round the faces and saw a room full of people who had been made for crime detection. She'd been lucky and she'd need them over the coming days. When it had all started, Macallan had worried that it might turn out to be one of those investigations that ran on forever with no result, where the team dwindled as they were drawn off to new enquiries and the public forgot what happened once it was no longer front-page news, but it wasn't going to happen that way – she knew it now, and events were drawing to a conclusion with a life of their own. She just had to stay with it and be ready to make the hard decisions when they were required.

43

Later that evening Christine Swan laughed at the antics of her friends in the pub where they'd met for a final bash before taking off the following day. The place was crammed with students determined to work off the energy of youth and damage their eardrums. Her boyfriend, way over the limit, kissed her wetly on the cheek and asked her (in the way of drunk men) if she was alright. She tried to suppress her giggles, but drunk or sober he knew how to make her laugh. Tall, maybe a bit on the skinny side, he was a looker – the guy every straight girl in college would have died for. They slept together a few nights a week, but he was away with the fairies and she decided she'd leave him to drink the rest of the night away with his mates – there was no way he was getting near her that particular night.

She kissed him back and said goodbye to her protesting friends. They were just getting started, but Christine never had more than two drinks and had to be in the mood to even do that. The memory of all those nights watching her father drink himself unconscious when he got back from the sauna couldn't be washed away, though sometimes it had been worse than that: like when he brought one of the girls home and Christine had lain in bed with her hands over her ears to blot out the sounds.

In a strange way she felt pity for her father, a weak man who by some quirk had found success in the only place he could. She always saw the desperation in his eyes when they met – how he watched for any sign of the affection that she was incapable of giving him. Some day she'd move away from Scotland, and hopefully in time she'd find a way to make sense of the life he'd given her. It had made her a strong and independent young woman who was determined that the sins of the father would not ruin her life. She was wrong in that respect.

It was a beautiful evening and when the storm had moved north it had dragged up balmy heat behind it from southern Europe. She walked slowly along the quiet streets towards her flat and thought about her upcoming trip to Italy.

Italy – the name itself almost made her tremble; there was so much she'd always wanted to see in Florence, Rome and Venice. She was doing the cities all on her own so that she could look, stare and touch as much as she wanted without worrying about anyone else. Her father was paying for it all, and though she'd tried to argue he'd made sure she was booked into the best hotels so that she would be safe from the dangers that lurked around single female travellers. Her instinct had been to say no, but the temptation of Italy had been just too much for her to refuse. She felt an element of guilt at taking the money from him, but she knew she could rob him blind if she was a different person and that would never happen. As soon as she could exist without his tainted money she would never take another penny – and that included any inheritance.

Most of the flats round about her were rented by

other students and there was the feel of a small friendly community where everyone knew everyone else. She started to punch the code into the flat's entry system but never reached the last number. Maxi Turner came out of the shadows and punched the side of her head then watched the girl's knees buckle. He grabbed her before she hit the deck and the three men did their work quickly and efficiently. Real pros. A rag was stuffed in her mouth, an old pillowcase rigged up with a drawstring pulled over her head and down over her arms as her hands were bound with a plastic tie. They bundled her into the van in under a minute and the driver pulled away calmly, keeping his eye on the speed limit all the time.

They'd worked on the van and she was dropped into a space under the floor then sealed in. By the time they stopped, a few miles away, the boiler suits plus Christine's shoes had already been stuffed into plastic shopping bags with the remnants of a couple of Chinese meals and the lot was tossed into a skip. The discarded food was usually enough to put off any skip rakers from investigating further.

Two of the men left the van and sauntered off casually to pick up their car, which was parked about two minutes' walk away, while Turner got in behind the wheel and wondered if they would pull it off. They'd switched the plates already but it only took a couple of bored traffic cops to pull him over, examine the old van for faults and find themselves with the case of their lives.

Handyside had arranged to rent an old shooting lodge no more than forty minutes' drive from Pitlochry and well into the wilds. There was nothing else near them for miles and on one side a small loch added to the privacy he wanted. It was perfect and they had an unrestricted view of the surrounding area if any nosey bastard started looking around. He was there on his own when he heard the van crackling the stone chips on the path leading into the grounds. He picked up a ski mask and went out to meet them.

'How did it go there?'

'Not a hitch and never saw a soul in the area. We were in and out before she knew what hit her.' Turner lit up a cigarette and tilted his head back as he eased off the knots in his neck muscles. 'What now then?' Turner knew the drill by heart and had already stopped using names.

'Let's get her inside and we'll go over it again before I make the call.'

As Handyside finished speaking the car with the rest of his crew turned up and they kept quiet, waiting for orders. They knew the girl was conscious and her senses would be on extreme alert. Abductions of young women got you a lifer and no one was going to break the rules with Pete Handyside leading the effort.

Christine Swan, still conscious but with a sore head, started to suck in more of the stale air under the floor of the van. She felt as if her lungs were burning with the effort to breathe through the filthy rag stuffed in her mouth. The engine had been switched off and she was aware of the muffled voices near to the van. They were just loud enough for her to hear that the accents weren't Scottish. English and perhaps North-east? The initial confusion mixed with extreme fear had shorted her senses for a few minutes after she'd been dropped below the floor of the van, but she'd tried to work out what she could do. Only the week before, her boyfriend had forced her to sit and watch two Liam Neeson films where his family had been abducted, and of course he'd saved them, and she'd tried to do what big Liam had done in one of them when he was taken. It had seemed so easy on screen: pick up sounds, remember when the van turned right and left or stopped at junctions. None of it had worked though, far more difficult in real life, and when she gave up trying, she'd tried to work out why on earth anyone would want to take her. It had to be about her father, but if not … the other option made her gag. If it was some sort of sex attack then she was probably going to die.

Swan was an intelligent young woman though and forced herself to think of the more rational options. Her father ran saunas and escort services and he was loaded. He probably mixed with all kinds, and if it was a kidnap for ransom then she might have a chance of surviving if he paid up. She was sure he would pay and all she'd have to do was cooperate.

She heard the sound of the van door being pulled open and lost control of her breathing again, her heart pounding like a clenched fist against the inside of her ribcage. The men lifted her out more gently than they'd put her in and she was pulled upright till she felt her bare feet on stone chips. She bent over involuntarily in an instinctive reaction to the fear that they might hurt her.

'Stay calm and no one will harm you. Nod if you understand.'

She did what she was told and tried to straighten her back. The words came through voice distortion equipment and if she needed confirmation that they were professionals then she had her evidence. There was a hand on each of her arms and she felt someone put what felt like slippers onto her feet. She was guided into some kind of building where she was pressed down onto a hard-backed chair. The pillowcase was pulled from her head and she blinked at the sight of the two men, both wearing balaclavas, who stood in front of her. One of them squeezed her cheeks with one hand, pulled the rag from her mouth and dropped it into a cellophane packet that he stuffed into his side pocket. The room was small, made of wood, and apart from a bed and large bucket with a toilet roll sitting next to it, there was nothing to see. Heavy blinds had been put over the windows so the room was in semi-darkness, the only glow coming from a night light that cast monstrous shadows behind the two men.

'What do you want?' She felt as if her throat was closing and she fought to get the words out.

The distorted voice that came through a speaker rigged up next to the door startled her.

'The men with you are there to help you if needs be. You're in no danger and our business is with your father. Do you understand?'

'Yes.'

'When that business is done you'll go back to your life. Do you understand?'

'Yes.'

'You'll be kept in this room and we'll bring you food and anything you need. You'll be given privacy when you need it. Do you understand?'

'Yes.'

'It's very important that you understand that if you do anything stupid then we'll hurt you. Not kill you, but hurt you. Do you understand?'

'Yes.' She managed to get the word out but couldn't contain her fear and she started sobbing uncontrollably.

'We may want you to speak to your father, and if we do, you can only say what we've told you. Do you understand?'

'Yes.' She nodded and wondered what the fuck they expected her to say.

'Okay, you'll be restrained by light chains, so you have some restricted movement. Is all that understood?'

'Yes.' Swan surprised herself and calmed down. They weren't going to hurt her – at least not right away. It was a small thing, but she was human and that was all she needed to keep her hopes alive.

One of the masked men stood behind her chair and the other one pulled out a small camera and took two photographs. It was just as well for her sanity that she couldn't see the man behind her quietly pull out a hunting knife and hold it at a forty-five-degree angle across his abdomen.

They left the room and the metallic voice crackled through the loudspeaker again.

'There's a pair of ski pants and a sweater lying on the bed. Strip completely, put them on, leave your clothes on the floor and sit down when it's done. My men are outside the door and window so please do as I say now.'

She knew the best thing she could do was comply. She pulled on the fresh clothes and sat down. The door clicked open at the same time and she realised there had to be a camera somewhere, but there was nothing obvious that she could see in the half-light. They didn't speak and shackled her left ankle to a length of chain running to a huge metal weight at the side of the bed. When it was done they left, closing the door behind them, and the voice came back on through the loudspeaker.

'You'll have food shortly and we'll make you as comfortable as possible while you're here. Now is there anything you want to know?'

She shook her head and stared at the floor.

'Very well. Every couple of hours I'll ask you if you need anything. Try and relax and this will soon be over.'

They were taking pains to hide their identity and for some reason that reassured her. If she'd known who'd abducted her and what they'd done in the past it would have had the opposite effect.

Turner pulled off his mask and sat down opposite Handyside. 'She seems okay. Don't think we'll have any problem with this one.' He lit up another smoke and

359

promised himself when he fucked off to the Med that he'd try to quit.

'Make sure the boys are disciplined with the girl. If anyone lays a finger on her I'll cut their hands off. As long as she can't identify anyone then there's no need to harm her.'

Turner puzzled again that a man who could give the order to kill without a moment's hesitation could care so much about Ricky Swan's daughter. He'd never been able to work that one out. He'd seen so many in the business who just enjoyed violence, but Handyside never hurt anyone if there wasn't a commercial case for it. Turner himself had handed out some serious damage in his time and put a few men in hell, and if they were deserving cases he would feel the high in the power of life and death just before he put them away. He was getting tired of it though; the pain he'd inflicted on other people had started to haunt him and he was no longer sure what it had all meant. He promised himself again that this would be his last match – he just wanted to feel the sun on his face and sleep easily at night. 'No need to worry,' he told Handyside. 'I've warned them and they know the score. They're our best men and they've been with us a long time now. They don't fuck about.'

That was when Handyside gave Turner his next order. 'I want you to get a hold of Tony Harrison and make sure he's on the end of a line if we need his expert advice at any time. No excuses unless he's dead.'

Turner rarely questioned his friend, as he tended to be right, but bringing bent filth into this game bothered him. He just never trusted dirty cops; they had no standards. He wondered if he was starting to suffer from pre-retirement nerves. Everything seemed to carry a portent of failure. He thought again about what they'd done to those girls on the *Brighter Dawn*. He'd been brought up in a Catholic home and though the priest had spent more time abusing the children of his flock than saving souls, Turner had never quite turned his back on his god – and he'd committed so many sins in his life that part of him still worried that the big man was up there in the sky, waiting to kick the shit out of him when the time came.

'Sorry, why do we need that rat involved?' he asked. 'Never trusted the bastard and he makes me choke.'

'Why do I trust a man like that?' Handyside had already seen the question in Turner's eyes. 'He is what he is, and apart from the corruption he's a top detective by all accounts. The best, and that's why we pay him so much for doing so little. When you think about it, we ask him the odd question, he gets the answer off his criminal intelligence system and we pay him a small fortune, all tax-free. The thing is, my friend, that despite all we've done over the years – and we've lifted plenty of men to have a little chat with them – we haven't done this sort of potentially high-profile thing before. The police are good at this game and are all high-tech now. If they get involved and we don't know it then we're in trouble. I want him on call so he can tell us if we're walking into a bear trap. It's about time he earned his wages.'

Handyside put his hand round Turner's shoulder, trying to reassure the man who'd stood with him all the way; he could see Turner was burning out and needed a break away from the game.

'When this is over I want you to go and have your time in the sun. You've earned it and I've put away a retirement bonus for you over the years. It's going to be all yours. Bad job if Tony Harrison can do it and you can't. What do you say?'

Turner was taken by surprise; he had been worried about how he'd break away from Handyside, but here was the man giving him the green light and bonus money

361

included. The weight dropped from his shoulders as he realised the man had it right again and bringing in Harrison was no more than insurance. It made perfect sense. His dream apartment overlooking the Med began to look like a real possibility; perhaps they might just make it and be forgiven for the *Brighter Dawn*.

Handyside had told him the truth but had left out some of his own concerns. He had as many doubts as Turner, and when he'd reassured him about retirement he had trouble believing that it would come true for the man who'd been with him since the beginning – who'd gone into the filthy waters of the Tyne and rescued him after he'd seen the rats. There was no turning back, however, and if he just sat and waited then Macallan would come for him, he was certain. There was no alternative – they had to finish cleaning up any witnesses who might hurt them.

They jumped into the car with one of the team in the back and drove twenty miles to a spot off the beaten track that was secluded but had a reasonable signal. Handyside rigged up the distortion kit with a clean phone and Turner and his man in the back seat got out of the car and changed into camouflage hunting gear. Both of them had rucksacks with all they needed for an overnighter and headed off into the woods to raised ground about a hundred yards from the car. They each prepared a hide that had an uninterrupted sight of the clearing from where Handyside would call Swan. Turner called him when they were settled in. It would have taken a trained dog to find them. Turner was used to this kind of work and had been a hunter all his life, and a few years in the army reserves had taught him a few more tricks of the trade.

Handyside settled himself for a couple of minutes and ran the job through his mind, looking for any detail they might have missed. He couldn't find one so picked up the phone and called Ricky Swan's number, praying that he hadn't changed it. He guessed it was unlikely – a man like Swan never had a backup for his numbers and would feel lost without access to his contacts. If the police weren't involved, as Harrison had said, then they wouldn't have given him any advice. That was the theory, but it could always go wrong.

The phone rang for too long, and Handyside began to worry till it was picked up by a man who sounded half-pissed.

'It's Ricky. Who's this?'

It took Swan a moment to realise that the alien voice on the other end was no wind-up or bizarre cold call. It sobered him up in record time and he couldn't believe that after all he'd just been through things were about to get worse. He reached his shaking free hand for the vodka bottle and emptied what was left into the glass sticking to the coffee table in front of him. Gnasher looked up at his master, understood there was no chance of 'walkies' and so padded through the open door and out into the garden to chase some dragonflies around the flower bed.

'What the fuck is this?' Swan tried to sound a bit like his hero Clint Eastwood, but he was a lightweight dealing with a heavy gun, and even with the gutful of vodka he'd consumed he couldn't hide the quaver in his voice.

'In a few seconds you'll receive a text with an attachment. Obviously you'll recognise your own daughter and I think there's enough there to show you that we're serious people. I'll call you back in one and a half minutes.' Handyside cut the call and stared at his watch. When he said a minute and a half that's exactly what Swan would get.

Swan stared at the phone, startled when the prompt came up that he had a message. He had the shakes and hesitated, knowing what he was going to see. He opened up the message and groaned at the little prompt telling him there was an attachment. The robot voice had said a minute and a half so he had no time to put it off.

'Please no.' The photograph of his daughter, terrified and confused, was bad enough, but the sight of the masked man behind her with a big fuck-off knife meant this was no wind-up. He was cynical about the whole world and to him women were no more than a commodity, but it was different with Christine, and there was no way she could be involved in staging the whole thing. It had happened to other men like him, but his daughter was the one and only person he trusted, even though he knew she would prefer that her life didn't include him in it.

The phone rang again. 'Did you see it?'

'Please don't hurt her. If it's money then I can sort that.' Swan closed his eyes and prayed that it was money. He had it in his power to find that if they didn't go over the score.

'It's not money. We only want to speak to you because you have information we're interested in.' Handyside was a highly intelligent man, but like all mortals he couldn't control what he didn't know, and he couldn't know that Swan thought his sauna recordings were gold dust, and despite two attempts on his life the kidnapper had used the words 'you have information'. Swan's world was full of bad men, so why wouldn't someone try to rip off his precious discs? Perhaps the police had tipped someone off. That was how his mind worked – and why he was completely out of his depth.

Misunderstandings have started wars and the small matter of crossed wires between the men at each end of this call meant that events would turn in ways they could neither anticipate nor stop. In that brief moment Swan understandably thought this was another crisis he could work his way through, because if these were men who

364

wanted to block something he had on his discs, or use it themselves for blackmail, then that was a price worth paying for his daughter.

He calmed down but needed time to think it through as there was always the possibility that the bastards might shaft him.

'Okay, maybe we can work this out. I want to speak to my daughter, though, before we do it.'

The answer surprised Handyside because he'd thought that someone like Swan would work out the eventual cost then try to buy time – because the cost would be his neck. He guessed, wrongly, that the power of a father's love had overcome the man's fear for his own life, but he'd spoken long enough and needed to get off the line in case the law was earwigging Swan's calls.

'That's it for now. I'll call you in the morning with the arrangements. If you involve the law we'll know about it and we'll start cutting bits off Christine. Understand?'

That image shook Swan up again and he started to panic.

'Just don't hurt her and you'll get what you want.'

The line died on him, and he stared at the window, wondering if he was ever going to get peace again. His options crashed about in his skull as he snorted a line of coke to try to clear his mind. What if it was a trap of some kind?

He went through a whole list of what ifs, did another line of coke and opened up a fresh bottle of vodka. When Gnasher trotted back into the house an hour later his master was spreadeagled on the sofa, having forgotten all about his daughter for the time being. For the dog, the fact that the creature on the sofa was soaked in urine meant nothing more than an interesting smell.

Handyside drove away slowly and left his team to see if the law came sniffing round; that would tell him whether there was a line on Swan's phone. It was worth the effort, and he wanted to take as few chances as possible with this particular can of worms so on the road back he went through a range of counter-surveillance moves he'd been taught by the detectives he paid off. When he reached the lodge he checked on the girl, who seemed calm enough and had taken some food, then called Turner.

'Everything's okay, the girl's in decent shape and there was definitely nothing behind me while I was driving. What about you?'

'Well I'd say that what we're watching at the moment is a man and a woman, who're probably married to other people, really getting to know each other. Unless the pigs are using a new undercover technique, it's so far so good.'

'Good man. The phone call went okay with our boy. He sounded a bit pissed but that seems par for the course. If nothing happens I'll pick you up around midnight.'

Handyside wanted to call his wife, but if things went wrong the less she knew the better. He just hoped that she'd done what he'd asked and he could stop worrying about her and the kids. She would send a text when everything was in order.

He watched the clock grind slowly towards midnight then called Turner, who told him it was still quiet and that, apart from the wildlife, nothing had moved. Handyside checked the girl again, got back in the car and spent another half hour on counter surveillance before heading off to pick up his team. They got back to the lodge about midnight and introduced a shift system to keep an eye on the girl during the night. Handyside spoke to her through the loudspeaker and told her that they'd made contact with her father and everything was going to plan. She would soon be home.

She nodded towards the speaker; she'd worked out that there was a tiny camera lens attached to it. She stared into it and Handyside saw the glint of anger in her eyes. Her mood had changed from fearful subservience to disgust for these invisible men who stared at her night and day. He'd expected it, as that was the way of these things, but he also knew exactly how to handle it – kill the instinct to rebel.

He pulled on the ski mask and walked into the room without breaking stride, watching the growing panic in her expression. He swung his hand though a wide arc and hit the side of her face with an open palm. The force of the blow knocked her off her seat and onto the floor, then Handyside pulled her up by the collar of her sweater and pushed his face two inches from hers. He wanted her to look deep into his eyes and know what he was capable of. She saw it burning like small points of light in the darkness and began to shake uncontrollably.

Handyside didn't say a word; Christine Swan had been taught the lesson she needed. The glimmer of confidence she'd found was gone.

He dropped her onto the floor, turned and closed the door behind him. He pulled off the ski mask and made himself a cold drink. Half an hour later he was asleep and it was as if nothing had happened. He'd done what he needed to do.

44

Handyside was up again before six and wanted to get on with business. He checked on the girl and saw that the left side of her face was bruised from temple to jaw. It made no difference to him, and he would use it to motivate her old man. He would make the call from another remote area to ensure the police couldn't locate him through his signals. It would be easier to take the straightforward option, but there was too much to lose if there was a problem. Although Handyside knew Swan wanted to speak to his daughter, there was no way he was going to move her from the lodge to make the call – the risk would be too great.

He was sipping the remnants of his second black coffee when he picked up the text from his wife. Her job was done and he felt a dragging weight of concern drop from his shoulders. Good girl. He smiled to himself; he could concentrate on the game now.

He sent one of his team on a twenty-mile drive to get a morning paper and then photograph the girl holding up the red-top headline in front of her. It would have to do for Swan – nothing else would be offered.

When Christine held the paper in front of her she was shaking so much she could hardly hold it still. The bruising on her face showed up clearly on the photograph, exactly as Handyside had intended; he wanted to make sure Swan saw that they were prepared to hurt her.

The location they picked for the second call was a long drive away in a beautiful spot next to a river. Handyside could see the surrounding countryside for miles so if anyone was approaching or following him he would spot them long before they could get close.

He sent the picture then immediately made the call to Swan. It rang for too long and Handyside couldn't believe that any man who loved his daughter wouldn't have been sitting next to the phone all night. It had the smell of the law about it.

In fact, another quirk of fate had come into play and by the time he made the call the intercept facility on Swan's phone had gone live. It was quite by chance that this would end up saving his miserable life. Swan himself was still comatose after his night of abuse and was close to having overdosed on booze after his dessert of high-quality coke.

Handyside was about to ring off when Swan finally managed to grope clumsily for his mobile and accept the call.

'That's too long to answer, Ricky. Do that again and I'll send you her lips.'

'Sorry, man, fuckin' head's mince.' Reality started to trickle back into his inflamed brain and his mouth felt like his saliva glands had gone on strike.

'Have you seen the picture we sent you?'

'What picture? Just woke up.'

Handyside was a supremely patient man, but Swan was pissing him off already. He told him to look at the

369

text he'd sent and that he would call back in one and a half minutes.

The policeman listening to the conversation perked up. Usually it took a while before you heard something interesting, but a distorted voice on one end of the call meant there was some serious business going on and he was all ears.

Swan sat up and stretched his aching body. Gnasher, who was hoping breakfast might be coming his way soon, stared up at him but was ignored as usual. When Swan opened the attachment and saw the bruising on Christine's face and the pleading fear in her eyes, he sobered up and felt the bile rise into his throat. He chewed his lip, impatient for the phone to ring again. Gnasher nuzzled his leg looking for attention, but the reward for the dog who'd saved his life was a kick in the gut.

Swan answered the next call on the first ring. 'Why the fuck was that necessary? Let me speak to her.' Swan had done a rare thing and let his anger rise above his fear.

'It was necessary, and we want to return her to you with no more damage than necessary.' The even tone of the Darth Vader voice on the other end of the line had a dampening effect on Swan equivalent to the blow to his daughter's face. 'Think carefully now before you make any rash decisions. She won't be harmed if you and your daughter behave and get this sorted.'

The policeman listening in to the conversation forgot all about his hangover and was already running through the lists of what to do next. It was a kidnapping and that mattered. He signalled to someone else in the office to make the necessary calls.

'We can't let you speak to her because it would put us at risk. You can see from the paper that the photograph was taken earlier today and that should be enough. In one and a half hours from now I'll call again and make an arrangement to meet you and hand over your daughter. Do you understand?'

'Okay. I'll give you all the information I have.'

Handyside thought it was no more than a strange choice of words so he didn't realise that Swan thought he was handing over enough dirt on discs to keep a blackmailer happy for the rest of his career.

'We can do this today, get it over with and Christine can get back to her life,' he replied then put the phone down before Swan had a chance to answer; it was part of keeping control.

45

Macallan got the call about the intercepted conversation only minutes after it had happened. She reached for the aspirin in her desk because she knew her head was going to hurt. At the same time, she was waving at Thompson to indicate that she should grab the seat opposite. Thompson could see the strain drawing the skin round Macallan's eyes and knew something was up.

'Please keep me posted on anything that comes in and we'll get things moving this end.'

When Macallan put the phone down she noticed she'd been biting the side of her forefinger again. She walked round the desk then closed the door, trying to think what they could do in the next hour and a half.

She called O'Connor at Fettes and asked if he had a moment because there was a critical situation developing with no time to deal with it. She'd already sent Thompson to request the chopper as soon as they could get it to her, knowing O'Connor would authorise it.

He agreed to that. 'What else do you need?' he asked, his face pale.

She thought for a minute. 'The problem is that we don't have much time before the next call so I'm going to phone Ricky and try to buy us some. If that works I'm thinking we can maybe get Handyside and his team to come to us. We'll use that bastard Harrison before we put him away.' She outlined her plan and he realised it could work with a bit of luck. He could also see the more likely scenario that it all went to rat shit, but what choice did they have?

'Get to it,' he told her. 'I'll clear my desk and work beside you on this. You'll need backing and it's yours.'

'Thanks, that means a lot to me. I'll call Ricky as soon as you leave the office.'

O'Connor walked over and pulled his door shut, realising that his career was about to end in either glory or flames.

Macallan's call was picked up right away. 'Ricky?'

'Who's that?' But he knew who it was. He was alert, his mind in near panic mode as the alcohol and dope flushed out of his system.

'We need to talk.' Macallan said it slowly and tried as far as possible to keep the emotion out of her voice. 'I'd rather do this face to face, but there's no time. Is there anything you need to tell us?'

Macallan had asked Thompson earlier to get a hold of Young, brief her and get her to come to her office. The analyst was peering round the door now, and Macallan waved her inside. She sat down opposite Macallan, pulled out her notebook and started to take notes as the detective put the call on loudspeaker.

Swan was a weak man, but he was no fool and he knew that her question meant they must have some knowledge of what was going on – but how?

'What do you mean?' he asked, stalling for time so he could decide what to say. They were sparring, but Swan guessed correctly that the woman on the other end of the phone knew how to play the game. He just needed to figure out how much she knew before he stuck his boot into the pile of dog shit that was his life now – and more importantly whether her involvement meant that Christine was safer or in more danger?

'Listen carefully, Ricky. I don't have time to fuck about, and you don't either. We know you're in trouble, but more importantly your daughter's in trouble. That's our business whether you like it or not. You can't deal with these men. They'll kill both of you, trust me on this.'

Swan tried to get his brain into gear and think, but his heart was hammering in his chest. They either had a grass inside the kidnappers' team … but if they did then why the fuck phone him? No, it must mean his phone was bugged. What had really sent his heart rate up was the suggestion that he could be killed. He'd been working on the theory that this was about his discs and if that's what it took to get his daughter back off the bastards then so be it. But why would they kill him? That would only bring down an investigation … and the police knew about his discs, just not (and more importantly) who was performing on them. They'd tear up the city looking for them. There was no point pissing Macallan about but he needed to know what the fuck she was on about.

'Look, they only want what's on these discs I've got. I just want my daughter back so you need to stay out of this. You said it made no difference to you what I've got on people anyway.'

Macallan was caught off guard. As far as she was concerned this had to be Handyside's work – and why would he want the discs? 'Ricky. You need to think very carefully because if you get this wrong then you lose big time. What exactly did they say and ask for?'

Swan began to pour sweat into his clothes, once again caught between forces he could do nothing about. He realised with numbing shock that the words used during his call to the kidnapper could be interpreted different ways so as far as he could, he told Macallan exactly what had been said and asked for.

Macallan and Young looked at each other and saw the crossed lines sticking straight up into the air.

'They don't want the discs, Ricky, they want what's in your head: they want to know what you know about them. They want to know it all just before they kill you.'

It was time to get Ricky Swan on-board.

'The other thing is that they'll torture you before they put you in the ground. You stuck an undercover officer into them. He's probably dead and buried and they'll put you in beside him. Is that clear enough?'

'Okay, I did the business with the undercover, but what the fuck have I got in my head that can hurt them?' He was confused and becoming more frightened by each disclosure.

'They believe on top of everything else that you have information linking them to the Flemings' business. You're the last problem still alive, Ricky, if we discount Big Brenda, who'll never talk to us.'

Macallan knew what his next question would be and it was time to twist the knife all the way round.

'Why the fuck would they think that?'

'Because I fed that information to them. You're the bait, whether you like it or not. If you want this finished you have to work with us or I'll drop you off at their front door myself.'

He whimpered like a small dog and Macallan knew she had his full attention. 'Now, we're going to finish this once and for all. One of my team will be on their way shortly, but when the next call comes in you have to buy time.'

The voice at the other end of the phone was like a beaten child. 'How?'

'When they phone, you tell them the murder team have been in touch and want to interview you and take a witness statement. Tell them they're on their way. Tell them you can do the business tomorrow. They'll buy it, and that'll give us time to get to you and wrap the bastards up. Can you do it?'

Swan felt more tired than he ever had in his life. It was too much, and if he survived then he was going to fuck off abroad and live the dream. He lit up a cigarette, saw Gnasher staring at him and realised the dog he'd been kicking about the place was the only friend he had. He patted the seat next to him and Gnasher's eyes lit up as he jumped onto the sofa.

He sucked in a lungful of air as he rediscovered his balls. 'I can do it.' His voice had steadied; there was no choice, and he was tired of being everyone's pet target.

'Someone's on their way and they'll be with you soon but maybe not before the call. I have something to do and then I'll be straight there myself. There's enough heavy squad to protect you from a tank regiment so go with us, Ricky. No more running away. Okay?'

'Okay, Superintendent.'

She ended the call and looked back at Young.

'Get your coat, Felicity, we're going to Newcastle. First things first though – I need to make a call to our best mate, Tony Harrison.'

Macallan saw the analyst's expression change to 'why on earth are we talking to that man?' She didn't ask, but Macallan gave her the answer anyway. 'Harrison is going to deliver Handyside to us, but we need to act the part: you should meet up with their analyst as normal and exchange a bit of information while I play kneesy under the table with Harrison and drop a story in his lap that he'll have to deliver to Handyside. It's simple.'

She felt nervous energy pulse through her at the

opportunities she saw opening up. They would only get one shot at this and she was going to take it. 'I'll explain on the way down, but when we're finished I want you to drop me off outside Newcastle and I'll get picked up by the chopper. Okay?'

'I think so.'

When Young left to pick up their car Macallan made a call to Jack but only got his voicemail. She told him she loved him and that it would be a long day and night but he wasn't to worry.

'Kiss the wee man for me,' she said before she put the phone down, picturing how they'd looked walking on the Antrim cliffs.

She took a couple of deep, steadying breaths then called Tony Harrison.

46

When his phone rang, Harrison stared at it for a long moment and wished he could avoid answering. The earlier call he'd had from Turner requesting he make himself available to advise on a kidnapping was a fucking nightmare, but he had no choice – he knew that if they went down on this one he'd burn just as brightly. He picked up the phone and had to suppress a sigh of relief when he recognised Grace Macallan's voice. She sounded warmer than she had the last time they'd spoken, so maybe his idea to make a move on her wasn't so daft. For a moment he forgot that he was running with the dogs as she reeled him in gently.

'Good to talk to you, though I'm actually about to head down your way. There's a development, and we might need to move quicker than we thought on Handyside. You available?'

It was an offer he couldn't refuse – in more ways than one. If she had something good and he could drop it on Handyside then maybe his feeling that things were going south would calm down.

'I'll be waiting,' he replied, 'and anything you need you'll get if it helps to put that bastard away.'

She had to work hard to swallow his words, but there was big prize money at the end of this game and she knew how to do it.

'We're just leaving. Felicity wants to have a quick meeting with your analyst when we arrive if that's possible?'

'Of course,' he replied.

'Great. I'll see you soon then, and if this goes well you can buy me dinner when they're all locked up,' she said, giving him that first hint that she might be interested in getting to know him more intimately.

He swallowed it whole, grinning down the phone. He'd have to cancel an appointment he'd made with an escort for one of his special massage sessions, but that could wait.

Macallan didn't speak for the first half hour as they drove down the A1 towards Newcastle. When she'd run it all through her head for the third time she was satisfied and feeling more confident. Thompson was already on her way to Loch Melfort with a small team to babysit Swan till Macallan could get there, and she'd planned for everything she could reasonably anticipate. It was a good feeling, and this was why she struggled to turn her back on the job. There was a gamble when people's lives were at stake; it could all go so very wrong, but that was why people gambled in the first place – when the dice landed the right way up there was nothing like it.

As Macallan wrestled with her thoughts, Ricky Swan stared at the clock as it wound down towards the time the next call was due, stroking Gnasher's head as he did. He wasn't frightened any more. He believed Macallan;

he'd underestimated her, but now he knew she was a ruthless bitch, and, what's more, she was a ruthless bitch who made sense. He'd realised how vulnerable he was in the lawless world he inhabited and he wanted out of it. There was no going back. Christine might escape all this, but Handyside was doing a cleaning job and he would be taken out no matter how long it took. He might as well fight back while he had the chance.

The phone rang.

'Okay, Ricky? You ready to do business?'

'There's a problem.'

'What do you mean, "there's a problem"? You have thirty seconds to convince me you're not messing me about or I start to work on Christine.'

Swan felt cold hatred for the man on the end of the phone. This was what he'd faced all his life as the runt, the weed who couldn't fight back. He wasn't going to let Christine die terrified and alone, buried where he could never mourn her, so he put on the best act of his life.

'What the fuck do you expect me to do? The murder squad are on their way to take a fuckin' witness statement. They didn't ask. If I fuck them around it'll look worse and they might get a warrant for me. Give it some thought, you cunt!'

The final expletive surprised even Swan, but it was just what a man in his position would say and Handyside could see where he was coming from.

'Okay, I'll call you again, same time tomorrow – but that's it,' he said. 'No more delays after that. Any new problem crops up then you know what happens.'

'One last question.' Swan had to ask it. 'What exactly do you want from me?'

'We just want to talk to you about the Flemings. Do that and you're on your way.'

'Nothing else?'
'Nothing else.'

Meanwhile, back on the road to Newcastle, Macallan snapped out of her thoughts as she realised Young was talking to her. 'Sorry, I was away somewhere else. What's happening with the team's work?'

'We're making real progress,' she said again. 'Ronnie took you at your word and got right on top of Billy Drew. House search, overt surveillance, the lot. Pulled him in and questioned him about every unsolved crime in the city. Last night Ronnie went back to see him for a witness statement in relation to the Flemings and wound him up so tight Drew took a swing at him. He was locked up for police assault. No evidence to connect to our investigation, but I don't suppose that was your point.'

Macallan knew that Young didn't quite approve of this kind of stroke, but she also knew that deep down she liked the idea of the bad guys getting it tight. That was what had first attracted her to Harkins. It certainly hadn't been his sharp dress sense or urbane line in conversation. Harkins was a rough bastard and the truth was that the men who'd inhabited Young's previous life at the badminton club and bridge nights bored the arse off her – and one thing you could never accuse Harkins of was being a bore.

'Anything else?' Macallan asked.

'Couple of developments. Ronnie's team interviewed a couple of junkies who were lifted the night the city went mad. Sweated them a bit and they admitted that they'd been paid by some of the Flemings' team to create havoc. I think we can be sure now that it was all a diversion, and a good plan when you think about it. The positive news is that the evidence is piling in from the financial investigation into Ricky Swan. There's enough to detain him as it stands but there's more to come. The point is that when you're ready you can take him. That's about it for the moment.'

'That's good enough for me. Think we need to get Ronnie on the team full-time when this is finished. There's a bit of the Mick Harkins in that boy.' She turned, smiling, to check Young's reaction.

The analyst tried to suppress a grin but it was there and Macallan thought again how lucky Harkins had been to find this woman. The way things were going he would probably have drunk himself into an early grave otherwise.

'Better dresser though,' Young replied. 'And he has some manners. Mick's never been good with manners.'

They saw the edges of the great North-east city starting to form on the horizon and lapsed into silence again as they headed on to the meeting.

'It's good to see you.' Harrison was all smiles and Macallan noted the glint in his eye, which was exactly what she'd wanted to see.

'Tony.' She shook his hand and held it for a moment longer than necessary.

Young was shown to the analysts' department while Harrison took Macallan into his office and closed the door behind him.

'Can I get you anything? Tea – or something stronger?'

'Next time, and over dinner. Too much to do and things on the move up there.' She watched him stiffen slightly – he was waiting for the pay-off. All the bastard had to do was pass the bait to Handyside.

'We're going to see Ricky Swan tomorrow; we think we can turn him now. We've been working on his financial background and it looks like there's enough money laundering and revenue avoidance to sink him several times over. On top of all that, we're finding links through

382

trafficked women to other criminals all over the country. Prison would break a man like Swan so it looks good. The murder squad are on their way to see him today, but that's only a routine action because they need his statement for their system. I'm going up tomorrow to work this one on him. He'll break, trust me.'

'What can I do for you then?' He wanted to ask her where the bastard was but that was too upfront.

'I need you to get surveillance on Handyside and Turner so that if we get in position we're ready to lift them straightaway.'

'Consider it done.'

Macallan watched his face pale and knew he was trying to find a way to get the answers she was going to give him for free anyway. Not all of it, which might spook him, but enough for a resourceful man like Handyside to work with.

'Sticks in my throat,' she said. 'Swan has a place to die for up there. Looks right down on Loch Melfort and only ten minutes' walk from the local boozer. Ever been up there? It's beautiful.' She watched him take it, his greed overcoming his survival instincts. 'Don't mention that outside the door,' she added. 'You know how it is with need-to-know.'

She hadn't given him an address, but it was enough for them to work on – a result as far as Harrison was concerned. 'How long will it take you to get the surveillance started?' he asked.

'It'll be up and running later tonight. Tomorrow morning at the latest. I'll email you with a few more details when I get back, and as soon as we get Ricky in I'll call you. When it's all done you can come up to Edinburgh for the piss-up.'

She stood up and squeezed his hand again before heading out the door.

Harrison watched her leave, pondering the gem she'd dropped in his lap with the reference to Loch Melfort. He'd never thought women made good detectives and it looked like she was no different, however much she pressed his buttons.

By the time Macallan was heading back out of the city she'd arranged for a team of specialists to head for an RV point near Oban. It was a race for time, because if she was right Harrison would have already made the call to Handyside. The information she'd fed them meant they only had what was left of the day to trace Swan and the cover of the brief summer darkness to move on him. A lot could go wrong and she needed a lucky break, but sometimes she got them.

On the way back she got the call she'd hoped for but didn't quite believe would happen: Swan had given an Oscar-winning performance when he got the call from the kidnapper on the other end of the line.

Macallan had been right about Harrison. He left the station as soon as he saw the tail of her car disappear from the yard and made the call. Handyside had been wondering whether Swan was at it, but Harrison was able to confirm that the murder squad were on their way to take a statement. The crucial information for Handyside was that Macallan thought she had enough to take Swan out and develop lines of investigation that might burn all the way back to his front door. He said, 'Good man,' but didn't mean it, when Harrison gave him the rough location for Swan. It was enough though, and when he looked up Google maps and a description of the area afterward he believed they should be able to find the little bastard with a bit of work. There were only a limited number of places Swan could be in the sparsely

384

populated area round the head of Loch Melfort, and he would have had no reason to use a false identity when he bought the place so that gave them another angle to work on.

He called Harrison back and told him to get to work on his contacts in the telephone companies and postal services to tie it down and within an hour Turner and the other two men on his team were on the road to Argyll, two in a car and one in the van. They headed for Oban and then the road south to Loch Melfort.

Handyside gave Turner one last order before he left. 'Remember, I want a call no more than thirty minutes after you tell me you're going in. If it goes dead then I clean it up here. You understand?'

'Got it. Take care.' Turner knew exactly what 'clean up' meant. If something went wrong at Melfort the girl wasn't going back to see Daddy.

The first of the police specialists were on their way to an RV point where they could brief and deploy to Melfort. Macallan was in the chopper when she got the call that O'Connor was going to meet her there. It surprised her, but it was his last show and in a way she was glad to have him beside her. They'd both made long journeys, but the past was where it was and she wanted to leave it there.

The rushing air froze her as the aircraft beat its way over the Scottish Borders and she wished she'd put more clothes on for the ride. She pulled out her wallet and grinned at the passport-sized picture of Jack and Adam smiling back at her.

Swan took Gnasher out into the front garden and when Thompson arrived he was throwing a ball for the happy-looking mutt to chase. She was surprised at how relaxed he looked, but the pimp and one-time runt had finally come to terms with what he was and what he'd been. They went inside and she started to brief him on what would happen and what they would need him to do.

Turner drove the car across the breadth of Scotland and despite all the plans and potential problems he had running through his mind, he marvelled at the country as they made their way through the Highland landscape. He thought that when this was all over he might spend a bit of time getting to know the place and follow his passion for the outdoors and fishing. The only thing in his way was the skinny little figure of Ricky Swan.

47

To reach Loch Melfort all a driver had to do was navigate the crowded streets of Oban and head south into some of the loveliest parts of Argyll, with its dazzling seascapes, ancient churches, gravestones carved with the images of long-dead island warriors and enough dramatic natural beauty to keep most people happy for a lifetime. Sixteen miles south, past the tiny village of Kilmelford, there was a turn to the right and Melfort sea loch opened up in all its glory. One road in and one road out to get round it, which was perfect for the police operation. If the killers arrived and went in then they couldn't get back out, at least not in a car, because there would be a small army of violent bastards with big fuck-off police guns waiting for them.

The teams were briefed before they headed for Oban and Macallan would take control when she arrived. O'Connor was the senior rank, but he would give way to let her run things unless they needed his authority for more resources or a critical decision. A command vehicle was also on its way so they could operate securely a few miles inland from Loch Melfort and well out of the way of public travel routes. There was too much risk of exposure in using the Oban police offices, and it would have been impossible to conceal the movement of so many officers and vehicles.

The CROPs men were first to go in, being well trained in camouflage and concealment. They could survive for long periods dug into hides and provided close-quarter information to the operational teams. They were hard, physically fit, and had to be, with nerves to match. They got close in to the targets they observed and acted as the operational team's eyes till there was an arrest.

The job Macallan had given them was a difficult one. Getting themselves into three positions to cover all sides of Swan's place in broad daylight was risky with too little preparation and no cover of darkness to prepare their hides, but there was no time to wait.

A heavy cloudburst came to their aid in the end, forcing the locals and tourists indoors and the three CROPs men managed to get under cover unobserved. Within an hour they called in that they were settled and had good eyes on all sides of Swan's house.

Over the next few hours, surveillance officers were deployed at points along the approach road both north and south of Melfort. Male and female officers booked into the few hotels in the area to act as backup if need be and in case the targets booked in anywhere themselves, and a firearms team was heading north as soon as they'd finished a full briefing in Glasgow.

Keeping the operation secure was the biggest problem, but the weather came to the rescue again as the occasional downpours joined up to rain in that unique way of the west Highlands. The CROPs men cursed it, but gave thanks at the same time that they had the natural cover of pissing rain and low cloud that killed the light.

Macallan was getting her bit of good luck, though she was being bounced around in the chopper and wanted to throw up with the motion. All she needed was to get on the ground and hear that Handyside's team were on their way. That was the hard bit – the waiting; never really knowing whether the killers would actually turn up, and the gnawing worry that all these men and women had been deployed for nothing. It happened – every senior detective knew it, and sometimes the police had to wait hours, days, even weeks before the villains turned up. And when they did it was invariably all over in minutes, and even though the operation was successful, the detectives involved would feel that crash after the high – and the realisation that somewhere else another team of bad bastards were planning to do the same things all over again.

The radio crackled into life – O'Connor was in the command vehicle, which had been set up in the grounds of an old deserted farmhouse well away from the routes used by the summer hillwalkers.

'Most of the teams have been deployed, and even if we miss them on the roads, the CROP boys have clear sight of Ricky's place. Lesley is babysitting him and she has a couple of firearms officers in there as well.'

'That's all good,' she replied. 'I should be with you in fifteen minutes. Are they ready to get Ricky out of there when we make the call?'

'Yes, as soon as we know the targets are coming for him we pull Ricky out the back of the house. There's good cover from trees and hills.'

Macallan felt her stomach attempting to escape through her mouth as she signed off. She hated helicopters, having spent too much time during the Troubles being ferried by Army flyers who not only accepted scraping the hills when they were flying but thought it was a laugh.

Turner lit up another cigarette to add to the fog that engulfed the inside of the car as they drove down the long hill that took them into Oban, where the streets were packed with soaked tourists. They drove down to a car park near the ferry terminal and got out to stretch their legs. After doing some foot anti-surveillance to make sure they hadn't picked up the law along the way, they decided it was safe to go and grab a coffee. Turner called Handyside and told him where they were, that it was pissing down and that the place was a dump.

'Okay, get some coffee in you. We might be able to get Ricky's place from our friend Tony. He's pushing some buttons with his contacts but he doesn't sound like a happy bunny. I'm starting to think we might need to make him redundant.'

'Sounds good to me,' Turner replied. 'You know how I feel about the bastard. He'll stab us in the back one of these days.'

'Not if we do him first. Take care and let me know as soon as you find Ricky, if our friend in intelligence doesn't come up with it first. Don't move in before I give you the okay.'

Turner hung up and they all squeezed into a badly ventilated café crowded with tourists waiting for the rain to clear. By the time they came back out, after being robbed for a cup of dishwater, the sun was blazing. It was a typical summer in the Highlands, all the seasons appearing in one day.

'Christ, are we in the same place?' Turner squinted into the sun and savoured the heat on his face. His mood should have lightened with the weather, but the whole job gnawed at his entrails. It was a massive risk taking Swan, and they might find out that he had nothing on them. He shook his head and headed back for the car.

Macallan was back on the ground, her stomach settling back into place almost the minute she stepped warily out of the chopper, which took off again to get some of the specialist firearms team and medics ready to go if need be. O'Connor handed her a steaming brew as soon as she stepped into the command vehicle and she accepted it gratefully; she was still shivering after the bare-knuckle ride through the rainstorm and she could feel each sip warming her. The sun had burst through the clouds and the light sparkled off the wet hills as they began to steam under the sudden burst of warmth.

'We're almost ready. The firearms team should be on their way soon enough and we have a couple of shooters in with Ricky and Lesley,' O'Connor told her.

Macallan nodded and sipped more tea before calling Thompson.

'It's fine here,' Thompson told her, 'and for some strange reason Ricky is calm enough. Don't know what's happened to him, but he just wants us to do the business and get his daughter to safety.'

'Okay, I want you to stay with him till we decide to do the extraction. Just one thing – let the dog run about the garden. I mentioned it to Harrison and, who knows, he might have passed that little titbit to the boys. I'll be here till this is resolved, so any problems just let me know right away. Get Ricky to show himself at the window every half hour. Our CROPs men would see anyone trying to get near enough for a snipe so he should be safe enough.'

Macallan put the phone down and passed out an order that the registration number of every car that passed the first surveillance team north of Kilmelford should be called in to the command vehicle for an intel search. The road was tight and carried very little traffic so it could be done easily enough. If those cars didn't pass the last surveillance team, at Arduaine, it had to mean they'd stopped somewhere. The cars' occupants would mostly be locals and a few tourists, but it might give them a start if anything came up on the numbers.

They settled down and the silence was only broken by the surveillance teams doing their communications checks and calling in the odd car number. The first of the firearms team arrived with the medics and Macallan breathed a quiet sigh of relief. They had enough people in place to tackle any unexpected developments that might crop up.

O'Connor watched her chew the side of her finger and knew she was running and rerunning every possible scenario through her head.

After a couple of hours the intelligence officer with Macallan gave her the list of cars that hadn't passed the last surveillance team at the south end of the operation.

'Anything stand out?' She didn't expect a miracle, but there was something. A few of the cars were locals and a couple of Home Counties wheels came up: posh 4x4s with nothing on the computer apart from expensive properties and double-barrelled names. Unlikely at best, but she kept them working the intelligence.

Macallan put down the cup that had been empty for twenty minutes when the intel officer mentioned the car and van. The hired car from Perth might be nothing but the van was registered in North Shields. She felt her skin prickle – they were near; she knew it in her bones.

'Anything on PNC for the van?' she asked.

'Nothing that we can dig up at the moment. All we know is it's a dodgy bit of town. Nothing else.'

'Call the surveillance teams and the guys in the hotels. Have a look for the van and give them the numbers of the other cars as well. Let's see where they are.'

She looked across at O'Connor who was staring intently at her. 'It's them.'

'You sure?' he asked.

'It's them.'

O'Connor stood up, called the firearms team leader and asked him for an update. The rest of his unit were just arriving and he was about to brief them on the job. They would be ready when the call was made.

'If we get a chance we'll put another couple of my guys into the house.' The firearms team leader was experienced, calm and knew exactly what needed to be done and how to do it. If he had to pull the trigger on these bastards he wouldn't hesitate. All he'd been told was that the men they might face wouldn't hesitate either. That was good enough for him – and the men and women on his team.

The atmosphere in the command vehicle was beginning to strain and Macallan stepped outside for some air and to ease the tension knotting up her muscles. She paced backwards and forwards but stayed close enough to the vehicle to hear any call from the teams.

'Superintendent.' The intel officer stuck his head out and gave her the nod. 'The van's in the car park of this hotel on the south side of the loch.' He pointed it out on an electronic map of the area. 'The hire car from Perth is there as well. The other cars have been traced to holiday lets around the loch and apparently they're in the second week of their hols.' The intel officer looked pleased and the mood lifted for them all.

Macallan looked across at O'Connor and smiled. 'Told you.'

'So you did. So you did.' He smiled back and, as he did every day now, wondered how he could have been daft enough to lose this woman.

She called the team in the hotel. They had a perfect view of the car park and could see the van and the hired motor. They hadn't seen the occupants arriving, but they would set up a watch on the cars for any movement and take it in turns to keep an eye on the bar in case they could get a physical description. Macallan moved another surveillance team to cover the entrance to the hotel and give the man and woman inside some backup.

The female surveillance officer was Pam Fitzgerald and she hung around the lounge area till the receptionist headed for the ladies. It only took a moment to clock the names from the register, which meant nothing to the intel officer, but they had used Newcastle addresses that were all bogus when checked out.

'They're pros – why would they put their true identities?' Macallan said to that and felt the knot in her stomach tighten.

Another half hour passed and Fitzgerald was sitting in the lounge trying not to get carried away by the stunning view across the loch when three men joined up at the bar. She sipped her Coke and appeared to study her paper, and though she struggled to hear what was said, it didn't matter – their Geordie accents carried across the bar and within two minutes she'd sent a text to the command vehicle.

'They're Geordies, the three of them. Description to follow.'

Macallan slapped the desktop, hoping beyond hope that one of them was Handyside himself. Everyone stared at the intel officer as he took the next message. He looked up and ran off the three descriptions.

'Pete Handyside isn't with that lot. Two of them mean nothing but the third man is almost certainly Maxi Turner.' Macallan was disappointed that there was no sign of Handyside, but she knew if they got Turner they could wrap up the boss with a bit more work. Tying Turner to Handyside shouldn't take Sherlock Holmes.

She turned to O'Connor and shrugged. 'Why would the main man be there anyway? He's the boss.'

They were interrupted by another text from Fitzgerald. The man they thought was Turner had left the bar and gone out to the car park. The surveillance officer in the room grinned. 'Gotcha.' He clicked off three pictures, which were with Macallan two minutes later.

'It's him alright.' She felt a bit more confident with a positive identification. Coincidences happened and sometimes an innocent punter wandered into an operation and looked like the real deal till he sued for wrongful arrest. A positive ID settled the nerves.

The intel officer asked Macallan if she wanted the identification confirmed with the intelligence unit in Ponteland.

'No. Absolutely no contact with them until this is over.' The command was sharp and the intel officer knew that could only mean there was a rat operating on their side of the game. It happened and he knew not to ask again.

Another report came in from Fitzgerald that the men had left the bar and appeared to have gone back to their rooms. Ten minutes later they came back into the lounge having all changed into warmer gear, as if they were planning to head outside. They finished their drinks, then picked up small rucksacks from the back of the van and stood around talking for a few minutes. It was obvious that Turner was in charge and giving the orders. Then Turner and one of the men left together, with the third target taking off ten minutes later, and soon they were all heading up the shore of the loch as if it was just another pleasant day out.

'Okay, make sure everyone is on their toes with this so we don't lose them, understood?' Macallan had started to fire out orders, glad it was all moving at last. Waiting was always a pain in the arse and action was easier to deal with than worrying about what might go wrong. She put out the call that Maxi Turner would be referred to as

Target 1 for the rest of the operation. The descriptions of the three men had been passed out and the picture of Turner flashed to all the units on the job.

Turner barely spoke to the man walking beside him. They knew exactly who they were looking for and roughly the area he was in and there seemed to be no need for discussion. The third man was a quarter of a mile behind them and would keep that distance in case they needed backup. To anyone passing they were just another pair of tourists sampling the spectacular scenery. Turner obviously thought they were well clear of any law, but all along the way they were under observation, and by the time they reached the left-hand turn taking them along the north shore of the loch they'd been photographed, videoed and every detail of their clothing and rucksacks was being fed into an intelligence system.

They stopped for a moment and Macallan stiffened, wondering if they'd been spooked somehow. Then the call came that they were looking at a map and everyone in the command vehicle relaxed again. They had walked another couple of hundred yards along the shore when Turner's phone signalled a text arriving. He looked at the screen to find it was a message from Handyside. Harrison had come up with the goods and had verified Swan's address, which was only another couple of minutes' walk in front of them.

'Looks like he's taking a message on his phone.' The intel officer was looking at a screen relaying pictures from an unmanned van parked at the road end with a view along the loch shore towards Swan's place.

They watched the two men look up and head towards the area covered by the CROPs team.

'We have them now.' The CROP man with eyes on the road running past Swan's cottage called it in, glad something was happening to take his mind off the fact that his camouflage outfit was soaked inside and out.

Macallan stood up and called Thompson. 'I want you to get Ricky to the window. They'll pass the front door shortly. Get your head down.'

Turner saw Gnasher running about the front garden and was sure Harrison or Handyside had mentioned some stupid breed of dog. Then he saw the main prize at the window, smoking casually as if he hadn't a care in the world. Turner had to work hard not to react and spook the man they intended killing.

'Nice one.' He grinned, and when they were fifty yards past the house they sat by the loch side and had another cigarette. They were about twenty feet from one of the CROPs men who'd dug into a camouflaged hole in the ground. He was indistinguishable from the surrounding vegetation and about an hour earlier a clearly uncomfortable tourist had taken a detour into the bushes and pissed all over the hide. It was an occupational hazard sadly – and the least of his worries. He could hear Turner talking quietly, but it was impossible to make out the conversation. He saw him gesture back towards Swan's place and it looked like they were happy they'd found their target. The third man joined them and Turner stood up and pointed again towards the cottage. He seemed to be giving them instructions. Then they split up again and turned back along the road.

The CROP officer called it in. 'Looks like they've taken the bait. All units beware they're on the way back.'

The three targets headed back they way they'd come, and as soon as they were well away Macallan gave the order to extract Swan. Barely five minutes later a van with a telecom logo pulled up in front of Swan's house, where it paused until the CROPs men confirmed there were no cars or walkers approaching. The moment it received the all-clear it reversed up the driveway and stopped parallel to the side of the cottage with about an inch clearance between it and the gable end, ensuring little or nothing of what happened next could be seen. Swan and Gnasher were virtually carried from the house, thrown in the van and it was on the move before the rear doors were properly closed. He sat between two very large policemen, who told him to relax.

He looked down at Gnasher shivering on his lap and stroked the dog's head. 'Hear that, son? We've just to relax. I mean, there's fuck all to worry about, right?'

The dog didn't get irony and continued to shiver at yet another change in his circumstances.

Another pair of surveillance officers had booked into the hotel while Turner and his team were away. They would keep their eyes on the car park so as to let Fitzgerald and her partner sit in the bar and chat like any other happy couple away for a few days in the country. When Turner and his team returned they went straight to their rooms before coming down for dinner an hour later. They stayed off the booze and talked all through the meal.

When Fitzgerald called to report that the three targets had then gone back to their rooms, Macallan guessed they would rest up for what they had to do later.

'Don't see them making a move before dark,' she said to O'Connor, before giving the order for the crews to rotate so they could eat and take whatever natural breaks they needed. Darkness came late in this part of the world and they had a long night in front of them.

Macallan stepped outside to stretch her muscles and gazed in the direction of Swan's cottage. 'See you there then, Maxi,' she said to herself, wondering where Handyside was and what he was doing.

*

Handyside sat quietly at the window, enjoying a cigarette. He'd cleaned the place as far as he could while the girl was still there and all he could do now was wait. Another short text came in from his wife, saying that everything was fine and she wished he was beside her.

He finished the smoke, put the stub into a jar and sealed it – the jar would be taken away when he left the lodge for the last time. The message from Turner was upbeat. They'd confirmed Swan was in the house so they would make a move after dark. No sign of any problems or the law.

He rubbed his chin and wondered what Macallan was doing with her investigation. He smiled as he imagined her face when she arrived the next day and found what was left of Swan. Barring accidents, that would be job done and he could join his wife – and Turner could get together with all the other old gangsters in the south of Spain.

As darkness fell the clouds closed in and it started to rain again. Not the monsoon they'd seen earlier but a steady drizzle that added to the discomfort of the men in the CROPs. Macallan checked again that everyone was in place and ready. She felt tired with the strain of the day and stirred more black coffee to help buzz up her grey matter.

'You okay?' O'Connor asked. He'd been outside to work his aching legs and was wet through.

'Fine. I always hate this bit, waiting for them to move. Running all the negatives through my head. Christ, I'm sure these operations take years off our lives. Though Handyside is probably doing something similar. We're so close to them, all waiting to meet up at Ricky's place.' She smiled wearily and O'Connor just nodded. There was nothing to say – she was just releasing tension.

'Let's get down there. We can give any commands from the car. If it's going to happen it'll be soon.'

'Okay, I'll drive and you can sit and worry for the two of us.'

They settled into a small car park behind the post office in Kilmelford so they could be with the team in minutes if required. The night was quiet and there was almost no radio traffic apart from the occasional comms check. She started a text saying goodnight to Jack—

'Standby. Standby. Standby!' It was always said three times so there was no doubt. Every man and woman on the operation came to life – this was it.

'That's the targets on the move,' said Fitzgerald, who was back in position watching the car park from her room. 'They're looking into the back of the van and it appears there's some kind of concealment beneath the floor.'

There was what seemed like a long moment's silence and the operator in the command vehicle acknowledged the call, checking that the operational units had received it.

Fitzgerald came back on. 'Can't be certain, but it looks like handguns being packed into their rucksacks. All three targets are into the van and they're off, off, off. Over to you.'

Macallan and O'Connor got ready to move, the tension in the car like an electric charge.

As the van turned left onto the road, two other vehicles were also on the move, but they remained inconspicuous, keeping well back and showing no lights. Although the night was darkest black with low cloud covering the hills all around, the police drivers didn't need lights because they were wearing night-vision goggles. The operation had a life of its own now, and all its components moved into place, ready for any action.

Turner was in the passenger seat, feeling more nervous than he normally would on a job. This was strange country and he was used to operating in a city environment. The overwhelming darkness spooked him, and he wished they were done already.

After sending a text to Handyside when he left the hotel, he'd thrown the phones into the loch and taken clean sets for the rest of the job. He had the boss's number in his head for security, and till they were done that was all he needed.

'Okay, boys, when we get there, stop the van outside. We cross the garden.' He nodded to the driver. 'You reverse up the drive. We crash the door if we have to. If we have to make a noise we throw him in the back of the van, stick him under the floor and find somewhere quiet to work on him. If we get in easy we can do him in the house. Okay. Now let's fucking do this, get the fuck out of this shithole and back to civilisation.'

The van swung left along the single-track road along the head of the loch. He pulled out the handgun and checked it again. There was no way he could know that on every side of the van there were cameras and eyes watching and waiting to arrest or blow the bastards to heaven and back.

The lights were on when they got to Swan's place and the main door was open. The interior lights shone through a glass vestibule door just inside and illuminated part of the front lawn.

'Thanks, Ricky, you cunt – you just made it nice and easy for us.' Turner grinned, his worries about the job easing slightly.

They drew up outside the garden wall, pulled the balaclavas down over their faces and jumped out of the van. When they were over the wall, Turner gave a thumbs-up to the driver, who started to reverse into the driveway. While he was running across the wet grass towards the front door a thought flashed through his mind: there was no sign of the dog...

A half-second later the place lit up like Hampden Park, and they discovered guns were aimed at them from every fucking direction. Turner was a hard nut and had always said he'd go down fighting, but this was what the Yanks liked to call overwhelming force, the Scottish version of which is, 'You're fucked, sunshine!'

The van driver thought for a moment that he might make a run for it, but they blocked him in, and Turner didn't even wait for the order; he dropped the gun and lay down on the grass so they had no excuse to fire. He regretted the decision immediately, because he realised he was probably going to die inside or be so fucking old when he was freed that he'd be terrified to walk back out through the gates.

They were kept face down and handcuffed just a bit too tightly for comfort. After a few minutes of waiting and feeling his clothes soaking up the water from the grass, Turner craned his neck up and saw a pair of sensible women's shoes and a nice pair of ankles.

'Let me guess; it's my fucking lawyer,' he said.

'Sit him up.'

He was pulled back and pushed down; after soaking his front the bastards clearly wanted to soak his arse.

'You have to be Macallan. Nice, very nice indeed.' Turner knew he was fucked, but like a good pro there was no way he was going to let them in on his misery.

'Where's the girl, Maxi? She's done nothing, for Christ's sake.' Macallan nodded to one of the uniforms. 'Get his phone and do last number redial.'

'Do we look that stupid, girl? The phones are clean. Anything you want is in my fucking noddle.'

She went down on one knee and put her face close enough for Turner to get what would be his last scent of a woman for a long time. 'We can do a deal,' she told him. 'Save the girl and you'll cut years.'

He moved his face even closer to hers, but Macallan didn't back away.

'If I don't make a call in the next ten minutes, she dies. Trust me. That's the arrangement. I'll make the call, tell him we have Ricky, you go and rescue the poor girl and I get a deal. Okay?'

'Give us the number and you get the deal. That's it.' She knew he had them over a barrel, but she had to try. If what he said was true then a man like Handyside wouldn't hesitate to do what he had to. He'd proved that already.

'No deal, Superintendent. Fuck you – I'll take my chances.'

Macallan turned to O'Connor and they walked off into the shadows behind the cottage. 'He's got us cornered on this. If the girl dies, it's down to me.'

'No, I'm the rank officer so it's down to me. Tell me what you think and let's do it.'

'We have to let him make the call.'

Turner was taken inside, the handcuffs removed, and he asked for a cigarette. He sucked on the smoke and smiled when Macallan handed him his phone. His eyes remained locked on hers the whole time. According to his timescale they had three minutes left.

He punched in Handyside's number and put the phone to his ear. 'Get the fuck out of there, Pete. They've got us.'

One of the uniforms put him in a headlock while Macallan grabbed the phone from his fingers and put the phone to her ear. It was quiet but hadn't rung off. She felt sick – there was no right way to do this.

'Let her go, Pete. What's the point now? It's over.' She waited for a reply that didn't come. 'Please.' It was all she got out before the call died in her hand.

'Take that bastard away,' she growled. She wanted to hurt Turner but the urge to see him inside was stronger.

403

The intelligence team got to work on the call that had been made to Handyside, but even at best there was more than enough time for him to do what he wanted and what the police team feared most.

'There's nothing more we could have done. We both know it. Now let's track this down and bring Christine home,' O'Connor said, then headed back to the command vehicle while Macallan waited to see the area cleared and Swan's cottage sealed off. It was a crime scene and there was work to do.

She watched the rear lights of O'Connor's car fade into the mist that was drifting up from the cold waters of the loch. The specialist teams were packing up and heading back to their units for a debrief and a rest before they made their reports.

Turner was the last of his team to disappear into the back of the van before they were taken away for process. It didn't matter if they said nothing – they were already fucked.

Macallan nodded to a couple of uniforms and told them to watch the cottage till it was sealed off, but that she had a couple of calls to make and she'd do it inside. She pulled the door shut behind her and walked slowly through the rooms. During the Troubles she'd been on several covert entries into terrorist homes and hides. She was trained in getting in, searching and getting out without disturbing the place.

Swan clearly travelled light as she found very little in the way of personal possessions. He wasn't careful, which seemed par for the course, and when she opened the bedside cupboard she shook her head when she saw the three discs inside. She took the laptop out of her bag, slipped on a pair of rubber gloves and it only took a few minutes for her to copy the discs onto her system. When it was done she relaxed – the copies she'd made would be stashed away in case there was any kind of cover-up.

She made three calls inside the cottage to make sure her story worked if anyone was ever asked why she'd been in there on her own. When she went back outside she asked the senior uniform to take anything they found in the cottage and log it. 'This is a crime scene and Mr Swan might end up as an accused for other matters.'

That was all they needed to know and they got to work while Macallan headed through the mist towards the command vehicle to join O'Connor and sweat it out till the intel teams worked on the call to Pete Handyside.

Dawn had started to light up the eastern sky as the police units closed in round the lodge where Christine Swan had been held. Angry purple and red clouds were rolling by and the air was cool and damp as Macallan and O'Connor stepped out of their car on a low rise about three hundred yards from the lodge. Macallan had hardly spoken a word since Turner and his team had been arrested. She was frightened – more frightened than she could remember being in a long time.

'All those women.' She looked round at O'Connor. 'The women on the boat, Ingrid ... We don't even know if we'll ever find her. Now Christine. We couldn't help them. What's the point?'

'We can't count who we save. We stop these bastards and somewhere along the line we've prevented someone being taken or killed by them. But I ask the same questions all the time. The difference is that you're good at cleaning up the mess. Me, I'm a politician.'

Two CROPs men were doing a creep round the lodge, looking for any signs of life. They had to be careful because there was still the potential, though unlikely, scenario that Handyside or some of his team were still there and fancied a shoot-out with the police. 'There's lights on in every room, but we can't see any signs of life,' the lead officer reported. 'We're going in closer.' The men were methodical and would take as long as they needed to make sure Macallan and the teams had all the information they needed before deciding to pile in.

'I wonder if he's taken her with him?' Macallan said.

There was another call from the CROPs men before O'Connor could answer her. 'The rooms that we can see into are clear. There's one room to the back of the lodge with the curtains drawn. Can't see in. Any instructions?'

'Fuck it. She might be dying in there.' Macallan made the call to send in the firearms team and she would be close behind them.

The front door was unlocked. The lead team entered the lodge and methodically swept one room at a time. They left the room with the curtains drawn till last in case of a trap, and once they'd cleared the upstairs part they repositioned round the door of the back bedroom.

The team leader carefully tried the door handle – it was free. He pushed down and burst into the room.

'Jesus Christ. Get the medic in here.'

Christine Swan's head hung forward, her chin resting on her chest. The team leader dropped his gun and went down on his knees. There was no sign of blood. He said 'Christine' several times and put his fingers against her neck.

'She's alive!'

Macallan came into the room as he said it and almost cried with relief. 'Thank God.' She knelt down beside Swan and saw she was unconscious but breathing noisily.

Within minutes the medics hurried into the room and set to work on the girl. When they cut her bonds and laid her on the floor she looked the colour of death, but they worked calmly – apart from telling the audience to fuck off out of it and give them room. Macallan nodded to the firearms team to clear the room and make space for what had to be done to treat the girl, then she turned back to the medics.

'Just one thing, guys. This is a crime scene so disturb as little as possible. Is she going to be okay?'

'I can't be sure, but my guess is she's drugged and it's a heavy dose,' the medic replied. 'We need to get her out of here as soon as possible.'

Macallan left them to it and wanted to hug O'Connor when he came in. He felt the same way, but they kept their distance. 'Thank God, John,' she said. 'I was sure they'd killed her.'

She got one of the team to make a call to Thompson, who was still with Ricky Swan, to let him know his daughter was safe and on her way to hospital. 'Take Ricky to the hospital. We can at least give him that.'

Ten minutes later Christine was in the back of an ambulance behind a traffic car burning rubber and making sure anything in their way was pushed off to the side of the road.

Macallan left O'Connor at the lodge to look after the forensics teams while she drove to the hospital, at a slower speed than the ambulance and traffic car leading it. By the time she arrived Christine was already being examined and hooked up to a drip. Ricky was in a waiting room with Thompson and a couple of detectives from her team. He looked like a broken man and seemed to have aged ten years, but given what he'd been through it was hardly surprising. He looked up then stood when Macallan walked in, his eyes puffy and bloodshot.

'They think she's going to be okay. Thanks,' he said, then broke down in tears for the second time that night. It was something he'd almost given up since his days as the runt, but the events of recent days were overwhelming him. The act and the self-delusion he'd relied on for years to get him through were gone; his dreams of doing it like Clint had been firmly put away. He sat down again and put his face in his hands.

Macallan gestured to Thompson to come with her. They found an empty waiting room and sat down.

'Did the docs tell you anything about Christine?' Macallan asked.

'It seems like it was some form of opiate and the dose could have been fatal. Doesn't seem like he wanted to kill her though. Let's face it, he has tried and tested ways to do that. It seems likely he just wanted to knock her out while he was cleaning the place and taking off. He's done a good job – there doesn't seem to be a trace of him or his team there. If she'd had any underlying health problems, however, he could have got that one badly wrong. What do we do with Ricky?'

'Keep him here for a few hours to see if she comes round. If not, lock him up. We have the evidence now and he's ours.' She waited for a reaction from Thompson. It might seem hard, but that wasn't what mattered. 'The fact is, Ricky Swan has a lot to answer for and it's time it was done,' Macallan added. 'Apart from anything else, we can't risk another attempt on his life. He's safer inside.'

'I'm sorry for what happened to his daughter, but if you want my professional opinion I'm with you a hundred per cent. Trafficking makes me sick.' Thompson said it like she meant it.

They went back through to see Swan and Macallan told him what would happen next. 'You go with us after this. Time's up. Do you understand?'

He nodded meekly – there was no fight left in him.

Macallan turned to head back to the lodge and meet up with O'Connor.

'What about the dog if I go away?' He looked old – lost

for answers in a world he'd only thought he understood.

'Do you want us to take care of it?' Macallan asked, already having an idea.

He nodded and she promised to make sure the dog who'd suffered so much was looked after.

As she drove back to the lodge she felt the crash starting to kick in. There was still a lot to do, but she was in control and whoever was left in Handyside's organisation was on the back foot and probably running for cover like their boss. She thought again about Ingrid Richter and the family who might never be able to take their daughter home.

She arrived back at the lodge to find everything was under control and O'Connor looked tired but relaxed.

'This working at night is a bit unusual for me now,' he said.

'And we're not finished yet,' she replied. 'Handyside is out there somewhere and we need to get the alerts out to arrest him. Let's get back to the office and you can make the calls to your counterparts in Northumberland. There are doors to kick in and a detective superintendent to arrest. They're going to need a rank above me to convince them to lift one of their own, though I must admit, I'd like to be the proverbial fly when our Tony gets the handcuffs on.'

She smiled and sent a text to Jack before she and O'Connor headed to the car and started their journey back to Edinburgh.

48

Macallan was further behind Handyside than she realised. He'd always had his Plan B, and by the time the messages were being read at ports and airports he was already on the early ferry from Cairnryan to Belfast. He was travelling under a carefully manufactured identity and later in the morning paid cash for a train to Dublin. He spent a pleasant night in a good hotel and followed the emerging story of the kidnapping and rescue in Scotland as it progressed.

Two days later, after a series of interconnecting train journeys, he arrived in Zagreb, and from there he travelled onwards to join his wife on the Istrian coast of Croatia where she was waiting for him in the sun. The trail behind them was already going cold and Handyside had been ultra-careful in planning the rest of his life – and, more importantly, his family's. No one, not even Turner, could have told the police where he was. Handyside knew that any man – even his friend Max – might be tempted, so it was better not to give them the chance.

His wife thought his shaved head and beard suited him, though the children seemed unsure of the look. He had some time to relax, and he checked the web every day to see how the hunt for him was going before they made their final move to South America.

Their old life was gone, almost as if Pete Handyside had never existed.

When Tony Harrison realised the rubber heels were starting to close in, he made a fatal mistake by panicking and trying to do a runner. Unlike Handyside, trying to leg it without planning in the modern world was a terrible mistake. He was a detective and should have known that better than anyone. He was already under surveillance when he made his move, and when they grabbed him at the airport he blubbed like an infant with a cut finger.

The rubber heels loved that – nothing gave them a bigger kick than watching a bent cop cry in front of an audience. It was what got them up in the morning.

Ricky Swan was locked up then bailed after his first appearance at court, but he knew, and his lawyer had confirmed, that it was game over. He sold all his legal businesses and made a decision to plead guilty when the time came; he just wanted to get it all over with. With no previous, he reckoned he could manage the rest of his life with his new way of viewing the world, and the acceptance of what he was and what he'd been.

Christine refused to talk to her father again and anytime he tried to call she put the phone down without speaking. When he asked the police about his discs he was told that there had been no trace of them when the cottage was searched. The truth was that they'd been locked in an ACC's safe after three members of the executive examined them and subsequently made some calls to members of the political class and the judiciary.

Swan basically said fuck it, realising the discs were

more bother than they were worth and wouldn't save him from a stretch inside. After three attempts on his life he just wanted to get below the horizon and hope the bad men out there would forget all about him. Cover-ups were just the way of the world and he wasn't the least bit surprised. He'd do his time then slip out of Scotland and sit in the sun for the rest of his life.

Macallan on the other hand had seen what was on those discs and still had her own personal copies. She didn't miss the fact that a number of cops of all ranks suddenly decided to retire quietly before their time. It was the same for a couple of senior civil servants and a rising political star, who all suddenly wanted to spend more time with their families.

She watched it happen till she'd had enough.

One morning when Jacquie Bell was nursing a cruel hangover, she arrived at her desk and ripped opened a jiffy bag that had been delivered in her mail. She tipped out three discs. There was no letter or sender recorded, and before she even looked at them she could smell they were Swan's bag of other people's dirty laundry.

'Nice one, Grace.' She said it quietly. There was no evidence to say it was Macallan, and it was better that way. 'I'll give them fucking cover-up,' she said to the reporter on the desk opposite.

'What?' The hack facing her was used to Bell talking to herself, but he fancied her rotten so he just grinned whenever he thought she was talking shite.

A month after Handyside disappeared, John O'Connor arranged his leaving do. They had a presentation for him, where the usual lines were churned out by a couple of reps from the executive. They didn't really want to be there, but O'Connor knew all the right people and might sort them with a job in the UN when they retired themselves.

Before they adjourned to The Bailie in Stockbridge and got down to the serious drinking, O'Connor pulled Macallan aside.

'They're giving Elaine Tenant my job. There's no sense in it, but she's the future: grey, robotic and with no personal life so she can't make any mistakes.'

He was concerned, and what surprised Macallan was that he thought she would be as well. She hadn't considered it, and most importantly, she didn't want it.

'Look, I want you to believe this – a promotion into your job would finish me,' she told him. 'Spending my time formulating policy and playing the touchy-feely politician is not for this detective. It's fine, and Elaine is perfect for the role. Anyway, Mick would disown me if I took a job like that.' She took his arm. 'Now come on, or Mick will have drunk you into serious debt.'

They found Jack, Bell, Thompson, Harkins, Young, and Jimmy and Sheena McGovern all there and going strong without the host. O'Connor had said the first hour was on him so a whole team of detectives of all ranks were squeezed into the bar. It didn't take too long for it to turn into a piss-up of epic proportions, and O'Connor let himself go, the legendary restraint finally tossed out the door as he did a medley of Beatles songs with Harkins – the pair of them somehow managing to forget half the words to some of the most enduring songs ever written. It was just the kind of night where everyone could forget the horrors of the past weeks and they'd already come to terms with the fact that Handyside was gone. It happened, and if nothing else he was out of the game.

Handyside's disappearance had left a gaping hole in the organised-crime business in the North-east of England, and particularly Newcastle, and just as it always was, the starting gun was fired and gang warfare broke out. It meant that every couple of days a fresh cadaver was found floating in the Tyne or buried on the moors not far from Hunter, Dillon and an undercover officer too far from his home and family in Northern Ireland. It suited the police, who made noises in the press about their concerns over the violence, though in private, detectives all over the force drank a toast to the latest bad bastard who'd bought their one-way ticket to the next life.

Macallan pulled Jack aside into something resembling a space near the toilets and as far away as possible from Harkins and O'Connor's singing. 'Hope you're not too shocked by the sight of all these officers of the law making complete arses of themselves?' she said.

The truth was that Harkins had made Jack drink whisky, even though he didn't really like the stuff, and after the fifth round the man was going under faster than he'd intended. He dropped an arm round her shoulders, pulling her gently to him, and realised she'd been nursing the same soft drink since she'd arrived. He picked it up and made what he thought was a questioning expression, though the whisky made it look like he was in pain.

'Not drinking? Not the woman I know and love.'

'Do you love me?' she asked.

'Of course I do.' He gave her a wet kiss, which his dulled brain told him should be proof enough for her.

Macallan laughed and, as always, thought that Jack was the most useless drunk she'd ever met. He was acting more like a detective than an increasingly successful lawyer and writer. 'That's good then because we should get this wedding arranged or I'll get a name as a scarlet woman.'

'What?'

'Another bun in the oven, big boy,' she said and smiled, taking another sip of her awful soft drink.

414

Jack made another strange facial contortion, which eventually evolved into a lopsided grin once his brain caught up with the conversation. 'We're going to have a bun?'

'No, not a bun, a baby – the second one. The first one's called Adam.'

He kissed her, punched his arm into the air and made a kind of primeval roar. 'I'm just going to tell the boys.'

Macallan kissed McGovern on her way out to get some air. He was suffering on the soft drinks as well but looked like a new man after his time off to recover. Macallan nodded towards Jack. 'Keep an eye on my man, will you? I'm going out for some air. I've warned him about drinking with detectives, and especially Mick, but he doesn't listen. He'll never learn.'

McGovern grinned, wishing his wife was making the same complaint. 'It's torture watching the team enjoy themselves when I'm on the soda an' lime. But such is life.' He put his arm round his wife's shoulder, pulled her a bit closer and she kissed his cheek.

'He's doing well. Lost ten pounds and sleeping like a baby.' There was no doubt she liked the life they were having despite his illness.

'Trouble is, I'm a picture of health but I wish I was in for a hangover like those reprobates over there.' There was a longing in McGovern's eyes and good health wouldn't take care of it.

'You should get a dog.' Macallan said it hopefully – she was sure McGovern was the solution to the problem she'd volunteered for. 'Supposed to be good for you, and I know where you can get one who loves you already.' She raised her eyebrows suggestively.

'Pity about that, but we just bought a spaniel. Anyway, do you really think I could deal with the piss-taking if I was seen with a spoodle? Mick would be unbearable.'

415

Macallan tried to suppress a small frown; she'd been sure McGovern would adopt poor old Gnasher. She kissed him again and headed outside, longing for some cold air on her skin. She turned at the door though, watching Harkins, O'Connor, Jack and Bell attempt a bad rendition of the old Frank Sinatra song 'New York, New York'. The whole pub joined in and it made her choke with emotion.

She stepped out into the warm night air and strolled along St Stephen Street looking into the basement windows of the bars and bistros where people were just enjoying their lives. She breathed in deeply, clasped her arms round her waist and thought about the future – a future that had some meaning.

A taxi rattled over the cobbles behind her in Circus Place, and unknown to the passenger in the back, he'd just passed by a pub full of detectives who'd like nothing better than to see him locked up or staring at the heavens from a skip. Mick Harkins, the man he intended to kill, was there as well, pissed as a newt and there for the taking. But Billy Drew was pissed himself. It had been a good night; he'd met up with the Scousers who were going to be his main suppliers and they'd shaken hands on a deal that would make him a fortune. DI Slade had started to leave him alone and moved on to harass some other villains, the hassle after the Flemings had been taken out was dying down and the people of Edinburgh would soon forget about it all – they always did when it was bandits killing each other. The world moved on quickly and the public was swamped with waves of bad news from the Middle East. It was hard to care about what had happened to some unfortunate foreign women when American journalists were being beheaded on camera.

He stuffed a bundle of notes into the taxi driver's

hand – he could afford it – and said, 'Take care, son.' The driver couldn't believe his luck, though he would end up putting the money straight into the bookies' pocket in the morning.

Drew was unsteady on his feet and fumbled for a cigarette. He'd decided that it was time to finish off old business. He'd got one of his boys to check that Jonathon Barclay was still drinking himself to death in Inverness. He'd do him first, then it would be time for the scalp he really wanted to hang on his belt: Mick Harkins. He'd have to take more care to make sure he had an alibi, but he knew where Harkins lived and he wanted to take some time with him. Harkins had never fully recovered from his injuries and physically he'd be easy, but he was a devious bastard and Drew would have to be on his toes when he did him.

He searched his pockets again for his keys, and like all drunks he had to go through them twice before he fumbled them from the pile of loose change he'd accumulated over the night. 'Life's looking up, Billy boy,' he slurred and grinned.

Drew turned and tried to navigate the key into the lock. When he eventually managed to push it in he spent the last few seconds of his life trying to work out what had just happened. He heard something like a dog growling and then he felt a blow to the back of his neck. It wasn't that hard or painful but he saw something at the bottom of his field of vision. The end of a long and very sharp knife was jutting out under his chin. It was there for a moment and then it disappeared, withdrawing from his sight. He tried to say, 'What the fuck?' but his lungs were filling up with blood and he was choking to death.

He was pulled round as he slipped down onto his arse with his back against the door. When he managed to force his eyes upwards, his last view of the world was of Big Brenda McMartin leaning over him with a long

417

dripping blade held in her right hand, which looked like a claw after the damage inflicted by Cue Ball Ross. She pushed her ugly face as close to his as she could so she could watch his lights go out with her good eye.

'Think you could fuck the McMartins and get away with it, Billy?' she said. 'That was for Bobby.'

She walked calmly back to the car and got in. Fanny Adams was the driver and he looked round at her, waiting for an order. She stared out of the window for a minute then turned on him. 'What the fuck you waiting on? Supposed to be a fuckin' getaway driver. Getaway driver my fuckin' arse. Now go.'

They headed for the M8 and Glasgow. When they were safely out of Edinburgh she dialled the number she'd been given. It was a bad connection, but of course Pete Handyside was a long way away, though Brenda had no idea exactly where.

'It's done.'

'Thanks, Brenda. Guess the business is all yours up there if you want to take it.'

Handyside was pleased that Drew was out of the way. He'd decided to make a gift to Brenda of the name of her brother's killer, though he'd left out the fact that Drew was working for him, as that didn't suit his purposes. As always, he liked to have several plans in the bag in case circumstances changed, and keeping Brenda onside was worth the risk. She was one of the few people he had complete faith in. Hell would freeze over before she would cooperate with the law so he'd decided he would let her live unless things changed. He could never be sure when he might need The Bitch's unique penchant for violence again.

No one made a statement against Handyside, including Tony Harrison. They knew he had a long reach and decided it was better to take what was coming no matter what they did. Handyside had cleaned up a lot of the problems and the Crown was happy enough that Turner, his team and Harrison were all inside. They would need to work hard to get a case against Handyside and it looked like he wouldn't be coming back anyway. His file was available if required, but it was slipped quietly onto a shelf and the world moved on.

The public hadn't forgotten completely about Ingrid Richter and the thousands of women trafficked across Europe though. A few astute politicians saw an opportunity to look like caring individuals and new tougher laws were put before Parliament.

In reality though, nothing changed.

Epilogue

One year later

Macallan sat on a large towel and sipped the fruit juice Jack had put into the picnic bag. She felt she was getting too much sun, pulled a soft hat onto her head and swatted a fly away from the food in the bag. They'd driven the car along the north coast of Northern Ireland and down onto the long sands near Portstewart. Jack had a week off so they were just enjoying being together. He was down at the water's edge with Adam and their daughter, Kate, who was like a small bundle in his big, strong arms. The dog raced backwards and forwards on the sand, chasing and playing with a couple of completely uncontrollable Jack Russells.

Kate's birth had been an easy one, and all round life was pretty good. Jack had become a real success as a writer as well as a barrister, but Macallan liked to remind him that behind every successful man was an even more successful woman. At least in his case.

The money that had come in from the book meant they were able to buy the cottage on the Antrim coast and keep the flat in Edinburgh. She felt well again, and her bad dreams were fading with time. She was still struggling over what to do with her future, but at least she had some time off to take care of Kate. Her daughter was a carbon copy of Macallan: even as a baby she looked a bit serious and the features were all her mother's. Adam on the other hand was all Jack, and she could see a boy developing who would have his father's passion for disfiguring his face on the rugby pitch. That was okay. The rugby pitch was fine; anything that was far away from the places she'd inhabited and visited in her dreams was fine.

'Jack, come and get something to eat,' she called. He waved and strode back up the beach towards her as Gnasher raced ahead, covering Macallan with sand as he skidded to a halt beside her.